TARGET: TOBRUK!

The bomb bay doors were partially open, creeping shut before his eyes. Harris stood on the catwalk, chilled, breathing cold oxygen, and pushed the lever on the bulkhead that operated the doors manually. The doors stopped closing, backed slowly open. Bombs hung from their shackles inches away from him. Below, the sea sparkled far beneath the narrow catwalk—his world until the bombs fells, a real birds eye view of Tobruk!

Then, abruptly and without warning, *Blonde Job* fell wildly to the left, throwing him hard against a strut. He teetered over the void, clutching the bomb bay door lever, panic frozen.

They'd been hit!

BLOCKBUSTER FICTION FROM PINNACLE BOOKS!

THE FINAL VOYAGE OF THE S.S.N. SKATE   (17-157, $3.95)
by Stephen Cassell
The "leper" of the U.S. Pacific Fleet, SSN 578 nuclear attack sub SKATE, has one final mission to perform—an impossible act of piracy that will pit the underwater deathtrap and its inexperienced crew against the combined might of the Soviet Navy's finest!

QUEENS GATE RECKONING   (17-164, $3.95)
by Lewis Purdue
Only a wounded CIA operative and a defecting Soviet ballerina stand in the way of a vast consortium of treason that speeds toward the hour of mankind's ultimate reckoning! From the bestselling author of THE LINZ TESTAMENT.

FAREWELL TO RUSSIA   (17-165, $4.50)
by Richard Hugo
A KGB agent must race against time to infiltrate the confines of U.S. nuclear technology after a terrifying accident threatens to unleash unmitigated devastation!

THE NICODEMUS CODE   (17-133, $3.95)
by Graham N. Smith and Donna Smith
A two-thousand-year-old parchment has been unearthed, unleashing a terrifying conspiracy unlike any the world has previously known, one that threatens the life of the Pope himself, and the ultimate destruction of Christianity!

Available wherever paperbacks are sold, or order direct from the Publisher. Send cover price plus 50¢ per copy for mailing and handling to Pinnacle Books, Dept.17-301, 475 Park Avenue South, New York, N.Y. 10016. Residents of New York, New Jersey and Pennsylvania must include sales tax. DO NOT SEND CASH.

RIDER ON THE WIND

DAVID WESTHEIMER

PINNACLE BOOKS
WINDSOR PUBLISHING CORP.

PINNACLE BOOKS

are published by

Windsor Publishing Corp.
475 Park Avenue South
New York, NY 10016

First Pinnacle Books printing: December, 1989

Printed in the United States of America

To Anthea Joseph

CHAPTER I

Here the Jezreel Valley, called in Hebrew Emek Ysrael, was brown and parched, bristling with the stubble of cut barley. To the south lay the mountains of Samaria and to the north those of Galilee with Mount Hermon thrusting up behind them in the distance. The hills of Nazareth were to the east and, clad in orchards and vines, Mount Carmel rose in the west.

The pink bomber was an anomaly in this storied setting. It sat on a hardstand in the stubble, ringed with sandbags. Its wings were slender, its belly swollen, almost touching the ground. Harsh sunlight shimmered on the pink taxi strip, the hardstand and the bomber's Plexiglass astrodome and top turret, but the voluptuous blonde painted on the fuselage below the flight deck looked cool and loose-limbed on her bed of cloud. The bomber's name, *Blonde Job,* was lettered below the cloud. Two black bombs were stencilled above the blonde just aft of the Plexiglass window in the navigator's compartment at the nose. A third, for the convoy strike in the Mediterranean the day before, was yet to be added.

A tanned young soldier, his face Semitic, leaned against the sandbags in the paltry shade of the revetment wall, a World War I Enfield rifle dangling from his shoulder. His uniform was British Army khaki. The shoulder tabs said Palestine and, in Hebrew, in brackets, the letters E and I.

It was 10 August 1942. The bomber was a four-engine B-24D Liberator, one of the forty-odd widely dispersed on the baking airfield called Ramat Jonas after the kibbutz just across the road. It belonged to the first squadron of the 108th Bombardment Group (Heavy) to arrive the last week in July by the Southern Route — Morrison Field in West Palm Beach, Florida, Trinidad, Belem and Natal in Brazil, Accra on Africa's Gold Coast and Khartoum in the Sudan. Fifty miles to the south, at Lydda, outside Tel Aviv, was a smaller force of heavies that had begun operations in the Middle East some weeks earlier. A handful of tired B-17s hastily transferred from India and the longer range B-24s of Halpro, the 1st Provisional Group.

The latter, as the Halverson Detachment, had been intended for operations against Japan from bases in China. When the bases were threatened by Japanese ground troops, and Rommel's forces rolled back the British on Alexandria, it had been diverted to support the beleaguered Eighth Army.

The British Eighth was now dug in for a last ditch stand on a thirty-two mile front stretching from the impassable Qattara Depression to El Alamein on the Egyptian Coast, sixty miles from Alexandria and some 400 air miles from Ramat Jonas. Should Rommel break through, the whole Middle East would lie helpless before him. *Blonde Job* was part of the British and American bomber force pounding desperately at his extended supply lines.

None of this was prominent in the thoughts of Michael "Tex" Harris, the navigator, and Terrence Gallegly, the co-pilot, as they approached the bomber,

8

sweating and waving off *barhash*, tiny mosquitos which attacked only by daylight. They had a more immediate concern. Hunger.

The 108th was on British rations prepared by British cooks, a combination they found defeating. Breakfasts of lumpy oatmeal and canned bacon warmed in the tin and served flaccid and greasy. At other meals: odd meats sometimes identifiable as mutton, which Harris and Gallegly both detested.

The group's own mess staff would not be arriving until later in the month with the bulk of the 108th's ground echelon and equipment, now at sea on the British ss *Pasteur*. The aircrews had flown over in their own planes, bringing with them only their basic personal gear, spare parts and key members of the ground echelon. British personnel from the RAF units they had replaced at Ramat Jonas were performing most ground functions.

Harris and Gallegly had skipped lunch, found the line too long at the NAAFI canteen truck where they had hoped to buy tinned fruit and biscuits, and were now on their way to raid the crate of C rations kept in *Blonde Job* for emergencies.

At five-eleven, Harris was an inch taller than Gallegly but looked more because he was rangy where Gallegly was thick. He was sandy-haired and fair, though as tanned as the plane guard. Both were second lieutenants and both wore flyer's sunglasses, short-sleeved British bush jackets, desert shorts, low-cut boots and sun helmets to which were screwed their officer's metal hat emblems. None of which was regulation except the sunglasses and hat emblems. Each had a holstered .45 automatic slung low on an olive drab web belt. All officers wore sidearms at Ramat Jonas.

They had fitted themselves out on the flight over-

9

seas. They bought the boots in Natal because everyone did and they cost only five US dollars. The helmets and British uniforms were from Khartoum, where they had RONed, Remained Over Night, for two nights before the final leg to Palestine. The desert uniforms were cooler than American khakis, and more overseas looking.

They stopped short of the revetment to extinguish their smokes. Harris field-stripped his cigarette reluctantly because he was running low on his US supply. Gallegly knocked the dottle from his pipe.

The plane guard grinned at them and said, *"Shalom."* They both said *"Shalom"* in reply. Members of the 108th had learned the first day or so that *"shalom"* meant "peace" in Hebrew and was both greeting and farewell. So far that was about all any of them had learned, or bothered to, about the country, except that the apples and grapes were abundant, good and, on the few occasions they were permitted to pay for them, cheap. And that Jewish farmgirls did not shave their legs or fraternize.

The bomb bay doors and the big waist windows were open. The bomb bays were the most convenient way of entering the plane and the waist windows had been permanently removed. The openings were firing ports for two flexible .50-calibre machine-guns. There were three more flexible fifties in the nose and turret-mounted twin fifties in the flight deck and tail.

They climbed in through the rear bomb bay and squeezed past the struts supporting the catwalk. The waist was baking. The familiar smell, enhanced by heat, enveloped Harris. Even now, after more than 400 flying hours in navigation school, crew training and combat, he was always conscious of the smell when he entered an aircraft. It was like sticking his head inside a radio that had been on a long time. In his first training flights the smell had made him a little sick but now it was familiar and comfortable. And, somehow, stirring.

The C ration crate, bound in wire, was against the bulkhead. They opened it carefully with a heavy screwdriver from the aerial engineer's toolbox so that their raid would not be obvious. Ordinary hunger pangs were not considered emergencies. Harris took a can of meat and beans, Gallegly a can of meat and vegetable stew. They pulled the keys from the tops, unwound the metal sealing strips and ate with their fingers, dripping sweat. The meat and beans reminded Harris just a little of the chili at James's Coney Island in Houston and the sign on the wall there. "The Eye Must Be Pleased Before The Stomach Can Be Satisfied."

They licked their fingers clean and replaced the crate in its original state. They took the empty cans with them.

Outside, a red-haired man in his forties was talking to the plane guard in Hebrew. He wore heavy British Army boots, knee socks, shorts and a short-sleeved shirt with the inverted three stripes of a British sergeant. The hairs on his muscular arms and legs were curling and reddish-gold in the, sun. He broke off speaking with the guard and said, "Hallo."

Gallegly said, "Hi," Harris, *"Shalom."*

"Gyorgy Weisz," the sergeant said. "Sergeant, Palestine Police."

"You're a cop?" Gallegly asked.

"Yes," said Weisz, smiling. "I am cop."

"About the C rations," Harris said gravely. "We can explain everything." He stuck out his hand and said, "Mike Harris. This here's Lieutenant Gallegly."

They shook hands.

"I come to see Liberators," Weisz said, looking at

11

Blonde Job with open admiration. "Until now I see only in air. You give Jerry much trouble, yes?"

"We try," Harris said.

"I am living in Aleenah," Weisz explained. "I listen always for Liberators. Until all come home safe."

Aleenah was the Jewish settlement half a mile from the airfield. From the air it was unique, being perfectly circular. A dirt road formed the circumference and another ran through the settlement, bisecting the circle. There was a scatter of buildings along the centre road but the houses were all set around the circumference, from which radiated tilled fields, gardens, orchards and vineyards. Outbuildings formed an outer belt between the homes and the fields. The homes were shaded by young trees and several symmetrical groves of pines had been planted in the open land of the circle. It all looked so resolutely functional that no one on the *Blonde Job* crew had visited the settlement.

"Is there somewhere to eat in Aleenah?" Harris asked, interested. "A restaurant or something?"

"Where I am living is private table. How you say in English, boarding house."

"Could we eat there?" Harris said hopefully.

"I think, yes. But why you wish? I think American flyers eat like princes, yes?"

"Not with English cooks and rations," said Gallegly.

"You don't like the English?" Weisz said carefully.

"We like 'em fine," Harris said. "Just not their chow." Weisz's face showed no expression.

"Can we come tonight?" Harris asked.

"At 1700 hours," Weisz said, nodding. "Ask anybody, Goldblum."

"Goldblum?" said Harris. "I got an uncle in Waco named Goldblum."

Weisz regarded him with the friendly interest that

12

had been there before he said he liked the English. "You are Jew?" he asked.

"Sure am. You, too?"

Gallegly shook his head in mocking appreciation of Harris's artfulness. "You joke me," said Weisz. "You know I am Jew. All in Aleenah are Jew."

"I know that. But you being a police sergeant and all . . . I figured you might just be stationed there."

"I am Jew from Hungary. Where from your people?"

"My grandfather came over from Germany."

"Goldblum also. In Aleenah much German Jew."

"Learn something every day, don't we?" Gallegly said, still amused at Harris's deception.

"I go now," said Weisz. "Seventeen-hundred hours. Goldblum."

He shook hands with the Americans and the guard before striding off across the fields toward Aleenah.

Harris and Gallegly threw their empty cans out into the stubble on the way back to their tent. On the other crews, the pilot and co-pilot and the navigator and bombardier bunked together in the two-man tents but Harris and Gallegly had become close friends during the weeks of training in Florida. Dan Wagstaff, the pilot, had not minded sharing a tent with the bombardier, J. Edward Silkwood, Jr. Wagstaff was probably the only member of the squadron willing to room with Silkwood.

It was hot in the tent even with the flaps folded back and the sides rolled up. Harris washed down a salt tablet with tepid, heavily chlorinated water from the canteen which was kept hanging in a soaked cover from a nail on a tent-pole. He sprayed a mouthful on the stubbly dirt floor to keep the dust down. He took off his shirt and sun helmet and sat on his cot. On the other cot, Gallegly already had his pipe going and his

13

nose stuck into Dos Passos's *USA*. When they wanted to read at night they usually went to the officers' club, a large, sparsely-furnished room in one of the field's few permanent structures. Only the permanent buildings had electricity.

Gallegly looked up from his book and grinned at Harris.

"What?" Harris asked.

"Tex, you're a pistol telling that sergeant that."

"Telling him what?"

"Telling him you're Jewish."

"I am."

"That's a crock. You think it'll help you with the local talent or something?"

Harris slipped off the dog tags he wore around his neck on a cord and handed them across to Gallegly.

"See that there H, *amigo?* It sure don't stand for Hardshell Baptist."

Gallegly looked at the dog tags and handed them back. Harris knew he was wondering if he had ever made any disparaging remarks about Jews in his presence. He hadn't that Harris could recall. Gallegly wasn't the type. And Harris did not notice such things anyhow unless they were really flagrant. He had never thought much one way or the other about being Jewish until he got to Palestine and found himself surrounded by Jews. He did not exactly identify with them, but it pleased him to see them farming and soldiering and to discover that they were admired by the men of the 108th. The Americans vastly preferred the Palestine Jews to the Palestine Arabs, regarding the latter much as coloured people were in the US south.

"If it works with the babes, let's tell 'em I'm one too," Gallegly said. "I look more Jewish than you do."

"Wouldn't work. You're not circumcised."

14

"By the time they noticed it'd be too late," Gallegly said, returning to his book.

Late in the afternoon they stripped to their boots, draped towels around their hips and walked across the barley stubble to the shower tent. The water was not as cold in the afternoon. After showering they got into the clean regulation khakis they kept for visiting Haifa, twenty miles to the west.

"We oughtta go get Wags," Harris said.

"If we can find the crap game he's in."

Wagstaff spent a lot of his free time shooting dice, and winning.

"We'll have to ask Silkwood too," Harris said thoughtfully.

The bombardier usually hung around Wagstaff. Their pilot was one of the few men in the squadron who could tolerate him.

"Wags wouldn't want us interrupting a hot hand anyhow," said Gallegly.

They angled across the stubble to the dirt road leading into Aleenah. There was nothing to mark the separation between the stubble of the airfield and the tilled fields of the settlement, except the widely spaced Palestine Buffs, as soldiers of the British Army's special Jewish units were called. The Buffs themselves were casual about the perimeter's location. For Arabs, they considered it just outside Aleenah. For Americans, just outside the tent area. Two nights before, a Buff had shot and killed an Arab trying to creep among the tents. The act had been generally applauded.

There were few people visible in Aleenah. The inhabitants not in their homes preparing the evening meal were still working in the fields. A boy in shorts and a mended shirt ran up to them, thrilled to see American flyers. "You fly yesterday," he said. "All back

15

safe this morning."

The boy led them to Goldblum's house, asking questions all the way. The house, like its neighbours, was whitewashed cement blocks, small, flat-roofed and set among half-grown trees. Goldblum flung the door open and called back inside in German, "Gyorgy, your American friends are here." His pants were baggy and his face deeply creased. He apparently had once been much heavier than he was now.

Weisz joined them in the tiny front room. Everybody shook hands. The furniture was of plywood, with framed old family photographs on every flat surface. In an adjoining small room, five places had been set on a table covered with an incongruously fine tablecloth creased from long storage. A mason jar in the centre held fresh flowers from the yard. Harris sensed that the cloth and flowers were something special for the American visitors. A comfortable-looking grey-haired woman smiled at them from the kitchen doorway. She came out to shake hands when Weisz introduced them. She looked from Harris to Gallegly, then at Weisz.

"This one is the Jew?" she asked in German, nodding at Gallegly.

"Nein," said Harris. "Ich bin."

"Oh," she said, pleased, still in German, "you speak German?"

"A little," Harris said.

"He doesn't look Jewish," Frau Goldblum said to her husband.

Everyone laughed except Gallegly.

"She said I don't look Jewish," Harris explained.

"Show her your dog tags," said Gallegly.

They hung their pistol belts over the backs of their chairs and Frau Goldblum began bringing in platters of food. Sliced tomatoes, fried eggs, fried potatoes,

16

boiled corn on the cob and a pitcher of cold milk. Frau Goldblum sat down in the chair nearest the kitchen. Goldblum bowed his head and said a prayer in Hebrew. Weisz looked at Harris and shrugged, as if to say this was something he had to endure at every meal.

Harris looked at the milk.

Gallegly looked at him and said, "Why not?"

Milk was not served in the Ramat Jonas mess. The local product had been declared unfit by the flight surgeon although the only local dairy Harris had seen, at Ramat Jonas kibbutz, had appeared spotless.

They drank milk copiously with their meal. Frau Goldblum watched them eat, beaming. She reminded Harris of his mother and grandmother. They loved watching him eat their cooking, too. He wondered if it were a Jewish trait. He had never thought of it that way before.

Goldblum asked about the Texas Goldblum, hoping to discover a relationship, however tenuous. Harris knew little about his uncle's antecedents; or even of his own. His grandfather, dead years now, never had much to say about the old country. He had been too resolutely American, and Texan.

They remained at the table talking after the meal. Harris quit struggling with his college German and let Weisz interpret. The Goldblums did not want to take money for the meal. Harris and Gallegly insisted, telling them it was the best meal they'd had in Palestine but they would not return if they were not allowed to pay. The Goldblums agreed reluctantly to take ten piastres—a hundred mils—from each of them. There were a thousand mils to the Palestine pound, which was pegged to the British pound. A hundred mils came to about forty cents.

Gallegly got out his pipe and Harris passed a pack

17

of cigarettes around. Goldblum took a long, loving drag and spoke earnestly to Harris.

"He is happy all bombers come safely home," Weisz translated.

"Does everybody here check us in and out?" Harris asked, recalling the boy who had led them to the house.

Weisz nodded. "We must know all come back safe," he said. "Also, those who pray, say prayer for you when you go. Goldblum, he always prays for you."

"Do you?" Harris asked.

Weisz's eyes flicked to the pistol hanging from Harris's chair. "I believe in other methods," he said. "The religious ones . . ."

He was interrupted by the appearance of two girls in the doorway. One, a teenager, was a typical farmgirl. Chunky, sun-bleached hair, sunburned face, tight shorts. The other, a few years older was less sturdy, even delicately made, and not bad looking. That was as much as Harris could tell in the brief glimpse he had of her, for they bolted almost immediately. Weisz was out of his chair in pursuit before Gallegly even saw them. Startled by Weisz's abrupt move, he fumbled for his gunbelt.

"Simmer down," said Harris.

"What's going on?"

Harris shrugged and shook his head.

Goldblum was undisturbed. The commotion brought Frau Goldblum from the kitchen. Harris could not understand what Goldblum told her. She went back to the kitchen and after a minute or so Weisz returned, greatly amused.

"Who were those girls?" Harris said. "Why'd they take off like that?"

"What girls?" Gallegly demanded.

"They think you are English," Weisz explained.

"Why should that scare 'em?" Harris said.

"We do things forbidden by English," Weisz said carefully. "You think this is bad?"

"Not if you don't. Whatever it is, I'm on your side."

"Lieutenant Gallegly also?"

Gallegly nodded and said again, "What girls?"

"Two girls peeked in and took off," Harris explained.

"Were they good looking?"

"Mine was. Yours had personality."

"They come for pistol training," Weisz said.

"What for?" Harris said. "You still having trouble with the Arabs?"

Harris was vaguely aware that before the war it had been like the pioneers and Indians between the Jews and Arabs in Palestine. Once in a while the Houston papers had carried news items about incidents. He had not read them very carefully. Palestine had seemed too remote to matter much.

"All young people learn pistol," Weisz said, getting up. "Now I must go. They are waiting. You are coming back again?"

"Can we watch?" Harris asked, wanting a closer look at the older girl.

Weisz hesitated. "You don't say to anyone?"

Harris shook his head.

Weisz's room was tiny, with a narrow bed, a wooden locker, a straight chair, a small plywood table and clothing hanging from nails driven into the mortar between the cement blocks. The girls were sitting close together on the bed studying a manual. Their eyes flicked to the Americans. The younger girl's look was frankly curious. She had what some people called a Jewish nose. The other girl's glance was cool and wary. Despite her typical settlement garb and lack of makeup she did not look like a farm-girl. She was too poised, and her brown legs were shaved. Good-look-

19

ing, Harris thought, city girl good-looking, not country girl good-looking.

Weisz spoke to them in Hebrew. A real language shark, Harris thought. A Hungarian who spoke English, German and Hebrew. The older girl gave Weisz the manual. He handed it to Harris. The diagrams and photographs identified it as a typical training manual. Typical except that it was in Hebrew. Harris had never seen Hebrew put to such use. He had been taught to read enough Hebrew phonetically to get him through his bar mitzvah ten years ago, but not to translate it.

Weisz unlocked the locker and took out a service revolver and a square of cloth. He spread the cloth on the table and put the pistol on it. At a nod from him, the older girl brought the chair to the table and sat down.

"You have handkerchief?" Weisz asked Harris.

Harris brought out a handkerchief and gave it to him. The younger girl kept glancing at Harris and Gallegly when she thought they would not notice. Weisz gave the handkerchief to the older girl, who inspected it. Harris was glad he had put a fresh one in his pocket before leaving for Aleenah but was annoyed with the girl for thinking it might not be clean.

She tied the handkerchief over her eyes and, blindfolded, deftly field-stripped the revolver and put it back together again. Harris and Gallegly applauded. She removed the handkerchief, unsmiling, and gave it back to Harris. He made sure that their hands touched.

"Zipporah is only now learning," Weisz said, nodding at the younger girl.

She blushed under her tan when she heard her name. Homely but cute, Harris thought, and way too young to think about. But the other one . . . He

20

looked at the watch on his left wrist. He would have liked to stick around and get to know the other one but everybody was going to a movie at the kibbutz. Major Beck, the squadron commander, had said that the Ramat Jonas people had been swell to invite them and he expected a big turnout from the 234th. And what Major Beck expected, Major Beck got.

Harris wore two wristwatches. All the navigators did. The one on the left wrist was for local time, the one on the right for Greenwich Mean Time, required for celestial navigation. Harris's left watch was Swiss, with a metal band. He had bought it cheap in Natal on the way over. The one on the right was a regulation Air Corps hack watch with a sweep second hand.

The act of looking at the time drew attention to his two watches. The younger girl was intrigued. The older one said something that made her laugh. Harris was sure it had not been anything complimentary.

"We don't want to be late for the movie," he said to Gallegly.

"Yeah," Gallegly said reluctantly.

It had been a while since they had been in the same room as a pretty girl.

Harris looked at Zipporah and pointed at himself. "Mike Harris," he said.

She got up and shook his hand, the standard brisk, single downward jerk. "Zipporah Barkowitz."

"And this is Terrence Gallegly."

She shook Gallegly's hand and said her name again. Harris turned to the older girl.

"It is better not to say names," she replied in surprisingly good English with traces of both a German and a British accent. "The English do not approve of what we do here."

"Is all right, Hannah," said Weisz. "They are friends. And Lieutenant Harris is Jew."

21

She regarded Harris with greater interest but with no increase in warmth. Harris wondered why she had taken a dislike to him. Most girls reacted just the opposite.

"Hannah Ruh," she said, holding out a brown hand.

It was hard and calloused. Despite that, Harris held it longer than necessary, partly because he wanted to annoy her and partly because he enjoyed touching pretty girls, even if it were only a hand. He wondered if she were all that good-looking or if it were only because the last woman he'd touched had been that coffee-coloured whore at Madame ZeZe's in Belem last month.

"Maybe I can see you again some time," he said, releasing her hand.

Her shrug was not encouraging.

"Well, *shalom*," he said.

"*Shalom*," Zipporah said shyly.

"Goodbye," said Hannah Ruh.

Outside it was totally dark except for the stars. Aleenah, like all of Palestine, was blacked out. The Arabs generally ignored the blackout except where it could be enforced but village Arabs went to bed anyhow with the descent of night. Out on the dirt road Harris stopped to look at the stars, thick and glittery overhead. It was instinctive with him now, searching the night sky, his vocation and his joy.

Once the night sky had seemed densely sown and without design. But in navigation school he had learned to know the stars and their constellations and pointers, to depend on them for guidance in the trackless dark. They were beacons, allies against his relentless antagonist, the wind. Now the night flashed patterns, changing with immutable precision as the earth moved in orbit.

Harris looked first to Polaris, the North Star, his

favourite of all stars. "Not bright but dependable," the instructor had said, joking, at star study class. Of all stars the most fixed in place, not wheeling in cosmic sweep like other stars and changing position from minute to minute and season to season but moving in a tight orbit at true north, its elevation never more than a fraction of a degree different from the latitude of the observer. He did not need the pointer stars of Ursa Major, the Big Bear, the constellation he had called the Big Dipper in childhood, to locate it. He knew where true north lay and had only to look for Polaris at an elevation of something less than thirty-two degrees, the latitude of Aleenah, and there it was, blinking at him.

At his elbow Gallegly said, "You can have Zipporah."

"It wouldn't be right," Harris said. "Any fool could see she's nuts about you."

"That Hannah's a real looker. Rue, that's a funny name."

"R-u-h," said Harris. "Means peace in German."

"How you spell it?" Gallegly said, laughing.

"P-i-e-c-e," said Harris. "I hope."

The movie had already started. It was being shown out of doors; against blackout regulations. But the beam of the projector gave no clue to its location, certainly nothing to reveal that an airfield lay close at hand. American airmen and kibbutznikim — men, women and children — sat on bales of hay, carts and planks supported by cement blocks. Cows stirred restlessly in nearby stalls. There was a pervasive odour of hay, manure and damp earth. The pumps that sent water to the irrigation tower went pock-pock, pock-pock over the sound of the film.

The picture was *Intermezzo*. It had both French and Hebrew subtitles. Harris had seen it before, in Hous-

23

ton, but did not mind seeing it again. He liked Ingrid Bergman and the music, especially Ingrid Bergman. He stood at the back with Gallegly trying to locate Wagstaff.

Wagstaff was not hard to find in the flickering beam of the projector. He was the one whose head stuck out above everyone else's. He was six-three, the tallest man in the 234th squadron.

They picked their way to the bale he was sharing with J. Edward Silkwood, Jr.

"Move your butt over a little," Harris whispered to Silkwood.

"Sssh," Silkwood hissed. "Not so loud."

It was Harris's theory that because of his personality, Silkwood was meant to be short and pudgy, but through some quirk of nature he was as tall as Harris and handsome: blue eyes, yellow hair and in great shape from regular calisthenics and interminable cold showers. Silkwood took a lot of showers. He liked to take them when no one else was in the shower tent. It was also Harris's theory, shared by Gallegly, that Silkwood did things to himself in the shower. They believed him to be a virgin. In Belem, Wagstaff had insisted that he go to Madame ZeZe's with them and learn about women. Wagstaff had even picked the youngest, prettiest girl for him. But Silkwood had resisted every wile and blandishment and remained pure.

Gallegly crowded next to Wagstaff.

"Where you guys been?" Wagstaff demanded.

He was loud but Silkwood did not shush him, Harris noted. You didn't shush your pilot. No one shushed Wagstaff anyway. Not because he was so big but because he was so likeable.

"We found a great place to eat in Aleenah," Gallegly whispered, trying to keep Silkwood from hearing.

He didn't want Silkwood tagging along next time they went. Not that they could keep Silkwood from it, Harris knew. Wagstaff always made them include Silkwood. Nobody got on Wagstaff's nerves.

After the show the kibbutznikim gave the airmen grapes to take back to the field. The *Blonde Job* officers all went to Wagstaff's tent, Silkwood leading the way. Silkwood never forgot his flashlight, a necessity in the unlighted tent area. Around them flashlight beams probed, men laughed and talked or swore when they stumbled over tent ropes.

Wagstaff hung the flashlight from a tent-pole and had Silkwood put down the tent flaps. They all put their grapes on Wagstaff's cot.

"I only got purple ones," Silkwood said, as if he thought there was some sort of conspiracy against him. "Everyone else got purple ones and green ones."

The purple grapes had seeds and thicker skins. The green ones were seedless but not as sweet.

"It's your blue eyes and blond hair," Harris said seriously. "Makes you look just like a Nazi. And you know what they think about Nazis around here."

"Yeah," said Gallegly. "I heard a lot of muttering going on around you back at the show."

Silkwood looked as if he half believed them. Wagstaff grinned, showing a lot of big white teeth in his rugged face with its bent nose. The nose had been broken in a basketball game during his playing days at UCLA.

"Get wise, Junior," he said, sweeping all the grapes into a single heap.

No one else called Silkwood "Junior" except to annoy him. Wagstaff did it out of sheer good nature and Silkwood knew it, and didn't mind.

"One for all and all for one," Wagstaff said, stripping purple grapes into his mouth and crunching

25

down. "Just like *The Three Musketeers*."

A ship in the 233rd was named *The Four Musketeers*, with a picture of D'Artagnan on the nose. Harris thought it was kind of raunchy, naming it that. They should have named it "The Ten Musketeers" There were six enlisted men on the crew, too.

A sergeant on Major Beck's crew stuck his head in the tent while they were eating grapes and said, "Mission tomorrow, sir."

Wagstaff stopped chewing and said, "Roger." He got to his feet. "Everybody hit the sack. Looks like a long day tomorrow."

Back in their tent, Harris and Gallegly stripped to undershorts and tee shirts and got under their mosquito nets. At night the *yatush*, the big mosquitoes, the "heavies" the men of the 108th called them, took over from the swarming *barhash* and attacked singly. Gallegly filled his pipe and began reading *USA* by flashlight. Harris put a forearm over his eyes to shield them from the light and thought about Hannah Ruh.

It was cooler now. The air smelled of dust and stubble and growing things. Out in the hills a jackal wailed. Their first night at Ramat, Jonas Harris had thought a woman was being tormented somewhere. The water pumps of the kibbutz and Aleenah made their rhythmic, monotonous sound. Harris fell asleep still thinking about Hannah Ruh. It did not occur to him that he might more reasonably have been thinking that tomorrow he was flying a mission, a mission on which a man could get killed.

CHAPTER II

The 108th had flown its first mission the night of 1 August, a week after the 234th landed at Ramat Jonas. Harris and the others had intended going into Haifa to see Fred Astaire and Rita Hayworth in *You'll Never Get Rich* at the Amphitheatre, but instead found themselves bombing Axis repair shops at Mersa Matruh on the Mediterranean coast between El Alamein and Sidi Barrani.

The bombers, only a handful, took off from Ramat Jonas the previous afternoon for the one hour, fifty minute flight to Fayid, a big RAF airfield on the Great Bitter Lake in Egypt. Veteran RAF staff officers did the briefing. A piece of cake, a British briefing officer said, smiling without condescension at their first-mission intensity. No flak, no night fighters, he said. And RAF pathfinder planes would be going in ahead of them to light up the target area with flares.

Multi-coloured tracers from light flak had curved away far below them on the bleak desert, leisurely as lobbed tennis balls, but everyone had been tense and silent until bombs away and the exultant turn for home. The interphone had been busy on the way back. Silkwood thought his bombs had started a

27

major fire and the tail gunner confirmed it. Wagstaff, who had been uncharacteristically serious on the flight to the target, sang "Show Me the Way To Go Home" and Harris responded with "The Eyes of Texas."

They landed at Ramat Jonas at four in the morning after six hours in the air. The others were weary but Wagstaff was as loud and jovial as if he'd had a good night's sleep. He insisted that Harris and Gallegly come to his tent, where he had a fifth of Vat 69 put aside to celebrate their first raid. Even the teetotalling Silkwood took a token swallow. After a couple of drinks on empty stomachs, Harris and Gallegly longed for their cots but Wagstaff insisted that they sit around and tell stories until they killed the bottle.

Later that day, when the *Palestine Post,* a four page English language newspaper, reported that British naval aircraft had attacked Mersa Matruh and started big fires Silkwood wanted to write a letter of protest to the editor. Harris and Gallegly egged him on but Wagstaff explained that he couldn't tell anything about military operations and besides, because of the timing, the article could not have been about their raid.

Three nights later they hit Matruh again, combat veterans. The next week they attacked a convoy in the Mediterranean, flying directly from Ramat Jonas to the target and landing at Fayid to spend the night. The fire from the two destroyers escorting the convoy had been ineffectual and there had been no fighters.

Now, two days after the convoy mission, they were going to Fayid again to be briefed for the next. The wake-up sergeant came through the tent area before dawn to get the crews out of bed. As on previous missions, less than a dozen planes were going. An old bus with a Jewish driver collected the crews and took them to the mess hall. On non-mission days everyone walked.

Major Beck was already in the bus when *Blonde Job*'s crew straggled aboard again after breakfast. He was a big-chested man, broader even than Gallegly, with hardly any definition between chest, waist and hips. He had a thick red neck and an auburn moustache shot with grey. He looked belligerent even when he was in a good mood, making it impossible to tell when he was in a good mood. He was the Old Man. He was thirty-four years old.

"Wagstaff, you overgrown bastard," he said fiercely. "Where the hell'd you go after the movie? We were supposed to play us some casino."

Everyone stopped talking to hear what Wagstaff would say. He was the only man in the 234th never intimidated by the major.

"Hiding," said Wagstaff, who had forgotten the game. "You get so sore when I cream your butt."

Major Beck's neck got redder. Silkwood paled. He was afraid that one day Wagstaff would go too far. And this might be the day.

"You know what's wrong with you, Lieutenant?" Beck demanded. "Outside of not being able to fly a four engine aircraft? You got no respect for rank."

"I've got plenty of respect for rank, Maje," Wagstaff said soberly. "I just wish I had more of it."

No one laughed until Beck did, then everyone joined in except the bus driver, who did not know enough English to follow the exchange.

The bus made a circuit of the revetments, dropping off crews at their planes. Harris struggled down the narrow aisle with his briefcase in one hand and his cased octant in the other, his leather flight jacket clutched under one arm. The rolled Mercator chart thrust under the two straps of the briefcase and

29

protruding at either end, made his progress awkward. Navigators were always more burdened than the other crew members.

The leather briefcase bulged with the tools of his trade. Maps, charts, Air Almanac, Ageton Tables for calculating celestial fixes, dividers, pencils, pencil sharpener, compass, triangles, Weems plotter, E6B computer, penlight, batteries and logbook. An E6B was a circular slide-rule especially designed for aerial navigation. Harris felt like a lawyer going to an office. He thought of his station in *Blonde Job*'s nose as just that, an office.

Silkwood offered to carry something for him. He always did. Harris let him take the flight jacket, not trusting him with the delicate octant.

The air throbbed with sound. The first planes to be taking off were already running up their engines. Harris liked the sound. It had become a part of his life from his first day as a cadet at Maxwell Field almost a year ago. Since then there had been no hour of the day or night when at one time or another he had not heard the sound of aircraft engines running up, taking off, passing directly overhead or landing.

At the revetment, Wagstaff, Gallegly and Trombatore, the aerial engineer, walking round *Blonde Job* in the first of the preflight checks, inspecting tyres, wheels, movable control surfaces and the Pitot tube. The rush of air through the Pitot tube translated into airspeed on the instrument panel. Ground crews had been known to forget to remove the protective cover before a flight and without airspeed readings it was exceedingly hazardous to take off or land.

The other crew members, navigator, bombardier, radio operator, assistant radio operator-top turret gunner, two waist gunners and tail turret gunner, climbed through the bomb bays to their takeoff stations. Silkwood hurried in ahead of Harris and reached down from the flight deck to help with the briefcase and octant. Silkwood did try to make himself useful, which was more than could be said of lots of bombardiers. He was really going to have to try and be nicer to Silkwood. But even Silkwood's helpfulness could be irritating. He was always so obviously *there*. Being around Silkwood could be like being in a crowd.

Wagstaff and Gallegly came aboard and climbed into their seats, Wagstaff on the left, Gallegly on the right. The seats were backed by thick slabs of armour-plate shaped like tombstones. "You think they're trying to tell us something?" Wagstaff said the first time he saw them. Wagstaff put his cigarettes and Zippo lighter on the instrument panel ledge. Gallegly did the same with his pipe and tobacco pouch. They started the checklist and slipped headsets over their visored caps. Outside, the British ground crew rolled up the energizer and waited. Wagstaff and Gallegly buckled into their seatpacks. Harris and Silkwood used chest packs. Their harnesses and cylindrical parachute packs were in the nose.

Silkwood took his place behind Wagstaff, holding on to the armour-plate, and Harris did the same behind Gallegly.

Gallegly said, "Clear on the right."

Wagstaff said, "Clear on the left. Let's get this show on the road."

He held his left hand out of the sliding window, thumb up. The ground crew plugged in the energizer and fired up Number 2 engine. The inside port engine was always started first. Gallegly ran up Number 2, its roar mingling with that of other engines around the field. He and Wagstaff started the other

31

engines in turn, resuming the checklist, shouting above the noise. A plane taxied past the hardstand on its way to the runway. The rachety beat of *Blonde Job*'s props enveloped Harris from both sides. *Blonde Job* throbbed and trembled. "Like a hound dog passing peach seeds," was how Wagstaff described it. Harris hardly noticed it any more.

The ground crew pulled the chocks. Wagstaff held the ship with the brakes while he received instructions from the tower. He released the brakes and *Blonde Job* moved heavily on to the taxi strip like a fat woman, not the lissom girl on the nose. In the air, though, she was graceful, as some fat women were on the dance floor.

Blonde Job joined a line of aircraft waiting to take off. Major Beck was already in the air in *Wrecking Crew*, orbiting. He was leading the nine-plane formation. *Blonde Job* rolled forward ponderously as the ship ahead of it wheeled on to the runway. At the far end, a plane was just getting airborne, its fat wheels lifting up into the wells as it rose. Gallegly held the brakes while Wagstaff increased power. The flight deck filled with thunder. *Blonde Job* shook and strained. Gallegly released the brakes and she wheeled on to the runway as the plane ahead of her lifted off. Harris held on to the armour-plate with both hands, his body relaxed, wishing he could be in the nose for takeoff and watch the earth fall away. You could do that in a B-17, which did not have tricycle landing gear. *Blonde Job* roared along the humming pink concrete, and was airborne. Harris checked his right wristwatch. He would record the time of takeoff later. *Blonde Job* climbed sluggishly, its wheels locking into the wells with a thump. Wagstaff said a combat-loaded B-24 took off like a fat lady climbing out of the sack.

Wrecking Crew was far up ahead, throttled back, one

plane on its wing and another moving in. The three elements of three would be climbing and forming on course. *Blonde Job* was leading the third element.

Harris reached around the armour-plate and tapped Gallegly on the shoulder.

"Going to my office," he said.

Gallegly turned, grinned, and turned back quickly to resume his methodical scan of the sky in the right quadrant. When they were forming, everyone in the ship kept a constant watch for other planes. Harris picked up his briefcase and octant and went to the back of the flight deck to the tunnel entrance. He hoped Silkwood would stay on the flight deck all the way to Fayid. There was nothing for a bombardier to do until they neared a target. He wormed his way under the flight deck, hampered by his equipment. An elbow dug into his ankle as he squeezed by the nosewheel. No such luck. He'd have Silkwood all the way to Fayid.

In the nose, he put on his headset, plugged it in, picked up the hand mike, plugged it in and said, "Navigator to driver," to let Wagstaff know he was in his position.

"Roger," said Wagstaff's filtered voice.

Silkwood started buckling into his chest harness. He leaned forward, lips moving. Harris could not hear him through the earphones above the beat of the engines. He flipped back one earphone.

"I said, do you think we'll see any fighters?" Silkwood said.

Harris shrugged and undid the strap holding up the work table at the back of the nose. He got out the maps covering Palestine, the Sinai and the Delta out of his briefcase and arranged them in order on the table.

"I hope so," Silkwood said at his elbow. "I'd give

33

anything to write my father I'd shot down a Nazi fighter."

Harris laid out his plotting equipment, E6B and logbook. The dividers slid forward on the vibrating work table. There was a metal ridge along the front edge of the table to keep things from sliding off. He entered time of takeoff in his log and began filling in the heading of the log page.

"I'd give anything to get a ME one-oh-nine," Silkwood said.

"You really think you could hit the side of a barn with one'a those fifties?" Harris said.

"If they came in head on."

"If it's all the same to you, Silkwood, I'd just as soon not see any fighters head on, sideways or upside down."

Silkwood went to his stool up front. He had the best seat in the house, surrounded by Plexiglass where he could see in an almost 270-degree arc. Harris went back to work. There was really nothing much he had to do on this leg because they were just following Major Beck's element. But he liked to keep in practice and it was necessary always to know exactly where they were in case *Blonde Job* had a malfunction and they had to abort. When you weren't leading you did "follow-the-pilot," entering instrument readings in the log and recording position at regular intervals.

The nine pink bombers flew tight formation, the wingmen tucked in and the three elements in crisp vee. It was not dictated by any threat of enemy fighters—none sortied this far behind the battle lines—but by Major Beck. He demanded that flying good formation be second nature to his pilots and missed no opportunity to make them practise it. The threat of his wrath was as compelling as threat of

German Me 109s and Italian Macchi 200s.

For a while, Harris was able to follow the route on his map. He had been taught map navigation at Turner Field, pilotage it was called, but it had not been stressed in the training missions. It was merely something navigators were expected to know. In this theatre he seldom had the opportunity to use a map. Their missions took them either over the Mediterranean or the trackless wastes of the Western Desert.

They flew south along the Jenin–Nablus–Latrun air corridor roughly paralleling the coast at first but soon angled away from it. The earth below was a green and brown patchwork of tilled fields and orchards, burnt pasture land and barren hills. The neat rows of irrigated crops most often surrounded the Jewish settlements. Jewish settlements and villages were precisely laid out, streets intersecting at right angles, buildings arranged in regular patterns. The Arab villages were clusters of mud huts, packed and formless. Tel Aviv lay off to the right, white and gleaming.

Farther south green fields gave way increasingly to sand, rock and brown hills, until only tenuous fingers of grassland probed the tumbled Sinai.

"Where are we?" Silkwood asked.

"I think we're lost," said Harris.

"You're kidding, aren't you?" Silkwood said, not sure.

"Yeah, Silkwood, I'm kidding. Just sit back down and enjoy the scenery."

The Sinai was heaped sand stretching out endlessly and crumpled hills in arid shades of tan, rust and copper broken by deep twisting wadis dark with shadow. Oases were marked on Harris's map but nowhere could he see palms or any glint of water.

The formation veered westward, approaching the

coast. Harris entered the new heading in his log and stared out of the right window.

Silkwood joined him and said, "What are we looking for?"

"El Arish."

The village should be coming up any moment. And there it lay, huddled against the coastline, pressed by sandy scrub with only here and there a vagrant patch of green. El Arish was a maze of mud walls enclosing courtyards and flat-roofed dwellings, from the air like a warren of small rooms in a building with its roof torn off.

After a while the straight silvery-blue thread of the Suez Canal split the desert. The formation went into trail to cross the canal through the designated corridor. Beyond the canal it turned south for Fayid, a great sprawl of sunbaked hangars, buildings, hardstands, runways and taxi strips merging on its perimeters with the monotonous desert. Twin-engine Wellingtons, obsolescent Blenheims with their caved-in noses and four-engine Halifaxes were dispersed about the airfield.

They were given lunch in the officers' mess before briefing. The British officers with whom they dined all looked terribly casual and competent. But the Americans felt battle hardened and combat wise, too, in their sweaty khakis and zippered flight coveralls, no longer diffident as they had been their first time at Fayid. The food was considerably better than at Ramat Jonas and served by Egyptian waiters in white robes, red sashes and black-tasselled tarbooshes.

"It's not fair," Silkwood complained. "Why don't the limeys have to live like we do?"

"Junior," Wagstaff said, "if you gotta gripe about something, gripe about how bad things are at Ramat Jonas, not how good they are here."

They were briefed for four Italian cruisers 650 nautical miles away in a Greek harbour, Pylos in Navarino Bay, within range only of the B-24s. The cruisers had been photographed by a high-flying RAF Spitfire reconnaissance plane the day before.

"That's swell," Silkwood whispered. "We ought to get a crack at some fighters."

Harris gave him a look. Going to Greece excited him, too, but he could do without fighters.

Crew members jotted down the information pertinent to their functions as RAF briefing officers gave them radio frequencies, course, bombing altitude and procedures, target data, intelligence estimates of enemy opposition and weather, including winds aloft. Harris's chief interest was course, target coordinates and winds aloft. He listened to the rest with half an ear, impatient to begin plotting the course on his Mercator. Navigators were always rushed. The other crew members had only to climb aboard and go. Navigators had to assemble maps, mark their Mercators and calculate headings, taking into consideration the vagaries of wind. As often as not the winds given them at briefing, the metro winds, had changed by the time the mission was under way. They were obliged to determine the wind in flight by other means.

They would fly at minimum altitude to evade detection, climb to altitude and split into twos on the bombing run. Each pair and a fourth three-ship element were assigned specific cruisers. Each plane was carrying six one-thousand pound bombs, two in each of three bomb bays. The fourth bay held the auxiliary fuel tank. The B-24s required them for the longer missions. They had been in the air twelve and a half hours on the shipping strike earlier in the week. They'd used two bomb bay tanks for the flight over from Morrison Field because of the Natal-Accra and Accra-Khartoum legs. *Blonde Job* had been in the air fourteen and half hours for the exhausting night flight across the breadth of Africa and Harris had been on his feet most of the way, falling asleep standing more than once. A 234th plane had gone down and been lost with all aboard on that leg.

The navigators remained behind after the time hack for setting watches and the crews went out to the planes. Harris spread out his Mercator, marked it to encompass the latitude and longitude of Fayid and Pylos, set down the coordinates of both, drew in the course and with his computer swiftly calculated the anticipated drift from the briefed wind. He was the first to finish.

Out at *Blonde Job*, Wagstaff made his usual joke.

"What were you doing, Tex, writing your will?"

Harris made his own ritual reply.

"Everything's going to charity. I cut you plumb out."

But he knew nothing was going to happen to him. Not flying with Wagstaff. Wagstaff was one hell of a pilot. And lucky.

CHAPTER III

The Nile Delta was a sudden burst of brilliant green after only empty, tawny desert all the way from Fayid. Lush fields patterned with canals, mud huts singly and in clusters, oxen and half-bare ploughmen, clouds of white birds rising in alarm at the roar of bombers flying low. Vivid green gave way to vivid blue as *Blonde Job* thundered over the coast. Harris entered the time in his log with compass heading, airspeed, altitude, free air temperature and co-ordinates of the crossing point. They crossed the coast just east of Rosetta, where the Rosetta stone had been found. Harris had known about the Rosetta stone, with its inscriptions in Greek and hieroglyphics unlocking the secret of Egyptian writing since elementary school, never dreaming that one day he would go to where it was discovered.

Rosetta was less than a hundred miles east of El Alamein. Men were shooting at each other and getting killed at El Alamein but here in the nose of *Blonde Job* he was no more aware of the fighting than the peasants the formation had just startled in their fields. He felt callow and a little guilty. Fighting on the ground, that was rugged. This was sightseeing.

Holding the hand mike he stood in the astrodome

and looked back at Gallegly. He called for an altitude check. Gallegly gave it to him, a hundred feet, and held up a thumb in salute. Harris reset his altimeter at a hundred feet. The pilots' altimeter had been adjusted before takeoff to reflect the atmospheric pressure given at briefing.

Harris studied the face of the sea for the surface wind. It was wrinkled and subtly ridged, with no whitecaps. That meant light surface wind, under five knots. A headwind. When you cruised at only 160 knots indicated a 5 knot headwind could make a difference on a long flight. Harris read wind direction from the surface. The wrinkles and ridges were at right angles to the wind and falling back into it.

The wind was different from that given at briefing, not unexpectedly. He entered the new wind in his log and calculated a new true heading and groundspeed. Whether the lead navigator caught it or not he would have it and know where they were. The winds would change as they climbed, of course. They shifted and changed force with altitude. The wind he read from the sea's face would be useless. For winds aloft he needed a driftmeter and, unaccountably, there were none in the 108th's pink bombers.

He had learned to get along without it but in school he had been taught to rely heavily on the driftmeter. It was a tube thrusting down through the floor, an eyepiece through which the navigator could track a point on the surface and measure the drift, the direction in which the plane was being carried off course by the wind and how far. Three such observations taken on different headings and plotted on the E6B's sliding grid gave wind direction and force. That and the instrument readings enabled a navigator to determine groundspeed and the heading necessary to maintain a desired course. That kind of navigation was called dead reckoning. "If you reckon wrong, you're dead," the instructor had explained, tongue in cheek. Harris had thought about that a lot until he became accustomed to operating without a driftmeter.

It was all because of the wind. If there were no wind to bully or coax you off course, slow you down or push you faster, a navigator would be about as useful as tits on a boar. The pilot or anybody could just read the flight instruments, make a few simple calculations and figure heading, groundspeed and time of arrival. The wind was the navigator's adversary but Harris was grateful for it. If it weren't for the wind, he thought, I could be in the infantry.

At his elbow Silkwood said, anguished, "I've got to pee."

He almost always had to as soon as they were off the ground on a long mission, like a kid on a Sunday drive. Harris let him by to the relief tube, a black rubber hose sticking out of the side of the ship with a little rubber funnel on the using end. There was another on the flight deck and third back in the waist. There was a chemical toilet in the waist as well, about the size of a wastepaper basket, but so far it had never been used. The user, whatever his rank, was supposed to clean it out.

Silkwood took the tube from its clamp, unzipped his flight coveralls and fumbled in his undershorts. As always, he kept his body between Harris and the tube. The plane rocked as Wagstaff made an adjustment. Silkwood tottered. Harris steadied him with speed born of practice. Coming over, Silkwood had sprinkled a considerable area of the nose. Once was enough. Silkwood put the relief tube back in its clamp, zipped up and looked at his hands with distaste. It really bothered him not to be able to wash up

41

afterward. He scrubbed his hands on his coverall leg and said, "When do we get to Pylos?"

Again like a child on a Sunday drive. Harris bit back a gibe. He was really going to be nicer to Silkwood. He estimated their position, measured the distance to the target, made a rapid calculation taking into account the slow climb to altitude and gave Silkwood an ETA. Silkwood thanked him, as always too grateful for small favours, and started back for his stool. Harris stopped him and pointed to the chute harnesses and yellow Mae Wests on the floor. They put on the life-jackets and buckled into the harnesses. They were supposed to wear life-vests over water but usually did not. This was a long one, though, and there might be fighters. The chute packs that snapped into the harnesses were under the work table.

It was hot in the nose and would be until they got higher. Harris was sweating under the triple layer of coveralls, Mae West and harness. Next time he'd wear khakis and a shortsleeved shirt. He would have removed the extras and let the coveralls down to dangle from the waist if he hadn't made Silkwood buckle up.

He read his flight instruments, made the log entries and sat down on his work table. It was the only place he had to sit. The ridge dug into the underside of his legs just behind the knees. He closed his eyes and tried to remember what Hannah Ruh looked like. He could not, exactly. Just that she looked good enough to be worth whatever trouble it might take. A sudden change in the tempo of the engines jarred him out of his reverie. He checked airspeed and altitude. No change. He had merely grown suddenly aware of the racket the engines were making. After a while in the air he always became so accustomed to the clamour that he forgot about it.

Harris cranked his radio around the dial and found

42

a news broadcast in English. Things were quiet on the desert front. RAF bombers had hit targets in Germany. US forces had made landings in the Solomon Islands. Good. They were finally taking the war to the goddam Japs. He was glad he was in this theatre instead of the Pacific, though. There was so much more to see and do here.

They droned on. Silkwood drowsed on his stool. Harris was grateful for the respite. Listening to Silkwood was bad enough at best but worse when he had to strain to hear him above the roar. Now there was a real, though subtle change in the tempo of the engines. The formation was beginning the long shallow climb to altitude. Harris entered the time in his log and made a note of cloud conditions. The metro officer always asked about that at post-mission interrogation. It supplemented the routine weather reconnaissance flights.

There were a few lonesome clouds four or five thousand feet above the formation looking out of place in an otherwise empty sky. Silkwood was awake now, tracking one of them with the starboard flexible fifty in the Plexiglass nose, pretending it was a Me 109 no doubt.

Climbing at last, Harris thought gratefully. They'd cool off at altitude. The interphone crackled. Harris motioned Silkwood to put on his headset.

"Big Wags to crew," Wagstaff said. "Clear your guns. And try not to hit my wingmen, OK?"

The crew called in, position by position, acknowledging the order. Silkwood gave Harris his hopeful little boy look. Harris nodded. When he was not especially provoked with Silkwood he let him clear all three nose guns instead of taking turns. Silkwood worked the charging handle and fired a burst.

"Gotcha," he said to an imaginary foe.

43

Harris could read his lips.

Blonde Job trembled as the turret and waist guns opened up. Streams of tracers laced the sky all around the formation.

"Pilot to crew," Wagstaff called. "That's enough. Let's save a few for Jerry."

Off to the right, the inboard port engine of one of the planes in the second element slowed to a stop, feathered. The plane continued in formation for a few minutes then, rocking its wings in a farewell salute, turned away in a wide arc on a heading back to Egypt. The other wingman floated back and filled the diamond beneath Wagstaff's element. The leader increased power long enough to catch Major Beck's element and slide in under it.

"Aren't you glad it's not us?" Silkwood said.

Harris nodded. He was. He wanted to see Greece.

He logged the time, calculated a position and logged that. If the plane didn't make it back they would want to know when and where it aborted for the search. He checked his Mercator position against a surface map. They were in easy fighter range of Crete now. They had been briefed on the possibility of enemy fighters from the Cretan airfields. Up ahead, as if in answer to his thoughts, *Wrecking Crew* rocked its wings in a signal for the formation to tighten up and for all to keep a sharp lookout. Wagstaff's voice came over the interphone putting the warning into words.

At 10,000 feet Harris got on the interphone to tell the crew. They went on oxygen at 10,000. He exchanged the hand mike for a throat mike and slipped on the black rubber mask. He did not feel restricted in an oxygen mask. He liked it. Breathing pure air, riding high on the wind in the clear and cold, masked like a bandit, visored like a knight. He wished Hannah Ruh could see him like this. And smiled, embarrassed, under the mask.

It grew cold. He shrugged into his leather jacket, a tight squeeze because of the Mae West and parachute harness. Nineteen thousand feet and minus six degrees centigrade. He made the conversion to fahrenheit on his E6B. Twenty-two degrees. It had been ninety on the ground at Fayid. The temperature dropped two degrees centigrade for every 1,000 feet they climbed. If it got much colder Wagstaff would be turning on cabin heat.

The formation levelled off at bombing altitude, 20,000 feet. Ahead and far off to the right, Crete jutted from the sea sombre brown in a pool of blue, lapped here and there in minuscule white where waves broke. Mountainous, menacing but with a stark beauty, like a great twin-horned lizard with its neck stretched out, its brown hide ridged and knobby. The horns, at the western end, pointed toward Greece. Harris moved as close to Silkwood as the restraints of headset, throat mike and oxygen mask permitted and showed him Crete and the Peloponnesus, with Navarino Bay at its south-western tip, on the map. Silkwood nodded, took the cover from his bomb sight and began fussing with knobs and switches.

Harris watched for fighters. The island lay off to the right for half an hour but none appeared. Maybe they wouldn't see any. Silkwood would be the only one disappointed. Another thirty-five minutes and the formation altered course for the target. According to Harris's calculations, right on the money. Major Beck's navigator was good too.

Then Greece emerged, a blurry nubbin on the horizon swelling into bold peninsulas thrusting out into the sea. Harris was the first of his family ever to see Greece. When the war was over he would come back and see it from the ground. He wanted some day to come back and see everything he had flown over.

Major Beck broke radio silence. The altered formation dictated a change in approach. Two planes of his four plane element would take the first cruiser, the other pair the second. Wagstaff's element would split up the same way for third or fourth cruisers. *Blonde Job*'s element fell back to make room for the two planes detaching themselves from *Wrecking Crew*. They did so sloppily. The pilots would be hearing from Beck when they got down. Then the four pairs of bombers were in trail, one behind the other, *Blonde Job* and her wingman third in line.

Navarino Bay was long and narrow, a finger of water between dark hills. The cruisers in Pylos harbour were lined up end to end between the plunging shoreline and a snaking protective boom. They looked like the protozoa Harris had seen under the microscope in biology lab at Rice Institute, narrow, tapering at the ends, with a blob in the middle.

Little tufts of black smoke materialized out of the thin air above the cruisers, thickly sewn, slowly dissipating to be replaced by new tufts: flak from the cruisers and shore batteries. Lots of it. Harris's belly tightened but he was not terrified, only nervous.

Douglas Fairbanks. *The Thief of Bagdad*. When Douglas Fairbanks wanted something he threw down a little pellet and what he wanted appeared in a puff of white smoke. He'd have to tell Gallegly about the crazy thing he thought about when he saw the flak bursts. But this was black smoke, not white, and not what he particularly wanted. Shards of steel.

"Bombardier to pilot," Silkwood called on the interphone. "Bomb bay doors open."

46

Competent, assured, not sounding like Silkwood at all.

The line of bombers pivoted and swung toward the cruisers as Wagstaff's voice replied, "Pilot to bombardier, Roger."

Not sounding like Wagstaff, either. Breathy.

Wrecking Crew would be first over the target, the other elements, having farther to fly, over theirs in quick succession.

Wrecking Crew's element was on its bomb run, pink bellies gaping, flying straight and level, ignoring the flak. The bombs popped out like water-melon seeds, tumbling, slanting down toward the harbour, vanishing quickly.

"Bombardier to pilot, follow the PDI," Silkwood said.

"You got her," said Wagstaff.

PDI, Pilot Direction Indicator. A needle on a dial on the flight deck instrument panel to be kept centred while the bombardier manipulated the complicated controls of his Norden bombsight, the plane always to be held within fifty feet or less of the intended bombing altitude. Not easy to do but Wagstaff was good at it.

Below, sharp flashing lights, like a pinball machine. The first element's bombs. They burst in the water in splashes of white; on the hills in spurts of black and red. One burst alongside its cruiser. The second element's bombs were falling. Silkwood, oblivious, hunched over his bombsight. Black tufts blossomed directly ahead of *Blonde Job*, concentrated and intense. She began weaving, taking evasive action, threatening the wingman, who had to weave with her.

Silkwood screamed into the interphone.

"Follow the PDI! Son of a bitch!"

Harris had never heard Silkwood say son of a bitch

47

before.

They would soon be directly over the target. Even a navigator knew it would then be too late. The bombs would slant over the cruisers into the hills. Silkwood was cursing. Nothing fancy, just hells and damns. Close to tears. *Blonde Job* stopped weaving, racking from side to side in a very narrow orbit, as if Wagstaff was having to fight the controls to keep her straight and level.

"Bombs away," Silkwood cried, *Blonde Job* lifting, lighter by six thousand pounds.

Blonde Job banked steeply, heading out of the flak.

Harris logged the time and looked back at their cruiser, waiting. Flashes in the mountains in a ragged pattern, one after the other. Silkwood had dropped long and the other bombardier with him. Black smoke with a red core spilled from the second cruiser. She had taken a direct hit earlier. As Harris watched, the bombs of the last element straddled the fourth cruiser. Some near misses, maybe better than direct hits. Near misses exploded below the waterline where the armour-plate was thinner. At least two out of the four cruisers damaged, three if *Wrecking Crew*'s miss was close enough. They had never bombed that accurately before. Silkwood was staring blindly, his eyes tear-filled above the black snout of the oxygen mask. Poor bastard. Harris pulled his oxygen mask aside and mouthed, "It wasn't your fault, Silkwood."

Silkwood turned away and hit the bombsight with his fist, real anger, not his usual petulance.

The bombers re-formed in four-plane elements on a course for home. Wagstaff usually started his chatter on the way back but the interphone remained silent. Probably concentrating on holding good formation, Harris thought.

Still no fighters.

They began the slow letdown. The airspeed picked up. Oxygen masks off at 10,000 feet. At dusk the formation began stringing out, purposely, to put space between the planes before full dark. Harris watched the other ships shrink in size and disappear into the gathering night. *Blonde Job* was alone in the darkness. This was the part of a mission where he earned his pay, coming home alone with only the stars to guide him.

He switched on the extension lamp over his work table and got his octant out of its wooden case. He had pasted paper over the lamp to cut down on the light and used the light only when necessary. Light impaired night vision. You needed your night vision for celestial navigation and strong light in the nose shone through the astrodome and bothered the pilots. They needed night vision too.

Harris used a squat A-7 octant, an older type than the long narrow A-10s the other navigators used and harder to learn but more accurate and better for dim stars. He had grown skilful with it through dogged practice on the ground and in the air.

He turned off the light and stood in the astrodome studying the skies for three good stars to shoot. At first glance, the sky was a maze of random brilliant pinpricks but to his practised eye it quickly resolved itself into familiar patterns. A single constellation, even a single star, in the slowly altering tapestry was all he needed to find the pattern. He found Orion. As Polaris was his favourite star, so Orion was his favourite constellation. Rigel, Bellatrix and Betelgeuse—"Beetlejuice" navigators called it—in their easily identifiable pattern and Orion's attendant star, blazing Sirius, the Dog Star, brightest star in the heavens. From Orion to the Square of Pegasus, Cassiopeia's Chair, Scorpio and the other patterns which held or pointed to the stars he used for navigation.

Fomalhaut, Spica and Canopus, Aldebaran and Dubhe, Procyon, Regulus, Arcturus. Others more obscure. Ancient names, and mysterious, Greek, Roman and Arabic. The Arabs they joked about at Ramat Jonas were descendants of men who had named stars.

Harris picked three stars he liked, stars at mid-altitudes and so situated in relation to one another that the Lines of Position would cross in approximately an equilateral triangle. One a good course line, directly off to the right, another a fair speed line. For the next fix he'd use one that gave a good speed line, a star directly ahead or behind.

Looking down into his octant he saw an inverted image of the pattern, brighter and clearer than with the naked eye. He centred the horizon bubble and lined up his star in the crosshairs, pressed the metal tab that made a pencil line on the celluloid disc, turned on the tiny battery-operated bulb that illuminated the disc and in its light read the exact time on his hack watch. Exact time was critical. Every four seconds you were off cranked in a one-mile error. Aerial navigation was inexact enough without that. He recorded the time. Then ten more sightings, rapidly, each one a new pencil line on the disc. He read the time again and recorded it, quickly estimated the average of the pencil lines, parallel or overlapping in a smudge, turned the knob to centre the average point and read the altitude off the Vernier scale. Recorded it. All in less than two minutes. He erased the lines and shot two more stars in the same manner. Seven minutes overall.

Silkwood watched from his stool. He never bothered Harris when Harris was shooting stars and plotting fixes. Even Silkwood understood that it required utter concentration. He continued to watch silently as Harris turned on his hooded desk lamp, got out his tables, calculated LOPs and intercepts and plotted them on the Mercator. It took just under fifteen minutes.

The LOPs intersected in a tiny triangle. Good. The tinier the better. If he had done everything right, their position at the time the fix was shot was in the centre of the triangle. The optimum three star fix crossed in a point but that seldom occurred.

The intercepts were long, indicating that the dead reckoning position he had used for the assumed position was considerably off. Not so good but not unexpected. Not when you'd been flubbing around in formation for more than an hour after the last visual fix with no wind to go on but the metro wind, which was usually wrong.

"Where are we?" Silkwood said.

Harris laid his hand palm down, fingers spread, on the Mercator.

"About here," he said.

On a Mercator a hand covered several hundred square miles and there were no surface features on a Mercator, only grid lines.

"Aw, come on, Tex."

"We're not too bad," Harris said, relenting. "I'll show you where when we get closer to land."

He couldn't trust a fix with such long intercepts. He shot another using a course projection of the first one for the assumed position. Again a small triangle, and this time short intercepts. He trusted this one. He calculated a wind from the difference between where they were and where they would have been with no wind.

They were twenty-eight miles to the left of the desired course and fifteen miles farther from Pylos

51

than true airspeed alone would have taken them. True airspeed was that on the airspeed indicator adjusted for free air temperature and altitude. He cranked in his new-found wind on the E6B, calculated a new heading, groundspeed and ETA and plotted the new course on the Mercator. They had been briefed to hit the Egyptian coast at Burg El Arab, thirty miles south-west of Alexandria, where there was a flashing code beacon. The landfall had to be precise. Off to the right, they'd be too near El Alamein and the fighting and would be shot at. Off to the left, Alexandria. Where they'd also be shot at. And chewed out when they landed at Fayid if the brass could find out who it was that caused the air raid alarm.

Harris called Wagstaff and gave him the new heading and ETA. Wagstaff was happy about the tailwind.

"My butt was getting so numb I was gonna make everybody get out and push," he said.

"Anything to keep my driver happy," Harris said.

He wondered why Gallegly had nothing to say. Gallegly usually called down to ask how he was doing, but not tonight. Probably sleeping. They were on automatic pilot.

Silkwood got his chest pack from under the work table.

"Wake me when we get close," he said.

Harris promised.

Silkwood lay down on the floor with the chest pack for a pillow. In minutes he was asleep. Harris sat on the work table. There was nothing to do until the next fix. He shot one every hour.

Under the wings, the supercharger blades glowed red hot. The surrounding blackness coruscated with stars. The new moon was up, a pale thin sickle shedding little light. Harris had come to dislike a full moon, so admired and aphrodisiacal when he was a civilian looking up at it with a girl: The light of a full moon washed out a wide swath of sky, obscuring stars around it, stars he might want to shoot.

He felt a deep repose. Contented, silent, riding the wind. He did not think it strange to think of the nose as silent with two great bellowing engines and thrashing propellers on either side of him. That sound was familiar, part of the silence. This was the time he liked best on a mission, only him and the plane beating through the night. Only him, on course, riding the wind. The wind was the only thing that could do you mischief. Once you had identified it, knew exactly what it was doing to you and compensated for it, it was harmless. Too bad about dropping long at Pylos. But that's how it went sometimes. His job was to see that they got back home.

Home. Not Houston, not even Ramat Jonas. Home was wherever it was you were supposed to land after a mission. Pilots said any landing you could walk away from was a good landing. So for a navigator any mission where you brought them home and on your ETA was a good mission. It was a crummy mission for Silkwood though. Even if it hadn't been his fault.

He wished it were Hannah Ruh lying there in the nose instead of J. Edward Silkwood, Jr. Ruh. Peace in German. Piece to a horny navigator. He hoped. Tomorrow night he'd eat at the Goldblums' again and find out where she lived. Go see her and take her a pair of the silk stockings he'd brought overseas just in case he met a girl who appreciated them. She was standoffish but she'd appreciate silk stockings. She shaved her legs.

Time for another three star fix. Silkwood was stretched out under the astrodome and he had to wake him to use it.

"Where are we?" Silkwood said, yawning and rubbing his eyes.

Harris said he'd let him know.

The wind hadn't changed much. Just enough to move them off course a couple of degrees and increase groundspeed a couple of knots. Not enough to bother giving Wagstaff the new ETA. He might be sleeping, anyhow, along with the rest of the crew. Tooling over the sea like this on automatic pilot, only one pilot had to stay awake. A one-minute change in ETA didn't mean much. Celestial navigation wasn't all that accurate. Any time you could hit your destination within ten miles and a couple of minutes of your ETA you were doing all right.

His fixes had been good though. Maybe he ought to call Wags and give him a new heading. Gallegly responded to his call. Wagstaff was sleeping. Gallegly sounded grumpy, not his usual self. Probably wishing he was sleeping too.

"OK, Silkwood," Harris said. "You can start looking for the Burg El Arab beacon."

It would be a while yet before they were close enough but it got Silkwood off his back. After Silkwood had his nap he liked to talk. Harris did, too, talk whiled away the hours, but Silkwood was so boring. He did have good eyes, though. He'd be the first one on the plane to see the beacon. He was 20/15 in both eyes. You only had to be 20/20 to be a pilot. You could be 20/30 in one eye and be a navigator.

That was why Harris was a navigator. He couldn't pass the pilot physical. Twenty-thirty in his right eye. And that was why he preferred the A-7 octant to the A-10. The A-7 was better for dim stars like Polaris. It magnified and there was no illumination in the bubble chamber.

Silkwood had started as a pilot and washed out in basic. Harris had heard his excuses in greater detail than he wanted, and more than once. Silkwood was ashamed of having washed out. Silkwood said his father hadn't answered his letters for two weeks after he washed out. That was one of the reasons why Silkwood wanted so badly to sink cruisers and shoot down Me 109s.

Harris didn't think washing out was anything to be so ashamed of. A lot of good bombardiers and navigators were washed out pilot cadets. Bombing and navigating just took a different kind of skill. Silkwood was a hell of a good bombardier. But that was about it.

Harris's stomach growled. He was hungry. They hadn't eaten for hours. You'd think the bastards would give them a lunch to take on missions. He thought about the case of C rations back in the waist. A can of meat and beans would sure hit the spot. But no chance, somebody would see him.

Wagstaff called.

"Big Wags to navigator. You awake?"

"Navigator to pilot. Navigators never sleep."

"Where are we?"

"Getting close. Thirty-seven minutes."

Blonde Job droned on through the night. Harris thought about a T-bone steak, cooked medium, and a big baked potato with all the butter you wanted. Maybe there'd be decent chow for a change after post-mission interrogation. But probably not, just the usual greasy canned corned beef sandwiches. "Corn willie," his dad called it. His dad had been in the First World War, a three striper in the infantry. Kidded him about being an officer. Saluted him after the graduation and commissioning exercises at Turner Field. Harris had given him a dollar bill. Tradition

55

said you gave a dollar to the first enlisted man to salute you after you got the gold bars. There'd been a lot of grinning enlisted men waiting outside the auditorium after the graduation ceremony. His dad had said he was going to frame the dollar bill. He said it was the first money he'd got back on his investment. And hugged him. Mom cried a little. She'd been afraid his new observer wings meant he'd be going off to combat right away and getting killed.

"I see it!" Silkwood cried, pointing.

At first Harris thought it was Silkwood's imagination because he could see nothing but stars up ahead himself. Wagstaff called wanting to know if it was a beacon out there just off to the right or a low star. Then Harris saw it himself, a winking spark in the far blackness. It could have been a low star, at night you couldn't see the horizon and didn't know where the sea ended and the sky began, but the winking was too regular.

It was a beacon all right, but too far away for the signal to be read. He turned on the lamp to check the flimsy, not long, because he wanted to keep his eyes accustomed to the darkness. The flimsy was a sheet of onion skin paper handed out to navigators at briefing. It listed colours of the day, radio frequencies and identification code word and the co-ordinates and signal letters of the flashing code beacons on the Nile Delta approaches.

He could not be sure it was the Burg El Arab beacon up ahead until he could read the letters it flashed. It should be, he'd had good fixes. And yet. On long missions with no visual fixes you were never really *sure*. Your octant could be off, or your watch, or a sudden, drastic shift in the wind after your last fix. A thirty or forty knot crosswind could carry you off course far and fast. And what were those irregular flashes way off to the right? There weren't any light beacons west of Burg El Arab. He had a moment of doubt. Not worry, just doubt.

He turned on the lamp and studied his surface map. If it was the Burg El Arab beacon that would be El Alamein off to the right. The flashes could be artillery. He'd forgotten there was a ground war going on. Silkwood read off the dots and dashes the beacon was flashing. It was definitely Burg El Arab. Something not quite relief flooded Harris. A release of tension, pride of craft. He called Wagstaff and told him to alter heading for the beacon. It was only a minor alteration. He had hit it almost on the nose.

They crossed the coast over Burg El Arab within ninety seconds of his ETA. Not bad.

Wagstaff called him on the interphone. "Just lucky, Tex," he said.

Harris knew Wags really didn't think so. Wags thought he was the best navigator in the 108th and said so to everyone except Harris. Wagstaff started singing "Blues in the Night," making up his own words, mostly dirty. And funny. The crew, awake now, joined in with their own versions. Everyone was always wide awake and happy when they knew where they were after a long mission.

There was an air corridor they were supposed to fly from Burg El Arab to Fayid. No problem. They were among a network of flashing beacons now, some looking close enough to reach out and touch, some too far away to be read. As beautiful in their own way as the stars, Harris thought, and a damn sight easier to read. He had marked the corridor and the beacon co-ordinates and code letters on his Mercator and it was as easy as reading road signs. He gave Wagstaff a heading for Fayid and sat back. He was just a passenger now.

Everyone was alert, watching for other returning planes. Flying back, you never saw another plane from your mission for hours and then they all seemed to be arriving at the same time, except those whose navigators hadn't had good fixes and let themselves be carried off course. They had their running lights on now, and the navigation lights winking red and green at the wingtips, and the IFF. IFF for Identification Friend or Foe, sending out a constant radio signal to let people on the ground know they weren't Axis planes sneaking in.

The officers' club, where they went after interrogation, was in awesome disarray, with overturned furniture and butt urns on their sides spilling sand and cigarette ends. The RAF officer who conducted them there said without apology it was always like that after a long evening of drinking.

Wagstaff, as usual, was the life of the party, wolfing down corned beef sandwiches as if they tasted good and making everyone laugh with his account of the mission. Gallegly sat a little apart, silent, sucking on his pipe. Brooding. Gallegly was sometimes quieter than most but this was unusual. Harris brought over two mugs of strong tea and sat down.

"What's the matter?" he asked.

"I'm not sure," Gallegly said, troubled.

"What are you talking about?"

"That bomb run."

"Hell, it could happen to anybody."

"We're not supposed to take evasive action on the bombing run, you know that. Straight and level's the ticket."

A long pause.

"I took her away from him."

"You took *Blonde Job* away from Wags?"

"I think he was scared shitless."

Harris stared at him. He looked over at Wagstaff, towering head and shoulders above the others, head thrown back, laughing. Everybody laughing with him. He couldn't believe anything could scare Wags, not flak, not anything. He looked back at Gallegly. Gallegly believed it, though. Gallegly didn't want to, but he did.

CHAPTER IV

They slept a few hours at Fayid, had a good breakfast and were back at Ramat Jonas by mid-morning. The kibbutzim and Aleenah settlers looked up from the fields when the planes started coming in. Counting, Harris thought, and he wondered if Hannah Ruh was one of them. She didn't look like a farmworker but she had the hands of one and must be. Everyone was in Aleenah. Except the Goldblums. They were latecomers and didn't have the customary twenty acres. That's why they ran the private table, Sgt. Weisz had said.

The bombers always tried to avoid flying directly over the kibbutz and Aleenah on their final approach. An ex-farmer on group staff said it was too upsetting to the chickens and livestock.

Harris did not have a chance to talk with Gallegly about Wagstaff until they were back in their tent.

"I don't believe it," he said. "Not Wags."

"Yeah," Gallegly said. "I must be wrong. He must have thought he could get her straight and level in time. And I screwed him up by jumping in. He didn't chew me out, though."

"That's Wags. You oughtta be glad it wasn't Beck you screwed up."

They walked to the officers' club to write letters. Most of them wrote more letters than they had thought they would. Conditions at Ramat Jonas encouraged it. There was little else to do except play cards, shoot dice or read the tattered copies of *Life*, *Time* and comic books some of the air crew had brought with them on the flight over and left in the club when they were finished. They had the *Palestine Post* every day but Saturday, when it wasn't published, but the paper didn't take long to read. Some, like Gallegly, had been foresighted enough to bring books even though they had been told to hold down the weight of personal gear. Harris had several books coming on the ss *Pasteur* in his footlocker.

They could have used their free time to explore the area but being somewhere simply because you had been sent there seemed to inhibit sightseeing. Ramat Jonas, just across the road, was worth only one visit anyhow. The kibbutznikim were cordial enough but always occupied with their many tasks, and very clannish. They all ate together in one big dining-hall and no one had his own house. The small children were cared for in a communal nursery. The adults marched off to work like a GI detail on fatigue duty and were gone from dawn until almost dusk. As bad as being a cadet in pre-flight, Harris thought. Except that there were men and women both. The women looked as rugged as the men. If it weren't for all the little kids he would have thought they'd be too tired at night to be interested in sex. Aleenah was different, being a *moschav ovdim,* a workers' cooperative, instead of a kibbutz, with families having their own homes and fields. But there, too, everyone worked all day, and there was nothing to see or buy, no shops, no movie house and no restaurant. Just the Goldblums' private table, which only Harris and Gallegly knew about.

Nazareth was within easy hitch-hiking range but few had bestirred themselves to get on the road and thumb a ride. When they had the chance they went to Haifa but not really as tourists. They bought souvenirs to send home but basically what they were after was a good meal and women. There were café's and hotels in Haifa with dance bands and live entertainment, places like the Ginat-Or on Herzl Street that had a folk singer and the Panorama and Park-Hotel El Dorado on Mount Carmel that had dancing in the garden on weekends, but there were always a lot more restless men in uniform there than women and the men of the 108th usually had to return to the field too early in the evening to do more than have a few drinks.

The club had no attractions but it was convenient. It was a one-room, flat-roofed stucco building hot in the day-time even with the wide overhangs shading the large windows. Instead of curtains there were wooden shutters on the outside, closed at night for the blackout. The furniture, chairs and a few plain tables, looked as if it had been scavenged. At that, Harris thought, it was probably better than the P-40 boys were having it in the desert up closer to the fighting. The 57th Fighter Group had been at Khartoum at the same time as the 234th. The men and their planes had crossed the South Atlantic on Aircraft Carrier *Ranger* and flown across Africa in stages.

Silkwood and Wagstaff were already at the club, Silkwood writing away with his tongue sticking out and Wagstaff shooting dice in a corner. Wagstaff was crooning, "Eighter from Decatur, the county seat of Wise." He had a name for every combination on the dice and knew the gambling odds for all the points.

Silkwood looked up and said, "You fellows want to

62

do some PT later?"

PT was Physical Training, anything from calisthenics to sports. There was no athletic equipment at Ramat Jonas except for the odd ball and glove someone had brought over so Silkwood had to mean calisthenics. Harris and Gallegly hadn't done any of that since cadet days.

"We just did a rugged thirty minutes," Harris said. "We're pooped."

Silkwood studied his face to see if he was joking but couldn't tell. He went back to his letter. There were already two completed ones on the table. He wrote a lot of letters, one a day to his mother unless they were flying. Others, it seemed, to just about everyone he'd ever known who had not been actively hostile to him. Wagstaff rarely wrote. "Let 'em read about me in the papers," he said.

Harris motioned for Gallegly to sit with him at Silkwood's table. It was part of being nicer to Silkwood. He felt sorry for him. Silkwood was as good a bombardier as any of them and had been the only one not to get at least a piece of the target at Pylos. Gallegly's fault, maybe, but Gallegly had only been trying to straighten out the bomb run.

"That's a dandy writing kit," Silkwood said.

He said it every time he saw it. Harris's folks had sent it to him at Lakeland when they realized he would be going overseas. Harris had made the mistake, which he regretted, of letting them know he was in combat crew training. The kit was of leather and had come complete with four books of six cent airmail stamps and a Parker 51 pen guaranteed not to leak at high altitude. Harris took the gift as hint that he was expected to write regularly.

Now he wrote his mother and father about visiting a Jewish settlement without naming Aleenah or re-

63

vealing how far it was from the field. He wondered if they knew yet that he was in Palestine. The only address they had, if they had started receiving his letters, was a New York APO number and he had written only that he was well, happy, working regularly and to send candy bars, magazines and the *Sunday Houston Post*. If they were in touch with Gallegly's folks they would know after Gallegly's parents got his first letter.

"Dear Mom and Dad," Gallegly had written, "I am in the land where Christ was born and I wish to Christ I was in the land where I was born."

Gallegly hadn't meant it, though. It was just his way of letting them know where he was. Gallegly was the type who settled in quietly anywhere. All he needed was his pipe, a book and now and then a woman. He hadn't had one since Natal. None of them had, Harris thought ruefully, although they had gone to Haifa looking. They had heard of a brothel there which had among its attractions a girl known as the Brown Bomber. When they found the place there was a waiting line and they hadn't bothered. Neither Harris nor Gallegly really liked brothels and whores. They had gone to Madame ZeZe's in Natal because it was notorious and supposed be fun. And it had been, but not like being with an eager amateur.

Ramat Jonas was the first place Harris had been stationed that he'd not quickly found an agreeable girl in the nearest town. One visit to the kibbutz and he had realized it held no promise. He had thought Aleenah would be the same, until he saw Hannah Ruh. She hadn't acted eager but you never could tell. And you never knew until you tried.

He sealed the envelope and wrote "Censored By" in the lower lefthand corner, signing his name and rank. Officers could do that. Enlisted men had to leave their letters unsealed to be checked. He used one of his dwindling supply of airmail stamps. He could have merely written FREE where the stamp went but the letter would go surface mail and take weeks to get to them.

After lunch, which was as unappetizing as usual, he went back to the club and played blackjack until it was time to shower and change into good khakis for supper at the Goldblums'. Wagstaff and Silkwood went with him and Gallegly.

Harris took two pairs of silk stockings in his pocket, one for Mrs. Goldblum, and an extra pack of cigarettes, in case Hannah Ruh smoked. He was into the next to last carton of the four he had bought in Trinidad for seventy cents each. He was trying to make them stretch until his footlocker arrived with the ground echelon so he wouldn't be reduced to Players and Craven A's from the NAAFI truck. Black-market American cigarettes were sometimes available in the harbour area at Haifa for a pound a carton but he didn't like being played for a sucker.

On the road just outside of Aleenah, a double file of young girls from the agricultural school marched by them carrying rakes, scythes and hoes on their shoulders like rifles, singing a jaunty, martial sound-ing song in Hebrew. All together, as if they practised a lot. They were swarthy from the sun, their strong legs hairy in short shorts. Wagstaff called out to them, loud and friendly, flashing his big smile. They all looked at him at the same time, like "Eyes right!" in the daily parade at Maxwell Field, and smiled back without breaking stride or harmony. Silkwood was embarrassed.

"I think the big one next to the end's got the hots for you," Harris said.

"Aw, come on," Silkwood said.

Supper was delayed a little when Mrs. Goldblum found out she had American guests.

"Is good when you come," Sgt. Weisz said dryly to Harris. "Is more to eat and better."

Both Goldblums were at first intimidated by Wagstaff's size and manner but before the meal was over, with Weisz as interpreter, he had them laughing to the point of tears. In the end they were laughing even before Weisz translated. It also took the Goldblums a while to overcome an instinctive hostility to Silkwood's poster Aryan looks. But he was shy, eating with his eyes fixed on his plate, and Mrs. Goldblum gradually sensed that he was just a boy a long way from home. She pressed food on him as she had Harris on the first visit and kept his glass filled with milk. Harris wished Silkwood would be as silent in the nose of their plane, and he had a brief twinge of jealousy. Before, Mrs. Goldblum had mothered him.

Harris gave her the stockings after supper. She was deeply moved. Wagstaff said she couldn't have them unless she modelled them for her American boy-friends. She pinched his cheek and said he was a terrible boy but left the room and returned to raise her long, shapeless dress calf-high. Wagstaff whistled and applauded, the others joining in. Mrs. Goldblum blushed like a girl and covered her face with her hands. She told Wagstaff he was a very terrible boy. She gave him grapes and figs clumsily wrapped in an old Hebrew newspaper to take back with him, saying he must share it with the others.

Harris took Sgt. Weisz aside and asked him where he could find Hannah Ruh.

Weisz looked him in the eye. "She is good girl," he said carefully.

"I know that."

Harris felt guilty, but he wasn't a rapist for God's

66

sake, and she was old enough to take care of herself. It wasn't any of Weisz's business anyhow.

"You don't forget it, OK? She is serious girl. She has important work to do."

Harris wondered just what he meant by that. He could hardly mean the work she did in the fields. In Aleenah that was important, sure, but everyone did it and there was no reason for Weisz to make such a big deal of it. It was something to do with her pistol training, maybe. But he hadn't thought they were still fighting Arabs. Not with a real war on.

"You understand?" Weisz said. "You are soldier, too."

Was Weisz telling him Hannah was a soldier? Harris nodded, thinking, I'm not a soldier, I'm a navigator. Soldiers carried rifles and got shot at. No one ever shot at him personally, just the plane he was in. That made a big difference.

Weisz told him where she lived. Harris wondered if Weisz would have done it if he weren't Jewish. She lived with a widowed aunt, Frau Waldvogel, a few houses away on the circular perimeter road across from one of the groves of young pines in the centre section.

"Waldvogel?" Harris said. "That means woodbird, doesn't it?"

Weisz nodded.

Ruh and Waldvogel. Peace and woodbird. Suddenly Harris was back in Dr. Freund's German class at Rice listening to Goethe.

Uberallen Gipfeln
    Ist Ruh.
In allen Wipfeln
    Spürest du
    Kaum einen Hauch.

Die Vogelein sweigen im Walde.
Warte nur, balde
   Ruhest du auch.

"Over all the mountaintops is peace. In all the treetops you feel scarcely a breath. The little birds are silent in the woods. Only wait, soon you will rest, too."

Harris couldn't believe he remembered the whole thing. Dr. Freund would be proud of him. If he had absorbed everything else that well in his two years of German he would have been a shark instead of just barely average.

He told Wagstaff he wasn't going back with them. He had things to do in Aleenah. Silkwood asked why didn't they all go with him.

"It's personal," Harris said.

"Has she got a friend?" Wagstaff said.

They hadn't told him about Hannah but Wagstaff knew it could only be a girl.

"You're going to see a girl?" Silkwood demanded, somewhere between envy and disapproval.

"Has she got two friends?" said Wagstaff. Looking at Gallegly, "Make that three."

Harris knew Silkwood was afraid they would get him a date.

"Remember that big one next to the end?" he said. "That's her best friend."

"Come on, fellows," Silkwood said nervously. "Let's go back to the club."

"You bastard," said Gallegly. "That's what you were talking to Weisz about. Good luck."

That was like Gallegly, not trying to horn in. Maybe later he could get Hannah to fix him up with somebody.

The houses were clumps of shadow showing chinks

of light around blackout curtains and shutters. Harris counted them, not looking up to check the stars. The pumps went pock-pock, the air smelled of pines. A familiar smell. Pines grew everywhere in Houston.

This must be Frau Woodbird's. He went up the dirt path feeling unaccountably nervous. Almost a reversion to his early teens, when he first began dating. Because of Weisz's attitude, and Hannah Ruh being so different from any other girl he'd been around before. Withdrawn. Not shy, he could handle that easily enough, but withdrawn. Able to fieldstrip a pistol blindfolded. Doing mysterious important things. And foreign. Most all, foreign. But she was Jewish and he was too. Small comfort. He didn't really know how to be a Jew. For the first time in his life he wished he did. But maybe she'd be interested in him because he was as foreign to her as she to him. Besides being good-looking and here, being foreign was something about Hannah Ruh that attracted him.

He knocked. There was no response. He knocked again, louder. There were light footsteps inside and a woman's voice asking something in Hebrew. He couldn't tell if the voice was Hannah's. He could not remember what her voice was like except that it had not been cordial. He could not even visualize her face.

"Does Hannah Ruh live here?" he asked the door. "Is this Mrs. Wood . . . Frau Waldvogel's house?"

The door opened. Light spilled out and Hannah Ruh stood looking at him, slender, stacked. Now he remembered the face. A delicate oval, eyebrows as heavy as a man's but a woman's challenging eyes, hazel, he thought, not sure in the uncertain light. A face on which surprise gave way to wariness as he looked into it.

"Lieutenant Harris," she said. "What a surprise."

Her tone was mocking. He wondered if she was like that with everyone or just him.

"Come in," she said, opening the door wider and standing aside.

She closed the door behind him and stood against it. Posing, he wondered? She had to know how great she looked in those short shorts, legs so brown and smooth and slim. But there was no artifice about her. She wasn't trying to attract him. Just the opposite. She wasn't posing, just sizing him up. He sensed he made her feel uncomfortable and that made him feel uncomfortable. She kept looking at him as if waiting for an explanation. What the hell was there to explain?

"Well," he said. *"Shalom."*

"Shalom, Lieutenant."

"I had supper at the Goldblums' and I thought as long as I was in the neighbourhood I'd say hello."

"Why?"

"Why not?"

Now she was the one at a loss. She looked at him uncertainly, came a few steps into the room and waved carelessly at a chair.

"Sit down, if you like."

Harris tucked his flight cap under his belt and sat. The chair was upholstered, rumpsprung. The room wasn't any larger than the Goldblums' but there was no local plywood here. It was crowded with old furniture, heavy, like that in his grandmother's house, but more worn. The couch was all hills and hollows with an unprofessional patch near one end. There were three cushions on the couch, two plain brown and the third with pine trees embroidered on it. There was an open book on the couch. Hannah'd been reading. Old family photographs were everywhere, as at the

Goldblums', and a print of Mount Carmel was on the wall.

Hannah sat on the couch and slid one of the brown cushions over the patched place. She leaned forward and crossed her arms on her thighs. Harris knew she was uncomfortable having so much leg showing. He had been looking at her legs. He looked away. She said nothing. She sure as hell wasn't trying to make him feel at home.

"What are you reading?" he asked.

"What?"

He nodded at the book. She picked it up and put it, open, on her lap, her arms, now freed, falling to her sides.

"Buddenbrooks," she said.

"Mann was always too heavy for me. Too German."

She was surprised he knew it was Thomas Mann. As he had hoped she might be.

"Too German?" she said. "In Germany it was not permitted to read him."

It was a reprimand. Try again, he thought.

"Sergeant Weisz said you lived with your aunt. Where are your folks?"

No sooner had he said it than he regretted asking. Maybe they were still in Germany. Every day the *Palestine Post* carried stories about the terrible things the Germans were doing to Jews all over Europe. He hated the Germans for that but it did not make him feel any closer to those Jews.

"You are not really interested, are you?" she said. "Is it just me you don't like or all Americans?"

"Mauritius."

"What?"

"My parents are in Mauritius."

He did not know where that was and his face showed it.

71

"A small British island in the Indian Ocean," she said, as if pleased by this confirmation of his ignorance.

"Why didn't they come here instead?"

"It was not permitted. The English do not permit Jews entry to Palestine."

There was bitterness in her tone, and hate.

"You're here."

"Obviously."

"If they let Jews in, how did you . . ?"

"Harris is not a Jewish name," she said, interrupting deliberately. "Yet you say you are Jewish."

"You mean it's none of my business how you got in?"

"Perhaps," she said, looking down at her book.

"I'm keeping you from your reading," Harris said sarcastically, sitting forward as if to rise, not really intending to but wanting to see if it mattered to her if he did.

"Actually, it's rather a bore," she said, unruffled, despite the trace of German accent sounding more English than the English she seemed to hate.

Where had she learned her English? He started to ask her but instead took out his cigarettes and offered her one. She hesitated, then accepted with a nod. He lit it for her, then lit his own. They smoked in silence, Harris watching her. She pretended not to notice, looking not at him but at a wisp of smoke drifting towards the ceiling. She grimaced. He followed her gaze. There were ugly brown stains where the roof had leaked. Maybe she didn't like it here and wished she had gone with her folks, he thought. Lonely, maybe. Good, lonely girls were eager.

"What do they do for fun here?" he said.

"We are not here for fun," she snapped, looking at him as if he were stupid as well as impudent.

Wrong move. Try again.

"The reason my name is Harris," he began.

"It is of no importance."

If she weren't the only good looking girl around . . .

"You know something, Hannah?" he said, smiling. "You're a real horse's butt."

She stiffened, eyes widening, and shot him a swift, reappraising glance. Well, he thought, I finally got her complete attention.

"The reason my name is Harris," he said affably, "is because of my granddaddy's first cousin, Max."

She smiled at the "granddaddy," as he had hoped she might.

"They were both named Max Hirsch and they both ended up in Houston, Texas when they came over from Germany."

"You are German?"

Interested at last.

"Yeah, if you go all the way back to my grandma and grandpa. Anyhow, everybody was always getting 'em mixed up. So they decided one of 'em was going to have to change his name and since my cousin got there first . . ."

"Some Jews change their names for other reasons." Sceptical.

"Grandpa Harris was not ashamed of being Jewish," he said coldly.

"Are you?"

He thought about it.

"No."

When he was a child he had sometimes wished he wasn't Jewish but not because he was ashamed of it. Until he was bar mitzvahed he'd had to go to temple on Saturdays and Sunday school on Sundays when most of his friends only had to go on Sundays. And for several years he had to take Hebrew from Mrs. Goldberg on Wednesday afternoons while other kids were out playing. He hadn't thought it fair and on Saturday mornings and Wednesday afternoons wished he was a Christian. After he was bar mitzvahed and stopped going to temple he never wished he was a Christian again. He didn't care much what he was as long as it was American. And particularly a Texan. He wouldn't much want to be a Yankee.

"Are you proud of it?" she persisted.

"You're whatever you happen to be born. So what's there to be proud of?"

Her smile was scornful. "Have you not looked around you, Lieutenant Harris?"

"Sure, but what's that got to do with me?"

"Yes," she said thoughtfully, "you are German."

"What do you mean by that?"

But he knew.

"Look, I'm right proud of what Jews are doing here but it's not me doing it. Just because I'm Jewish . . ."

He was Jewish and they were Jewish but they were also Germans, Poles, Russians or, like Weisz, Hungarians. He was American. Like Gallegly and Wagstaff and the others. Why couldn't she understand that?

"You are more American than Jewish, I think."

Could she read his mind?

"Just as German Jews were more German than Jewish," she continued. "Or so they thought."

Her face grew sombre as she retreated into memory. Damn, he thought, just when she was starting to get a little more friendly.

"Hannah," he said, "it's real nice outside. How about taking a walk?"

"No, thank you."

She was wary again.

"What are you afraid of?"

But he knew without asking. She knew what was on his mind. Her face hardened.

"I am not afraid of you, Lieutenant Harris. I am not afraid of anything. Not ever again."

"Well, then?"

"I'll just tell Tante Frieda I'm going out for a moment."

She was gone only briefly. When she returned the door to the rear of the house remained ajar. Harris was sure Mrs. Woodbird was studying him from behind it.

"Shall we go?" said Hannah.

Outside, the air had grown cooler. The pumps sounded louder and the pine scent was strong, mixed with the smell of damp earth from the water coursing through the irrigation ditches. A sound of engines floated in from the airfield. The limey ground crews were working late. Harris looked up instinctively at the stars and stumbled in a rut. Hannah took his arm to steady him but quickly dropped her hand.

He put his arm around her waist. It was a slender waist, firm, with not an ounce of fat. She would be like that all over. What luck to find a girl like Hannah in a place like this. She removed his arm as if picking off a bug but said nothing.

No one else was out on the dirt road. The houses were dark. It was as if they were all alone in Aleenah. The pine grove loomed dark across the road beneath the thin edge of the new moon. Harris angled toward the grove. Hannah did not protest. That was promising. The trees were small and widely spaced, with no undergrowth, but all the same providing a screen from the dark houses.

"Why don't we sit down?" he said.

"You invited me to walk," she said.

"Now I'm inviting you to sit down."

"Very well."

She sat down carefully, her back against a tree, her knees pulled up against her chest and her arms around her shins. A defensive position. But at least he was alone with her, with no Mrs. Woodbird peeking from a back room. And no mosquitoes. They must do something about them in Aleenah.

"This sure beats Houston," he said.

"Indeed?"

"It'd be hot and we'd be fighting off mosquitoes."

"Tante Frieda said there were many mosquitoes here when she and Onkel Karl came to Aleenah."

Harris laughed.

"You are amused?"

"A knockout of a girl and a horny navigator sitting out here in the dark like this and they're talking about mosquitoes."

"What does it mean, horny?"

"Wanting a girl."

"That was quite obvious from the beginning. You're dreadfully transparent, Lieutenant."

She was not insulted, but she wasn't responsive, either. Just matter-of-fact.

"Why don't you call me Mike?"

"You should find a girl quite easily in Haifa. Such a handsome American Lieutenant. And quite—practised, I think. But in Aleenah I am afraid you must be content with speaking of mosquitoes. We are serious people here."

Gyorgy Weisz had said she was a serious girl. What exactly did they mean by that, other than that he shouldn't try to make time with her.

"How about talking about something else that knows how to draw blood? You."

"What do you wish to know? Now that you have

76

learned what most concerns you; that I am not . . . available."

She was, though, he thought. Just wouldn't admit it. Maybe she didn't even know it. And she was afraid. A virgin, most likely. Well, what the hell, he was a virgin once himself. It was going to take longer than he'd expected, that was all. But he had plenty of time. What was there better to do between missions? She was worth the trouble.

"Now that's settled," he said, "how'd you learn to speak such good English?"

"In Mainz I had an English nanny. And we were first in England some months after Germany."

"A nanny? You mean like a governess?"

He'd never known anyone with a governess, had only read about it in novels.

"Were you rich?"

"Yes."

She said it without boasting and with less regrets than he would have expected.

"Are you?" she asked, mocking again. "But all Americans are rich, are they not?"

"Not hardly. My dad's in the lumber business. I'd probably be in it with him if it wasn't for the war."

He shifted position to sit back to back with her on the other side of the tree. It was a small tree and their backs were only inches apart but far enough away that she wouldn't feel he was trying to move in on her.

"After all that it must be tough living here in Aleenah like this."

"I am not surprised you should believe so," she said icily. She rose and brushed pine needles from her shorts. "I would be nowhere else. For a Jew there is only Palestine. Here we can fight back." She glared down at him. "You think you know everything, but

77

you know nothing. And so smug. Bringing me here, expecting . . . as if I were some little tart."

He was disconcerted by her attack. And by its accuracy. At least the part about bringing her here. He stood up and faced her.

"I know you're not a tart, Hannah."

"Thank you."

Cold.

"I must go back. We go early to work every day in Aleenah. Unfortunately we are not American flyers."

He should be angry with her for that. Hell, he was fighting a war. Getting shot at. Bombing hell out of the people that had run her and her family out of Germany. And he was angry with her. But not for that. For knowing all he wanted was to get in her pants and making it so plain he wasn't going to. He wasn't going to let her know he was sore though.

"It does beat working for a living," he said lightly.

"I am sorry, Michael," she said, unexpectedly. "I think it is because I am so jealous."

"Jealous?"

Of the girls he could find in Haifa?

"You are fighting back. Killing those swine. While I . . ."

"While you what?"

"Can only envy you. Now I must really go."

They walked back in silence. He wanted to ask her why she hadn't gone to Mauritius with her folks and what the pistol training was for, why Weisz had called her a soldier when, as she said herself, she had no one to fight. But he sensed it was better for now to honour her silence. She had unbent enough to apologize and to call him Michael. He'd made a little progress with her tonight and he wanted to hang on to his gains.

Her hand on the doorknob, she turned and said,

"Shalom."

"Ruh," Harris said.

"What?"

"Means the same thing, doesn't it? Peace?"

"Not really."

"Hannah?"

"Yes?"

"I'd like to kiss you goodnight."

She hesitated, then offered her cheek as if to show how little it mattered. He turned her face towards his and kissed her lips. They were taut and unresponsive. He felt her teeth through them. It usually made him angry when a girl kissed like that. Now he was only disappointed.

"I want to see you again."

"As you wish."

He fumbled the stockings out of his pocket and put them in her hand, closing her fingers over them.

"Shalom," he said, and left her standing at the door before she could say anything.

He looked back when he got to the road but the door had already closed behind her.

CHAPTER V

Harris woke up in the morning to find Gallegly, still in his undershorts, looking across at him expectantly. Harris shook his head.

"Must be losing your touch," Gallegly said.

"It's like barbecuing hot links," Harris replied. "Good stuff shouldn't be rushed."

Wagstaff stuck his head in the tent. "How'd you do last night?"

"Struck out."

Wagstaff pretended not to believe him and accused him of not wanting to share with his comrades in arms. Silkwood, who came into the tent right behind Wagstaff, looked pleased that Harris had failed.

"You better get your strength back quick, Tex," Wagstaff said. "We got a mission today."

Damn, Harris thought, they'd never be back in time for him to see Hannah tonight.

"Target, Haifa," Wagstaff said. "We're gonna take Junior in to the Brown Bomber and get him bred."

"I'm not going," Silkwood said quickly.

"Junior, when are you gonna learn to tell when somebody's kidding you?" Wagstaff said. "I wouldn't let you loose on the Brown Bomber. You'd ruin her for the troops. How about it, men? Want to run a reccy to Haifa?"

"Can we go to Mount Carmel for banana splits?" Silkwood asked.

"Why not? Everybody fall out in Class As after morning chow. OK, men?"

"I'd like to," Harris said, "but I've got things to do."

When you went to Haifa with Wagstaff you got back late.

"Same things you did last night?" Wagstaff said. "Junior, what do you think of a man who'd rather mess around with some eager babe than be with loyal friends who risk their lives with him on an almost daily basis?"

Not much, Silkwood's expression said.

Watching them heading for the road to hitch-hike, dressed for town, Harris had a moment of regret. He should have gone with them. They were a crew. Wagstaff had been joking but they really were loyal friends. Even Silkwood. And when you were with Wagstaff you had fun. What was it Hannah Ruh had said? "We are not here for fun." The 108th was here to help fight a war but it didn't mean you couldn't have fun when you got the chance. His job was to convince her of that.

Without Gallegly to knock around with the day stretched out ahead emptily. He wrote his married sister, Betty Lee, and a friend of his who hadn't gone into the service yet, and a girl in Lakeland he'd promised faithfully to write every day but was just getting around to for the first time. He spit-shined his GI shoes, lunched off bread, canned New Zealand butter and marmalade in the mess and hurried back to his tent to shoot the sun in transit. If you shot it a few minutes before its zenith and a few minutes after, the LOPs gave you a one-body fix. His was eighteen miles off. Shooting stars from the ground he could almost always get within four or five miles but some-how he never had the same accuracy with sun shots or moon shots.

He still had the whole afternoon to kill. He could go out to *Blonde Job* and eat C rations but it was a long walk in the hot sun and he didn't want to raid the emergency rations without Gallegly. He dipped into Gallegly's copy of *USA* but didn't feel like read-ing, either. He might as well go over to Aleenah and fool around until it was supper time at the Gold-blums'.

There was nothing to do in Aleenah when he got there. He'd expected that really. He took the circular dirt road to Hannah's house and knocked on the door. She was probably out in the field working but it didn't hurt to try. He waited, knowing she wasn't in the house. He should have gone to Haifa with the others and come back early. As he turned away, a woman came around the corner of the house and spoke to him in Hebrew. She had an old farmwo-man's face, creased and weatherbeaten. She wore a kerchief and the knotty legs below her kneelength shorts were patterned with varicose veins. She was sweating and holding a scythe, the same kind of scythe he'd seen used cutting tall grass back home. A long wooden handle with two knobs sticking out, one for each hand. Hard to use until you got the knack.

"*Ja?*" she said.

Could she be Hannah's aunt? He hadn't expected her to look like that. More like Mrs. Goldblum. This old lady looked like she'd been farming all her life. Sharecropping.

"Mrs. Waldvogel?" he said, walking towards her.

She sure didn't look like a woodbird, or any other kind of bird. Hannah Ruh would probably look like that when she was old if she kept working in the fields.

The tanned, creased face broke into a smile. She had a gold tooth near the front. She leaned the scythe against the side of the house, wiped her palm on her shorts and held out her hand.

"Lieutenant Harris, *nicht wahr? Shalom.*"

She gave his hand a brisk, downward pump. She'd been watching through the crack in the door last night, all right, if she knew who he was. But why so friendly? He'd have thought she'd be suspicious of him for taking her juicy niece out into the dark. She sure wasn't acting like any Jewish mama he knew.

Her hand was like a workingman's. She was speaking German too swiftly for him to understand a word.

"*Bitte,*" he said. "*Nicht so schnell.*"

Not so fast. One of the few phrases he still remembered. She spoke more slowly. There was a lot he didn't get, just enough to know she was thanking him for the silk stockings he had given Hannah, Hannahle, to give to her. He tried to conceal his resentment. That goddam Hannah. Afraid he'd expect something for the stockings. But he did. A word of thanks if nothing else. If she didn't want to accept them she should have given them back. This was her way of getting even with him for thinking he could get anywhere with her. Or maybe just because he was an American, an American Jew, who didn't appreciate how goddam wonderful she was for coming to live in Palestine.

In a halting mixture of German and English he told her he was glad she liked the stockings and hoped they fit. He asked where Hannah was working. He had intended to maybe give Hannah a hand but now he'd just watch her sweat. Mrs. Woodbird was reticent at first. Maybe Hannah had told her he'd

83

made a pass. Hell, Hannah wouldn't know what a real pass was.

Mrs. Woodbird decided he was OK. Hannah had gone to Nahariyah on an errand. He was disappointed. He had wanted to watch Hannah sweat. His disappointment showed. Mrs. Woodbird was sympathetic. It took some searching for words and some gestures but she managed to convey that Hannah had taken a bathing suit with her and if he hurried he might find her still on the beach. Nahariyah was only twenty kilometres north of Haifa on the coast road.

What made her think he gave a good goddam? He thanked her and hurried back to his tent for a towel and a pair of desert shorts. His swimming trunks were still somewhere at sea in his footlocker. He'd only packed them because it was too much trouble to send them home. No one had thought there would be any use for swimming trunks overseas.

He left his .45 under the sleeping bag that served as a mattress and went out to catch a ride. He'd never been to Nahariyah but knew it was some kind of a resort settlement because of all the ads in the *Palestine Post*. Cohen House, Pension Hirsch, Hotel-Café Flatow. He remembered the names because when he first saw the ads he had not yet grown accustomed to everything sounding Jewish.

A British lorry took him as far as the highway on the southeastern outskirts of Haifa, close enough to the coast to see the sweep of the Bay of Acre and, at its northern end, the ancient fortress town of Acre itself hanging over the Mediterranean like a cliff.

He stood with his thumb out. He would take the first ride offered, whatever the direction, letting luck decide whether he'd go looking for Hannah in Nahariya or Wagstaff and the others in Haifa. A black 1935 Cadillac heading north picked him up. The driver was a plump Arab, middle-aged and amiable, wearing a business suit despite the heat without a drop of sweat showing. He had keen dark eyes and a black, pencil-line moustache. He spoke excellent English with a French accent and was going all the way to Beirut.

He was delighted to make the acquaintance of an American officer and seemed to find silence unbearable. Just like Silkwood, except that he was interesting, telling Harris what to look at when he learned Harris had never been north of Haifa before. The limpid little stream they crossed was the Kishon River. There was the Haifa airfield and there the famous refineries. Harris knew the harbour and refineries were what the Germans were after when they raided Haifa at night and were the big reasons the B-24s weren't supposed to approach Haifa from the sea even with their running lights and IFF on. He hadn't been this close to the refineries before. They smelled just like the ones he passed on the highway on the way to Sylvan Beach back home.

After the railway shops the highway ran close to the bay for a while with only a band of marshy ground between it and the water. Harris was reminded of part of the bayshore back home, except that here the water was blue and back home the bay was brownish close in. And of course there weren't any hills in the distance back home. The driver pointed up ahead at the heavy stone battlements hanging over the sea.

"You know Acre?" he said. "Very historic."

"I haven't been there yet but I've read about it. The Crusades and everything."

Wishing he hadn't added that. This man was an Arab. He wouldn't be too crazy about the Crusades.

"Yes, yes," the driver said eagerly, pleased that Harris knew. "By the way, I am a Christian."

Harris was tempted to say, "By the way, I am a Jew," but didn't think it would go over too big, knowing how things were between Jews and Arabs. But maybe Christian Arabs were neutral, although a lot of plain Christians had it in for the Jews too. The driver offered to stop and show him around Acre but Harris said he was meeting a friend in Nahariya.

Nahariya was very nice, the driver said, a pleasant little middle-class resort. But of course it did not compare with Beirut. Beirut was a very cosmopolitan city, very French.

"No rationing, marvellous restaurants. Not like Palestine. Marvellous women also."

When he mentioned women he looked sidewise at Harris, smiling slyly.

"You wouldn't mind that, I imagine."

"Sure wouldn't," Harris said.

It was something to think about if they ever got leave.

The driver asked if he flew one of those marvellous Liberator bombers at Ramat Jonas. Harris was inclined to ignore the question. You didn't discuss military information with civilians. But what the hell, the man knew there were B-24s stationed at Ramat Jonas and could see he was US Air Corps and wearing wings. He told the man he was an observer, not a pilot. He did not say navigator because everybody around here was RAF oriented and in the RAF the navigator-bomb aimer was an observer, and wore half wings instead of full wings, which was probably why the driver had thought he was a pilot.

After the old aqueduct they reached Nahariya, a cluster of houses between the highway, the railroad and the sea. The driver let Harris out and shook his hand saying, "One day you must visit my beautiful city. You will not be disappointed."

The white sand and the blue sea beat anything Harris had ever seen at Galveston or Corpus Christi. Though it was a working day there were more people than Harris had expected swimming, sunbathing or buying food and soft drinks from stands open on four sides with palm-thatched roofs. He did not see Hannah among them. The keenness of his disappointment annoyed him. His only consolation was that she wouldn't have the satisfaction of knowing he'd come looking for her. He should have gone to Haifa with the others. But as long as he was here he might as well take a swim. He hadn't been in the Mediterranean yet, and some of the women looked passable. The trip might not be wasted after all.

There was a hut for changing. He got into his shorts and left his wallet and hack watch with a gap-toothed woman at one of the stands. Among men of the 108th, Palestine Jews, even taxi drivers, were legendary for their honesty. It was just the Arabs they didn't trust. They were probably wrong both ways, Harris thought, although he did think he could trust any Palestine Jew. On the other hand, the Arab who gave him a lift had seemed like a decent guy.

The sand was hot. He hadn't been barefoot on a beach since Fort Myers, before the group moved to Lakeland. The sand was finer than at Galveston and the water was great, too. This time of year the Gulf of Mexico would be tepid. Here the bottom sloped off quickly. At Galveston you had to walk out a way to get to water over your head. He swam out, floated on his back a while, making frustrating fantasies about what might have happened if he'd found Hannah, and returned to the beach.

His dog tags were cold against the fading summer tan of his chest. His face was still deeply tanned, except for a wedge of forehead usually covered by his flight cap, as were his arms up to where his shirtsleeves covered them and his legs between his shorts and where his socks would have been. Now was a good time to make his tan more uniform, he thought. He got his towel and went looking for a girl to spread it near.

He saw a girl who looked good. She was lying on her back, a leg flexed with the raised brown calf muscular but shapely, and not hairy. She was slim, with nice knockers rounding out the top of her suit and showing an edge of white where a strap had slipped. A forearm thrown across her face to shield her eyes prevented him from seeing if she were pretty but it didn't matter too much, not with a build like that. He walked toward her. No wonder she looked so good. It was Hannah Ruh.

Harris looked down at her covertly. There was something arousing and maybe just a little bit shameful about studying her body without her knowledge. Like peeping in a bedroom window. She was built for speed, not comfort, but there was comfort there, too, in her swells and hollows. For a slender girl, she was well rounded.

Something made her aware of his presence, his feet in the sand, his breathing or his shadow falling across her body. She moved her arm and opened her eyes. They were hazel, as he had thought. Her eyes widened. He'd startled the hell out of her. She sat up quickly and started to speak, then stopped. Why was she disconcerted? Because she sensed he'd been undressing her in his head?

"*Shalom*, Hannah," he said.

"How did . . . ? You will not tell Sergeant Weisz you found me bathing?"

Now wasn't that a goddam funny thing for her to say? Was the old bastard getting that?

"I am here on an errand for him," she said carefully, more composed. "I thought no one would be the wiser if I took a few moments to enjoy myself. Am I not wicked?"

Her laugh was forced. It was the first time he had detected any hint of falseness in her.

"Tante Frieda told me you'd be here."

"What else did she tell you?"

"Not that you're Gyorgy Weisz's girlfriend. I can tell that myself."

Why should he be so goddam jealous? And worse, show it?

Now her laugh was genuine.

"How incredibly . . . My errand was . . . business. Gyorgy Weisz's girlfriend! He has a wife and children in Natanya." Earnestly, "You will tell no one I had business in Nahariya?"

"Why should I?"

He believed her and was relieved.

"By the way," he said solemnly, "Tante Frieda thanked me for the stockings I gave her."

"That was wicked of me. But I could not accept them. I had nothing to offer in return."

"I wouldn't say that."

"I would, Lieutenant."

"Mind if I join you?"

"The beach is for everyone," she said, without the undertone of sarcasm he was prepared to hear and ignore.

He spread his towel beside hers and lay down, propping himself on an elbow, ready for a chat. But instead of doing the same she lay back and closed her eyes again, gratefully taking the sun. For want of a better topic he started telling her about the Arab who had given him a ride, watching her hungrily, achingly aware that she was white and supple under the bathing suit. At Galveston one day, in full view of a crowded beach, he had taken a girl out in neck-deep water, peeled off her suit and made love to her with no one the wiser. No chance of that with Hannah. But if she'd stretched out like that last night, tempting, relaxed . . .

"I am surprised you didn't go to Beirut with your Arab friend," she said, not opening her eyes. "Where the marvellous women are to be found."

He gave a start. He didn't think she'd been listening.

She opened her eyes and looked at him, lips twitching mischievously. "Or does food also interest you?" She got up without waiting for an answer and said, "Do you swim?"

She ran towards the sea without looking back. He ran after her. When the water was above her knees she arched in a clean, shallow dive to reappear doing a sidestroke, the way old men swam. He dived after her, passed her doing his powerful, economical crawl, wanting her to see how well he swam. He had learned to swim in Bray's Bayou, naked, having to be sure his hair was dry before he went home so his mother wouldn't know, and later learned the crawl from Sammy Howard in gym class at Albert Sidney Johnston.

"Albert Sidney Johnston Junior High,
Now our voices rise to thee in song.
Southern hero's name we proudly bear . . ."

If he sang that to Hannah he'd probably get a laugh out of her. Getting them to laugh was a good start. He lifted his head to breathe under his crooked left elbow and she passed him: doing a hell of a crawl. He picked up the tempo, digging, but couldn't catch her. He could only keep her from opening up more distance between them. Her brown arms flashed in the sun, dripping jewels. She stopped and turned to face him, her face merry and triumphant — who said she was a serious girl? — treading water, shaking the hair from her eyes. He dog-paddled to her, stopped a yard short and trod water, looking at her, wanting to kiss her laughing wet mouth.

"You can really swim," he said, panting.

She was winded too. At least he'd made her work.

"I had professional instruction," she said between breaths. "My father insisted I do everything as well as a boy."

"Must have been tough on you."

"Oh, no. It pleased me to please my father."

"But it didn't please you to go to Mauritius with him?"

It was the wrong thing to say. She got that bitter, angry look again.

"He did not go by choice. It pleases both of us more for me to work for Eretz Israel."

His expression told her he did not know what she meant.

"You have been how long in Palestine?"

"Two or three weeks. Why?"

"And you still know no Hebrew? Even Eretz Israel? The land of Israel?"

"Just *sh' ma yisroel adonoi elohanu.*"

That was the most common prayer and the only one he still knew by heart. He could still even read it in Hebrew after all these years. He'd had to say it nearly every Saturday of his life from seven to thirteen.

"You are Jewish, if only a bit," she said less severely. "I must confess I did not know Hebrew, either, until I came to Aleenah. Do you ride?"

"What?"

"Do you ride? But of course. You are from Texas."

She meant horses.

"Some. I'd rather swim."

"I was quite good at it."

He never thought he'd see Hannah Ruh looking wistful.

"I think what I miss most is the riding. My father displayed my ribbons in his office."

"You must have been good."

"At the end they would not permit me to compete," she said, her face grim with the memory. "They said a Jewess could not compete with Aryans. They knew I would take the blue. My mother had a new habit tailored for me especially for the competition. I never wore it. And it was so lovely."

"With everything else they must have done to you you're still burned up about that?" he demanded.

"Droll, is it not?"

She turned over on her back and floated, waving her feet a little to keep them from sinking. He had to do that, too, when he floated on his back but most girls didn't. They were more buoyant than men. Not Hannah. It was all that working in the fields. Her body must be as sinewy as a snake's. He paddled closer and kissed her salty lips. Then he was under water, gagging. She had ducked him. He pulled her under. She struggled, her limbs smooth and slippery, her snake-supple body yielding only at the bosom. He released her, reluctantly, before she could feel threatened.

She swam towards the beach at a leisurely pace, not competing. He swam at her side, wondering if she was sore at him for kissing her. They waded the last yards.

She looked at the watch on his left wrist, her face

showing no resentment. "It's waterproof, I hope."

He nodded, encouraged.

"What is the time?"

It wasn't five yet. The sun was still high.

"I must hurry."

"Aren't you hungry?"

She hesitated. "Ravenous. But I must pick up a package no later than 1800 hours."

Harris retrieved his hack watch and wallet and they bought food from the stalls—corn on the cob, salted without butter; butter, like sugar, was rationed and rare in Palestine; round flat bread stuffed with mashed chickpeas, and Mits Paz grapefruit juice in little chianti-shaped bottles. Hannah ate with gusto. He watched her the way Mrs. Goldblum watched him.

From the south came the sound of aircraft engines, growing louder. Everyone turned to look. A pink B-24 erupted out of nowhere, flying low over the water just offshore. It thundered past the beach less than twenty feet above the surface. Immense, pounding them with sound. It was *Pink Lady* from 234th, close enough for Harris to see the navigator and bombardier grinning in the nose, waving. The co-pilot waving, too, from the right seat, and three gunners waving from the waist window. If Major Beck found out they'd buzzed the beach there'd be a royal reaming. The only time he'd given Wagstaff a serious chewing out was when Wags had buzzed the beach below Sarasota and an irate citizen had got the plane identification number.

None of these citizens was irate. They all waved back, flapping towels, cheering.

Hannah waved, too. "How exciting!" she cried. "Do you know them?"

"Yeah. Crazy bastards."

93

"It must be glorious. Is it glorious? Flying like that?"

Harris nodded. "But it gets old after eight or ten hours. Especially when they're shooting at you."

"Are you never frightened?"

"Let's say I get very nervous."

"I think you must be very brave."

"Not as brave as you."

"What do you mean?" she said quickly.

"Coming to Palestine all by yourself."

"Oh, that," she said.

After they changed he went with her to a house. She made him wait while she went inside. After a few minutes she came out with a dented tin suitcase pulling at her arm.

"I'll take that," he said, reaching for it.

She pulled back instinctively, thought better of it and gave it to him saying, "It might be better."

He thought that was a peculiar thing to say.

The suitcase was heavy.

"What's in this, anyway? Bricks?" he said.

"Books," she said without hesitation.

They caught a rattletrap bus for Haifa. Hannah insisted on paying her own fare. She wanted the suitcase on the floor at her feet and Harris had to sit with his legs in the aisle.

"Are you angry with me for giving away your silk stockings to Tante Frieda?"

"You can do anything you want with 'em. They're yours. With legs like yours, you don't need stockings anyway."

"Thank you, I'm sure."

"I've got more coming in my footlocker. I'll give you another pair."

"Why are you so obsessed with my legs? American girls do not have them?"

94

"There aren't any American girls around."

"I see. Any legs will do."

"Hannah, don't start that stuff again. Wasn't it fun today?"

But he'd forgotten. Hannah didn't like fun.

"Yes," she said. "I'm sorry, Michael." Slyly, "You were very nearly a gentleman today."

It was almost dark when they got off the bus at the junction with the Haifa-Nazareth road.

"We must take another bus here," she said. "We leave it at Shimron. I hope you do not object to walking."

Shimron was on the main road a couple of miles from Aleenah.

"Carrying this?" he protested, nudging the suitcase with his foot.

"Nothing else for it, I'm afraid. You needn't come with me. I'll manage quite well, thank you."

Not sarcastic, just independent.

"I'm going that way anyhow," he said, resigned.

He could go on in to Haifa and try to find Wagstaff and the others but he wasn't going to leave her with that heavy suitcase. He wouldn't leave her even if there were no suitcase. Things were looking too promising.

"You don't even have to tell me what's really in it if you don't want to," he said.

"Books," she said evenly.

He thumbed a passing British lorry to a halt. "Got room for me and my girlfriend?" he asked.

The lorry driver gave him a thumb's up and a knowing smile and said, "Just nip in the back, sir."

Hannah didn't want to. "I accept nothing from the English," she whispered angrily.

"I'll get him to take us all the way to Aleenah," Harris coaxed.

"No!" she said, more emphatic than the situation demanded, Harris thought. "We go to Aleenah alone."

"Aw, come on, Hannahle."

"To Ramat Jones only, then."

He lifted the suitcase into the back of the lorry and turned to help Hannah. She had already climbed nimbly aboard. He went around to the driver's side and said, "You going as far as Ramat Jonas?"

"Anything for a Yank, sir. Nice bit of frippet you've got there, if I may say so, sir."

Hannah didn't say anything when he joined her. The lorry spun along the highway in the night. Hannah still wasn't talking. He moved closer to her. She moved away.

"The limeys are real swell about giving us rides," he said.

"I dare say."

She sounded sore at him. So she wasn't too crazy about the English. Tough titty. It beat waiting for a bus and lugging that suitcase all the way from Shimron.

"I am not your girlfriend."

So that's what she was so sore about. He laughed. He knew it made her madder but he couldn't help it.

"I know that but I had to tell him something, didn't I? You care what he thinks?"

"No."

"Well, then."

She touched his hand fleetingly.

"I'm behaving wretchedly," she said. "I am not so brave as you think."

So it wasn't just accepting a ride from an Englishman or him calling her his girlfriend. It was what was in the suitcase. If she didn't want to talk about it he wasn't going to pry. It wasn't any of his business. If he could just get her into the sack she could have all

96

the secrets she wanted.

She offered to carry the suitcase after the lorry dropped them at Ramat Jonas. He refused, shifting it from hand to hand as they trudged the dirt road to Aleenah. He stopped once to rest and looked up at the sky. A little cloud cover, about two tenths. It was challenging to pick out the stars when it wasn't clear and to know which stars were obscured.

"You know the stars, Hannah?"

"No."

"I'll teach you sometime, if you like."

"Michael? When you wish you can be quite nice."

"So can you."

He put the suitcase down at her door and said, "I'd like to come in for a while."

"I'm really quite tired. I'm sorry."

"That's OK."

He was tired, too, and his arms felt like they were coming out of their sockets. And there was always tomorrow.

She opened the door and he put the suitcase inside for her. She held out her hand. Ignoring it, he put his arms around her and kissed her. She didn't pull away. He hadn't thought she would. Even if a girl thought you were trying to make her, she'd usually respond a little anyway if she knew you were leaving and she was safe at home. Her lips weren't rigid and he couldn't feel her teeth. He kissed her again, more hungrily than he had intended because he didn't want to scare her off now that she was starting to be comfortable with him. She pulled free and shut the door in his face. He hoped he hadn't ruined everything by moving in too fast.

"Hannah?"

"Yes?"

So she was still there on the other side of the door.

"Goodnight."

"Goodnight, Michael."

So it was OK.

"See you tomorrow night?"

"Yes."

All the way back to the field he thought about how she'd looked in her bathing suit and how she would look without it. Tomorrow night might be the night. A Buff challenged him outside the tent area. Harris gave the password immediately. You didn't mess around with a Buff in the dark when he couldn't see you weren't an Arab.

He tripped over a tent rope. A flashlight pinned him in its beam.

"That you, Harris?"

Major Beck.

The squadron commander moved closer. Harris could see his hard gaze.

"Where's your goddam sidearm, Lieutenant?"

Harris felt desperately for the .45 that wasn't there.

"I forgot it, sir."

"Sometime you may wish you had it," Beck snapped.

"I wished I had it when you asked me where it was, sir."

Major Beck didn't smile. Harris braced himself for a royal chewing.

Surprisingly, to his great relief, all Beck said was, "Next time I catch you without your sidearm it's gonna be your happy ass. Where's that goddam Wagstaff?"

"I don't know, sir."

When Beck was on the warpath it was best not to know anything. Especially if it involved a friend.

"That a fact? He better not be too late dragging his ass back from Haifa, Lieutenant. We got a mission tomorrow."

"Yes, sir."

Beck turned on his heel and charged off like a retreating bull, leaving Harris to find his way to his tent in the dark. Inside, Harris kicked his cot. Another goddam mission, just when he was going so great with Hannah.

CHAPTER VI

The target was Tobruk.

The ten combat crews jammed into one end of the mess hall cheered when the group commander announced it. Tobruk was famous. The British and Italians, then the British, Italians and Germans had been fighting back and forth over it since before the United States entered the war. Harris had read about Tobruk in the papers and *Time* and *Life* before he ever had any notion he would one day seeing it himself. In a way, bombing Tobruk would be like participating in the real war for the first time. The ground war was the real war.

The Tobruk raid would be the first originating from and returning to Ramat Jonas without staging through Fayid. Harris didn't like missing a Fayid breakfast but, on the other hand, Tobruk was only a 1,400 mile round trip, under nine hours if the wind didn't screw things up, and with any kind of luck at all he could be back in time to visit Hannah.

They were going after supply dumps, harbour installations and shipping.

"Don't waste any bombs on sunken hulks," the briefing officer cautioned. "The harbour's full of 'em."

Bombing altitude was 21,000 feet.

100

"Too goddam high," Major Beck growled.

Each plane would carry twelve five hundred pounders. They would come in from the sea and return inland, giving a wide berth to the Axis forces strung out along the coast. There were Italians as well as Germans but Harris thought of the enemy as the Germans. The 108th hardly ever mentioned the Italians, except jokingly, though they did respect the Italian fighter pilots, who attacked at least as persistently as the Luftwaffe.

The briefed route meant they would not be exposed to enemy fighters for very long at a time. But it also meant they wouldn't get a look at any land action either. Harris was disappointed. Not about the fighters, Silkwood was the only one with a hard on for fighters, but about not getting a bird's eye view of the real war. Except over the target there would be nothing to see but a lot of water and sand. They'd be flying to a point well off the coast before making the turn to the target, hoping to surprise the defenders.

They flew towards the Mediterranean on a 270 degree heading, due west, over Arab villages and fields, scattering goats herded by robed men. They flew strung out behind the group commander's *Follow Me*, taking their time forming up. They crossed the coast at Athlit.

Athlit. Petra Invisa, "Hewn Out of Rock," Castle of the Pilgrims. Knobby and sea-girt, in medieval times fortified by the Knights Templar and chief seat of the order. But to Harris, only a visual fix, co-ordinates to be marked on his Mercator as the last checkpoint until Tobruk itself.

They were over the sea in formation now. There was nothing to do for four hours but check instrument readings, make log entries, nod at Silkwood as if he were listening to him, and look at one hell of a lot of water. Harris tuned his radio to Cairo. He did not have to worry about missing any calls from the flight deck because the interphone overrode everything.

He listened to Arab music and thought about Hannah Ruh. All Arab music sounded alike to him, wailing, up and down, monotonous. But endurable because it was something he'd never have heard if he'd spent his life in Houston. The first time he tuned in Arab music he'd thought he was on a jammed frequency. The Germans interfered with radio transmissions by sending out a constant eerie annoying signal that drowned them out on some frequencies.

The free air temperature was minus 20 degrees centigrade at bombing altitude. Twelve degrees fahrenheit. It was almost that in the nose. Cabin heat came on while Harris was making up his mind to ask for it. He would rather be cold than hot. A dead fly was feet up on his Mercator. He wondered what got it first, the thin air or the cold? Silkwood pulled away his oxygen mask to dab at his runny nose with a sodden rag. Sometimes the cold brought out his sinus drip. Not enough to block the passages though. They wouldn't let you fly with a blocked sinus or a cold. At altitude you couldn't equalize the ground atmospheric pressure in your head and the reduced pressure upstairs even by swallowing air, as Silkwood was doing now, trying to make his ears pop. Harris could see his Adam's apple bobbing. When you couldn't equalize the pressure it messed up your ears and hurt like hell. It could do permanent damage. If Silkwood weren't so eager, he could use his sinus condition to get grounded permanently. But nobody wanted to get grounded. It wasn't the flying pay either. Who wanted to be a groundgripper?

The sea below was as much silver as blue, smooth

and curved as a shield. At 21,000 feet you could see the coast, a faint smudged line to the south looking as if it were at your own altitude instead of far below. There were German and Italian troops there, cloaked in distance, with tanks and artillery, inspiring in Harris no sense of imminent peril. When you were miles away and four miles up it was the same as if they weren't there.

Random puffs of cloud appeared below them at 12,000 feet, balls of purest cotton bursting from the boll. Wagstaff's voice on the interphone, tight.

"Pilot to crew. Keep your head out. We're in fighter range."

No jokes.

Silkwood sat forward on his stool, swivelling his black-snouted head from side to side, up and down, hoping for 109s. Harris searched, too, knowing he would not be the first to see the fighters if they came up. Not with that 20/30 eye.

The formation altered heading ninety degrees left. Harris entered the time and his DR position in the log. According to his dead reckoning they were turning nine miles short. It didn't matter much, except to his professional pride, if *Follow Me*'s navigator was right and he was wrong. After four hours of DR with or without a driftmeter nine miles was nothing, not when you'd eventually be able to see what you were after.

The coastline no longer a smudged pencil mark. It dropped farther and farther below, thickening and growing clearer like a photographic print in its bath of hypo. Tobruk was just a hair to the right, splitting the difference between Harris's estimate and the lead navigator's. From this distance it was but a slight excrescence on the desert coast. Then definitely Tobruk, though still without much detail except the flecked harbour. The flecks were hulks with, if they were lucky, floating targets of opportunity among them.

Tobruk and the coastline took on greater definition as *Blonde Job* approached. There was no longer the illusion that it was not four miles below. Silkwood fussed with his bombsight. Harris searched the sky for fighters. He would have preferred watching Tobruk but they weren't paying him to sightsee.

The four planes in *Follow Me*'s echelon went into trail. They were bombing individually today, not in echelon. Up ahead of *Follow Me* but well below it the black puffs blossomed. Pinball lights winked all around the ruined toy village. Muzzle flashes from 88-millimeter batteries. Lots of them. More than at Pylos. Not terrifying but gut-tightening. Hannah Ruh thought he was brave. He wasn't. He just knew that a plane was hard to hit at 21,000 feet.

The black puffs rose to meet *Follow Me* as it neared the target. Four planes in a line, plodding. Major Beck's three-plane element fell into trail behind them. Wagstaff's element would be next. Still no fighters. Maybe there wouldn't be any today. Tough titty, Silkwood. *Blonde Job*'s wingmen fell into trail. *Follow Me* was in the flak, spilling bombs.

The interphone crackled. "Fighters at ten o'clock!"

Not where, not how many, not who was calling in, the way you were supposed to report fighters.

"Where, goddammit, where!" Wagstaff, high-pitched, sore about the sloppy reporting.

Other positions reporting in. Three fighters. Twenty-one thousand feet. Still ten o'clock. Closing in on Major Beck's element. Silkwood off his stool, grabbing the left fifty. Remembering he had other work to do, gesturing like a disappointed child and getting back on the bombsight. Harris took over the guns, eyes straining. Nothing. Then black specks, *barhash*, little mosquitoes, swelling swiftly into recognizable shapes. Not three fighters, five. Darting toward *Wrecking Crew*. From all angles, making their passes, climbing or diving to come in from the other side. Three 109s and two Macchi 200s. Tracers flicking toward *Wrecking Crew*'s element. Tracers flicking back at them, all short. The fighters weren't all that eager today.

Bombs slanting from the belly of the last plane in *Follow Me*'s element. High over the mottled desert beyond Tobruk, a Liberator already on *Follow Me*'s wing and a third ship moving to back on. *Wrecking Crew* bored into the flak. The fighters broke off, keeping out of it, working their way back along the line of bombers. Coming their way. *Blonde Job*'s element flying straight and level. Shouts, curses and tracking reports flooding the interphone. A fighter grew in size off to the right, coming in at an angle. An Me 109. Harris dived for the starboard fifty. The top turret clattered. *Blonde Job* shook. Lights winked in the leading edge of the 109's wing. Tracers danced, going and coming.

Harris couldn't get the goddam fighter in the sights. Like trying to track a goddam mosquito. He fired a short burst anyhow, partly out of frustration, partly to let the son of a bitch know he didn't have a sitting duck.

"Bombardier to pilot."

Unruffled, conscious of nothing but his bombsight. Too goddam dumb to be scared.

"Pilot to bombardier, go ahead."

Wagstaff sounded excited, though.

"Follow the PDI."

"Pilot to bombardier. Roger."

"Got darn it!"

Silkwood raging on the interphone.

"The dumb doors are precessing!"

He meant the bomb bay doors were creeping closed. The bombardier opened them from his position. A warning light told him when they were closed. The bombs wouldn't drop if the doors were closed.

"Son of a bitch!"

That was Wagstaff. Harris had never heard him lose his temper before.

"Pilot to navigator! Get your butt back there and hold 'em open."

He was not making a joke. A lever on the bulkhead at the front of the bays operated the doors manually. The navigator was the one who was least busy under attack on a bombing run.

"Navigator to pilot. On my way."

He got the metal walkaround oxygen bottle from its clamps, removed mask and throat mike, turned off the oxygen flow, stuck the bottle's rubber hose in his mouth and opened the valve at the top of the bottle. Unplugged his earphones, crawled under the flight deck and into the bomb bay.

The doors were partially open, creeping shut before his eyes. Cold, thin air whistled through the cracks. Harris stood on the catwalk, chilled, breathing cold oxygen, and pushed the lever down. The doors stopped closing, backed slowly open. He held the lever down to keep them from precessing again. Bombs hung from their shackles inches away from him. Below, his view curtailed, the sea sparkled far beneath the narrow catwalk at his feet. His world until the bombs fell. He'd get a real bird's eye view of Tobruk. Not even a sheet of Plexiglass to interfere. Hot damn!

Then, abruptly, what the hell am I doing here? Looking past my dirty GI shoes into 21,000 feet of empty space, not scared, just creaming to see Tobruk get pasted. Sucking on a rubber tube, freezing my tail off, getting shot at, up to my neck in high explosives, acting like it's the most natural goddam thing in the world. Back home it made him nervous just to look out of an open window on a tall building.

Without warning, *Blonde Job* fell off wildly to the left, throwing him hard against a thick strut angling from the catwalk to the top of the bay. He teetered over the void, clutching the bomb bay door lever, panic frozen.

They'd been hit!

He had to get back to the nose for his chute pack! Why had he come back here without it? *Blonde Job* continued to fall away, but more gently, losing altitude slowly, curving gracefully to the left, over the coastline. Tobruk off to the right, just in view. A quick, tormenting view of the harbour patterned with widening circles of bomb splashes, smoke billowing from fires, ground batteries winking, somebody's bombs popping red and black.

He released his frozen grip on the lever, flung open the door to the flight deck and scrambled through it. No panic, no sign of damage. The radio operator in his seat, the assistant standing in the top turret, traversing, Wagstaff and Gallegly at the controls, *Blonde Job* flying straight and level again, Tobruk falling behind to the right. Ahead and to the right, *Follow Me*'s four-plane element back in formation, *Wrecking Crew*'s two wingmen still closing in on their leader harassed by three fighters spitting tracers. Behind them, *Blonde Job*'s wingmen were coming off the target. Whatever it was that happened, they were OK now.

Harris crawled up to the nose, heart no longer racing. Silkwood was pounding a fifty with his fist, his eyes streaming tears. Harris spat out the oxygen tube and put his face close to Silkwood's.

"What happened?"

Silkwood, furious, jerked his oxygen mask aside and bawled, "Ask them!" pointing back towards the flight deck.

Harris hurried to his station, put on his oxygen mask and throat mike, plugged in his headset and stuck the walkaround bottle in its clamps, got on the starboard fifty. *Blonde Job*, full throttle, climbing, ran for *Wrecking Crew*'s element, all formed now, and closing on *Follow Me*'s element. The fighters switched to *Blonde Job*'s wingmen, stragglers now without a leader. They broke off and plummetted towards *Blonde Job*, all by herself, coming in high and head on, trying to cut her off. *Blonde Job* turned towards her wingmen instead of seeking the shelter of *Wrecking Crew*'s element. That was Wags for you. The fighters attacked desperately. Both Harris and Silkwood were firing now, Harris on the starboard fifty, Silkwood on the nose gun. The three planes headed for the seven ahead, forming as they caught up, trading chasers with the fighters.

The two advance elements throttled back to let *Blonde Job*'s element catch up, increasing power when it got in close. The fighters fell away, unwilling to challenge the firepower of ten Liberators in tight formation. They tilted and dived for the desert. Silkwood shifted to the left fifty and chased them with a long, frustrated, useless burst.

Three elements again, all nice and tidy. The skirmish was over.

Back to work. Time of turn off target—he had to estimate it—altitude, airspeed, compass heading, free air temperature logged, DR position calculated, plotted and logged. He sat slumped on his desk, sweaty at crotch and armpits despite the cold, beat. Silkwood sat on his stool staring out at nothing. Harris knew what he was thinking. Two missions in a row without hitting anything and the fighters too chicken to come in close enough to be shot down.

He pressed the mike more firmly against his throat and called Wagstaff. The first time he used a throat mike he'd felt silly. Like talking to himself.

"Navigator to pilot, go ahead."

"Big Wags to navigator, go ahead."

"What the hell happened back there? You damn near lost me."

"Controls jammed. Right in the big middle of the bomb run. You OK?"

"Yeah."

"Swell. Hey, Junior?"

"Bombardier to pilot, go ahead."

Sulking.

"Cheer up. You'll get 'em next time."

"Dan? Could we cut over to El Alamein and drop 'em on Jerry?"

"If it was up to me . . . But I just work here."

The formation levelled off at 2,000 feet after a long, gradual descent. It was hot in the nose again. Harris took off his chest harness and shirt. He'd worn shirt and pants instead of flying coveralls.

"Why couldn't it have happened after bombs away?" Silkwood demanded querulously.

"I'll take it up with somebody," Harris said. Relenting, "It wasn't that great a target anyway. All bombed to hell. Nothing left. Didn't you see how beat up it was?"

Silkwood refused to be comforted.

"They wouldn't have sent us there if it wasn't important. They always put it in the papers about Tobruk. My dad's gonna read about it and know I was on the raid, I bet."

"OK, he'll read about it. He won't know you didn't get to drop your bombs."

"You don't think I ought to tell him?"

"You can't tell him. It's a military secret. You don't tell civilians military secrets."

"Yeah," said Silkwood, relieved.

He went back to his stool but returned immediately.

"What if I just say I was among those blasting Tobruk? That wouldn't be lying, would it?"

"No. You tell him that, Silkwood."

The flat, scruffy desert stretched away endlessly below them. They were too far inland to see the coast. Harris figured a position, plotted it on his Mercator and checked the coordinates on his surface map. He had them thirty-five miles south of the coast between Sidi Barrani and Mersa Matruh. They wouldn't be seeing any Germans. Nobody got that far from the coast road back here. If his DR wasn't too far off they'd be over the Qattara Depression in twenty-five minutes. Too far from El Alamein to see any fighting. To get rid of Silkwood he showed him the Qattara Depression on the map and set him to looking for it.

"You've got the best eyes on the crew," he said.

When he thought they were getting close he called the crew and announced if anyone was interested they'd shortly be flying over the Middle East's most famous hole in the ground. He was looking forward to seeing it himself. Wagstaff came on the interphone to tell Silkwood he could jettison the bombs when they got there. They didn't land with a load of bombs.

"Can I drop 'em armed?" Silkwood said, perking up.

110

"Sure," said Wagstaff. "They got a delay on 'em."

Two thousand feet was a bit low to be dropping bombs with instantaneous fuses.

Silkwood got on his bombsight and opened the bomb bay doors. They didn't precess this time. The desert fell away into a great, irregular trench stretching out across their path as far as they could see. Steep, broken sides, floor a sandy waste gouged as if by giant machines.

"Bombs away!" Silkwood cried, gleeful.

He'd salvoed them, dropped them all at the same time in one cluster. Puff, puff, puff, twelve spurts of sand not quite simultaneously. Harris pressed his face against the Plexiglass, looking back at them. Flashes of red fire, sand geysers erupting, the sound of explosions barely audible above the roaring engines. Silkwood, euphoric, turned and called to Harris.

"Wow! Wouldn't it be swell if we could go in that low on raids?"

Harris figured a new ETA for Ramat Jonas. They'd never be back in time for supper at the Goldblums' but if post-mission didn't take too long and he wasn't too beat he might make it over to see Hannah.

Wagstaff started singing the Air Corps song on the interphone. After "Nothing can stop the Army Air Corps" the crew joined in, Harris with them.

"Except the weather."

Pause.

"Except the women."

Pause.

"Nothing can stop the Army Air Corps."

Over the lush wet green of the Delta in formation, monster pink birds startling white flocks from the fields. More desert. The narrow ribbon of the Suez Canal. The Canal was a restricted area. They had to

111

cross it in a prescribed air corridor or the Hurricanes would come up, IFF or no IFF. Across the Canal, across the Sinai. After El Arish altering heading for Ramat Jonas. East of Gaza, west of Bethlehem and Jerusalem, none of them close enough to see. Between Ramle and Ramallah, between Tulkarm and Nablus. Closer to home, Jenin. Then Afula, far off the right wing. Almost home. Ramat Jonas at last, eight hours and thirty-two minutes after takeoff.

"Big Wags to navigator. You missed it a minute. I'm gonna dock your pay."

"Navigator to driver. You just drove too slow."

Not a peep out of Gallegly. Harris hadn't heard him on the interphone since Tobruk.

The formation broke up to land in the order in which the planes had taken off, circling, pelicans playing follow the leader. A red-red flare arched from one of the planes. Trouble aboard. It left the pattern to land first. By the time it finished its roll, an RAF ambulance and crashtruck would be there to meet it. Somebody hit by flak or fighters, Harris thought, or battle damage or just plain old mechanical failure. Wagstaff should have fired a red-red, too, after the way the rudder controls had jammed over Tobruk. As good an excuse as any not to flub around in the pattern waiting their turn to land. Time wasted in the air was time he could be with Hannah.

He tapped Silkwood on the shoulder and they crawled back to the flight deck to take their landing positions. Harris let Silkwood carry his octant. He stood behind Gallegly, holding on to the armour-plate. Gallegly didn't turn around to grin at him as he usually did.

Wagstaff let Gallegly land the plane. Not all first pilots were so generous with their co-pilots. Wagstaff said Gallegly was going to be the first co-pilot in the

108th to get his own crew.

It was pretty good for a right seat landing. Just a couple of short bounces and then straight as an arrow down the rushing pink runway streaked black with tyre marks. Wagstaff grinned and held up thumb and forefinger in the standard congratulatory circle. Gallegly didn't smile back or even look at him. Harris thought it odd.

They had to wait for the crew bus's second trip. Wagstaff went back to the tail with Sgt. Trombatore, the aerial engineer, to check the vertical stabilizers. Gallegly, sombre, didn't go with them. That was odd too. The crew stood around stretching, scratching and talking about the mission. No one except Silkwood was particularly concerned about not dropping their bombs on the target. It was enough to have got there and back. Gallegly did not join in the chatter.

"You got the trots?" Harris asked.

The trots, diarrhoea, had been common in the 108th ever since they'd been at Ramat Jonas with its medicated water and British rations.

Gallegly shook his head. He walked far enough away from *Blonde Job* to fire up his pipe.

Harris followed him. "What is it, then?" he asked.

Gallegly examined his pipe to see if it was burning to suit him. He looked back at Wagstaff, who was entertaining the crew with a story.

"There wasn't anything wrong with the rudder controls," he said.

"What?"

"You heard me."

"Aw, come on, Terry."

"Have it your own way."

Snappish. Unlike the normally serene Gallegly.

"What was it, then?"

The crew bus lurched to a stop in front of *Blonde*

113

Job, worn brakedrums groaning.

"Later," said Gallegly.

They filed in with the rest of the crew. The bus was crowded. The next crew it picked up would have to stand. After long missions, ten hours or more, when they'd flown through the night, the bus was quiet. It was noisy now. Nine hours from takeoff to touchdown and no lost sleep. Gallegly said he'd tell Harris about it when they got back to the tent.

Someone said the plane that fired the red-red flare had had its ailerons knocked out by flak. No one hit, though. So far the only men lost had been those on the plane that went down somewhere between Accra and Khartoum. Maybe *Blonde Job* had been hit, too, Harris thought. A piece of flak could have lodged somewhere, jammed a control cable and been dislodged without doing any permanent damage. He told Gallegly his theory. Gallegly shook his head. He didn't contradict Wagstaff at postmission when Wagstaff reported the malfunction and said he wanted *Blonde Job* gone over from one end to the other before he flew her again.

The mess hall had held chow for the mission crews. It had not been improved by being kept warm. Harris and Gallegly made do with bread, New Zealand butter and marmalade. Wagstaff ate with his usual gusto. He could eat anything, and enjoy it. Harris envied him that. He could usually eat almost anything himself, but not British rations after the Ramat Jonas cooks finished with them.

Someone had gotten hold of a copy of the day's *Palestine Post* and everybody was talking about a front page story about their Pylos mission. The paper reported three Italian cruisers damaged by American heavy bombers in a dusk raid. Silkwood asked Harris if he thought it would be all right just to send a clipping home without mentioning he had been on the raid, his father would get the picture without that, and also without mentioning he hadn't contributed to the damage. Harris said it was a great idea.

It was after eight by the time Harris and Gallegly got to their tent. After dark. Night fell late here in August, and almost without dusk. The sun seemed to hang on the horizon for a moment, then drop. Quenched. Almost like turning off an electric light.

Gallegly hung his flashlight from its nail on the tent-post, got a couple of apples out of the net bag he kept under his cot and handed one to Harris. He sat down on his cot and took a bite of apple.

"A whole mess of flak burst just up ahead of us," he said without preamble. "Right at our altitude. Wags kicked left rudder and jerked the control post outta my hands."

He sounded as if he didn't want to believe it.

"Maybe a burst threw the plane off," Harris said. "I damn near fell out of the bomb bay."

Gallegly shook his head. "He thought they had us ranged. If we kept going straight and level the next bunch'd get us. What else could it be?"

"He could have been right. Maybe if it wasn't for him we wouldn't be sitting here eating apples."

"You know better than that. Once we're on the bomb run we're supposed to stay on it. That's what they pay us for."

He sighed. "I just can't believe he'd pull a stunt like that," he said unhappily. "Not Wags. And then lie and say it was the rudder controls."

"Maybe it really was the controls."

"Dammit, it wasn't just the rudders! I told you he snatched the control post away from me! And what about Pylos?"

Harris knew it wasn't him Gallegly was mad at.

115

Maybe he wasn't even mad at Wagstaff, either, just mad because it had happened.

It was hard to believe that about Wags. He didn't want to believe it. But Gallegly couldn't be mistaken about anything Wags did to the rudder bar or control post. When the left seat controls moved, so did the right seat controls.

"What are we gonna do, Terry?" he said miserably. "You're not gonna tell anybody, are you?"

Gallegly got up and threw his apple core out into the night.

"You know I wouldn't do that," he said.

"Maybe if we talked to him . . . Just kind of let him know we knew so he'd watch it from now on."

He wasn't sure he could talk to Wagstaff about it though. It would be so embarrassing. And hurtful.

"It's not like Wags," he said. "It won't happen again."

"Yeah," Gallegly said. "The least we can do is give him another chance."

Harris looked at his left watch, the one with local time on it. Too late to go to Aleenah. He didn't feel like it, anyhow. Not tonight.

They sat up late, talking. About everything but Wagstaff.

CHAPTER VII

At breakfast Wagstaff acted as if nothing suspect had happened over Tobruk. Observing him more attentively that he ever had before, Harris wondered if anything *had* happened. Nobody who'd chickened out could be that natural and good-natured afterwards. Today, because *Blonde Job* was redlined for a check of the rudder controls, they were missing a mission. Another convoy. One of the few 108th missions without them. Anyone devious enough to cover a moment of panic with a claim of mechanical failure would have pretended to be disappointed. Not Wagstaff.

When he saw the crews heading for the flight line he'd called out to Major Beck, "Hey, Maje. Maybe you'll find out you can fight a war without us guys and make some other jokers take turns. I'm a lover, not a fighter."

Gallegly was not quite as sure as he had been last night. Not as ready as Harris to believe it possible Wagstaff hadn't panicked but not completely convinced of it either. Still convinced enough, though, to make an excuse when Wagstaff suggested another run into Haifa. Harris begged off too. He'd thought of a new tactic to try with Hannah. Work in the fields

117

with her. Show her he wasn't as different from the local Jews as she thought. And that he had something on his mind besides getting her into the sack. Even if she suspected that's why he was helping her she couldn't be sure.

He started out of the tent with his canteen clipped on his pistol belt. It would be thirsty out in the fields.

"Where you going that I'm not invited?" Gallegly demanded, looking up from his book.

"Courting."

"Looking that way?"

"It ain't the clothes that makes the man. It's the man that makes the babe."

"You getting anywhere?"

"Not yet. But one 'a these days."

Gallegly marked his place with a barley straw and closed the book.

"Tex?"

"Yeah?"

"I don't think she's used to guys like us."

What was Gallegly trying to say? He sounded almost like Sgt. Weisz warning him she was a serious girl.

"I'm gonna taxi out to the ship," Gallegly said, dismissing the subject. "I want to be around when they check out the cables and vertical stabilizers."

Aleenah was unusually active. People on the dirt road, others sitting in the shade on straight chairs in front of their little houses. Harris tried to remember if any Jewish holiday came in the middle of August. But they'd be in temple if it was a Jewish holiday.

No one was home at Mrs. Woodbird's. He went around to the back. Two figures stooped among rows of green plants, one of them with a twist of cloth around the head and hanging down over the neck. What the Arabs called a *kefieh*. The other wore a

118

scarf. That must be Mrs. Woodbird. Had she hired an Arab boy to help out, with no man around the place? He didn't think the Jews did that even if they could find an Arab willing to work for a settler. And where was Hannah?

Mrs. Woodbird straightened and bent sideways from the waist, easing her back, one wrist on her hip and the other wiping sweat from her brow. How many times had he seen his mother do exactly that in her zinnia beds, groaning with relief? He felt a wave of homesickness. It had been five months since he'd last seen his folks. At graduation. It seemed longer.

"Shalom," he called.

Mrs. Woodbird turned and looked his way. So did the other one. It was Hannah. He hadn't recognized her right away. Just like at Nahariyah. Looking for her too hard, maybe. Afraid she wouldn't be there and he'd wasted the trip.

"Shalom." Mrs. Woodbird called back and, in German, "Hannahle, see who is here."

He joined them and shook hands. Everybody shook hands in Palestine, and the same way. That one quick downward jerk.

"What an unexpected surprise," Hannah said.

A little sarcastic, but not displeased.

"If it wasn't unexpected it wouldn't be a surprise," Harris said.

She and her aunt were picking tomatoes into shallow baskets.

"We grow tomatoes every summer back home," he said. "In the rose beds."

Hannah found that amusing and translated it for Mrs. Woodbird.

"Can I help?" he asked. "I might get to like it."

"Of course," Hannah said, her expression quizzical.

He took off his gun belt and got a pannier from a

119

nest of them. He began picking the row next to Hannah's. The sun lay on his back like a hot towel. Maybe he should have found some other way to impress Hannah. She picked in silence, deftly, seemingly oblivious to the stooping and the heat, glancing at him from time to time and, he thought, suppressing a smile at his discomfort. So she could do two things better than him, swim and pick tomatoes. Mrs. Woodbird picked steadily, too. Tough old bird. How long did they keep this up? Even in the service you got a five minute break now and then.

"What's everybody in Aleenah just sitting around for?" he said, sitting back on his heels, panting, drenched with sweat.

"It's Saturday," Hannah replied, her face impish. "What kind of Jew are you, not to know?"

Saturday. He'd lost track of days of the week. His days had no names. There were only days you flew and days you didn't. No such thing as Saturdays off, or Sundays. All a navigator had to know was the right date. For celestial navigation you needed the right date as well as the exact time.

"What kind are you?" he said, grateful for the excuse to take a break. "You're working."

"The tomatoes must be gathered or they will spoil. Here we do what must be done. Otherwise, we take Saturday as our day of rest."

"Do you go to temple?"

"Temple?" Hannah said, working and speaking at the same time, as if trying to goad him with her example. "Do you mean synagogue?"

"Yeah."

"We are not religious here."

"Then how about quitting picking on me for not being a good Jew?"

"In Eretz Israel there are better ways of being a

120

good Jew."

Sounding like Sgt. Weisz that first time he and Gallegly went to the Goldblums' and Weisz had disparaged prayers.

Someone whistled from the house. Speak of the devil.

Sgt. Weisz was motioning for him to come. Harris got up and started walking toward him, welcoming the break.

Hannah caught his arm. "I believe it is I he wants."

"Don't blame him a bit," Harris said.

Hannah and Weisz conversed briefly but earnestly. Hannah returned and spoke briefly to Mrs. Woodbird in Hebrew. Mrs. Woodbird did not seem pleased with what she heard but accepted it philosophically.

"I must go now," Hannah said.

"I don't guess I could tag along, could I?"

But it would be kind of raunchy, running off and leaving Mrs. Woodbird to do all the work by herself. And anyway, Hannah and Sgt. Weisz must be up to something they didn't think he should know about.

"Maybe I'll stay here and help Tante Frieda," he said.

The "Tante Frieda" evoked a big motherly smile from Mrs. Woodbird.

"That is really quite decent of you, Michael," Hannah said. "I may have misjudged you. But perhaps not."

She walked a few steps towards the house, hesitated and came back.

"I can't take advantage of you like this," she said. "Come along if you like."

"What'll Sergeant Weisz say?"

"Nothing. Why should he?"

"Where to?"

"Haifa."

"Haifa?"

He looked down at his sweaty desert uniform.

"I can't go into town like this. My CO'd have my . . . my hide."

Hannah took his wrist and looked at his watch.

"There is a bus in forty minutes," she said. "I will meet you on the road by the kibbutz Ramat Jonas."

He hurried back to the field at a dogtrot, wondering why Hannah had changed her mind, and if he took a room in Haifa would he be able to get her into it. Probably not, but it was still a good sign that she wanted his company. He took a quick shower and was sweating again by the time he got back to the tent. He got his money belt from under his sleeping bag-mattress and put it on under his uniform. He intended showing Hannah a good time in Haifa.

Hannah was waiting for him on the road in front of the kibbutz. She was wearing a dress. The tin suitcase was at her feet and her brow was beaded with sweat. Several kibbutznikim were waiting for the bus, too, dressed for town, which meant pants and skirts instead of shorts. They all said "Shalom" to Harris but eyed Hannah covertly and with tacit disapproval when he joined her.

"Tell 'em I'm Jewish," Harris whispered.

Hannah did not smile. She was uneasy. Did it really bother her that much that the kibbutznikim might be thinking she was sleeping with him?

On the bus he said, "You sure must read a lot."

"What?"

Preoccupied.

Touching the suitcase with his toe he said, "All these books."

"I am taking them to a friend."

"How about lunch at Pross's when we get there."

Pross's was a restaurant a taxi driver had taken him

and the others to on their first visit to Haifa. It was the only one they had tried so far. "It's quite dear, isn't it?"

"Not too. You can't get a meal for more than twenty piasters there. On account of the rationing."

"You do not think 200 mils dear?" she said, amused.

Two hundred mils was only eighty cents. There were plenty of places in Houston you could eat cheaper. than that but not swanky ones like Pross's. Funny Hannah should think 200 mils was expensive when she'd been rich in Germany.

"But I forgot you Americans are so well paid," she said. And, with her disconcerting knack for following his thoughts, "In Aleenah I have learned to be frugal. I detested being poor in London. But here . . . It is of no consequence. We do not think rich or poor."

He carried the suitcase for her when they left the bus at the Haifa station. The station was busy. Hannah made a quick survey without being obvious about it.

"Wait for me around the corner," she said, not looking at him. "I will join you presently."

He followed her gaze.

Two watchful British MPs, feet spread, batons clasped behind their backs, were eyeing the throng. Now Harris understood why Hannah had asked him to come along. Not for his company. For his goddam uniform. Nobody was going to pay any attention to an American officer carrying a heavy suitcase.

He waited for her around the corner, leaning against a building. Hot. Angry. Hannah quit smiling when she saw his face.

"What is it, Michael?" she said.

"You know goddam well."

"But I do not."

But she did.

"I've got a good mind to go off and leave you with your goddam . . . books."

"Oh." Carefully. "Perhaps it might be better."

Sure. She didn't need him any more. And didn't want him to know where she was taking the suitcase. Whatever was in it, it was something she wasn't supposed to have. And she didn't even trust him enough to tell him.

"You act like I'm a goddam spy or something."

"I haven't the foggiest notion what you're talking about."

"Oh, sure. Do we walk or take a taxi?"

She sighed, accepting his company. "It is too far to walk."

Too conspicuous, too, he bet. He hailed a taxi. Hannah gave the driver an address in Hebrew. As soon as they were rolling the driver introduced himself. They usually did in Haifa. They were almost always middle-aged German refugees, often college professors or musicians in the old country, educated men who couldn't find any use for their training in Haifa. They liked Americans.

Soon the driver and Hannah were in animated conversation in German. Harris caught a word here and there, feeling left out. Hannah was leaving him out of a lot of things. He should have left her with her suitcase and gone looking for Wagstaff. Americans usually went to the same places in Haifa. Favourite bars and cafés with entertainment where they bitch about no bourbon and the high price of scotch and drank Carmel hock, they called it Camel Hockey, Stock brandy, egg brandy or local gin mixed with Mits Paz grapefruit juice or lemon squash. Or they might wander aimlessly along Jaffa Road or Kingsway, window-shopping, or take a taxi up to

Mount Carmel and have what passed for ice-cream in Palestine at one of the hotels, sitting outdoors and looking down at the view.

The driver had his free arm flung over the seat and kept looking back. It made Harris nervous even though the taxi was just creeping along and the traffic was light. Few of the refugees were good drivers even when they kept their eyes on the road. Some of them hadn't even driven a car before coming to Haifa.

"He was a portrait painter in Dresden," Hannah said. "Isn't that interesting?"

Harris didn't bother to answer. He kept looking out the window, hoping to spot Wagstaff. They were in the shopping district on a broad avenue with light standards rising from concrete islands in the centre. The sockets in the reflectors at the ends of crossbars arching out over the pavement were empty because of blackout regulations but the iron scrollwork supporting them made them look ornamental. Pedestrians were dressed in their Sunday best. Saturday best. Shirtsleeves or coats without ties. A few Arabs in soiled white drawers tight at the ankle but baggy in the seat. To catch the prophet when he was reborn of man, Gallegly said. Harris hadn't known if he were joking. It sounded like the kind of thing you told Silkwood. Some of the white modernistic buildings with long rows of windows were six or seven stories tall. The shops were closed. Saturday wasn't a good day for visiting Haifa, with or without Hannah, the way she was using him.

Out of the shopping district and into an Arab quarter. The streets and sidewalks were narrower. Shops all open, some of them with their entrances directly on the street. Narrow sidewalks crowded, Arabs walking in the streets among donkeys the size of burros loaded down with crates and bags, and carts

with the drivers sitting on the loads or walking alongside. Sidewalk cafés. Men only. Drinking coffee from
tiny cups and smoking waterpipes. The waterpipes,
hookahs, were to fool the prophet, Gallegly said, not
just to cool and flavour the smoke. Moslems weren't
supposed to smoke tobacco. Against their religion.
The same way hardshell Baptists back home weren't
supposed to drink or dance.

Harris felt a stirring of interest. This was more like
it. The shopping district was like some brand-new
uptown back home. This was more like being in a
foreign country. Maybe they even had a Madame
ZeZe's kind of place here. Americans didn't go to the
Arab quarter after dark. They had been warned
against it. Wagstaff said an Aussie he met in a bar
told him if you had on an Australian uniform you'd
be safe among Arabs any hour of the day or not. The
Aussie said it was because in World War I an Australian soldier had been killed in an Arab village and the
next night his friends had gone back to the village
and killed everybody they could find. And the Arabs
had never forgotten it.

It smelled different here, too. Not quite a stink but
damn near. Donkey manure in the street. Burning
charcoal braziers. Ancient dirt. Urine. Khartoum
had smelled a lot like this.

The driver was still talking with Hannah but
watching more carefully. If you killed an Arab you
had to pay his relatives blood money.

"Tell me," the driver said in English, "what do you
think of Haifa?"

"You talking to me?" Harris asked. "I like it fine.
Do you?"

"Not so well as Dresden."

With a grin and a shrug, "But for a Jew, Haifa is
better, yes? Your friend says you also are a Jew?"

"That's right."

They'd been talking about him then.

"What else did she say?"

Looking at Hannah.

"That you are friends, only."

She looked away, embarrassed.

"Not very good friends," Harris said.

Her jaw tightened. He was beginning to enjoy himself.

"What a pity," the driver said, enjoying himself, too. "When you look so well together."

"I think she's a Lorelei," Harris said.

The driver turned all the way around to look at him.

"You know 'Die Lorelei'?" he asked, pleased.

It was one of the poems Harris had been obliged to memorize in German class and sing with Dr. Freund. He could still visualize Dr. Freund striking the *Stimmgabel*, the tuning fork on his desk and holding it up to his ear before leading the class in song. Harris had forgotten most of the poem. It was a lot longer than "Wandrers Nachtlied"; about this beautiful golden-haired maiden sitting on a rock in the Rhine luring sailors to their deaths.

"Don't you think she's a Lorelei?" Harris asked.

"I think not. Such a charming young lady could not be so cruel."

"You are not amusing," Hannah said.

But her lips twitched.

They were out of the Arab quarter. The streets were wider, though only a little, and much cleaner. Almost deserted. Old dwellings of one and two stories shoulder to shoulder and an occasional apartment house newer than the other buildings. Jews must live here, Harris thought.

The driver began singing.

127

Ich weiss nicht was soll es bedeuten,
Dass ich so traurig bin . . .

"I do not know what it means, that I am so sad."
Harris joined in, skipping parts he couldn't remember. Then Hannah was singing beside him, her voice pure and sweeter than he would have expected. He covered her hand with his. She left it there.

"Heine," the driver said. "In Germany it is not permitted to sing Heine."

"Here," Hannah said. "Stop here."

The street they were on was intersected by a narrower one, little more than an alley, with closed doors and shuttered windows facing each other across it. Empty.

"Please wait for me here," she told the driver.

All business again. In English, for his benefit, Harris thought.

"I'll carry it," he said, taking hold of the suitcase and opening his door.

"No," said Hannah sharply. Then, placatingly, "No, thank you, Michael. I will only be a moment."

She walked down the narrow sidewalk, leaning away from the weight of the heavy case. The driver watched her, curious.

"Books," Harris said. "For her aunt."

"I think she is fond of you," the driver said.

If he only knew. But Harris liked hearing it anyway.

Hannah did not stop at any of the doors. She walked all the way to the end of the block and disappeared around the corner. She didn't want him to know where she was going. But maybe it was the driver she didn't want to know. Both of them, probably.

"You have had lunch?" the driver asked.

"Not yet."

"Neither have I. We go all together? I pay for my own."

Haifa taxi drivers were like that.

"Sure," said Harris. "Only it's my treat."

"Oh, no. I invited myself."

"But you don't get flying pay."

"After the war I will come to New York and paint your portrait. Gratis."

"I live in Texas. Houston."

"You are a Jewish cowboy! Bang! Bang!"

Hannah returned without the suitcase.

"Your aunt is well?" the driver asked.

"My aunt?" said Hannah.

"The one you took the books to," Harris explained.

"Quite well, thank you," Hannah said. "Now, if you will please drive us to the bus station."

"I thought we'd have lunch," Harris said.

"I must get back. Tante Frieda is working without help."

"You must eat lunch somewhere," the driver said, putting the taxi in motion. "Why not here?"

"He's right," said Harris. "Take us to Pross's."

"I'm afraid not," Hannah said reluctantly.

"Tuna cocktails," Harris said. "Maryland fried chicken. Chips. English peas."

She was weakening, he thought.

"Perfection," the driver said. "Tell me, dear lady, where it is you must go."

Harris and Hannah answered simultaneously.

"Aleenah," Harris said.

"Ramat Jonas," said Hannah.

Really being cagey, he thought.

"Aleenah, Ramat Jonas, it is quicker by taxi than by bus, yes? We have a little lunch, you are still there

129

before the bus."

"Taxis are too dear," Hannah said.

"Live a little," said Harris.

"I will make a special price," the driver said. "All inclusive. All driving in Haifa, plus Ramat Jonas, one pound."

Four dollars. Dirt cheap. Refugee taxi drivers were mostly casual about money but even the most unbusinesslike among them charged at least a pound to drive all the way to Ramat Jonas, without any Haifa driving thrown in.

"You've got a deal," Harris said before Hannah could say no. "Pross's."

Hannah was subdued in the restaurant at first.

"It is my first time here," she said. "We do not dine in restaurants."

By the time they finished their tuna cocktails she had changed noticeably, demanding attention from their waiter unselfconsciously, as if she lunched here every day and expected no less. She spoke to the waiter in German, not Hebrew. He hovered, in thrall, keeping Harris's glass filled — Harris was the only one drinking water with the meal — bringing bread without being asked, neglecting other tables. In Harris's two previous visits the service had been good but not slavish like this. It was as if the waiter and Hannah were playing a game. They were not in Pross's in Haifa but in another, more elegant, restaurant in another city and another time. It was easy to believe Hannah was once a rich girl.

The taxi driver grew nostalgic.

"As in the old days," he said to Hannah in German.

Harris remembered enough German to know what he had said.

"I'd order us a bottle of Carmel hock but it'd put us over the maximum allowed," Harris said.

Hannah tilted her head at the waiter, who was at her elbow in two strides. After a whispered consultation he hurried off to return with three glasses and a chilled bottle.

"It is uncivilized to lunch without a little wine," Hannah said.

Not at all the Hannah he had seen sweating in a tomato patch a few hours ago.

"It will be billed separately," she said. "My treat."

"No," said Harris.

"Permit me," the taxi driver said gallantly.

"I insist," Hannah said.

In a tone not to be denied. This Hannah was intimidating. He liked the one who had let him take her hand in the taxi better.

"I think I shall have the beefsteak," she announced. "Despite the white wine. It has been how long? More than two years, I think."

She gave the waiter instructions how it was to be prepared. Harris and the taxi driver had the Maryland fried chicken. Not like Harris's mother's or Bill Williams's Chicken Shack but, compared with Ramat Jonas chow, ambrosia. Hannah ate exactly half of her thin steak.

"Aren't you hungry?" Harris asked.

"I am taking it to Tante Frieda," Hannah said. "I hope it does not embarrass you, asking the waiter for scraps from my plate."

"Not at all," Harris said. "But why not let's take her a steak all her own?"

"That will not be necessary."

Period.

In the taxi again, Hannah and the driver spoke in German, laughing, interrupting each other again and again, excited. Talking about old times, Harris sensed. They were five miles outside of Haifa, passing the Nesher Portland cement factory, before nostalgia and the wine began losing their effect. By Shimron, where they turned off for Ramat Jonas, Hannah was back to normal, speaking English again.

"It was extravagant of me," she said ruefully. "The wine."

"You should have let me pay. How much was it?"

"No. I do not regret it, actually. For a few moments . . . I had forgotten . . ."

"I guess you do miss the way it used to be."

"I regret nothing."

Firmly, and not meaning just a few mils spent foolishly on a bottle of Carmel hock.

"Aleenah or Ramat Jonas?" the driver asked.

"Ramat Jonas," Hannah said promptly.

In spite of the camaraderie at Pross's still not wanting the driver to know where she lived.

The driver shook hands with them and refused a tip.

"One pound only was the agreement. And you bought me a most excellent lunch, in such charming company. I should pay you, my friend."

Hannah waited until he drove away before setting out for Aleenah.

"You're suspicious of everybody, aren't you?" Harris said.

"It is the times," she replied.

"But he was such a good egg. A German Jew, like you."

He would have said "like us" if he'd thought he could get away with it. But Hannah knew he really wasn't one of them.

"You are making too much of it, Michael."

He liked it when she spoke his name. Wondering if she knew that and did it by design to get him off the subject. Not Hannah. She was without artifice except in her dealings for Sgt. Weisz. She didn't even use makeup.

Hannah stopped him in front of the Goldblums'.

"I must pop in for a moment," she said, giving him the little parcel with Tante Frieda's piece of steak in it.

Weisz came outside with Hannah, looking grave. She looked chastened.

"*Shalom,* Gyorgy," Harris said, wondering what it was all about.

"*Shalom,*" Weisz said, studying him. "You forget everything today, OK?"

"Sure."

They walked on. Harris looked back. Weisz was still out in the yard, watching them.

"What's eating him?" Harris demanded. "I don't know what's going on. And if I did, who would I tell?"

"It was wrong of me. To involve you in . . . in internal matters."

"Dammit, don't you people trust anybody?"

He wished he hadn't said "you people."

The slip went unnoticed but the closeness of the drive from Haifa had already dissipated.

"It is not simply a matter of trust. It is unfair to you to be placed in such a position."

"What position?"

"To appear to be helping us."

"What's going on, anyhow? I thought all that trouble with the Arabs was over."

"May we consider the subject closed? Please?"

Tante Frieda had finished gathering the tomatoes and was in the front yard tending some dusty flowers. There had been no need to hurry back after all. If he had worked it right he might even have got Hannah up to a hotel room. Instead, here they were in

133

Aleenah, the rest of the afternoon shot.

Tante Frieda was relieved to see Hannah back home safely.

"No trouble?" she said anxiously.

Harris caught enough of Hannah's reply to know she told her aunt they had lunch at Pross's and she had a lovely time. Tante Frieda told Harris he was a good boy, adding quickly perhaps she should not call a *flugleutnant* a boy. Hannah did not have to translate it for him.

Tante Frieda went inside to put the steak away for supper.

"I guess I'll go on back," Harris said. "Is it OK if I come back tonight?"

"Of course."

Tante Frieda came out of the house carrying two straight chairs. She put them in the shade of a tree and motioned for Harris and Hannah to sit. She whispered in Hannah's ear. Hannah nodded, amused by something.

"She wants you to stay for dinner later," Hannah said. "She will kill a chicken. Would you mind terribly if it isn't Maryland fried?"

Gallegly was back at the field all by himself. But of all the crew, Gallegly minded being alone the least. Harris wondered what he had found out about the rudder controls.

"*Dankeschön*, Tante Frieda," he said.

She beamed. She went around the house and came back pushing a two-wheeled cart loaded with panniers of tomatoes. Hannah jumped up and began arguing with her.

"She wants to take the tomatoes," Hannah explained.

She pronounced it "tomahtoes." I say tomatoes and you say tomahtoes. Fred Astaire and Ginger Rogers.

134

"Shall we dance?" said Harris.

"What?"

"Making a joke."

"It is for me to do." Hannah said, not pursuing it. "She was working in the sun while I drank wine at Pross's."

"I'll help you."

Hannah went in and changed into shirt and shorts. Harris looked at her legs and wished they were in a hotel room in Haifa.

The cart and its load were not heavy. With one pushing and one pulling it rolled easily. A young girl with a large nose greeted Hannah, trying to hide her interest in Harris.

"You remember Zippie, do you not?" Hannah said. "Zipporah?"

The girl from pistol class.

"Sure," said Harris.

They shook hands. Zipporah looked as if she wanted to tag along, but didn't.

"I think you have made a conquest," Hannah said slyly as they moved on.

"She's not the one I had in mind."

Hannah made no reply.

"Where are we going, anyhow?"

"Tnuva. The co-operative producers' society."

He'd seen small ads in the *Palestine Post* saying simply, "Tnuva, pears, grapes, apples, plums," and thought they were for a store.

"I thought you owned your own land here," he said.

"So we do. But we market co-operatively. Tnuva for fruit and vegetables. Also eggs, poultry and milk. Yakhin for citrus. But I think I am boring you."

"No. It just makes me feel stupid, that's all. Being Jewish and just down the road all this time and not knowing any of that."

"Don't be embarrassed, Michael. Until two years ago, neither did I."

I say neether and you say nyther.

"We are all members of the Histadrut Ha-Ovdim, the General Federation of Jewish Labour," she continued.

"For a labourer, you're pretty sexy looking."

She made no reply to that either.

They unloaded the cart at a long low building on the dirt road dividing Aleenah down the middle. Two lean bronzed men working on the loading dock spoke to Hannah, grinning. She laughed and shook her head. He knew it was something about him . . .

Tante Frieda was in the back killing a chicken when they returned with the empty cart. She wrung its neck vigorously, just like their coloured girl back home did. When Harris had to kill a chicken for his mother he used a hatchet from his Boy Scout days.

Tante Frieda boiled the chicken with herbs, carrots and onions on a kerosene stove. Of all the ways chicken could be served, boiled was the one he liked the least but he raved about the meal for Tante Frieda's sake.

"I think you will turn into a chicken," Hannah whispered.

"As good as your mother's?" Tante Frieda asked.

"Better," Harris replied before Hannah could translate.

Which was true, if you were talking about boiled chicken. His mother never boiled chicken except for soup. She fried it coated with her own special batter in deep fat or sometimes in a skillet, or baked it, stuffed, in the oven.

Tante Frieda had divided the steak into three equal strips.

"Not when I can have your chicken," Harris said.

Hannah refused a share too. Tante Frieda fell to with great relish.

After the usual grapes and apples, with cigarettes from Harris's pack, Hannah and Tante Frieda went to the kitchen to wash the dishes. Harris followed them and led Tante Frieda back to the front room. He sat her down with another cigarette and ordered her to stay put.

Back in the kitchen, he looked at Hannah and said, "Flip you for wash or dry."

He got a blank look.

He took out a silver hundred mil coin and said, "Heads you dry."

Hannah wouldn't believe he helped with the dishes at home. He did, though, except for the two days a week they had the coloured girl. With his sister before she got married and later with his mother.

Hannah washed the dishes in a pan of water heated on the kerosene stove and he dried, standing close to her. It was kind of nice.

Tante Frieda talked with them for an hour or so, Hannah translating when necessary, then yawned and said it was time for old ladies to be in bed. She shut the door firmly behind her.

Harris moved closer to Hannah on the couch and put his arm around her shoulder. She stiffened but did not move away. Scared to death. She'd delivered a suitcase full of something illegal for Sgt. Weisz without turning a hair but got all frozen up when a man put his arm around her. Was she frigid or just inexperienced?

He talked until she relaxed. Stories about home. About himself and Gallegly. Asked her about her life in Germany and Aleenah, avoiding disturbing questions about the suitcase. After a while her answers grew longer. He leaned to kiss her. As before, she

137

averted her face, presenting only a cheek. He turned her face to his and sought her mouth. She wasn't frigid. He let his hand fall to her breast, casually. She twisted from his embrace as if he'd given her an electric shock and moved to the end of the couch. Not looking at him.

"You sore at me?" he said.

She shook her head, still not looking at him.

"Michael, isn't it enough just to talk?"

"You like somebody else or something?"

"You think that is the only reason for me not wanting to be . . . pawed?"

"I'm sorry."

He wasn't, though. He knew she'd get over that if he didn't rush her. She'd liked kissing him. He could tell. He could always tell. She was like this because it was a new experience for her. There wasn't anybody else. There never had been. He would bet on it. A rich sheltered girl in Germany, a refugee in England, working her butt off here. Not like the American girls he knew.

They talked without touching until Hannah said she had to go to bed. Sunday was working day in Aleenah. He didn't protest. He hadn't intended trying anything again until they said goodnight.

He kissed her in the doorway. She had expected it. He held her against him and stroked her back from shoulder to leg. She shivered when he touched her hard buttocks. Then, like the first time, pulled free and closed the door between them. With one important difference. This time she waited longer to do it.

CHAPTER VIII

There was nothing demonstrably wrong with the rudder controls. Sunday Wagstaff insisted on taking *Blonde Job* up to check her out in the air. He took only Gallegly and Trombatore with him.

"That way Beck'll still have you guys to chew out if we buy a farm," he said blithely.

Buy a farm. Crash. If Wagstaff didn't think there was really something wrong with the controls he was sure doing a good job of acting like it.

Harris and the other crew members stood in the stubble and watched Wagstaff rack her around. Major Beck came out on a bicycle and joined them. Everyone was uncomfortable with him around.

"What's the overgrown bastard trying to do?" Beck demanded of no one in particular. "Tear the goddam wings off?"

It was his way of praising Wagstaff's skill and daring.

Wagstaff emerged from the ship looking perplexed.

"Handled smooth as a baby's ass," he said.

Gallegly said nothing, then or later. He and Harris did not discuss it as if by silent agreement. But Harris sensed that Gallegly's mistrust of their pilot was fading.

They went four days without a mission. During that week the 12th Bombardment Group (Medium), B-25s, began bombing targets in the Western Desert from Egypt, there was fierce fighting in the Solomons and British commandos raided Dieppe. And the ss *Pasteur* entered the Suez Canal with the 108th's ground echelon and equipment. In a week or so the group would be complete.

During the day Harris read a borrowed book, wrote letters and played poker or blackjack at the officers' club. At night he ate at the Goldblums' and visited Hannah. Tante Frieda, always pleased to see him, would sit with them for half an hour and then leave them alone. Harris knew she thought he was serious about Hannah. He was, but not the way she thought. It made him feel a little guilty. He liked Tante Frieda a lot.

Hannah permitted him small, increasing liberties, though not without initial hesitancy. It was clear to him this was a new experience for her. Her responses were like those of a junior high school girl. When he had necked with junior high school girls he was in junior high school himself and was as awkward as they. It was different now. He felt like a teacher.

She responded to his kisses and let his hand linger on her breast but would not let him unbutton her shirt. And she would not go walking with him as she had the first time he came to see her. He considered that a good sign. It meant she was afraid she would be unable to resist him. All he had to do now was just get her alone. He asked her to go to Haifa with him on Saturday if she didn't have to work and he didn't have to fly. If she did have to work, he would help her again so she could finish early. She was reticent. He promised to have her home before dark. She said she would go.

Thursday night she came to Goldblums' with Zipporah as they were finishing their meal. It was their pistol night. Harris was keenly disappointed. It wouldn't leave much time for him to sit with Hannah on the couch and see how much farther he could get with her. Nights, horny under his mosquito net, he had thought about that couch. Sleepless, inventing reasons for Tante Frieda to be away, leaving them all alone, having Hannah on the couch all night, her resistance weakening until she was naked and panting in his arms. There was still some junior high school boy in him, he thought ruefully.

He practised his German with the Goldblums until he thought the pistol lesson was almost over. It had just been revealed that day in news broadcasts and the *Palestine Post* that Winston Churchill had recently visited the front at El Alamein and that the Middle East Forces and the British Eighth Army had new commanding generals, Gen. Harold Alexander and Lt. Gen. Bernard Montgomery. The Goldblums were anxious to have Harris's opinion as to whether that was a good or a bad sign about how the desert war was going. As if a second lieutenant in the Air Corps knew anything. Weisz knew a hell of a lot more about what was going on than he did. Weisz had, for example, already known about Churchill's visit and the change in command. He didn't say how he knew. Harris assumed it was because of his position in the police.

Harris told the Goldblums he thought it meant the Eighth Army must be getting ready for a big attack, which cheered them enormously, and said he had to be getting back to the airfield. He went outside and waited on the road for Hannah. He'd rather Sgt. Weisz didn't know he was seeing her every night. Weisz wouldn't approve. He acted as if he thought he was Hannah's father. Not her father, exactly, her CO. Maybe he was.

Harris smoked two cigarettes and studied the stars. The moon was in its first quarter. Five more days and it would be full. Screwing up navigation. But it would be great to be under a full moon with Hannah somewhere if he wasn't flying missions.

The door opened. Harris stepped back into the shadows in case Sgt. Weisz was seeing her out. Hannah emerged with Zipporah. Zipporah saw him first and nudged her.

"*Shalom*, Lieutenant Harris," Hannah said.

He had not expected such formality. Then he understood it was for Zipporah's benefit. Hannah must not have confided in her the way girls did back home.

"May I walk you girls home?" he said.

"We should be delighted," Hannah said, translating his offer into Hebrew for Zipporah.

Zipporah gave him a big smile. She was homely but cute. Everybody's kid sister. He was glad she didn't speak English. It made him feel less ignorant. All these people spoke so many languages. Hannah three, fluently. Maybe more, for all he knew. All he knew was English and a smattering of German. He wished he'd studied harder at Rice. But how was he to know he'd get a chance to use it in a couple of years?

Hannah and Zipporah walked ahead of him with their arms around each other's waist. Hannah said something that made Zipporah giggle and look back at Harris.

At the dirt path in front of Tante Frieda's Hannah said, "Zippie lives only a bit farther on. I'm sure you will gallantly see her to her door."

Then she was gone.

It was because she didn't want Zipporah to know

he was coming back to see her, he thought. If Zipporah didn't know he'd been waiting for Hannah she really must be dumb. Hannah must think Zipporah would tell Sgt. Weisz.

Zipporah kept looking at him, pleased with herself. It was flattering. Too bad she wasn't older. If she were, he'd fix her up with Gallegly. She wasn't pretty but you took what you could get when you were a long way from home.

She lived a hundred yards or so beyond Hannah on the circular road. Harris shook her hand and said, *"Shalom."* She knit her brow in concentration.

"Hannah say you very neese," she said, as if she had been rehearsing it in her mind. *"Shalom."*

Hannah was not as completely different from American girls as he had supposed. She'd just had to tell somebody after all. Girls did that when they had a crush on somebody. And she wouldn't have told Zipporah if she hadn't wanted him to know. Maybe he wouldn't have to wait until they went to Haifa on Saturday. He hurried to Tante Frieda's. Hannah wasn't waiting for him outside as he'd expected. He knocked lightly on the door. No response. He knocked louder.

"Who is it?"

Hannah, mischievous.

"Come on, open the door."

"I'm going to bed."

"It's not late yet. Let's go for a walk."

"Zippie is fond of hiking. Perhaps if you hurry . . ."

Merriment in her voice. She was teasing him.

"Hannah, dammit . . . if you don't open the door, I'm gonna wake up everybody in the neighbourhood."

"You wouldn't!"

He began singing the bombardiers' song, "I Don't Want To Set the World on Fire." Not loud enough to wake the neighbourhood or even Tante Frieda. The door opened just enough for Hannah to reach out and put her fingers on his lips.

"You sing like a bird," she said. "A crow."

He captured her hand and kissed the palm.

"That tickles."

He tried to draw her outside. It was a tug of war which he let her win. She shut the door and led him at once to the couch.

"That Zipporah sure can kiss," he said.

Her look was angry, incredulous, and he could suppress a grin no longer. She hit him on the chest. His wings hurt her knuckle.

"*Affe,*" she said.

Monkey.

She sat in his lap. After a while he unbuttoned her shirt. She resisted only half-heartedly, her hand pulling at his without strength. He groped under a strap. There. So warm and silken. The beginning of his nightly fantasy. He stopped kissing her and looked at her rapt face. Her head was thrown back. Eyes closed. Lips parted. Breathing as if they were at 20,000 feet without oxygen. And he had once thought she might be frigid.

"Hannahle," he murmured.

Her eyes flew open.

"No!" she said, frightened.

She scrambled from his lap. Stood looking down at him, breathing hard, hands fumbling at her shirt buttons.

"We must not!"

"We," not "you." He knew it was only a matter of time. Not tonight, maybe, or even tomorrow night. But Saturday in Haifa. He tried to draw her into his lap again. She pulled free and sat down in a chair, buttoning her shirt, not looking at him, embarrassed.

He knew he wouldn't get anywhere with her tonight.

He went to her, tilted her face to his, kissed her chastely, reassuringly.

"It's late," he said. "I'll see you tomorrow night."

"Yes."

He looked back at her before he closed the door. She did not look up.

Blonde Job flew a mission Friday. One of twelve planes, the most yet on a raid. A convoy believed heading for Tobruk, expected still to be within fighter range of Crete at the time they would intercept it.

There were three merchantmen and a tanker escorted by Italian destroyers. The ships moved ponderously, leaving curving wakes as they took evasive action. The destroyers skittered around them like waterbugs, their batteries belching pinpricks of fire and trickles of smoke. The flak was sparse and inaccurate. The Liberators bombed in elements of three, raining down five hundred pounders that burst in towers of spray, roiling the sea among the ships. Wagstaff flew a perfect run.

They left a merchantman sinking, spouting columns of black smoke, ribbons that broadened, thinned and twisted as they ascended through changing winds. The crew of *Blonde Job* cheered on the interphone. Shouting, congratulating Silkwood, Harris looked back at the smoking ship. And, unbidden, a memory from a high school history class.

"Don't cheer, boys, the poor devils are dying."

The captain of the battleship Texas at the battle of Santiago Bay. 1898. The Spanish American War. A Spanish cruiser beached and burning.

Harris kept on cheering. Their job wasn't to kill people. It was to sink ships. And a damn good job of it today. From up here he couldn't see anyone dying. They'd have plenty of time to get into lifeboats or get

145

picked up by the other ships. Even if they didn't . . . They were the enemy. They'd get you if they could. Your life was on the line just like theirs. That made it OK.

Coming off the target a plane in the last element began falling back, a prop feathered, its three blades turned edgewise to the rushing wind so they wouldn't windmill. There was something ugly about a still prop on an airborne plane. Like a deformity.

The formation throttled back to let the straggler catch up. The gap closed slowly. Silkwood grabbed Harris's arm and pointed, his voice shrill on the interphone.

"Bombardier to pilot, fighters at eight o'clock!"

Three motes dancing towards the straggler. Exchanging tracers with it, diving and twisting to attack from new angles. Two Me110s, Harris identified them by the big greenhouse canopy, and an Me109. Competing to get at the straggler like birddogs after a bitch in heat. The Liberators nearest the straggler poured in supporting fire. Their tracers fell away harmlessly. The straggler and its tormenters were out of range. A plume of smoke trickled from the engine next to the one with the feathered prop. It grew, trailing like a banner. Its prop flailed to a stop, feathered, stark and still like the one next to it. Harris watched, fascinated. Were the fighter pilots cheering?

The straggler lost altitude, falling off towards the feathered props, belching smoke from the damaged engine. The fighters were gamboling puppies now, pouncing on a bone. The wounded plane's wing came off between the two dead engines, leaving an ugly stub protruding from the fusilage. Someone cursed on the interphone. Harris gritted his teeth.

"Don't cheer, boys, the poor devils are dying."

The cripple just hung there for an instant, transfixed between sea and sky, then fell toward the Mediterranean, gyrating.

"Oh, Jesus," someone moaned.

Three men tumbled from the waist windows, two out of one side, one after the other. The flight deck escape hatch fell free, glinting in the sun, planing down through the air in a series of widening arcs. Two chutes opened. The third roman-candled out above its doomed wearer. Another man got out of the flight deck hatch. He hit the flailing tail and fell languidly towards the sea. The two open chutes were still floating, tiny puffs of white, when the plane, shrunk by distance to a miniature, struck the surface and broke up in a welter of spray.

The fighters pursued the rest of the formation for a while, breaking off their attack when the answering fire grew too strong and testing other angles of approach. The Me109 left first, then the Me110s, one after the other, fuel running low, going back to Crete.

"Anybody know who it was?" Wagstaff asked on the interphone.

"*Flat Foot Floogie*," someone answered.

"Minto," said Wagstaff.

Harris couldn't place Minto. *Flat Foot Floogie* wasn't from the 234th. He knew the name of every pilot in the 108th but not always the name that went with it. He knew *Flat Foot Floogie*'s navigator though. Had danced the *schottische* with his wife at a group party in Tampa when the 108th was drawing overseas equipment at MacDill Field. Hell of a nice guy. Harris couldn't think of his name. It was right on the tip of his tongue. He could see the guy sitting there, drinking a Cuba libre and smoking a big Tampa cigar, flushed, laughing while he danced with his wife. But not his name. Harris felt crummy about that.

Silkwood pulled the oxygen mask away from his mouth and shouted over the roar of the engines.

"I knew their bombardier. Bourdillon. I wonder who it was got out."

Everyone was wondering that. And if the two who did get out OK were just going to drown, anyway.

There was no singing and joking on the long flight back to Ramat Jonas. Harris knew everybody was thinking what he was thinking. It could have been us. For the first time he really understood that this was a war, not a game, and you could get killed. If Wagstaff had been scared over Tobruk maybe it was because he already knew that. He felt disloyal thinking Wagstaff had been scared. Even if he had been scared it shouldn't have prevented him from doing his job. You did that no matter how scared you were.

Parsons. That was his name, *Flat Foot Floogie*'s navigator. He couldn't have gotten out. He wouldn't have had time to get all the way back to the waist. Nobody up front got out of the plane except the man who hit the tail. Harris wondered what it was like, being in a plane going down and not being able to get out, knowing when it hit it was all over.

When they got back to Ramat Jonas, everybody in Aleenah would know a plane had been lost. They always counted. Hannah might think it was his. He wondered how she would take it. No matter what time they got in he'd go see her. Maybe she'd be so glad to learn he was alive . . .

He was ashamed. He'd just seen one of their planes shot down, men killed, and he was thinking about how it might help him get a girl into the sack.

Silkwood was talking to him.

"Don't you think so, Tex?"

"Don't I think what?"

"I'll get credit for that ship? I know it was us

148

straddled it. A direct hit and two near misses."

Harris was less ashamed. He wasn't the only one who gave less of a damn about men being killed than his own concerns. Everybody on the plane must have something on his mind more important to him than *Flat Foot Floogie,* unless he happened to have a close friend aboard. But your closest friends were usually on your own crew. He even felt closer to Silkwood than to guys on other crews, even good guys.

It wasn't as cold-blooded as it might seem to somebody outside, somebody who didn't fly missions. Because you took the same chance as the men on *Flat Foot Floogie* did. You were just luckier. This time. If you brooded about what had happened to them you'd start thinking about what could happen to you. So it was better to think about something else.

Wagstaff had everybody gather around him while they waited for the bus. He was grave. Harris had never seen him so serious. This was a new side of Wagstaff, and reassuring.

"What happened to Floogie was rugged," he said. "But I don't want any of you guys letting it get you down. It's not gonna happen to us. The only reason they bought it was because they had to fall out of formation."

He looked at Trombatore.

"We've got the best aerial engineer in group and those engines are gonna keep on purring."

Trombatore looked down at the concrete, embarrassed but pleased.

"And any goddam fighter that gets in close is gonna get the living whey shot outta him. We also got the best goddam gunners in group."

Harris was proud of Wagstaff. He wanted to hug the big son of a bitch. He looked at Gallegly. Gallegly was impressed, too. Wags might clown around a lot but he was a leader. Their leader. And what had happened at Tobruk wasn't going to happen again.

Wagstaff grinned. "And your pilots ain't too bad either," he said, dispelling the sombre mood.

Blonde Job's crew was the only one not steeped in uneasy silence on the bus. Harris sat next to Wagstaff, beating out Silkwood who, scowling, squeezed in next to Gallegly. Harris wanted to be near Wags, to make up for any doubts he'd had about him.

"You're gonna claim a ship for Silkwood at postmission, ain't you?" he asked.

"Roger. Junior got himself a shack."

"You flew one hellova run."

"You noticed? Me and Gallegly add up to a pretty damn good pilot, don't we?"

That was Wags, always sharing the credit.

"Those M-es were sure eager today," Harris said.

"Yeah, when they had 'em a cripple," Wagstaff said, looking thoughtfully out the window and then back again. "Fighters don't really bother me that much."

Harris knew that was true. Wags may have frozen on the bomb run at Tobruk but later he'd turned into the fighters to pick up his wingmen when their planes were under attack.

"With fighters," Wagstaff said, "you always get a chance. You can fight back. It's when you can't fight back . . ."

Harris expected him to continue but he didn't. He just looked out the window.

There wasn't any joking or horseplay at post-mission. Major Beck, who hadn't been on the raid, acted sore at everybody. He made every first pilot give his own meticulous account of the battle, sometimes making them repeat details.

"If Minto hadn't had his goddam head up he could've maintained formation on three engines," he

150

said angrily.

He's mad at Minto for getting shot down, for God's sake, Harris thought.

"If you bastards are telling the truth about throttling back to let him catch up," Beck said.

"We did, Maje," Wagstaff said quietly.

He was the only pilot daring to speak up.

"The next son of a bitch who falls outta formation with three good engines better get his ass shot off like Minto," Beck snapped. "Because that ass is mine if he gets back."

He glared at all the sullen faces. And chuckled deep down in his thick chest.

"Bunch'a goddam schoolgirls. The first combat casualty is always the roughest. The next one won't bother everybody so much."

The mess hall, which had been kept open to feed the returning crews, was crowded with men who had not gone on the mission, all eager for details of *Flat Foot Floogie*'s destruction. Harris brushed aside questions, eager to finish eating and get to Aleenah. Hannah and Tante Frieda would be worrying about him.

Everybody was going to the officers' club. It was too early to go to bed. Harris said he was going for a walk. Silkwood wanted to go with him.

"Maybe we can do some PT and loosen up," he said. "Don't you get stiff, all cramped up for ten hours?"

"I want to be by myself," Harris said. "You know how it is."

"I understand," Silkwood said solemnly.

Thinks I want to ponder life and death, Harris thought.

There were cracks of light around the shutters at Tante Frieda's. Hannah was waiting up. He knocked.

"Hannah?"

There was a flurry of movement inside. A door closed. The front door opened and Hannah was in his arms.

"Michael! I was afraid . . ."

She'd counted the planes out and back, all right. And really been worried. If he could get her outside to the pine grove he'd see just how worried. She freed herself from his embrace and closed the door behind them. She said something in Hebrew to the door at the back of the room. A tall, wiry youth with an indoor pallor, black hair a shock of curls, came out. He looked quizzically at Harris, unembarrassed. Hannah wasn't embarrassed either. And he'd thought she was so innocent and guileless. She spoke to the youth in Hebrew. Harris heard his name spoken. The youth held out his hand.

"My friend, Judah," Hannah said without explanation.

That quick, downward handshake.

"What's he doing here?" Harris demanded, releasing Judah's hand.

He could have been getting himself killed and she was entertaining some overgrown kid. And not even acting guilty about it.

Hannah was taken aback by his tone.

"A visitor. From Tel Aviv."

Compressing her lips, as if she'd revealed too much.

"Next you're gonna tell me he's your cousin."

"My cousin?"

Then she understood.

"You are insulting."

Eyes bleak.

"What's he doing here? You knew I was coming over."

152

Judah watching, looking from one to the other, missing nothing. Wary old eyes in his kid's face.

"Lieutenant Harris . . ." Hannah snapped.

Her face lost its severity.

"You are jealous of Judah! I am flattered. He is on his way . . . elsewhere. He required a place to sleep tonight."

"He's spending the night here?"

"Yes, Michael. And in my bed."

The bitch!

Now she did laugh.

"And I am sleeping with Tante Frieda."

Judah sat down on the couch, looking bored.

Maybe it wasn't anything after all. They couldn't be such good actors.

Hannah spoke to Judah in Hebrew again. It couldn't have been about their conversation because Judah didn't smile. He got up, said "*Shalom,*" and left the room.

"If you could have seen your face," Hannah said. "Like a thundercloud." Complacently, "Perhaps you are fond of me. Just a little."

"A lot more than that."

He knew she wanted to hear it.

"I guess I did act kind of dumb, didn't I?"

"Tell no one you saw Judah here tonight. In any case, his name isn't actually Judah. He is only called that."

"Why?"

Knowing it had something to do with Sgt. Weisz and mysterious tin suitcases but wanting Hannah to confide in him instead of treating him like an outsider. He was a Jew, too.

"Must I always remind you it is better for you not to know such things?"

She let him turn out the light and take her in his

153

lap in the dark. And allowed him to put his hand in her shirt. So smooth and round, so warm and resilient. She let him kiss her there, both of them breathing like runners. Would she be so eager if she hadn't thought she might never see him again? He yearned for her with numbing intensity. Ached. Was it just because he hadn't had a girl in so long or because it could have been *Blonde Job* instead of *Flat Foot Floogie?*

She wouldn't go outside with him or let him unbutton her shorts.

"No, *Liebchen,* no."

"Hannahle."

Don't beg, Harris. Never beg, no matter what.

"You're still going to Haifa with me tomorrow?"

"Yes, but not for . . ."

"I know."

But she would. If he could just get her off alone somewhere. He'd find a way. He always had.

She lifted his head between her palms and kissed him.

"When one bomber did not return . . . I thought . . ."

"Not me. I'll always come back."

As long as Big Wags was sitting back there in the left seat.

Ships burning. Billowing smoke. Black tatters fluttering in the wind like rags. "Don't cheer, boys, the poor devils are dying." A pink Liberator flopping around like a duck with one wing. Blue sky. Blue sea. Men spilling out. The next one won't bother everybody so much.

He returned her kisses. Roughly.

"I know, *Liebchen.* I know."

But she couldn't know. Not really.

154

CHAPTER IX

Gallegly was going to Haifa with Wagstaff. Silkwood wasn't going because he had volunteered to go through Bourdillon's personal effects and weed out anything that might upset the Floogie bombardier's folks. Rubbers, dirty pictures, letters from girls he might have promised to marry. Mothers always worried their sons were going to meet some scheming camp follower and do something dumb. Even Harris's mother. The way mothers of girls in Air Corps towns were afraid those wild flyboys were going to ruin their daughters.

Silkwood hadn't really been that good a buddy of Bourdillon's, he didn't have any buddies except Wagstaff and, however reluctantly, Harris and Gallegly, but in retrospect seemed to think he had.

"Can you ditch Wags for a couple of hours?" Harris asked.

"Did your girl find a girl for me?" Gallegly said, interested.

Harris felt like a heel. He hadn't even tried. But he hadn't really had a chance to. Maybe after he'd had Hannah in the sack and she knew the score.

"Get me a room at the Savoy. Then meet me at Pross's about twelve-thirty. Just you."

"And?"

"You know the drill. Invite us to your room for a drink or something."

Gallegly was not enthusiastic.

"I'd do the same for you, Gallegly."

He would, and had. At Fort Myers, Lakeland and on cross countries, if one of them had a girl and the other didn't, and the girl was balky about going to a hotel room, the other would make some excuse for all to go up together. That made the girl feel safe. What worked best was for one of them to say he wanted to make a long distance call to his mother. They made the call, too, which made everybody happy, the mother, the one with the girl and, eventually, the girl. A phone call wouldn't work in this case. You didn't just pick up a phone in Haifa and ask to be put through to the United States. But Gallegly would think of something. He always did. So did Harris, when he was the one without the girl.

"You sure you want to pull that on her?" Gallegly said. "She's . . . hell, you know what I mean."

"She's eager. All she needs is an excuse not to look like she is."

"You could'a fooled me . . . OK."

Judah wasn't around when Harris picked up Hannah and neither she nor Tante Frieda mentioned him. Harris asked about him on the bus but Hannah turned all questions aside.

"See, just over there?" she said. "There is Yagur, a workers' settlement. In ten more years it will be so changed you won't recognize it. And just over there, Nesher, the Portland cement factory."

"You showed me that last time," Harris said, defeated.

"We are very proud of our Portland cement fac-

156

tory. One would think it a museum or a cathedral, we are so proud."

She was teasing him.

"See, there is Carmel on the left. Will we go to Carmel? Please?"

Not teasing.

"Sure," said Harris.

Anything she wanted. After the Savoy.

They reached Haifa too early to run into Gallegly at Pross's. Harris took Hannah window shopping on Jaffa Road. On Saturdays there wasn't much else to do in the new part of the city where almost all the businesses were owned by Jews. He wished the shops were open so he could buy Hannah something. Not to soften her up, just to give her a present. He was the same as rich. More money than he knew what to do with and nothing to spend it on. Fourteen Palestine pounds won at blackjack, fifty dollars in traveller's cheques and, back in the tent in his money belt, another hundred in traveller's cheques and three US twenties. And payday coming up in another ten days. A lot of dough when you had no expenses. More ready cash than he'd ever had before in his life, not counting his college savings fund.

Hannah lingered at Nagler's Bookshop, squinting to read the titles through the window. Harris had been there his first visit to Haifa looking for something to read. There had been books in English but he hadn't bought any. He'd already read the only ones that interested him.

"Did you finish *Buddenbrooks?*" Harris asked.

"No."

"Too German, huh?"

"Most certainly not. I've had no time to read. Far too many interruptions. An annoying visitor every night when I'd much prefer my book."

They looked in the window at Paras & Madi. Curios and souvenirs. He'd sent his mother and Betty Lee silver filigree brooches from there. Jerusalem silver it was called. If it were open he'd buy one for Hannah. He looked at his watch. Still way too early to meet Gallegly at Pross's. He wished he'd asked Gallegly to show up earlier. He was wasting time he could be spending in the sack with Hannah.

"Would you mind going to the Arab quarter?" he said.

"Why should I mind?"

"I just thought . . ."

By rights she should hate Arabs too much to want to be around them.

"Come along, then," she said.

Poking around the Arab shops turned out to be fun. Shopkeepers called from doorways, some even taking his arm and hustling him inside. Bargaining in English. Hannah joshing them in Arabic. Four languages, for cripe's sake. She was enjoying herself. The shopkeepers loved it too. Arguing with her, feigning anger, despair. They watched a cabinetmaker at work. There was a tang of sawdust as his saw bit through a plank. It overrode the Arab smell. The little shop was redolent of pine and olives. There was a pile of olive wood in the corner, creamy, streaked in patterns of brown.

The cabinetmaker tried to sell him a crucifix carved from olive wood, speaking not a word of English. Hannah said something that stopped his sales pitch for a moment, but only for a moment.

"I told him you are a Jew," she said. "So buy it for a Christian friend, he says."

Harris bought it. The price was right. The cabinetmaker gave them each a piece of Turkish delight and they all shook hands.

"Salaam aleikum," said Hannah.

"Aleikum salaam," said the cabinetmaker with evident sincerity.

"You get along pretty well with Arabs," Harris said outside, wonderingly.

"Those who mean me no harm," Hannah said. "In any case, at the moment they are not the worst enemy."

"I don't get it," Harris said, waiting for an explanation.

Hannah popped the Turkish delight in her mouth and sighed with rapture. "We almost never have sweets," she said.

"I'll buy you a whole box."

"No, thank you."

"For Tante Frieda, then."

"She will be your slave. She is already, I think."

They found a shop that sold it packed in souvenir olive wood boxes.

"It will taste of olives," Hannah warned. "But Tante Frieda will like the little box."

They went back to Kingsway in the new section, still too early for Pross's. Three English soldiers were arguing in front of the Post Office, two short, knotty ones, the other Harris's size. The tall one popped to when he saw Harris.

"Begging your pardon, sir," he said.

Hannah pulled at Harris's arm, not wanting him to stop. The other two soldiers were waiting expectantly.

"P'raps you can settle an argument for us, sir," the tall soldier said.

"Glad to, if I can," Harris said, ignoring Hannah's insistent hand.

"Do Yanks have sergeant pilots, sir?"

"No. Only commissioned officers."

159

Harris's questioner shot a triumphant look at his companions. Hannah walked on a few steps and stood waiting with her back to them, shoulders rigid. One of the soldiers beckoned to the one who had stopped Harris.

"Excuse me, sir," the tall one said.

He rejoined his companions. They spoke in low tones, now and then looking over at Harris to detain him with a glance. Hannah looked back over her shoulder.

"Michael," she said tightly, "are you coming?"

"Hold your horses," he said.

What the hell was eating her?

The tall one approached Harris again.

"Begging your pardon again, sir. Do you know Haifa at all, sir?"

"A little."

"Our first day here, sir. Why is everything all shut up?"

"It's Saturday."

"Saturday, sir?"

"The Jewish sabbath."

"I see. Right, sir."

He turned to his companions.

"Bloody Jews," he said. "It's their Sunday."

"Always mucking things up," said one of the soldiers. "Even our bloody free day."

Hannah whirled on him, eyes blazing. "It's you who muck things up here!" she cried. "Murderers!"

All of them, Harris, too, stared at her, startled. Why'd she have to say a thing like that, Harris wondered. So a limey said, "Bloody Jews." It wasn't that big a deal. People said things like that without meaning anything. And just who the hell did she think was keeping the goddam Germans out of Egypt, fighting the Nazis that had run her and her

160

folks out of Germany? He was embarrassed for her.

One of the short ones laughed. The others did, too.

"She's a proper Tartar, your little Jewess, sir," the tall one said.

Harris didn't like that himself. "Bloody Jews" didn't bother him so much but "Jewess" was something else. And talking about Hannah like she was a tramp.

"Come on, Hannah," he said, going to her and taking her arm.

She refused to budge.

"You are all cowards and bullies," she said.

"See here," said the tall one.

"Turning our ships away. Hounding refugees. Betraying us."

"You should take your belt to that lot, sir," the tall one said.

"I shouldn't think it's his belt the lieutenant would want to lay on that lovely little Jew arse," said one of the short ones.

"Just a goddam minute!" Harris grated.

The other short one looked at him appraisingly. "Dear me, chaps," he said. "We've provoked the Yank lieutenant."

"We beg the lieutenant's humble pardon," the tall one said, obviously not meaning it. "But if the lieutenant can't manage the little baggage himself . . ."

"That's about enough, Private!" Harris snapped.

It was the first time he had ever pulled rank. Not that a second lieutenant had all that much rank.

"Is it now? Sir?"

Things were getting nasty. The limeys were spoiling for a fight. Something to do on a dull Saturday, nothing personal intended. And they weren't completely to blame. That goddam Hannah had started it. Just the same, he had a savage desire to punch the tall one in the mouth. If he wasn't in uniform, if he didn't have to meet Gallegly in a few minutes. He might just do it anyhow.

The two short soldiers, sensing Harris's mood, ranged themselves beside the tall one.

"Let's go, Hannah," Harris said.

Despite the odds, if they didn't leave now he was going to have to punch somebody and there'd be hell to pay. Not just because he'd get his plough cleaned by three limeys but also because Major Beck might find out he'd been fighting in town. Back in the States, Beck had a reputation as a brawler, not caring who or where, but he'd announced there wasn't going to be any of that overseas.

"Hop to it then, Yank," the tall one jeered. "Take your little Jewess and run while you're still able."

Civilians were hurrying by them, pretending not to notice the argument. No help there. It was just him against the three of them, Harris thought, re-signed, but thinking if he could just get the big limey one good one in the chops it might be worth it.

"Wait for me at the corner, Hannah," Harris ordered.

"They do not frighten me," she said fiercely.

Sure, thought Harris. Let's you and them fight. He clenched his fist, poised. If he could put the big one down quick the little ones might get discouraged. Wishful thinking. They were too tough and ready. Limeys didn't quit. Well, here goes.

"Problems, Tex?" said Wagstaff's voice from behind him before he could throw a punch.

And there stood Big Wags, casual, looming. As welcome a sight as the beacon at Burg El Arab.

"Hi Wags," Harris said, trying to sound as casual as Wagstaff looked. "No sweat."

He didn't think there was, now. Not with Wags there, looking big as a bull and twice as tough. One of the short ones licked his lips nervously.

"This is between me and your mate," the big one said, impressed by Wagstaff's size but not intimidated. "So why don't you just bugger off? Sir?"

The short ones closed ranks with him.

"Why would I want to do that?" Wagstaff said conversationally. "Why don't I just buy you all a beer?" He turned to Harris and said, "You and the little lady go on. I'll have a beer with your friends."

One of the short ones, mistaking Wagstaff's mild tone for timidity, said, "Rather drink than fight, would you, Yank?"

"Try us," Harris said.

"Shut up, Tex," Wagstaff ordered. To his challenger, "Don't you know it, soldier. You don't get your uniform so dirty that way." To Harris again, "Dammit, take off."

"I'm not gonna do it," Harris said. "There's three of 'em."

The limeys were going to start swinging any second now. Harris knew the look. Let 'em, he thought joyfully, Hannah forgotten. He and Wags could take them. He'd handle the big one and Wags the two little ones.

"Oh, hell," Wagstaff said, resigned.

Before anyone could move Wagstaff grabbed a short soldier by wrist and elbow and, swinging him like a flail, launched him into the other two. The big soldier and the one Wagstaff had thrown into him went down in a heap. The other soldier staggered back, off balance. Harris started for him, fists cocked. I'll show you about Jews, you bastard! Wagstaff shouldered Harris aside, stooped, picked up a kicking man from the tangle on the pavement and threw him bodily into the one still on his feet. Three down.

"Now take off with your girl, you dumb son of a bitch," Wagstaff said calmly, not even breathing hard.

Harris shook his head. The three limeys were already struggling to their feet. He wasn't going to leave Wags to fight them all by himself. Wags wouldn't be able to take them by surprise again. A whistle sounded down the street. Feet pounded.

"Michael!" Hannah cried.

Harris looked around. Two British MPs, batons poised, were charging towards them. The three soldiers took one look and started running. Wagstaff with them. Not after them, with them. The tall soldier stumbled and would have fallen if Wagstaff had not reached out, dragged him erect and pulled him along. Wagstaff looked back, grinning.

"See you around, Tex."

Harris stepped in front of the MPs, blocking their way.

"What the bloody . . . !" one of them, a corporal, cried, breaking off at the sight of Harris's gold bars.

"Sorry, Corporal," Harris said. "I didn't mean to get in y'all's way."

"That's all right, sir," the corporal said angrily, his eyes still fixed on Harris's bars. More controlled, "What seems to be the trouble, sir?" To Hannah, politely, "You all right, miss?"

Hannah nodded curtly, still indignant and unwilling to accept any courtesy from an Englishman.

"Nothing, really," Harris said. "My friends were just horsing around, that's all."

The MPs looked dubious.

"Thanks anyway," Harris said.

He hustled Hannah away while they were thinking it over. He stole a glance at his watch. After twelve-thirty. If he didn't hurry, Gallegly might think he wasn't coming and take off. Where were all the taxis? If Gallegly didn't wait he wouldn't even know if he had a room at the Savoy or not.

"Who was your marvellous friend?" Hannah said.

"My pilot," Harris answered curtly, still angry with her, searching the street for a taxi. "Dan Wagstaff. What the hell's wrong with you, anyhow?"

"You were marvellous too," she said, unabashed.

"What was all that? They were OK until you started it."

"You are defending them?"

It was an accusation, not a question.

"Yeah. I am. You called 'em names. If it wasn't for the British . . . Whose side are you on, anyway?"

He saw a taxi and flagged it down.

"Eretz Israel," she said.

He opened the door and pushed her in.

"Swell," he said. "I guess fighting the goddam Germans don't count."

"That is important, certainly, but it does not mean we must love the British."

"How true," said the taxi driver. "Where should I take you?"

He was a middle-aged man with a German accent, as usual, wearing metal-rimmed glasses with smudged lenses. Harris hoped he could see to drive.

"Pross's," Harris said. To Hannah, "Well, I like 'em. You can't go by those three back there. I don't even blame 'em all that much the way you acted."

"So sorry you don't approve of me," Hannah said stiffly.

"So what do you think of Haifa," the driver asked,

turning to look at Harris.

"I like it," Harris said impatiently.

He was sore at Hannah. Everything had been going so great until she started popping off at those limeys. Who'd have thought she was such a fanatic? Scrunched over in the corner now, madder at him than he was at her. If he was going to get anywhere with her today he'd better do something about that.

"I'm sorry, Hannah," he said. "I guess the reason I don't see things the way you do is because I don't know as much about it as you."

Not really believing that, just wanted to make peace with her.

"It is too beautiful a day for young people to quarrel," the driver said.

"Roger," said Harris.

"You are learning though, I think," Hannah said, mollified.

Harris reached over and took her hand. She twined her fingers in his. Everything was going to be just fine.

"They do the Arabs' bidding," she said bitterly. "The English. Even though Jews support the war effort and the Arabs do not. They turn away the ships bringing Jews to safety here. Or drag so-called illegal immigrants to detention camps and get rid of them at their convenience."

"Aw, come on, Hannah, the English wouldn't kill Jews."

"Only those who fight back. Like Abraham Stern. Those who cannot defend themselves they send to Mauritius."

"Abraham Stern was a madman," the driver said.

"And you call yourself a Jew?" Hannah snapped.

"There are Jews and Jews," the driver said mildly.

"Is that what happened to your folks?" Harris

166

said. "They got sent to Mauritius?"

He remembered her telling him that the first night he went to see her.

"They were in the camp at Athlit."

"Athlit?"

Athlit was his last visual fix sometimes when they crossed the coastline at the start of a mission. He hadn't any idea illegal immigrants were kept there.

"The English came one day with clubs and curses and forced them into lorries. My father and mother and everyone. And herded them on a leaky ship and sent them to Mauritius. And you say to me I should love them."

"I'm sorry, Hannah. I didn't know."

He squeezed her hand. No wonder she hated the English. But somehow he could not hate them. They were fighting a war together. If it weren't for the English the Germans might have already conquered the world. And the ones he'd run across, except for those three today, couldn't have been nicer. But he wasn't about to say so to Hannah.

"We have arrived," the driver said, sounding relieved.

The driver, as they always did, refused a tip.

Gallegly was at a corner table, already eating. He must have thought they weren't going to make it.

"Say," Harris said, feigning surprise. "There's my co-pilot."

Hoping Gallegly had gotten the room and had a good story to go with it. Gallegly looked up and saw them. He stood up and waved for them to join him. Harris guided Hannah to the table.

"You remember Gallegly," he said.

"Of course," Hannah said, shaking hands. "I must confess Lieutenant Gallegly made a better impression on me than you did when we met."

Gallegly grinned at Harris and held Hannah's chair for her, saying, "That's understandable. I'm a much nicer guy than he is."

Harris asked Hannah if she could persuade the waiter to get them a bottle of wine on a separate cheque.

"And this time it's not your treat."

"I have no intention of treating you," she said.

She arranged for the wine. Except for that she did not behave as she had the first time. Pross's apparently no longer had the power to evoke memories.

Harris told Gallegly about Wagstaff and the limeys, leaving out the part about Hannah starting it.

"He's a pistol, all right," Gallegly said.

He had a glass of wine with them while they ate. He asked Hannah questions about herself, Aleenah and Palestine. Harris had rarely heard him talk so much. Not trying to move in, just interested. Hannah was much freer with Gallegly than she'd been with him before they got to know each other. Jewish or not, Harris was glad he'd got to know her before she had a chance to spend any time with Gallegly. Gallegly got more girls just half-trying than most guys did working at it.

To stay under the maximum allowable cheque they skipped the tuna cocktails to have dessert. Apple pie. OK, but not like mama used to make. Hannah ate hers with fork and spoon, using the fork as a holder and pusher, chasing down the last crumb. Harris could see Gallegly got a large charge watching her. Seeing Gallegly appreciate her made him realize all the more how lucky he was to have stumbled on Hannah. He was impatient to get to the Savoy. Gallegly had gotten the room, hadn't he?

Gallegly suggested another bottle of wine if Hannah could arrange it. Harris kicked him under the table.

"But I guess I don't have time," Gallegly said, wincing.

"We're going to Mount Carmel," Hannah said, disappointed. "I was hoping you might join us. Such a lovely view."

"I'd really like to," Gallegly said. "But I'm meeting Wagstaff later. And I've got things to do before that."

"That's too bad," said Harris.

Dammit, what about the room?

"Got to get some things wrapped to mail home," Gallegly said. Offhand, "I'm staying over tonight."

"Yeah?" said Harris.

"At the Savoy. If you're not in a hurry, why don't you come with me to pick up the stuff I'm sending home?"

"OK, Hannah?" Harris said.

"Of course. And perhaps we can go with you to meet Lieutenant Wagstaff. I must thank him. Do you think he would enjoy going to Carmel?"

"We wouldn't want to push it," Gallegly said.

"But we would be delighted. Would we not, Michael?"

"Sure," Harris said, knowing Gallegly had no intention of ruining things for him.

Gallegly had the room key in his pocket. They never turned in their keys at the desk. That way, if you found a girl you could take her right up without having to fool with some nosey room clerk.

The Savoy desk clerk studied them, pretending to be busy with the register. Hannah was self-conscious under his furtive scrutiny. She hid her discomfort by talking loud enough for him to hear, as if assuring him there was nothing censurable about her going to a hotel room with two American flyers.

Gallegly actually had souvenirs laid out on the bed. A pair of droopy-seat Arab pantaloons, a cross and chain of Jerusalem silver and a *yarmulke,* the skullcap pious Jews wore. Good old Gallegly.

"Something for every religion in Palestine," Gallegly said. "Not that Arab pants are all that religious."

"How very clever," Hannah said.

"Send this to somebody, too," Harris said, taking out his olive wood crucifix.

"That's really dandy," Gallegly said. "My mother'll love it."

He gathered up his souvenirs.

"I'll take 'em down and get 'em wrapped," he said. "And run 'em over to the Post Office. Why don't you two wait for me?"

"Why do we not go with Gallegly?" Hannah said.

Calling him Gallegly because Harris did and she was feeling the wine.

"I'd just as soon not run into those three characters again," Harris said.

Gallegly paused at the door, not looking too happy.

"Tex?"

Harris went to him.

"How much do I owe you for the crucifix?" Gallegly asked, slipping him the room key.

"Nothing."

Gallegly, low, "I don't know who's the biggest bastard, you or me."

Harris shut the door quietly behind him. Hannah was looking at him quizzically.

"What?" he said. Instead of answering she went to the window and looked out.

"It is so warm here," she said. "I had too much wine."

170

Harris put his arms around her from behind. She didn't flinch. He put his face in her hair and inhaled. It smelled of perspiration and strong soap. She was very still against him. Less jittery than he was. Don't be too goddam impatient, Harris.

"You think you are so clever, do you not, Michael?"

Amused.

"What are you talking about?"

"I think you know."

"I didn't think you'd mind us having a few minutes alone."

He nuzzled her neck. She snickered.

"That tickles."

He turned around and kissed her lightly. She kissed back.

"Gallegly is very nice," she said. "I like your friends. They are nicer than you, I think."

He took her hand and led her away from the window. She took a few steps and pulled back. She thought he was leading her to the bed. She wasn't ready for that. Not yet.

"We might as well sit down," he said.

She sat in his lap, as she had so many nights on Tante Frieda's couch. Settling back comfortably, trustingly, against his chest. She sighed when he kissed her. He drew back to study her face. Her eyes were wide, staring at him.

"What?" he said again.

She closed her eyes. He kissed the lids. She liked that. Kissed her neck. She liked that, too. He handled her breasts gently. She liked that even more. He tried to slip his hand in her dress. The neckline was too high. It buttoned down the back. He'd already checked that out. Two buttons. Kissing her, he fumbled at the buttons.

171

"No, Michael."

"Why not?"

"Gallegly."

"The door's locked."

"He will know."

"He won't be back for a while. I'll unlock it before he gets back."

She waited patiently while he undid the buttons. Shivered at the touch of his questing hand on her uncovered breasts. Resisted weakly when he began undressing her. Gasping, at last, in only virginal white cotton pants. Exactly as he had imagined it in the tormenting, restless nights under his mosquito net. Only this was real. He pushed hard against the floor to stand erect, bearing her in his arms towards the bed. She opened her eyes as if waking from a stupor. They had been shut tight until now. Shutting out or shutting in?

"No!" she cried, frightened.

"It's all right, sweetheart," he whispered. "He's not coming back."

She seemed to collapse in his arms. She wanted him as much as he wanted her.

But why did she look so sad?

CHAPTER X

She lay naked on the bed at last. As in his fantasies. But inert, scarcely breathing. An arm flung over her eyes to shield them from something. The other arm rigid at her side, her hand clutching a fistful of the spread as if to keep from sliding into an abyss. She had not moved since Harris had laid her there to hurry out of his uniform.

He had to arrange her limbs to make her accessible. She neither helped nor hindered or made a sound. Like an articulated clothing dummy. Her only acknowledgment of his existence was a gasp of surprise and a grunt of pain. She was a virgin. And except for that first moment of shocked recoil, totally unresponsive. He had imagined her impatient and eager, squirming and panting, clutching him to her. Not like this. Despite her woodenness it was over quickly. He hadn't had a woman in more than a month and whatever Hannah's problems in bed she had a great body.

The ebbing of his hunger left him filled with guilt. He should have prepared her better for her first experience with a man.

"Hannahle," he whispered. "I'm sorry."

"Why?" she said dully.

"I hurt you, didn't I?"

"Yes."

"It wasn't any fun for you, was it?"

"Fun?"

She opened her eyes but did not look at him. The sadness was still there, intensified.

"I mean you didn't like it, did you?"

"Was I meant to?"

With a hint of her old spirit. Better she should be sarcastic than so damn sad. One cut but the other crushed.

"Yes. It'll be better next time. I promise."

"There will be no next time."

She sat up and covered herself with her arms. What a hell of a shape she had. Too bad she didn't know how to use it. But as much his fault as hers. Maybe more. He put his arms around her. She averted her face from his kiss.

"Don't be like that," he said.

Feeling like a dog. Tricking her into bed and then not even pleasing her. They couldn't leave until he'd done that. Pleased her. He brushed her cheek with his lips, holding her.

"Hannahle," he whispered.

"It isn't necessary for you to pretend any longer," she said. "You have accomplished what you wished."

"That's not quite true."

"Indeed?"

"I wanted it to be great for you too."

"Oh? And was it great for you?"

"No."

"I disappointed you, then?"

"I disappointed you, didn't I?"

"Yes."

"It'll be better next time."

"Do you think it is that?" Exasperated. "Do you

174

think it matters so much you are not good in bed?"

That stung. He had never had any complaints before.

"It is how you brought me here. Tricks and lies. Scheming with your friend. I suppose you will laugh together about it tomorrow?"

"No. He didn't want to. I had to talk him into it."

"Why did you not simply ask me to come with you here?"

"I didn't think you'd do it. Would you have?"

"I do not know. Perhaps. But it should have been my choice."

"Dammit, it was your choice. You could have stopped me any time."

"I thought you cared for me in other ways. As well as that way."

"I do, Hannahle, I do."

"Let me go."

Impatiently.

"No."

"I only wish to go to the wc. I am not . . . clean." There was blood on her thighs. On both their thighs.

"All right."

He watched her go, relieved. She wasn't all broken up any more. She didn't seem to think losing her virginity was such a big deal. Just unhappy with him for being sneaky. Saying he wasn't any good in bed! What a smooth back she had, and such a cute little butt. The bathroom door closed behind her. Water running for minutes and minutes. Stopping. After a while he grew impatient. He was restored, ready to prove to her he was good in bed. Then he became alarmed. Was Hannah OK? Had her non-chalance been a pose to get away from him?"

He ran to the bathroom door. It was locked. He

pounded on the door.

"Hannah!"

"What do you want?"

Annoyed, not despondent.

"Are you all right?"

"Of course I am all right. I am bathing. What a luxury."

There weren't any bathtubs with running hot water in Aleenah.

He went back to bed to wait for her. This time he'd be damn sure she was good and ready. She came out holding a towel in front of her and headed for her clothes. They were in an untidy heap on the floor where he had dropped them.

"No, you don't," he said, intercepting her.

"Do you wish to hurt me again?" she said coldly.

"It won't hurt this time. I promise."

"Very well."

Resigned. As if it were of no importance to her one way or the other.

She lay beside him, eyes open, staring at the ceiling. Looking bored. To get back at him, he knew. Despite that bored expression she was tense. He could feel it. She was afraid but determined not to show it.

He was patient and very deliberate, doing everything he knew aroused women, waiting until she was as responsive as she had been in the chair and on Tante Frieda's couch. Waiting even beyond that, until she was distraught with expectation.

Now I'll damn well show you who's not good in bed.

She shuddered. Not in surprise this time.

"Does it hurt, sweetheart?" he whispered.

"Only a little. *Ach. Ach.*"

Moaning in German and not from pain.

She was very noisy. Sighing, moaning, gasping. Quivering, with intervals of rigidity as he methodically postponed his own release. But not responding with any movement of her own. Taking, taking, not giving anything back. Not knowing how, or unable, to make a contribution. He didn't care. She would learn. What mattered now was that she was enjoying it as much as he. He wouldn't be going back to Aleenah feeling like a heel and she wouldn't despise him for having tricked her and then been lousy in bed to boot.

He lay beside her. They were both sweating, both spent. She twined her fingers in his.

"Was it as marvellous for you?" she murmured, content.

"More. The best it's ever been."

They always liked to hear that. But then, so did he.

"Honestly? I am . . . skilful, I imagine."

"You just have to be you, sweetheart. That's enough."

"Sweetheart. That is only a word with you, isn't it, Michael?"

Not accusing, not sad. Just matter-of-fact.

"No. I really mean it."

Lying a little, but not very much. He did like her a lot.

"You called me *liebchen*. Did *you* mean it?"

Liebchen. Sweetheart in German.

"I don't know. Perhaps . . . perhaps if I believed you actually cared for me."

"I do. I really do."

He kissed her to prove it. Some girls he hadn't wanted to kiss afterwards. Should he tell her that? Don't be stupid, Harris.

"Well," he said, propping himself up on an elbow,

"you still want to go to Mount Carmel?"

"Do you?"

"Sure."

"Then I would like it very much. Michael?"

"Yes?"

"Will I have a baby?"

"I took precautions."

"Of course. I should have guessed. You plan so carefully."

"Look, I'm sorry about that. The way I did it. Are you still sore about it?"

She sat up and put her face against his.

"You are not so clever as you think," she said. "I saw through you and your friend. But I wanted you, too."

"You sure as hell didn't show it."

"I was frightened. When my fantasies became real."

So she'd had fantasies just like he did.

"And then, the first time you made love to me . . ."

"I guess I was kind of rough, wasn't I?"

"It was not only that. It hurt. And was so . . . so empty. Ugly. And you did not seem to care for me nearly so much as when we only kissed and touched. I thought you might not want to see me again."

"Just try to get rid of me."

More Saturdays in Haifa. Nights in the pine grove on a blanket.

The desk clerk accepted the room key in reproving silence. Hannah swept by him with regal unconcern. Odd, Harris thought, when she'd been so self-conscious before they'd done anything. He wondered if he would really ever understand her. Not that it mattered that much as long as he could keep on seeing her whenever he wanted.

178

She stopped halfway into the taxi and said, "Oh, dear. I forgot your gift for Tante Frieda."

"We'll buy her something else."

"How wasteful! If it embarrasses you to return, I'll fetch it."

The desk clerk was still stonily disapproving. Harris retrieved the olive-wood box of Turkish delight and looked at the bed. They had smoothed out the spread and plumped up the pillows. It looked as if no one had been there. Not much of a room, really, without Hannah in it. Hard to believe he'd been making love to her in that narrow bed just a few minutes before. Almost like a dream, because in the end it had been so much like his fantasies. No need for fantasies from here on.

Their taxi driver had taught romance languages in Heidelberg. He and Hannah talked happily in German all the way to the crest of Mount Carmel. They chattered of Heidelberg and Mainz, of Wiesbaden, Frankfurt, the Rhine and the River Neckar. Sounding as if they missed them. The driver paused only to point out places of interest to Harris; Haifa taxi drivers always did that whether you asked them or not. The Bahai gardens, the view of the Bay of Acre, still and as contrived looking as an amateur's painting, the Kishon River catching the sun, the rolling hills of Galilee and the checkered Valley of Zebulon. The road led up through groves of cedar and green carpets of heavy brush, past summer residences, hotels, the big convalescent home.

"That part of the Carmel is French," Hannah said, pointing. "The home of the Carmelites. We must visit the monastery one day, Michael, when next we are in Haifa."

At the Mount Carmel Hotel Harris invited the taxi driver to have ice-cream with them in the garden.

"I'll pay for the waiting time," he said.

"Not necessary."

The garden was on the seaward side, set with spindly chairs and tables. Most of the tables were taken, civilian couples, a few British officers, men from the 108th, all the Americans looking at Harris enviously. Suffer, he thought. There were no British Other Ranks. The best places usually had signs, "Off Limits to Other Ranks." American enlisted men disregarded the signs. All three of them ordered parfaits. Palestine ice-cream was beginning to taste like the real thing to Harris although it was water-ice sweetened with honey or the dates, figs, bananas and apricots that flavoured it. Because of sugar rationing and the shortage of fats there was no real ice-cream in Palestine.

Hannah ate her parfait greedily, looking across at Harris straightfaced and saying, "I wonder why I am so ravenous."

Sitting eating ice-cream with a good-looking girl he could have any time he wanted her, euphoric, looking down at the blue Mediterranean, Acre across the bay, the hills and green valleys, and getting paid for it. What a way to fight a war.

They drove back down the mountain. He kissed Hannah whenever the road demanded the driver's full attention. He started to want her again. They went back to Pross's for dinner. He hoped they wouldn't run into Gallegly there. It might be embarrassing for Hannah.

He asked Hannah to spend the night with him in Haifa. Impossible, she said, much as she would like to. Tante Frieda would worry. And suspect. And she had to be at work early in the fields. Harris did not press her. She was right about Tante Frieda. He didn't want her to suspect anything either.

Driving home after dark, he kept kissing her in the back seat of the taxi until she made him stop because he was getting her too excited and the driver was sitting there close enough to touch.

Hannah was nervous.

"Tante Frieda will surely guess."

"No, she won't."

"She will. I feel . . . so different. She will surely notice."

"You are different, sweetheart. I like the way you're different. But I'm the only one who knows it."

"And Gallegly?"

"He won't say anything if I tell him to keep his mouth shut."

"Tell him . . . tell him we did not make love."

"Sure."

He'd have to tell Gallegly, though. Just not all the details.

"I would not like him to think me cheap."

"No one could ever think that about you."

"You do not think I am cheap?"

"I think you're expensive. Two dinners. Two parfaits. All these taxis."

She rested her head on his shoulder, more reassured than if he had protested he didn't think her cheap. As, of course, he had intended. And she wasn't cheap. She was loving and passionate and now, trusting. He was the one who was cheap. Dammit, why should he think that all of a sudden? They hadn't done anything she didn't want to. All the same, he wished he'd just asked her to go to the hotel with him, not pulled all that stuff with Gallegly. That's what made him feel cheap, and the fact she'd been a virgin. And he felt dumb, too, because she had seen through it.

She made him wait a few minutes before they went into the house, while she composed herself.

"I must look . . . innocent," she said. "Not like a fallen woman."

She was trying to make a joke of it and not succeeding. She was making him nervous now. You didn't want a girl's folks to know you'd been in the sack with her. Especially if you wanted to keep seeing her. And it wasn't only that. He wanted Tante Frieda to keep thinking well of him. Looking at it through her eyes, it hadn't been so charming. Luring her niece into a hotel room and taking her virginity. So don't look at it through her eyes. What Tante Frieda didn't know wouldn't hurt her.

"I am ready now," said Hannah. "I think."

She took a deep breath and opened the door. Harris expected Tante Frieda to be sitting there waiting for them. The room was empty.

"Tante Frieda?" Hannah called.

Tante Frieda came from a back room. Benign. Harris was relieved.

"You are home," she said. "You enjoyed yourselves?"

He was getting to where he could understand German better and better. Or maybe Tante Frieda was using easy words on purpose.

"Sehr viel," he said.

Thinking, dammit, Hannah, don't look so guilty.

"Look what we have brought you," Hannah said brightly, thrusting out the box of Turkish delight.

"It is beautiful," said Tante Frieda. "You shouldn't have."

"Look inside," Hannah said.

Tante Frieda opened the box.

"It is too much!"

She shut the box and said, "I will make tea. You

182

will stay a while, Michael?"

She'd always called him "lieutnant" before. It was good and not so good. Good because it showed she liked him, not so good because maybe she was accepting him as one of the family, thinking he was serious about Hannah. He really didn't want to stay and have tea. He didn't feel completely comfortable with Tante Frieda right now, so soon after having been in the sack with Hannah. Especially with the way Hannah was acting; babbling away nonstop to Tante Frieda about what a marvellous time she'd had in Haifa. Eating at Pross's twice, going to Mount Carmel to look at the view. It wasn't like her at all. Tante Frieda had to know Hannah was trying to cover up something. If the old lady did know she wasn't showing it. And it wouldn't look right if he didn't stay.

"Sure, Tante Frieda," he said. "Thanks."

Hoping it wasn't a mistake to call her that. It might give Hannah ideas.

Tante Frieda served the tea in glasses, with pieces of Turkish delight on a blue plate that looked as if it must have come from Germany a long time ago. His grandmother had plates like that, and cups and saucers too. He'd broken one of the cups when he was little and grandma had dusted his butt for him. He told Tante Frieda the story with just a little assistance from Hannah when his vocabulary failed him. Talking about his childhood was a safer topic than their day in Haifa.

The glasses had a gummy dark substance dissolving in the bottom, giving the tea a peculiar, chocolatey taste.

"Russian tea," Tante Frieda explained. "But it should be raspberry preserves."

Hannah had to translate the "raspberry preserves"

for him.

"We have none these days," she said. "This is made from St. John's bread." Seeing that it meant nothing to him, "Carob. In Hebrew, *charuv*."

The word struck a chord. Schwartzberg's, in his childhood the only Jewish delicatessen in Houston. Across the street from the Farmer's Market, smelling of sawdust on the floor, pickles and salami. *Charuv.* Dry black pods you were supposed to eat like candy. He hadn't liked them.

"It isn't very good, is it?" Hannah said.

"It's fine," Harris protested. To Tante Frieda, taking a swallow, *"Sehr gut."*

"Schrechlich," said Tante Frieda. Terrible. "But better than nothing."

Hannah, gaining confidence, was settling down and not so voluble, entertaining Tante Frieda with a droll account of Lieutenant Wagstaff's victory over three perfectly beastly English soldiers. Tante Frieda was not amused. She scolded her for provoking them.

"You, of all people," she said.

Warning her, if Harris interpreted her tone and the German correctly. She was disturbed that Hannah had drawn attention to herself. If Hannah was doing things the British didn't allow it had been reckless of her, he thought. And dumb. Dumber than just putting him in a spot where he could have got his tail whipped if Wags hadn't come along when he did. But gutty, too. If they had jumped him he bet she would have been right in there, kicking and scratching.

Tante Frieda asked Hannah to take the empty glasses to the kitchen. As soon as Hannah left the room she regarded Harris in grave silence. It was hard for him not to squirm. She didn't look sore,

184

just serious.

"*Sie dürfen nicht meinen Hannahle wehtun*," she said quietly.

He couldn't quite make it out. You something not my little Hannah something. *Wehtun. Weh.* Woe. *Tun.* Do. Do woe, hurt. You something not my little Hannah hurt. A chill danced up his back. She knew, all right. Did it mean she wasn't going to let her see him again? And, almost as bad, that she thought he was a bum? But she hadn't sounded mad at him or disappointed with him. He looked down at his shoes, not knowing what to say.

Tante Frieda sat with them a while after Hannah came back, not indicating in any way that she had said anything significant to Harris. Soon, as was her custom, she said it was time for old ladies to be in bed and left them alone. If she objected to him seeing Hannah again she wouldn't have done that.

Hannah immediately snuggled up to him on the couch. He could not generate much enthusiasm. Exactly what had Tante Frieda meant? Whatever it was, it had been important to her.

"You are through with me then?" Hannah said bitterly, drawing away.

"You know better than that."

He pulled her back and went through the motions.

"Sweetheart," he said casually, "what does *dürfen* mean?"

"Why do you ask?"

"Just wondering. I heard it somewhere."

"How was it used?"

"Like, '*durfen nicht*'."

"Dare not. Must not. Depending upon the context."

She looked at him impishly.

"If you are trying to improve yourself, *Liebchen,* why not learn Hebrew? Or is it too difficult for a Jew from Texas?"

You must not hurt my little Hannah.

Not exactly a warning, not exactly a plea.

He felt like a goddam dog.

CHAPTER XI

Gallegly was waiting up for him. Harris figured he would be, wanting to know how he had made out. He hadn't decided how much to tell Gallegly except that he'd done OK.

He was not bothered as much now by what Tante Frieda had said as he had been at first. He would be uncomfortable around her for a while, sure, knowing that she knew, but it meant he wouldn't have to worry about her finding out. Tante Frieda didn't have to worry. He wasn't going to hurt Hannah. Hannah knew it couldn't be anything permanent. Nobody knew how long they'd be at Ramat Jonas. When the time came to move he'd have to move. Nothing he could do about it. Hannah knew that. And he hadn't told her he was in love with her or anything. Some guys would tell a girl that to get her in the sack but he never had. So Hannah just had to realize it would be fun while it lasted and that was it.

He hadn't told her Tante Frieda knew. Hannah wouldn't go to Haifa with him or anything any more if she knew Tante Frieda knew what was going on. He didn't think Tante Frieda was going to tell her either.

"I don't guess you heard the news," Gallegly said.

"What news?"

"The ground echelon's getting in tonight."

"Hey! That's swell!"

They'd be getting their footlockers. He had four cartons of cigarettes in his and a whole box of almond Hersheys and a big can of Planter's peanuts. Other stuff he couldn't even remember, it seemed so long since he'd packed his footlocker at Lakeland and stencilled his name, rank, serial number and squadron on it. Some books, uniforms and some more silk stockings. He'd give the stockings to Hannah.

"No more British cooks," Gallegly said.

The way he said it sounded like that kid's chant when school let out for summer vacation. No more school, no more books, no more teachers' crazy looks.

Not a word about Hannah.

"How much do I owe you for the room?" Harris asked.

"Forget it."

Acting like he didn't want to talk about it.

"Come on, Gallegly."

"OK. Seventy piasters."

Seven hundred mils. Two-eighty. Best bargain he ever had.

He gave Gallegly a 500 mil note and two 100 mil coins. Gallegly shoved the money in his pocket without looking at it.

"You jealous or something, Terry? Next Saturday I'll see if she's got a friend."

"You son of a bitch," Gallegly said, grinning reluctantly, "You did all right, didn't you?"

"She's no tramp, though. She's a swell girl."

He felt a sudden urge to defend Hannah. You must not hurt my little Hannah.

"I could have told you that," Gallegly said. "Glad you know it."

"About next Saturday. It may be a little sudden, to ask her to fix you up. She's still kind of . . . selfconscious. You know?"

"I found my own. She lives in Haifa. Got her own room."

"Swell! Pro?"

"Eager amateur. But I'll be paying her rent from now on." Casually, "Major Beck says two squadrons are moving up by Acre."

"Oh, hell! Not us!"

Just when he was all set with Hannah. Acre was a good twenty miles away.

"Brand new buildings," Gallegly said. "No more tents. Indoor hot showers and a real club."

"Dammit, Gallegly! Is the 234th going? We are, aren't we?"

"No such luck. The 231st and 232nd. Major Beck's sore as hell."

"It's not so bad here," Harris said, relieved.

"That's not what you said before you latched on to Hannah Ruh. You must be the only son of a bitch in the squadron glad we're not moving to Acre."

In the morning Major Beck flew *Wrecking Crew* over for a look at the new field. No one thought it unusual that he took his four-engine bomber instead of borrowing a staff car. Beck would fly his plane to the latrine if it had a runway. Wagstaff wangled a ride on the plane for everybody. He was flying co-pilot with the major. None of Beck's regular crew except his aerial engineer and radio operator were going.

Harris wanted to see what he was missing, but not if there was a chance of getting back to Ramat Jonas too late to see Hannah. Wagstaff said they were coming back right after lunch.

Wrecking Crew had a demolition ball and rig painted on the side. That was Major Beck to a tee. It was odd being just a passenger, even for a ten minute flight. Major Beck jerked his ship off the runway as if by main force and skimmed over the valley, flying so low, fields and groves and pastures, Jewish settlements and Arab villages popped up and fell away like a speeded-up movie. They were on their final approach at St. Jean d'Acre so soon they would have still been climbing after takeoff on a normal flight.

The airfield at St. Jean was at least half again as big as Ramat Jonas, its western boundary within spitting distance of the coast road between Acre and Haifa. The runways and taxi strips were camouflaged to look like country roads crisscrossing the field. From *Wrecking Crew*'s altitude it was obvious which roads were fakes and which were runways and taxi strips. Harris thought it probably wouldn't be that obvious to the German bombers that raided Haifa at night and the high-flying German reconnaissance planes that came over in the daytime. There were already pink B-24s in the widely dispersed revetments, looking frivolous in comparison with the soberly painted RAF Libs, Beaufighters and Hurricanes parked elsewhere around the field. Typical, Harris thought. Despite the fact he was a combat veteran now, he still couldn't shake the feeling the British were somehow more seasoned and military than the Americans. The British had been fighting for years and they had barely just got here.

The 108th officer quarters were in an olive grove, constructed to simulate a kibbutz. Two long, low flat-roofed concrete block buildings at right angles to each other partially enclosing a squarish building housing the officers' mess and club. There was grass, flowers and shrubs.

The four officers of each combat crew shared a cell-like cubicle. The rooms were cramped but they had windows and an electric light dangling nakedly from the ceiling. The washroom at the end of each barracks building had washbasins and showers with hot water. The 231st and 232nd had been issued folding camp beds with steel springs instead of canvas and were already moving in in a fever of self-congratulations. Harris felt a twinge of envy, thinking about the dust and stubble of Ramat Jonas. But he had Hannah. Let them have their electric lights, hot showers and officers' club. There wasn't one of them who wouldn't trade with him if he could.

The latrine was a round brick building with a conical roof, like a miniature silo.

"I've finally seen the famous brick outhouse babes are supposed to be built like," Wagstaff said. "I don't think I could go for a babe built like that."

"It sure beats the Obstacle Course back at Lakeland," Harris said.

At Lakeland they had lived in tents in a humid stretch of pines and palmetto swamp where shoes grew mildew overnight. The Obstacle Course, the latrine, was two freshly debarked pine logs straddling a lye-sprinkled trench. You hooked your knees over one log and leaned back against the other to keep from falling in, getting resin on the crook of your knees and on the back of your shirt when you didn't remember to take it off.

"Roger," said Wagstaff. "That was rugged. Worse than a three-engine landing with the co-pilot flying." Looking at Gallegly, "Present company excluded."

Two Arabs in dirty white pantaloons and black knit caps down to their ears were working among the flower beds near the club. Harris had never seen a bareheaded adult Arab except a few in regular clothes in Haifa. Like the coloureds in Houston they always wore something on their heads. Only those knit caps or *kifeyehs* or a twist of cloth instead of big caps with visors or felt or straw hats. Just the same, it reminded him a little of home. The oleanders, too. They had oleanders in the front yard at home. Pretty, but if you got the white sap in your eyes it hurt like sin. Oleanders were supposed to be poisonous.

They had sliced tomatoes and swiss steak for lunch, the meat tender and served hot instead of lukewarm as at Ramat Jonas. For dessert, canned fruit salad with evaporated milk from cans with two holes punched in the top, just like at home except that these cans were bigger. At home they had real cream but Harris had liked evaporated milk better. To drink there was purple passion, made with artificial flavour crystals, cold and with plenty of sugar in it. Coffee, as well. Too strong, the way it always was in the service, but OK if you used enough sugar and plenty of evaporated milk. There were jars of strawberry preserves and cans of apple butter on every table. The mess had individual tables and chairs, not long trestle tables and benches. If he didn't have Hannah he'd really be browned off about the 234th not moving here—the first squadron to come over and with more missions than any of the other squadrons.

"It's not fair," Silkwood said petulantly.

They were all sitting at one table, Silkwood, Wagstaff, Gallegly and Harris.

"Quit your bitching, Junior," Wagstaff said. "You want to live soft when the folks back home are making all those sacrifices for the war effort? We fly around like birds and they can't even get tyres."

Major Beck was eating with the 231st and 232nd COs, cussing them for drawing St. Jean. Harris didn't think Beck really gave a rat's ass if he lived in a tent or a two storey house as long as he could drop bombs on somebody. He just liked to chew butts for the fun of it.

Harris screwed the lid tight on a jar of strawberry preserves and slipped it under his shirt, where it made a telltale bulge. It would go good in Tante Frieda's Russian tea.

"You're not supposed to do that," Silkwood complained.

"Shut up, Junior," Wagstaff said. "When those guys at the next table leave, taxi over and get us one."

"Somebody'll see me."

"That's an order, Junior."

There was a real bar in the officers' club, with running water. It wasn't supposed to be open during duty hours but because it was moving day the bar was being tended by a GI. The bar had nothing alcoholic to sell yet except Carmel hock and egg brandy, but somebody said they were trying to make arrangements with 205 Group to get the same kind of Australian ale sold at the NCO club at Fayid.

Major Beck sat in the club drinking Carmel hock with the other COs, playing poker dice to see who paid.

Wagstaff proposed that the four of them have some camel hockey and Honest John for the tab. Silkwood protested he didn't drink camel hockey.

"Drink orange squash then," Harris suggested.

The bar stocked local soft drinks and Mits Paz juices.

Wagstaff numbered the four slips of paper and put them in his hat. Silkwood drew the four and had to pay for the drinks. What he didn't know was that Wagstaff had written a four on every slip. Wagstaff let him moan a few minutes before telling him and paying him back.

They sat around on the new rattan furniture, so much more comfortable than the castoffs at the Ramat Jonas club, smoking and listening to the short-wave radio that had arrived with the ground echelon.

"Why do they get everything?" Silkwood demanded.

"We'll probably get one, too, Junior," said Wagstaff. "If we don't we'll fly over here some night and steal theirs. OK?"

Major Beck showed no sign of leaving. They went outside to watch the 231st and 232nd finish moving in. Two US Army two and a half ton trucks drove up and began unloading footlockers. Everybody clustered around looking for their footlockers and hauled them away like ants in a sugar bowl. By the time the trucks left, all the footlockers were either in rooms or on the corrugated iron-roofed porches running the length of each barrack. Except four. They sat side by side between the club and the barracks. Harris walked over to see if by any chance they belonged to *Blonde Job*'s crew and had been delivered to St. Jean by mistake.

The first name he saw was Minto. The others were Smith, Parsons and Bourdillon. From *Flat Foot Floogie*. The four olive drab boxes sat there in the heat, brass fittings shining in the sun. Accusing. Parsons and the others had been dead only three days and he'd already forgotten them. Wagstaff and the others came over to join him.

"Poor bastards," said Wagstaff.

Noticing them standing there so solemnly, men from the two squadrons drifted out to join them. Soon there were a dozen or so clustered around the footlockers, speaking in hushed voices about the day Floogie went down. About as close to a funeral as Parsons and the others were likely to get, Harris thought. A few of the guys just standing around, laughter and loud talk from the rooms, engines running up somewhere out on the airfield.

Here today, gone tomorrow. Not like they were dead, just gone somewhere. That was how it was in the service. Men got reassigned and you never saw them again. He probably wouldn't even have remembered Parsons if he hadn't danced with his wife. He wondered if she knew yet Parsons was missing in action.

All but the four of them drifted away. The others had things to do, scrounging nails to drive into the mortar between the concrete blocks for hanging clothes, mattresses to get from the piles on the porches for their steel camp beds.

"They could at least all stand around for a minute and say the Lord's Prayer or something," Silkwood said, not petulant, just sad.

For once Silkwood was the most decent guy around, Harris thought. It hadn't entered his mind

195

they ought to do anything.

"Dan," said Silkwood. "Why don't we? Say the Lord's Prayer for 'em?"

Harris didn't think he could. He'd feel too silly standing out there mumbling with everybody else yelling and making jokes.

"Let's just say it to ourselves," Wagstaff said.

He always knew the right thing to do.

A truck came back and loaded on the four footlockers. They went back to the club.

About four o'clock Harris started getting fidgety. Major Beck was still drinking with the squadron commanders and Wagstaff, who had joined them and was winning at poker dice and razzing Beck about it.

If he left now, with any luck at all he could catch rides to Aleenah and be there before dark. But if Beck decided to get back to Ramat Jonas by afternoon chow they could wait an hour and still beat him back if he hitch-hiked. He'd feel like a dope if he got stranded somewhere between St. Jean and Aleenah with Wagstaff and the others already back home. He drew Wagstaff aside and asked him to ask Major Beck when they were going back.

"Ants in your pants, huh, Tex?" Wagstaff said. "I would, too, if I had a babe waiting in Aleenah. You getting that?"

"We're just good friends," Harris said, grinning.

"This is old Wags you're talking to, pal. I've seen you operate."

All the same, he didn't feel like talking about Hannah the way he had about other girls, not even with Wags. He'd sort of promised her not to say anything.

He watched while Wagstaff asked Major Beck. He

knew Wags hadn't let on why he was asking because neither of them looked his way.

Wagstaff came back and said, "Sorry, Tex. We're staying for chow. He said he wasn't going to fly till he'd bled the camel hockey out of his hydraulic lines."

"Is it OK if I take off now?"

"Sure. If he says anything, I'll tell him something."

He got a ride right away to the Haifa-Nazareth highway. After that it got harder. Short rides and long waits. It was after dark when he reached the turnoff at Shimron. It was an easy walk to Aleenah. He was hungry, wondering what kind of chow he'd missed. And if he should take the time to drop by his tent first and get a blanket. He decided not to. Any time he wasted would be that much less to spend with Hannah in the pine grove.

He looked up at the stars as he walked. The full moon was on the rise. When it got high enough it would wash out some of his favourite stars. He felt the jar of preserves in his shirt. Maybe Tante Frieda could fix him a strawberry jam sandwich. He and Hannah wouldn't be going out until Tante Frieda went to bed anyway.

A dark sedan without even the usual blackout lights sped past, scaring him.

He yelled after it, "Son of a bitch!"

It looked like there were two people in it. He was mad enough to take them both on if they heard it and stopped. But the car went on. Wouldn't it be something if he'd got knocked off by a hit and run driver on a country road right in the middle of the war?

"Dear Mr. and Mrs. Harris, we regret to inform you that your son got his butt clobbered by a hit and run driver while chasing tail."

He wasn't mad any more. The car hadn't come all that close. It had just surprised him, was all. He heard another car coming fast. He stepped off the road and looked back. It had its headlights full on. The lights swept over him. The car slid to a stop and backed up. It was a sedan with four men in it. Two limey soldiers in front wearing berets, and two civilians in the back. A spotlight came on, dazzling him. He put his arm over his eyes.

"What the hell?"

The spotlight went off.

"Excuse me, sir."

One of the soldiers.

One of the civilians said, "Did you see a motorcar go by just now, Lieutenant? Two men in it?"

"No," said Harris.

Now why the hell did he say that. Maybe because whatever was going on was none of his business. But what if they were German saboteurs or something? He started to say he had seen the car but the sedan was already making a screeching U-turn. It kicked up a cloud of choking dust when it went off the road, showering him, and headed back the way it came without a thank you or kiss my ass.

He was glad he hadn't told them anything. Maybe it had something to do with Hannah and Gyorgy Weisz. And that Judah character.

Harris told Hannah about it when she let him in.

"Are you sure you told them nothing?" she demanded, alarmed.

"Sure I'm sure."

Tante Frieda looked on anxiously, knowing from Hannah's reaction it was something serious. Maybe thinking it was a lovers' quarrel.

"I must tell Sergeant Weisz," Hannah said.

Tante Frieda's expression changed when she heard Gyorgy's name mentioned.

"Who were they, anyway?" Harris asked.

He expected an answer now that he and Hannah were so close.

"I'll not be gone long," she said, slipping out the door.

You'd think that after they'd been in the sack together she'd stop being like that.

He didn't like much being alone with Tante Frieda. So soon after she'd asked him not to hurt Hannah it was still a little embarrassing. He told her about the two cars in his halting German. She made a clucking sound, just like his grandmother, and went to look out the door as if wanting to see Hannah safely on her way. She didn't say a word about him and Hannah. Harris felt much more comfortable.

He gave her the strawberry preserves. How did you say sandwich in German? He asked for bread instead. She brought half a crusty loaf, cutting towards her flat chest, expertly. He had four slices, spreading the preserves thinly. He'd bought it for her, not himself. Now that the ground echelon had arrived he'd be able to bring them a lot of stuff. Even sugar and coffee.

Hannah returned while he was on the third slice. He offered her a bite. She took it.

"Sergeant Weisz said to thank you," she said, chewing.

"You're still not going to tell me what it's all a . . ."

The sound of a car starting up and speeding away cut him short.

"It is better for you that you do not know."

"Was it that Judah?"

"It is better that you forget Judah. May we change the subject now, please?"

"I think you'd start trusting me. Now."

Hannah looked at Tante Frieda and shot him a warning glance. As if he'd let something slip.

"It is not a question of trusting you or not trusting you, Michael. I do not tell even Tante Frieda everything."

"I should hope not."

It drew an involuntary smile from Hannah.

"You know very well what I meant," she said.

Tante Frieda made Russian tea with the preserves, had a glass with them and went off to bed.

Hannah wouldn't go for a walk.

"It is better to remain here," she said.

"But Tante Frieda . . ."

"You are impossible, Michael. Thinking always of . . . We must remain indoors because the Englishmen may come to Aleenah, searching."

"Who were they anyhow?"

"Always questions."

She turned out the lights, opened the shutters a crack and stood peering out into the night. He sat on the couch, expecting her to come to him, but she remained at the window. He went to her and nuzzled her neck.

"Not now," she said impatiently.

But when he kissed the back of her neck, tasting perspiration, she bent her head to give him a better target. Satisfied nothing was going on outside, she let him lead her to the couch. She did not respond fully when he fondled her.

"What's the matter?" he said.

"Nothing, *Liebchen*," kissing him, pulling away abruptly.

He heard nothing at first, then the sound of a car creeping along the dirt road. In a night silent except for the water pumps, sinister. Hannah ran to the window and looked out. A band of moonlight glimmered. She remained at the window for some minutes, standing very still, one eye and part of her face ghostly in the moonlight.

When she returned to him she said, "It was they. They've gone now. If you had not warned us . . ."

"Now can we take that walk?"

"It is much too late now. Tomorrow night."

"I might be flying."

He was beginning to dislike the goddam English as much as Hannah did. If it weren't for those characters in the car he'd be out in the pine grove with her right this minute. But Hannah's goddam friends were as much to blame. If the British hadn't been chasing them they'd have never showed up in Aleenah and messed up his evening.

"Don't be angry, *Liebchen*."

"I'm not. Not about that."

It was about that, though. He wasn't mad at the English, not really. He was mad at Hannah. He'd spent almost three hours on the road for nothing. He'd be going to his tent all hot and bothered after a session on the couch that didn't lead to anything.

"What is it, then?" she said.

She knew he was sore. He wasn't going to admit the real reason, though.

"The way you act like I'm an outsider."

He was an outsider, really, but he didn't like being treated like one.

"I have explained to you it is better for you that

way."

"I don't see it that way."

"If it is that important to you . . . We have been stealing arms from the English."

"What!"

"We must get them somewhere."

"What for? The Arabs aren't acting up, are they? With all the troops around."

"It is for the war. If we do not need them before that to fight the Nazis."

"They're 400 miles away, for cripes sake!"

"If they break through at El Alamein there is nothing to stop them. We know the British do not intend a defence of Palestine. They will withdraw to the north."

"What could you do against the Afrika Korps?"

"Our best," she said simply. "We will fight to the last. Make a second Masada on the Carmel."

"A second Masada?"

"Surely you know Masada. But I forget. You are an American Jew. Not really a Jew at all."

"Sure I know about Masada."

Vague memories from Sunday school history. A bunch of Jews had held out against the Romans and then killed themselves. Men, women and children. But it couldn't happen now. Not on Mount Carmel or anywhere. It was just yesterday they'd been sitting in the hotel garden on Mount Carmel eating parfaits and looking down at Haifa.

"They won't break through," he said. "We're knocking the whey out of 'em."

"Would you be so confident if you could not merely get in your Liberator and fly away?"

"I never thought about it that way."

"Then do, if you do not wish to be treated as an

outsider."

"You'd have plenty of time to leave even if they did break through. They'd have to regroup and cross the Sinai. I've seen the Sinai."

"To go where?"

"I don't know. Wherever the British go."

"Iraq? You think Jews are welcome in Iraq? Or anywhere?"

"You could be evacuated to the United States."

She laughed. Bitterly.

"If your country would not admit a few hundreds from the *St. Louis* do you think they would admit thousands from Palestine?"

"The *St. Louis?*"

He felt stupid. He didn't know a goddam thing.

"The passengers were refused entry to Cuba," she said with exaggerated patience. "And your great President Roosevelt would not permit them to land in your country either."

He remembered now. Not the details like the name of the ship or why. It hadn't seemed all that big a deal at the time. Just some kind of political thing.

"So we will fight," she said. "And that is something. To be able to fight back. Do you know some of the old people have obtained poison? To use if the Nazis come?"

"No!"

"The Goldblums have poison."

That nice old man and lady!

"Do I shock you, Michael?"

"Yes."

He groped for an answer. Something to reassure her.

"The British would protect you."

"The British!"

Scornful.

"They have never protected us. The 1939 White Paper gave the Grand Mufti everything he wanted."

White Paper? Grand Mufti? What was she talking about? But he wasn't going to ask. He'd already made a jackass of himself.

"But they're fighting the Germans now. They hate 'em as much as you do. You're on the same side now."

He'd seen articles in the *Palestine Post* about the British forming a Jewish regiment to help fight the Germans. And almost every day articles about the Jewish Agency and something called the General Council of Palestine Jews encouraging Jews to enlist. It sure as hell sounded to him like the Jews thought they were on the same side.

"There are those who agree with you, of course. I do not happen to be among them. In June, the Haganah gave up stealing weapons from the English. Uniting against the common enemy, so they said. But some of us do not agree with our superiors in all things."

"You and Gyorgy Weisz and that Judah?"

" 'We will fight the Germans as if the British Mandate does not oppress us and we will fight the British as if Hitler does not exist.' "

He could tell from the way she said it she was quoting from somewhere.

"I figured you all belonged to the Haganah. You and Gyorgy and Judah."

At least he knew what the Haganah was.

"I have said too much. You will forget what I have told you."

"You know I can't do that. But I won't say any-

204

thing to anybody. Not even Gallegly."

"Did you tell him we made love?"

Why did he have to mention Gallegly? And who'd have thought with all her talk about a second Masada, she'd still be worried about anybody finding out they'd been in the sack?

"No," he said. "Hannah?"

"Yes?"

"You're really something. You know that?"

"Something to make love with?"

"That's a lousy thing to say."

"I suppose it was. I am sorry."

She sounded like she meant it.

"It was only because I know you want me only for that. Don't be angry with me, Michael. I will learn to accept it."

"You won't have to. Because you're wrong."

"Am I, *Liebchen?*"

Sure she was. He liked her for a lot of other things, too. He liked being with her, and not just in the sack. It had been fun in Haifa, except when she popped off at the soldiers, and he'd even got a boot out of that after it was all over. And she had guts and brains and humour. And class. No ordinary shack job. He was one lucky son of a bitch.

CHAPTER XII

Breakfast was American, prepared by American cooks. Corn flakes with evaporated milk, scrambled eggs, hot, thick slices of canned New Zealand bacon fried crisp, hot, strong coffee. Even stewed prunes tasted good for a change.

"Take me to the chef," Wagstaff said. "I want to marry him and eat like this the rest of my life."

They were getting a shower building, too, with hot water.

"Otherwise the groundgrippers said they were moving to Cairo," Wagstaff said.

Groundgrippers were non-flying officers, most of whom had come over on the *Pasteur.*

Harris went back to the tent for his canteen and Gallegly's. He got the cook to dry them out in the oven and persuaded a KP pusher to fill one with ground coffee and the other with sugar for the promise of a carton of American cigarettes. They would be getting their footlockers later in the day and he could afford to be prodigal with his four cartons. Major Beck had told Wagstaff they'd be able to buy American cigarettes now that the group was full strength.

The footlockers were distributed early in the afternoon. Harris's box of almond Hersheys was a gooey mess. The chocolate had melted and hardened many times on its long journey and was runny now after sitting out in the Palestine sun in his footlocker. The brass fittings were almost hot enough to raise blisters. Harris spent the time until afternoon chow picking out the candy wrappers and salvaging what he could of chocolate, now and then scooping out a gob with his messkit spoon. Gallegly, who was not normally a sweets eater, took a couple of spoonfuls too.

After chow Harris hurried back to the tent and folded a GI blanket tight enough to fit into his musette bag. He wanted to do it when Gallegly wasn't around. That way he was sort of keeping his promise to Hannah. If Gallegly saw him taking a blanket to Aleenah he'd know what it was for. Gallegly came in while he was eyeing the pile of loot spread out on his cot, the two canteens, his messkit containing the salvaged chocolate, two cartons of cigarettes and a pair of silk stockings, and wondering how he was going to carry it all to Aleenah.

"Hey, Gallegly. Can I borrow your musette bag?"

"Who do you think you are, Santa Claus?"

"Just some stuff for our friends in Aleenah."

"*Our* friends?"

"You know. Gyorgy and the Goldblums. Tante . . . Mrs. Woodbird. And Hannah."

"I never met Mrs. Woodbird."

"One 'a these days . . ."

Gallegly grinned. "From what you said, she's kind of old for me, ain't she?"

Harris waited until dark. He didn't want anyone in Aleenah seeing him cache a blanket in the pine grove.

Two men carrying a load of concrete blocks were on the circular road by the grove. Harris said, "Shalom," and waited until they had gone on. He hid the blanket in the grove and divided the other articles between the two musette bags.

Gyorgy wasn't home. He was somewhere on police business and wouldn't be back that night, Goldblum said. Harris was relieved. He'd be pretty nervous with Hannah in the grove with Gyorgy right across the road. For all he knew, Gyorgy patrolled around Aleenah at night. He'd have to ask Hannah about that. He wondered if it was really police business Gyorgy was away on or if he'd only told the Goldblums that. Except for the pistol sessions, Harris didn't think the Goldblums knew what was going on.

It was hard to talk to them the way he usually did now that he knew they were scared Rommel was going to win and they'd kill themselves if he did, even when Frau Goldblum told him his German was getting better. He wanted to tell her everything was going to be all right but they'd think it was odd. And anyway, he didn't know for sure, did he?

He gave them a carton of cigarettes to split with Gyorgy and half the coffee and sugar. He just felt so goddam sorry for them. Even if Rommel wasn't going to win. He understood for the first time that the Goldblums really didn't belong here any more than he did. They just hadn't had any other place to go.

Tante Frieda gave him a big hug. He didn't think it was just the chocolate and coffee and sugar, or even because she thought he had a crush on her Hannahle. It was because she liked him. He hugged her back. He liked her, too. She reminded him of

208

his grandmother. She was probably closer to his mother's age than his grandmother's but she didn't remind him of his mother.

He could see Hannah was touched by his display of affection. That ought to show her he had other things on his mind than getting in her pants. It hadn't been meant to. Even if Hannah wasn't around he'd come to see Tante Frieda now that he knew her. Tough old Woodbird.

Tante Frieda shaped the chocolate into little patties and served them on the blue plate with the coffee. There was only regular milk for the coffee. Next time he'd bring a can of evaporated milk. Not that it made any difference to Tante Frieda. Every time she took a sip she would say how long it had been since she'd tasted *echte Kaffee*. Real coffee.

Time for old ladies to be in bed. He was anxious to be alone with Hannah but somehow he hadn't been as impatient as in previous visits for Tante Frieda to go to her room. Maybe it was because he didn't have to wonder any more how far he'd be able to get with Hannah.

She came to his lap immediately.

"Let's go outside," he said.

"But it is nice here."

"It's nicer outside. Wait'll you see that moon."

Wondering, if they stayed inside would she let him make love to her on the couch with the chance of Tante Frieda catching them. And not wanting to take that chance.

The road was empty. It was barely nine o'clock but there was not a lot of going and coming in Aleenah at night. Everybody worked too hard all day.

The moon was so bright he wondered if it was

209

such a good idea after all to go to the grove. Maybe they should go out in the fields behind the house. Whichever, he'd want the blanket.

"Let's go over here," he said, guiding her towards the trees with his arm around her waist.

Her arm was around his waist, too. She'd put it there when they found the road deserted.

It was darker among the trees than out on the road. Even if somebody should walk by they wouldn't be able to see them. It took him several minutes to find the blanket. Hannah watched silently while he spread it in a little hollow. Nobody'd be able to spot them from the road for sure when they were lying down. Even if they were looking for them, which nobody would be. He sat down and motioned for her to sit beside him, patting the blanket. She didn't move.

"Come on in," he said. "The water's fine."

"Everything is still so planned with you, isn't it, Michael?" she said unhappily.

"We couldn't do anything in the house. With Tante Frieda there and everything."

"We did before. Every night."

"You know what I mean."

"Yes. I know what you mean."

He pulled her down beside him. She drew her legs up and wrapped her arms around them, resting her chin on her knees, staring out into the trees. Just like the first time he brought her out here.

"Come on, sweetheart, relax."

He rubbed her tense back until she did. He stretched out beside her on the blanket. Her lips were unresponsive, her eyes staring up blankly at a patch of moonwashed sky among the treetops.

"Are you mad at me for bringing the blanket?"

210

"Disappointed."

"Why? You knew we came out here to make love."

"Did I?"

"Didn't you?"

"Could we not wait until Saturday? This is so . . ." Not finishing.

"You might have to work. I could be flying. Anyway, Saturday's a long way off."

"Isn't just kissing and . . . touching enough until then?"

"Not any more. You wouldn't want to stop either. After last Saturday."

Even after she began responding to his caresses she didn't want him to take her clothes off.

"Someone will see us."

"Nobody can see us here. Look for yourself. You can't even see the road from here."

In the beginning it wasn't a whole lot better than it had been the first time in Haifa. Until he made her forget they were not safely locked behind a door in a hotel room.

He lay beside her, wanting a cigarette but unwilling to strike a match. It would be like a beacon.

"Michael?"

"Yes?"

"I feel so strange. I have never before been naked out of doors."

"Swell, isn't it?"

"Delicious. Have you?"

"Have I what?"

"Been naked out of doors. But I know you have. Many times. With other girls."

"Not really."

She rested her head on his chest. Her hair tickled.

"You are lying, I think. You are too practised. I

211

am sure you have been naked out of doors with other girls."

"I used to swim naked in the bayou."

Remembering.

"Bayou?"

"It's kind of a river. We call 'em bayous back home."

"And there were also girls swimming naked in the bayou with you?"

"I was just a little kid."

They used to feel each other's hair to make sure it was dry before they split up to go home. Mothers worried about their kids swimming in the bayou. Snags and deep places and water moccasins. He hadn't been afraid of water moccasins when he was little. Not when he was in the water. Everybody knew they didn't bite under water. It was only after he grew up and quit swimming in the bayou he realized it wasn't true.

"You are so quiet, *Liebchen*. Do you care for me just a little?"

"A lot. A whole lot."

"You do not ask if I care for you?"

"You wouldn't be here if you didn't, would you?"

"I am pleased you are aware of it."

Teasing him.

She stroked his stomach awkwardly. Her hand strayed. Harris gave a little start, taken by surprise. And he was sensitive again.

"I hurt you," she whispered contritely, snatching her hand back.

He wanted to laugh. She really and truly didn't know anything.

"No," he said. "You surprised me, that's all."

"I surprised myself. I have never touched a man

212

there. Not even you. Before now."

"I'm glad."

"I wish . . . "

"What do you wish?"

"It is of no importance."

"Come on, what do you wish?"

"That with you it was also the first time."

"If we were both all that innocent we'd never have gotten together."

"Perhaps it would be better if we had not."

"You're not sorry, are you?"

"Yes and no."

"What kind of an answer is that?"

He knew, though. He felt tender and protective. I won't hurt your little Hannah, Tante Frieda. Not on purpose anyway.

They made love again and lay contented and quiescent. The water pumps made their insistent sound. The air was cool, with a tang of pine mixed with the wool smell of the blanket. He wondered what time it was. It must be getting late.

"Michael?"

She propped herself on an elbow and looked down at him. Now she's going to ask me if I love her. What'll I tell her? Not wanting to lie but not wanting to hurt her by not saying what she wanted to hear.

"Are you ever afraid?"

"What of?"

He was relieved.

"Do you ever think of death? Of being killed?"

"Sometimes, I guess. But not for long at a time."

Only when the fighters were boring in or the flak was thick up ahead. Even then he wasn't afraid of being *killed*, exactly. Just scared and excited in general. Except the time he almost fell out of the bomb bay. He couldn't picture being killed. That happened to unlucky people. He could picture *Blonde Job* being hit, but not getting killed. They shot at *Blonde Job*, not at him.

"Why?" he asked.

She sat up, hugging her knees, her smooth back arched in the moonlight.

"I have thought about it quite often."

He sat up and put his arm around her.

"We're gonna stop Rommel," he said fiercely.

"It could be the English," she said matter-of-factly. "Or after the war, the Arabs. But it does not frighten me. To die for Eretz Israel . . . It is only that now I am selfish."

"Selfish?"

"I don't want it to be so soon."

Wryly.

"What did you mean, 'now'?" he said.

"I am afraid I am in love with you."

The only thing that really surprised him was that she would come right out and say it. Women usually thought they were in love with you afterwards. Except the tramps, and sometimes even them. It stood to reason Hannah would think so, him being the first one. He wished she hadn't said it, though. It put him on the spot. He was supposed to tell her he loved her too. Still, he wasn't exactly sorry to hear it. It was really something to have a girl like Hannah Ruh in love with you. Or thinking she was, anyway.

"You have nothing to say to that?" she said, looking into his face. She touched his cheek. "Poor Michael. It is inconvenient for you, isn't it? For me, also."

The next night, instead of looking down at Hannah stretched naked on a blanket he was looking down at Greece from 16,000 feet, washed by the same full moon. They were trying to block the Corinth Canal. It did not strike Harris as at all bizarre that he should be making love to a girl in Palestine one night and be over Greece in a bomber the next. And if he had to choose which of the events was most out of the ordinary it would be, without question, lying with Hannah in the pine grove. Navigating a bomber was what he did. He had been trained for it, conditioned to it, sent overseas for precisely that purpose. Just one of several hundred men whose regular work it was to see that bombs got dropped on targets. But having Hannah, that was unbelievable luck. He was the only man in the 108th with a regular girl practically next door to the field as far as he knew. And what a girl.

He wasn't all that unhappy about not getting back to see her tonight. Not that he didn't want to be with her. He'd rather be with Hannah than any girl he'd ever known. It was just that he wasn't sure yet how he wanted to handle the situation. Whether to kid about it, tell her how much he liked her without actually saying he was in love with her or just not mention it at all. He'd never had that kind of problem with girls in the past, he'd said and done the first thing that occurred to him, but this wasn't the same. Do not hurt my little Hannah.

The Corinth Canal cut across the thin neck of the Peloponnesus, connecting the Gulfs of Saronic and Corinth, a narrow channel cut deep into solid rock less than fifty miles from Athens. Harris welcomed the opportunity to see another part of a foreign country — Pylos had been down in the south-west corner of the peninsula and Corinth was way up in the north-east corner — but he wished they were after a target with a closer connection to the front line fighting.

What he really wished they were doing was bombing the Afrika Korps standing before El Alamein. After what Hannah had told him he wanted to take a personal hand in stopping the sons of bitches. The heavies had a necessary job to do, cutting off Rommel's fuel and material, and it was the job of the mediums and fighters to work closer to the front, but all the same he'd like a crack at some close support missions.

The object of the Corinth Canal raid was to try to catch shipping in the canal and block it. Because of the moonlight they wouldn't have any trouble spotting anything as big as a ship even from 16,000 feet. If they didn't catch any ships in the canal they were supposed to bomb the canal itself and cave in the high, steep sides of the cut. Major Beck had got up at briefing and said that was stupid. The Corinth Canal was through solid rock and even the thousand pounders they were carrying wouldn't do more than chip it. He wasn't going on the raid but he always sat in on briefings.

He said if they didn't find any ships in the canal, Tobruk should be their alternate target. They had enough fuel to hit Tobruk if they landed at Fayid instead of Ramat Jonas. Harris thought it was a good idea. Tobruk was the next best thing to El Alamein. It was Rommel's headquarters and main supply base. There'd be Afrika Korps there, too, and material Rommel was stockpiling for the big attack everybody knew was coming. Harris could see from Wagstaff's expression that Wags didn't agree.

The group commander got up and said the Corinth Canal was the primary target with or without shipping in it. They had been given the target by 205 Group and that was that. If it turned out they found an undercast at the canal and couldn't see to bomb, which the metro officer said wasn't likely, they were to return by way of Crete and bomb targets of opportunity in harbours and on airfields. And return to Ramat Jonas. Fayid was not prepared to receive any 108th ships except for emergencies. Fayid had its own missions to run.

Seven planes took off late in the afternoon for the five hour flight over the Mediterranean which would find them over the target after moonrise. The intelligence officer told them they could expect little flak even at the comparatively low bombing altitude of 16,000 feet.

It would be the first time they had bombed by moonlight.

The crew bus had been driven by a stolid GI, not a cowboying Palestine Jew. The sentries were GI now, too, not Buffs, and the English ground crews had been replaced by Americans who had come over on the *Pasteur*. Harris missed the international flavour. The way things were now, it was almost like being on a field back in the US. Without advantages like permanent quarters and a big PX.

Going out to the ship, Harris wondered if Hannah would start thinking he'd had enough of her when he didn't show up that night. Maybe that she'd scared him off with that love stuff.

He was over that now. She'd hear the planes taking off and realize he must be on the mission. If

217

she still had any lingering doubts, he'd remove them tomorrow night.

They were between Crete and Rhodes at dusk, at bombing altitude and still in formation, flying directly over Karpathos. It was easy to identify the little island from his surface map. It was shaped like a turkey gobbler with its neck stretched out. When he took the co-ordinates to mark *Blonde Job*'s position on his Mercator he showed Silkwood where they were. They were eight miles off his DR course. He calculated the new wind and heading and plotted the new course to Corinth. They would soon be splitting up to approach the target individually.

The last daylight drained away. *Blonde Job* droned over scattered, ridged islands dark and clearly visible against a sea silvered by moonlight. No wine dark sea here. The islands were shaped like birds and animals. The last time Harris had seen so many islands was on sub patrol in the Caribbean out of Lakeland. They'd never located a sub to attack with their depth charges but they had seen burning ships.

The lights were on in Corinth. Nobody below knew they were up there. Gallegly called the nose in disbelief. It was the first time they had seen lights on the surface since they left the States except for tiny fires in the jungle on the Accra-Khartoum leg through holes in the undercast.

Even from three miles up the canal was as plain as a heavy Number 2 pencil line on a Mercator. The canal was shadowed by the towering stone through which it was carved. The lights of Corinth stayed on even after the ground batteries opened up. Nothing burst at their altitude. Multi-coloured tracers of light stuff fell away far below them. Flak that couldn't reach your altitude was a beautiful sight. As

218

beautiful as the Burg El Arab beacon after a long night of shifting winds.

Puffs of orange blossomed along the canal. The first planes were already bombing. Silkwood hunched over his bombsight searching for ships through it. *Blonde Job* flew the length of the canal without him finding one. Wagstaff made a one eighty over the Gulf of Corinth and came back on a bombing run. Using a penlight clenched between his teeth—he didn't want to turn on his hooded desk lamp on a bombing run—Harris plotted Athens on his Mercator, drew in a course from Corinth and calculated a heading.

"Bombardier to pilot, bombs away."

"Pilot to galvinator. Let's go home."

Harris gave Wagstaff the heading for Athens. He'd never seen Athens and might not get another chance.

"Pilot to galvinator. Roger. What the hell! That won't take us home!"

"It's the heading for Athens. With this much moon we oughtta be able to see the Acropolis."

"Screw the Acropolis! What about the flak?"

"There won't be any if we steer clear of Piraeus."

He couldn't be positive but it stood to reason the Germans wouldn't be wasting any ground batteries to protect Athens. Not with a fat target like the harbour at Piraeus so near.

"It's less than fifteen minutes," Harris said. "How about it, Wags?"

The crew began calling in.

"Hey, Lieutenant, we want to see Athens."

"Come on, Big Wags, be a sport."

"Pilot to crew. If anybody tells Major Beck I'll break his thumbs."

219

A searchlight came on when they flew over Salamis, probed nervously and went out almost immediately, as if fearful of drawing attention to itself. Harris took *Blonde Job* north of Athens to avoid Piraeus. He flew out his ETA and gave Wagstaff a new heading to put them east of the city on course for Ramat Jonas.

"Navigator to crew. This is your friendly guide. Athens coming up on our right in two minutes."

There she lay, leached by moonlight, riding the swell of hills. A white city, sprawling. Athens, Greece. Hot damn! He pulled aside his oxygen mask and yelled in Silkwood's ear.

"You got good eyes. Can you see the Acropolis?"

Silkwood pointed. Harris aimed along his finger. There it was, a bump on the landscape. Stark in the moonlight, the outlines of buildings as sharp as those on the toy model some teacher's pet had built for Broadening and Finding at Albert Sidney Johnston Junior High. Looking as if it had been bombed, almost like something out of Tobruk but not that cluttered. He wasn't disappointed, though. He'd seen the Parthenon.

Off to the right, at two o'clock, searchlight beams wove a nervous pattern, probing the bleak sky. The sky always looked bleak when there was a lot of moon. Harris looked from the shifting anxious beams to his map. Piraeus. It was a good thing he hadn't taken them over the harbour. Wagstaff would have had a piece of his butt.

"Pilot to navigator, go ahead."

"Navigator to pilot, go ahead."

"OK, we've seen Athens. What's our heading?"

"We're on it. Wags?"

"Yeah?"

"If Beck finds out, just say we got a little lost, OK?"

"He'll believe it, too. Considering who our navigator is."

Gallegly's voice, kidding. Happy, Harris knew, because Wags had made two runs over the target and let himself be talked into flying over Athens. Proving that Pylos and Athens had been flukes.

Blonde Job was the last plane in because of the side trip. Not by much, though, because a couple of navigators had missed a wind shift and let their planes get way off course between fixes. And definitely not late enough to start anyone wondering.

At post mission a bombardier claimed to have hit a ship in the canal. Silkwood choked on a swallow of coffee and called him a liar. He couldn't stand to see anybody else get credit for a shack when he hadn't hit anything. And even worse, for somebody to get credit for something that hadn't happened. There would have been a fistfight if Wags hadn't made them both shut up.

"In the first place there weren't any ships in the canal," he said. "And in the second place it's none of your business, Junior. Let's just wait for the snapshots."

An RAF Spitfire would be flying a high altitude reconnaissance mission over the Corinth Canal to take pictures.

"They won't show a goddam thing," Major Beck said. "You didn't even kill any goddam anchovies."

On shipping strikes, when a bombardier missed badly, someone almost always consoled him by saying at least he'd killed a lot of anchovies.

"We tried hard, though, Maje," said Wagstaff. "Put us in for a medal. For trying so hard."

"Only medal you'll ever get is for bullshit, you overgrown son of a bitch."

"Yes, sir! You heard the major, chaps. I'm gonna get a medal."

There wasn't anybody as much fun after a mission as Big Wags.

CHAPTER XIII

Instead of going to bed, Harris stayed up to see the total eclipse of the moon. The *Palestine Post* had said it would start just after 4 a.m. When nothing happened, he thought he'd been mistaken about the date until he realized it had been the paper's error. The *Post* had failed to take "summer time" into account and 4 a.m. was really three. At just under two minutes past five, local time, a dark shadow began eating away at the moon's perimeter. The sun rose ten minutes later. Exhausted, Harris crawled under his mosquito net as soon as the moon was totally obscured.

He saw Hannah for three nights running. He kept the blanket in its musette bag under his cot. If Gallegly knew what was in the bag he took to Aleenah every night Gallegly didn't let on.

During those three days, news broadcasts and the *Palestine Post* hinted that the desert war was heating up. It was revealed that Churchill had visited Cairo and the front lines the previous Saturday and the news was full of phrases like "the desert lull may soon be broken," "the Eighth Army is ready for battle." The *Post* reported a desert race of supplies, which made Harris fidget because *Blonde Job* was doing nothing about it, and increased patrol activity. Meanwhile, the Nazis were closing in on Stalingrad and the battle in the Solomons was reaching a decisive phase. Neither seemed as important to Harris as what was happening at El Alamein even if it was American troops doing the fighting in the Solomons. He knew it was because of what Hannah had told him about a second Masada and old folks having poison ready.

Tante Frieda asked him what he had seen of the build-up in the desert and he had to admit he had seen nothing. He didn't consider it a breach of regulations to tell her he never flew over the battle lines.

After Tante Frieda left them for the night they would head for their little hollow in the pine grove without Harris having to suggest it. The first night she was still a little shy but the next night she took off her own clothes. She grew less inhibited and more adept, no longer so passive when they made love and, when they were not, easier with him resting naked at her side, taking frank pleasure in having a man's body to fondle and explore as she fancied. As if now that she'd found out what she'd been missing she wanted to make up for lost time.

She did not again mention being in love with him. He thought it might be because she'd come to understand just because she liked making love with him it didn't mean she had to be in love with him. Any more than he had to be in love with her. He hadn't expected to be disappointed by it but he was. When the 234th left Ramat Jonas, which it would sooner or later, she'd find out other guys could take care of that department. Local guys. Like the ones who took their tomatoes at Tnuva. Or that Judah.

Guys she had a lot more in common with than Tex Harris, who liked the British and was just passing through. Maybe even before the 234th left Ramat Jonas.

The thought chilled him.

He couldn't stand the thought of somebody shooting him out of the saddle. That thought was to plague him when he was back on his cot under the mosquito net.

The third night after Corinth he could stand it no longer. They had grown bolder in their hollow, lying on their stomachs propped on their elbows smoking and concealing the glowing butts in cupped hands, talking low instead of whispering.

"Hannahle?"

"Yes?"

"Do you still love me?"

"Of course. Why do you ask?"

"I was just wondering."

He field stripped his cigarette to cover an awkward pause. Hannah thought it was a terrible waste to scatter the unsmoked shreds of tobacco like that. Everyone in Aleenah saved butts.

"You haven't said so lately."

"One does not send a message knowing there will be no answer."

"Huh? Oh. I really do like you. More than any girl I've ever known."

"Known in the biblical sense, my Michael?"

She was kidding him.

"Do you make love with every girl who attracts you?"

"I try."

Feeling a need to be as honest with her as he could. Hannah knew when you were lying.

"And do you always succeed so easily as with me?"

She seemed curious rather than bitter. Next she'd be asking if she was as good as the others.

"You weren't easy."

"Oh? I rather thought I was."

"Well, you weren't. You know something? At first I thought you didn't even like me."

"I didn't. You were too sure of yourself. Too . . . American. Your intentions so obvious."

"That was before I got to know you."

"In the biblical sense?"

Kidding him again.

"Be serious."

Knowing she was in control, not him, and not liking it particularly.

"Before I knew who you *were*. Before I met Tante Frieda."

"I don't think she would be so fond of you if she knew what you did with me after she goes to her bed."

He didn't say anything. Hannah might not be here if she realized Tante Frieda damn well knew what he was doing with her. Or maybe Tante Frieda didn't. She might think they were just smooching on the couch. Maybe he'd been wrong about what she meant when she told him not to hurt her little Hannah. She could have just meant not to take advantage of her innocence.

"When we come back from Haifa tomorrow try not to be so gabby, sweetheart. It could make her think you're trying to cover something up."

"Tante Frieda has no idea what a wicked person I have become." Carefully, "I'm afraid I will be unable to go with you to Haifa."

"More tomatoes?"

He didn't mind too much. It would be swell to have a real bed and eat at Pross's and maybe go up to Mount Carmel again but as long as they could come here every night it didn't really matter all that much.

"No. I must go . . . elsewhere. I must say, you do not seem terribly disappointed, *Liebchen*."

"Yes, I am. I was really looking forward to it. Can I go with you?"

"I hardly think my friend from the Palmach would be pleased."

The Palmach. That was a new one.

"I thought you were in the Haganah."

"And so I am."

"What's the Palmach, then?"

"It is part of the Haganah. The combat units which will fight Rommel should he succeed in destroying the British at El Alamein."

He couldn't believe she said it so casually. She was like that Russian girl sniper he'd read about in the *Palestine Post* just that afternoon. Liudmilla something. She was in Washington being honoured for having killed or wounded 300 German soldiers on the Russian front. Only twenty-six years old, not a hell of a lot older than Hannah.

"You're in that?"

"No," she said regretfully. "But I often work with some who are and think as I do. And one day . . ."

"I thought you were just helping hide arms stolen from the British."

"And why do you think we have been stealing those arms?"

She really thought she would have to fight the Afrika Korps. And so matter of fact about it. Just like he was about going on bombing raids. But there

227

was no comparison. She knew if she had to fight she was sure to be killed while he knew when he went on a raid he'd be coming back to hot chow and comfortable sack so far from any real fighting there might as well not be a war going on. Long-range bombing was like a one night stand. Wham, bam, thank you, ma'am.

He was a little in awe of her for that. Lying there naked as a jaybird and taking it all so calmly.

"I don't want you to die!" he blurted, unexpectedly close to tears.

He was embarrassed. Not just for being such a goddam emotional boob but also for letting her talk him into believing it could happen. The Germans weren't going to break through. They were taking too big a pasting from the RAF and the Air Corps.

"You surprise me, *Liebchen*," she said, touched.

"You're not gonna die," he said, harshly. "It's just a lotta talk."

"Of course," she said. "It is only talk. *Vehen hayu beosher veosher ad hagom haze*. We will all live happily ever after."

He had a flash of insight, rare for him with women.

"If all this wasn't going on would you have let me . . ."

She wouldn't answer. He held her in his arms, not wanting to make love again even with the feel of her nakedness against him, just wanting to hold her. Even if nothing bad was going to happen to her she thought it was, which made it just as rough for her as if it were true. But he wasn't going to think about it any more.

It turned out that it didn't matter that she couldn't go to Haifa with him. He couldn't go himself. When he got back to the tent Gallegly woke up and told him they were on alert for a mission.

They went after another convoy. Harris could not work up much enthusiasm over a shipping strike. It was nothing but a long grind over a lot of water. Almost eleven hours this time. When a girl like Hannah was willing to take on the Afrika Korps practically with her bare hands it was almost cowardly to sit up here out of flak range dropping bombs on targets that didn't want to do anything but get away. Especially when there weren't even any fighters to make trouble on this one. Not that he wanted to mess around with any fighters. He wasn't as dumb as Silkwood. What he wished he could do was paste Germans and come back and tell Hannah about it.

The news said aircraft and patrols were active in the desert. If things were getting ready to pop maybe the heavies would see some real action. Funny, before he got to know Hannah he'd thought bombing supply lines in rear areas was real action. All the action he wanted, for sure.

They got back too late for him to go to Tante Frieda's but he and Hannah made up for lost time the next night. He hadn't dreamed she'd turn out to be so eager. She didn't say where she'd been or what she'd done Saturday and he didn't ask. She did tell him she loved him. More than once, now that she knew it didn't bother him to hear it. He damn near told her he loved her, too, but he didn't want to lie. She was really starting to get to him though. It bothered him a little.

Monday he wandered around restlessly, unable to get interested in any of the books that had arrived in his footlocker or in writing letters, wondering what

Hannah was doing. He hadn't been like this about a girl since his junior year at Rice, when he was younger and dumber. He caught the bus to the officers' club—they had regular service around the field now that the ground echelon was there—and sat in on a fifty mil limit poker game. He liked poker and it was as good a way as any of whiling away the hours until it was time to go to Hannah.

They were all at the club, Wagstaff shooting craps, Silkwood writing his interminable letters home and Gallegly playing deadly earnest chess with a hawk-faced navigator named Rosenfeld. Rosenfeld had been "Rosey" until they got to Palestine. Now he was "The Arab" or "Camel Jockey." He didn't mind. "Arabs are Semites, too," he said. Wagstaff had bought a burnous in Haifa and offered him five pounds to wear it past a Buff perimeter guard some night. Rosenfeld said he would if Wagstaff would try to slip past a British sentry at the RAF field at Fayid wearing an Afrika Korps uniform. He wore the burnous occasionally in the club, though, and went around begging other officers to sell him a pocket compass so he'd pray to Mecca in the right direction.

"I get mixed up and forget which way is east," he would say. "Sometimes I'm up to fifteen degrees off. Prayers don't count when it's over five."

That was a popular 108th Arab joke. Another was, "How do you tell a bundle of rags from an Arab? If you kick it and it gets up and runs it's an Arab."

Harris thought it was cozy, all of them being there together, relaxed and comfortable. He knew he wouldn't be that relaxed if he didn't have Hannah waiting for him in Aleenah.

He got on a winning streak and the other players started kidding him, telling him to peel down to his undershorts so he wouldn't have anywhere to hide aces. Silkwood came over to watch. He circled the table to see what everybody had, his face mirroring what he saw.

"Beat it, Junior," somebody growled.

"Deal, cried the losers," said Harris, feeling a need to defend Silkwood because Silkwood was his bombardier.

It was all right for him to razz Silkwood, but not for an outsider.

"Let him stay behind you, then," said another player.

"Can I, Tex?" Silkwood implored.

"Sure."

If this were pot limit he wouldn't want Silkwood back there tipping his hand but they weren't playing for all that much in this game.

Major Beck came over to watch. The players had been joking and bitching. They fell silent, intimidated. Silkwood drifted away. He always got nervous when Beck was near. He was afraid of him. Major Beck was seemingly oblivious to the dampening effect of his presence on everyone.

A pilot with a air of deuces showing tossed a fifty mil piece in the pot and said, "Just to get the shoeclerks out."

They were playing five card stud, "the gentleman's game," with the last up card to come. Harris had queens wired. The other two queens were showing elsewhere on the board. Everyone called but Harris.

"I used to sell shoes at the Vogue on Saturdays," he said, folding his hand.

Major Beck reached over his shoulder and looked

at his hole card, the queen of clubs. If it had been anyone but Beck, Harris would have rapped his knuckles smartly. Anybody wanted to see how he played poker, they had to pay for it by calling his bet.

The pilot with a pair of deuces showing took the pot with three of a kind. He had a third deuce in the hole.

"You've played this game before," Beck said approvingly.

It was the first nice thing he'd ever said to Harris.

Major Beck left the poker game to sweat Wagstaff, who had Palestine one and five pound notes folded lengthwise between every finger on his non-shooting hand.

"Can't you clowns see the big bastard is palming and slick rolling?" Beck said, giving Wagstaff a friendly boot in the tail.

"Jesus," said the pilot who took the pot with three deuces, "I thought for a minute the sumbitch was gonna want to sit in. Can you imagine betting into old Beck?"

Silkwood came back and resumed his post behind Harris. They were playing stud again. Harris had a red ace in the hole and four clubs showing. The player across from him, the only one left in the pot, had four cards to a jack high straight showing.

"You got it, don't you, you lucky bastard?" he said.

"Cost you five piasters to find out," Harris said, shoving a fifty mil piece into the pot.

"Does a flush beat a straight?" Silkwood blurted. The other player folded.

"You're OK, Silkwood," Harris said, wondering if Silkwood had said it to help his bluff or had just

232

forgotten he had a stranger in the hole.

The game broke up for afternoon chow. Harris pocketed his winnings and went back to the tent. He thought he'd eat at the Goldblums' for a change. He hadn't done that since the chow improved at Ramat Jonas and he'd started taking Hannah out to the pine grove. Gyorgy Weisz might start wondering why. And besides, he felt like being with the Goldblums, knowing how shook they were about the war and all.

There wasn't a soul out of doors in Aleenah. He could hear radios playing in almost every house. It was loud but he couldn't tell what it was except that it was talk. The radio was on at the Goldblums', too.

He left the musette bag with the blanket in it against the side of the house. Goldblum answered his knock looking paler than usual and after a distracted welcome hurried back inside. Weisz and Mrs. Goldblum were listening to the radio, too, Mrs. Goldblum with her ear almost against it. Her shoulders were hunched. Gyorgy looked up, too, his face wooden. Mrs. Goldblum didn't even turn around to see who it was.

"What's going on?" Harris asked.

"The attack has begun," Weisz said.

Harris didn't have to ask what attack. But he was surprised. There hadn't been anything about it on the club radio. Maybe the Hebrew language broadcast had later news.

"When?" Harris asked.

"Last night."

"There wasn't anything about it on the news."

"Of course. They say nothing yet."

"What's everybody listening to, then?"

233

"They wait for official statements."

"You mean there hasn't been any bulletin or anything? How do you know, then?"

"I know," Weisz said quietly.

Being a policeman and all, and being in the underground, he must be able to find out things before they were officially announced. Harris knew better than to ask him how he knew.

"Did they break through?" Harris said.

"It's in the balance."

Oh, God, what if Hannah was right? And why wasn't the 108th in there bombing the hell out of them instead of sitting around cracking jokes?

Weisz said German and Italian tanks and infantry had launched the attack at the southern end of the British defences. The last he'd heard, they'd had some early success but the issue was still confused. Harris wanted to rush right over to Tante Frieda's but thought he should stick around for a while for appearance's sake.

The talk changed to classical music without anything having been announced about the attack. Nevertheless, Harris did not doubt that Weisz knew what he was talking about. And that the whole settlement knew it. They left the radio on loud while they ate in case there was a news bulletin. The Goldblums were too shaken to eat. Harris did not have much of an appetite, either, thinking about Hannah. Weisz ate as if there were no reason not to. He was one tough cookie. Harris left as soon as he could. He hesitated on the road, wondering if he should stash the musette bag in the grove. It was dark enough now.

He ought to get his butt kicked. What kind of a son of a bitch was he, anyway, thinking about taking

234

Hannah out there at a time like this?

He left the musette bag in Tante Frieda's yard, out of sight. He could tell from Hannah's face she knew about the attack, too. Tante Frieda looked grim but undaunted. What a woodbird.

"They'll stop 'em," Harris told Hannah. "We've got too much air power for 'em."

Yeah, and not using it, at least not the 234th.

"We shall see," Hannah said quietly.

They kept the radio on but there still wasn't anything about the German attack.

"If it was serious, there'd be bulletins, wouldn't there?" Harris said.

"Sergeant Weisz believes the English will suppress all news until the outcome is no longer in doubt."

Tante Frieda did not seem disposed to leave them alone, as had been her custom. She was talkative. Harris understood most of what she said. She reminisced about her life in Germany many years ago, her early days in Palestine with her husband, Karl. Joking about the early hardships. After a while Harris realized it was for Hannah's benefit.

Hannah was fidgety. She did not seem frightened, just unable to sit still. Tante Frieda said something to her in Hebrew. Hannah shook her head angrily.

"What did she say?" Harris asked.

"If worse comes to worst I must not be foolish. I must go beyond the reach of the Germans."

"It won't happen. But if it does, it's not such a bad idea."

"You also, Michael!"

She was sore at him for siding with Tante Frieda. "I will not run!"

She sat down and clenched her fists. He yearned to put his arm around her, resisting the impulse not because Tante Frieda was there but because he sensed Hannah would resent any attempt to reassure her. He looked at Tante Frieda and shrugged helplessly. She didn't notice. She was watching Hannah, her unguarded expression one of ineffable sadness.

Harris wanted to tell her, I'll save your little Hannah whether she wants to be saved or not. I'll save her if I have to stick her in a GI uniform and drag her on to *Blonde Job* by her hair. Knowing what he was thinking was a lot of baloney.

He made conversation with Tante Frieda. It wasn't easy because Hannah wasn't interpreting for them. Hannah was like a fighter between rounds. Damned if she didn't act like she *wanted* a crack at the Germans.

He kissed her goodnight, not caring if Tante Frieda was watching. She touched his cheek, preoccupied, as if reassuring him. *Her* reassuring *him*, for God's sake!

He walked along kicking the dirt, depressed, frustrated because there was nothing he could do to change anything. He was nothing but a goddam overpaid windfinder. He was passing the Goldblums' before he realized he'd left his musette bag in Tante Frieda's yard. The radio was still on loud at the Goldblums'. He could picture them sitting there, their heads practically in it, wondering if they were going to have to be on the run again. Thinking about the poison Hannah said they had. He went back for the musette bag. He walked towards Ramat Jonas feeling stupid for bringing the blanket. He looked up at the stars. The moon was waning and the patterns were mostly visible. Polaris was in its place, not bright but dependable, the showier stars glittering and none of them giving a good goddam about anything going on here or at El Alamein. They'd still be up there no matter what happened.

It was sort of reassuring. The farther he got from Aleenah the less he thought there was to worry about. Why get all shook about a battle going on 400 miles away, a battle he couldn't even be sure was really going on because there'd been no official news. Even if Rommel did win at El Alamein anything could happen before he could get to Palestine. But he wasn't going to win. The Eighth Army had stopped him once at El Alamein and they'd do it again. The British fought like bastards.

The next day, 1 September, was payday. The finance officer and a sergeant sat at a table covered with stacks of Palestine banknotes and coins in the officers' club. The officers lined up and got their pay in cash, giving name, rank and serial number to be checked off in the finance officer's ledger. Harris drew under twenty pounds, his flying pay and overseas pay. His base pay was allotted. He'd have a nice little nest egg when the war was over.

It was like a big party. Banter in the pay line, paying and collecting loans and gambling debts, groups settling down to blackjack, poker and craps. The fears and tensions of Aleenah seemed distant and unrealistic. Rumours about the action south of El Alamein had begun circulating but there was hardly any mention of it except conjecture about whether they would be flying some new kinds of missions. No one seemed to think Rommel had a chance. If they thought about it at all.

Harris felt sort of dumb for letting himself get so worried last night just because the people in Aleenah took it so seriously. But at the same time peeved at all these guys sitting around carrying on as if nothing very important was going on a few hundred miles to the west. Not knowing, and probably not caring if they did know, what it meant to the Jews of Palestine. He damn well knew. And cared. He wondered if it was because he was a Jew himself or only because he knew Hannah and Tante Frieda and the Goldblums. He didn't think he would feel so close to them, the Goldblums, anyway, if he weren't a Jew, realizing this was the first time he had felt close to anyone just because they were Jewish and he was too. And for the first time in some way closer to the people of Aleenah, all of them, not just the ones he knew, than to the Americans in the 108th except Gallegly, Wags and Silkwood. Not more like them, just closer to them.

There wasn't much about the desert front in the *Palestine Post*, mostly optimistic stuff about other fronts. The Nazis halted on a thousand mile front that included Stalingrad, a turn for the better in the fighting at New Guinea, Malta bagging its 807th plane. Wendell Willkie was coming to Cairo, the Armon Theatre in Haifa was showing Joan Crawford in *A Woman's Face* and Henry Armstrong had kayoed Rodolfo Ramirez in Oakland, California. It was like they were deliberately avoiding what was going on around El Alamein. Maybe Gyorgy Weisz was right about the English suppressing the news. Maybe things were really bad at El Alamein.

Harris ate with the Goldblums again that night. He didn't take the blanket. It didn't seem right. There was a stranger visiting Sgt. Weisz, a short, gaunt civilian wearing a rusty old suit and a tieless white shirt, needing a shave. Weisz introduced him as "Dr. Jacobs" and, in answer to the civilian's unspoken query, said something to him in Hebrew.

238

Explaining to Harris, "I tell Dr. Jacobs you say nothing. OK?"

The Goldblums still showed strain but they ate their dinner. With the radio on loud. Dr. Jacobs stuffed himself. Harris thought he ate a lot for such a little skinny man. Weisz wasn't exactly deferential to him but he treated him with obvious respect. Harris wondered what kind of doctor he was. There were plenty of middle-aged refugees in Haifa who were doctors of something or other, driving taxicabs or clerking in hotels, things like that.

"Is he a medical doctor?" Harris asked Weisz.

"Philosophy," said Dr. Jacobs.

There had been no previous indication he spoke English.

"Oh," said Harris. "Do you live in Aleenah?"

"Visiting, only."

Harris couldn't place his accent.

"Dr. Jacobs has been free since only a few weeks," Weisz said.

"I have been a guest of the English at Acre," Dr. Jacobs said dryly. Seeing Harris did not understand, "In prison."

Harris could not hide his surprise.

"They had the quaint notion I sabotaged a pipeline," said Dr. Jacobs.

Weisz smiled.

"Oh," said Harris. "They found out you didn't?"

"Amnesty," Dr. Jacobs said. "A change of heart. Of late they have graciously consented that Jews may be permitted to join the war effort. As Jews."

So Dr. Jacobs was Haganah, too, or Palmach. He didn't look like a fighter. But neither did Hannah. The way Gyorgy was treating him he must be high up. Harris wondered if he was in Aleenah for any particular reason, and if it had anything to do with the fighting at El Alamein.

"Gyorgy," said Harris. "What's the situation in Egypt?"

"The British seem to be holding their own," Dr. Jacobs said. "You are concerned?"

"Sure. Who wouldn't be?"

Weisz said something to Dr. Jacobs in Hebrew.

"I understand you are sympathetic to our cause," Dr. Jacobs said. "Is that typical of American soldiers?"

Hell, Harris thought, thinking about the payday activities at Ramat Jonas, they don't even know about it. And realizing he hadn't, either, until recently.

"Of American Jews then?" Dr. Jacobs said when he didn't answer.

"Sure."

Ashamed to admit he hadn't thought about it much one way or the other before he came to Palestine.

"Splendid. After this war we will need much help from America. Unless the English have another change of heart, which I doubt. What is your opinion of the English, if I may ask?"

"I like 'em."

He hadn't lied to Hannah about it and he wasn't going to lie to this joker.

"Perhaps I should say what is your opinion of the policies of the British Mandatory?"

He didn't know anything about the British Mandatory and its policies. Except that Hannah had said the 1939 White Paper was something bad for the Jews.

"I don't know too much about 'em."

He could see Dr. Jacobs wasn't too much impressed with his answers, or with him.

"Now that you have seen what we are doing here, do you think you should like to emigrate to Palestine? After the war?"

"Why?"

He didn't like Dr. Jacobs too much. Needling him like that.

"Why, indeed?" Dr. Jacobs said.

After that he paid little attention to Harris. Harris was more chastened than insulted.

There were more people outside after dark than he'd seen on any of his previous visits. They stood around talking in low voices. Aleenah was still tense. He could feel the tension. It was infectious. He lost some of the confidence he'd gained back at Ramat Jonas.

He thought about Dr. Jacobs, if that was his real name, and grew angry. Why the hell should he want to move to Palestine? What business of Dr. Jacobs's was it anyhow.

Hannah and Tante Frieda were more like their usual selves, as if their initial reaction was behind them and they were waiting philosophically to see what happened. When Tante Frieda said it was time for old ladies to be in bed Harris could swear she almost winked.

He wasn't sure just how to behave with Hannah. Even if she had settled down it didn't seem quite right to rush her out to the grove. Anyhow, he hadn't brought the blanket. And he was still thinking about Dr. Jacobs, wondering who he really was, about him asking what he thought about living in Palestine some day. Trying to recruit him, maybe? He wasn't a farmer or even a fighter. He was a navigator. There wouldn't be any use for navigators here after the war. Or back home, either, for that matter. He wasn't sure what he wanted to do after the war but he sure wouldn't be coming back here. Except maybe on a visit, when he came back to see every place he'd been in the service. It was too far off to think about. It looked like a long war.

And thinking of endings, realizing that once he left here he would never see Hannah again. No more nights in the pine grove or days in Haifa. No more sitting and talking, drinking Russian tea with her and Tante Frieda. He'd miss it all, not just the lovemaking. He had not expected the thought of never seeing Hannah again would bother him so much.

"You are very quiet," Hannah said.

She sat in his lap.

"And so backward. You have not asked me to go walking."

"Do you really want to?"

"And why should I not?"

On the way he said, "Who's Dr. Jacobs?" When she did not answer, "I met him tonight. At the Goldblums'."

"He is in Aleenah?"

"Who is he, anyway? He said the British just let him out of prison."

"A very brave man."

"Did he really sabotage a pipeline?"

"Who told you this?"

"He did."

"Truly?"

"Well, not exactly. He said he was accused of it. But the way he said it, I know he must have. He's the one Gyorgy gets his orders from, isn't he? And you get yours from Gyorgy."

"I do not ask you about your squadron, do I, Michael?"

They made love on the ground, uncomfortably, pricked by pine needles. But not caring. Harris was fierce and greedy, driven by his awareness that one day there would be no more nights like this. No more Hannah. Despite his ardour she was more tender and gentle than he had ever known her to be. Was she thinking about that, too?

"Michael?"

Lying quiet in his arms.

"Yes?"

"It was different for me tonight. So sweet."

"Sweet?"

"Because it was not all so planned."

"What do you mean?"

She bit his shoulder, playfully but hard enough to hurt.

"You did not bring your blanket."

Serious again. "It was different for you also, wasn't it?"

"Yes."

"I wonder why."

"Do you love me, Hannahle?"

"Yes."

A whisper.

"And I love you."

It just slipped out. Unexpected. Startling him.

"Did you hear me?"

"I heard."

Almost too low for him to hear. He touched her cheek. It was wet. She was crying. Hannah Ruh, who was ready to fight the Afrika Korps, was crying.

243

"Why, Hannahle?"

He needed no answer. She was thinking about it, too. One of these days he'd climb into his plane and fly away.

Never to return.

CHAPTER XIV

At last, two days after Weisz said the battle of El Alamein had begun, his words were confirmed by radio and press. The attack was called "a supreme Axis drive against Alexandria, the Nile and Suez." Rommel was reported to have between 100,000 and 140,000 troops and 600 tanks. His drive had been held in the centre but had advanced eight miles in the south and heavy fighting was in progress at the southern end of the El Alamein line in the area of El Himeimat hill overlooking the Qattara Depression. Harris could not tell if the tone of the reports was optimistic or foreboding.

He felt frustrated because *Blonde Job* flew no missions. He thought if they'd just send all the heavies from Ramat Jonas, St. Jean and Lydda over the ground fighting to drop two hundred and fifty pounders it would make a big difference. Not being sent on raids had its compensations, though. For three straight days he saw Hannah every day and every night. During the day he worked with her in the fields until his hands blistered and Tante Frieda put him to tending the chickens and fetching water. He just wasn't cut out to be a farmer, he thought ruefully.

The first night he was too tired even to think about taking Hannah to the grove. Instead, he sat with her on the couch, exhausted, hands burning, kissing and talking. With more talking than kissing. In some ways it was as satisfying as making love, and a totally new experience for him. In the past, it had only been frustrating to fondle a girl and not be able to do anything about it. Though this was only Wednesday he could wait contentedly until Saturday if it came to that. He noticed days of the weeks now because Saturdays had special significance. That was the day when, if things worked out right, he could have it all to himself with Hannah in Haifa with nothing to do but eat, go sightseeing and make love in a real bed.

The next day a big tank battle was reported raging on a twenty mile front with US tanks in action for the first time and giving a good account of themselves. The mediums of the 12th Bombardment Group were busy, too. Maybe that was why they hadn't had to call in the heavies, Harris thought. The day had been declared a National Day of Prayer. It was mostly a Christian affair although the *Palestine Post* reported some Jewish groups had participated. Harris didn't see any group praying going on in Aleenah but he thought maybe some of the settlers might be doing some praying on their own. Not Gyorgy Weisz or Hannah or Tante Frieda, though.

The day after, a Friday, it looked like Rommel had shot his wad. The headline said, "Eighth Army Holds Axis Desert Drive." The RAF and Air Corps P-40s and B-25s were pressing relentless attacks on Rommel's troops and armour. It was officially revealed for the first time that, just as Weisz had said days earlier, the whole of the Afrika Korps had been thrown into the attack in the early morning hours of the previous Monday.

It was also reported that Rommel had been sorely handicapped by a shortage of fuel. Harris felt good about that. The 108th had contributed to the land battle after all by helping to cut off the flow of supplies. He was never again going to complain about those long, butt-grinding convoy missions.

There was no overt rejoicing in Aleenah. The settlers went about their work as always. The only obvious change was that they no longer hovered near radios or stood outside talking quietly at the end of the day. Looking back, Harris did not think they had been frightened. Just in suspense. Except the Goldblums. They had been frightened. He didn't blame them. Of everyone in Aleenah, even Hannah, they had most recently experienced German barbarism. So Hannah hadn't been able to compete in a horse show. The Goldblums had barely escaped with their lives. Weisz had told him they were in one of the last groups permitted to leave Germany. In Aleenah they'd thought they were through with all that. Then to be threatened all over again. Who wouldn't be scared?

That night Mrs. Goldblum served Harris's coffee with supper. It was a celebration. Mr. Goldblum's prayer was longer than usual and Gyorgy was twice as bored with it.

Tante Frieda had a candle burning in a holder. Religious Jews did that on Friday nights but Harris hadn't thought she was religious. Maybe she'd lit it in gratitude for the Axis defeat. Even that didn't seem like Tante Frieda.

"*Jahrzeit* for Onkle Karl," Hannah explained.

247

He knew what that was. Commemorating the anniversary of her husband's death. His grandmother did that every year for his grandpa. The one Friday night a year his mother could get him to temple was when it was around the anniversary of his grandpa's death and they stood up to say *kaddish* with others also mourning loved ones.

They didn't talk about the war. Tante Frieda, pensive but not melancholy, talked about her early days in Palestine with her husband. Life was not as hard now as in those days, she said. They had seen days of bitter deprivation and grinding toil, survived Arab raids. But it had been joyous, even for a couple already approaching middle age and who had never before touched a farm tool.

Their first settlement had been on land purchased by Karen Kayemet Le-Israel, the Jewish National Fund. They had moved in quietly at night and begun fortifying the portion where they would live and house their animals with barbed wire fences, a wooden stockade and a watchtower. It was standard practice in those days. *Homeh u-Migdal,* "stockade and tower." If they tried to settle by day on land bought from the Arabs there was a good chance they would be attacked and murdered or driven off by other Arabs, or even by those who had sold the land. After that, Aleenah had seemed like Eden. Eighty families, unconfined, each with twenty acres to cultivate, protected against Arab incursions by vigilant patrols.

Tante Frieda made it sound like a picnic. Harris knew it hadn't been. His three unmenaced days playing at being a settler sure hadn't been any picnic. He still had blisters on his hands.

He felt as if he were getting a history lesson.

From someone who had made the history. He wanted to know more. If he could get into Haifa when Nagler's bookshop was open maybe he could find a book about it in English.

Tante Frieda fell silent. She went to bed earlier than usual. To be alone with her memories, Harris knew.

She'd put Hannah in a reminiscent mood. Instead of sitting in his lap she sat at the far end of the couch, looking at the flickering *jahrzeit* candle.

"Without Tante Frieda I'm sure I don't know what I would have done after my parents were taken away," she said. "At first I loathed working in the fields." Mischievously, "Just as you do, my Michael. I had not known it was such hard work. Now it doesn't seem so hard. But still it is not what I really wish to do with my life."

"What do you want to do?"

"Make it possible for Jews everywhere to have a homeland." Fiercely, "And one day they shall."

Her intensity made him uncomfortable. He preferred the tender Hannah who panted in his arms.

"I guess now Rommel's stopped, your bunch'll quit stealing stuff from the British," he said, joking, trying to lighten her mood.

It had the opposite effect.

"Quite the contrary," she snapped. "Any reason we had not to hinder them no longer exists. Their arms stores in Palestine will not be needed against the Germans. If we do not get them, one day they will be turned over to the Arabs. You may be sure of that."

He wasn't though. The British wouldn't do a thing like that. Hannah just said it to justify what her bunch was doing. She knew he didn't think Jews should be doing anything to bother the British while there was a war on. He wondered if that was why Dr. Jacobs had been visiting Gyorgy Weisz, to tell him if the Eighth Army held it was open season on the British. Harris knew there were a lot of Palestine Jews who didn't agree with Hannah and her bunch any more than he did. His first week at Ramat Jonas he'd seen an article about Jews helping the war effort. Something like 2,500 Jewish pilots and observers in the RAF and 6,000 in ground crews in Egypt.

He was about to bring that up when Hannah said, with obvious relish, "It is a great disappointment to them."

"What is? To who?"

"Rommel's defeat. To the Arabs. They were all praying for a German victory. It would have ended their problems with the *yishuv* once and for all."

Yishuv? What was that? Was Hannah really right about the Arabs? She ought to be. She lived here. But he'd thought everybody was against the Germans. And why would the Arabs want the Germans to win if the British took their side against the Palestine Jews like Hannah claimed they did? But it did make sense, when he thought about it. The British might be partial to the Arabs but they weren't against the Jews like the Germans were.

"What's the *yishuv?*" he said.

"The Jewish community of Palestine."

She wasn't sarcastic with him for not knowing as she'd been when he first started seeing her. She'd sure changed since then. But so had he. Thinking about what he'd told her that night in the grove, that he loved her. Wishing he hadn't said it. He wasn't quite as sure of it now. That night in the grove he'd just been carried away.

"Let's get an early start tomorrow," he said. "Is there an early bus?"

"If we leave from Shimron." Teasing him, "Will we chance to meet Gallegly and learn to your surprise he has taken a room?"

"He's already got a room in Haifa."

He wished immediately he hadn't said it. Now he'd have to explain that a girl went with it. Hannah might start comparing her situation with that of Gallegly's girl. When it wasn't like that at all.

"I thought there would be no more planning," she said, hurt.

"It's not for us, Hannahle. It's OK if I get us a room, isn't it?"

"I will be disappointed if you do not. But please, at another hotel."

He knew she did not want to be reminded of all his scheming the other time.

For the second week in a row the war interfered with his personal plans. He had to go on a mission. It was a night takeoff, though, and he was able to slip away to Aleenah to tell Hannah he couldn't go. It was, of course, against regulations to reveal anything about military operations, and it troubled him a little. But he felt an obligation not to let her sit there expecting him. It wasn't as if he were telling her where they were going. He didn't know himself, and wouldn't until briefing. And anyhow, she'd trusted him with things she wasn't supposed to.

Hannah was as disappointed as he. And beneath the disappointment something she tried to conceal. Her concern that something might happen to him. In that respect she was no different from other civilians. They all thought bombing missions were more dangerous than they really were. In this theatre, anyway. The only bad flak was over the target and the fighters never hung around for long at a time, either. The only plane they'd lost to enemy action had been *Flat Foot Floogie*. And Floogie wouldn't have bought it if it hadn't been for mechanical failure.

They went after harbour installations at Candia, on the northern coast of Crete. On the back of the big brown lizard. They were to hit it late at night. The briefing officer pointed out the landmarks the navigators were to look for to locate the target, saying even on a moonless night it should present no major problem.

Not for you, anyway, Harris thought. You ain't going.

"Yeah," Major Beck grunted. "When you see a pisspot-full of flak, it's Candia."

Well, the intelligence officer said, they could expect a fair amount of flak here, here and here. Which meant a hell of a lot of it. Otherwise he would have said it was negligible. That was probably why they were hitting it at night instead of dusk.

Harris was glad they were flying to the target individually. It gave him something to do besides standing around moping about his lousy luck to be sitting in the nose of a B-24 instead of having a big day in Haifa with Hannah. He thought about being in bed with her but also about all the other things that were fun to do with her. Maybe he really was in love with her.

He didn't think about Hannah while he was shooting stars and calculating winds but between fixes he thought of nothing else, snapping at Silkwood when he tried to make conversation.

Crete was a dark hulk dimly outlined against the darker sea. There was a glow in the direction of Candia. One of the first planes in must have started a fire. The glow was at one o'clock, not dead ahead. Harris was annoyed. He'd thought his fixes were on the nose. He gave Wagstaff the new heading.

The target was readily identifiable when they drew closer, picked out by scattered muzzle flashes of flak batteries. There was a fair amount of flak, all right. Harris wished the intelligence officer was sitting up in the nose with him to count the guns. Several fires burned, red beacons in the night. A pattern of bomb bursts blossomed and died.

Silkwood started his bomb run. Flak batteries winked up at them. *Blonde Job* climbed steeply. Silkwood ranted over the interphone. *Blonde Job* stopped climbing. Held. Steady as a rock. Then bounced a little but remained on course, maintaining constant altitude. It was flak bursts that were bouncing them around. A wonder they weren't hit.

"Bombardier to pilot. Bombs away. Swell run, Dan."

"Navigator to pilot."

Harris gave Wags the heading for home and looked back to see their bombs hit. A tongue of flame licked the darkness behind them. It shrank, but kept burning. Silkwood had hit something juicy.

"Navigator to bombardier. Good going, Silkwood."

A parallel row of lights came on far below them, circled by a pair of other lights moving and winking off and on. Jesus Christ! A German airfield with planes in a landing pattern! As Harris stared, a beam of light flicked on and approached the end of the parallel lights. Landing lights. A German plane was landing almost immediately below them. And

Blonde Job with no bombs.

"Navigator to pilot! Do you see what I see?"

"Co-pilot to navigator. Roger."

Gallegly. Calm.

Why did he answer instead of Wagstaff?

"Bombardier to pilot! Let's go down and strafe!"

It wasn't as dumb as it sounded. The planes would be bombers coming back from the battlefront, not fighters. They could get in the pattern without Jerry even suspecting. Except that by the time they got down to the deck all the Jerry planes might already be on the ground. It took a while for a B-24 to let down from altitude.

"Co-pilot to bombardier. Negative."

Why wasn't it Wagstaff?

Half an hour off Crete, Silkwood saw running lights in the distance heading in the opposite direction. He pointed them out to Harris. It couldn't be one of theirs. It was too late and too low. And they didn't put on running lights until they were almost home. It had to be a German plane. Harris watched it disappear into the night with nothing more than mild curiosity. It was no threat to *Blonde Job*. Nor *Blonde Job* to it. They'd both done their jobs and were returning home. Ships that passed in the night. The incongruity struck him. If either plane had been a fighter its job would be to attack the other. Instead they'd merely plodded on their way, not mad at one another, just guys in the same business working different territories. Having more in common with each other than with their own kind trying to kill each other at El Alamein.

They had almost flown out their ETA for the coast below Haifa before Wagstaff started singing on the interphone.

An undercast had built up. The nearer they got to the coast the more solid it became. The radio operator reported ceiling unlimited and visibility ten miles at Ramat Jonas but they couldn't just head straight for the field. They were not permitted to fly directly towards or over Haifa. Even with the IFF on they'd cause an air raid alert and the British flak batteries would open up on them. SOP was to make a landfall above or below the city, get a visual fix on the coastline and head for the field from there, avoiding Haifa.

Harris gave Wagstaff a heading parelleling the coast. He stared down at the undercast looking for a break. If they could find a hole he'd get a visual fix. No luck. He had Wagstaff do a one-eighty and tried again to the south. Still no hole. Wagstaff wanted to home in on Lydda and fly to Ramat Jonas from there. They couldn't home in on Ramat Jonas because Ramat Jonas had no ground radio homing facility. Harris considered Wagstaff's suggestion a reflection on his professional skill. He'd had good fixes all the way back and had done accurate DR during the search for a hole in the undercast.

"Navigator to pilot. We're OK. Let's take a chance."

He gave Wagstaff the heading for Ramat Jonas. According to his DR they should be well south of Haifa and just off the coast.

"Pilot to galvinator. You better be right, Tex."

They were on course for Ramat Jonas. Harris hoped. Haifa should be off to the left. If he was wrong and they flew over the city it would be his happy ass. Wagstaff's, too. The pilot would be held as much to blame as the navigator. More, because he was plane commander. The prospect of facing a

255

wrathful Major Beck was more chilling than flak or fighters.

A searchlight beam pierced the undercast off the left wing. Then another. Lifted, shifting. Descended to lay pointers of light across the undercast. Pointing the way to Ramat Jonas. Hooray for the limeys down there on the searchlights.

"Big Wags to navigator. Jolly good show."

Coming in for the landing, Gallegly was curt and aloof calling out airspeed and altitude. It was the co-pilot's job during landings, leaving the pilot free to devote his full attention to the runway lights rushing up at them.

Gallegly remained locked in harsh silence on the crew bus and during post-mission. Just like after Tobruk. Harris could not understand it. They'd had a flawless bomb run, almost flawless, anyhow. Just that climb at the beginning. Maybe he and Wagstaff had had an argument about something. That wasn't like either of them. It took a hell of a lot to make Gallegly sore and Wagstaff never got mad. He'd just jolly you out of it if you tried to argue with him.

Harris waited until they were back in the tent getting ready for bed in the dark.

"Well?" he said.

"He did it again," Gallegly said tonelessly. "He froze on the controls when we got into the flak."

"I guess that was you flying the bomb run, wasn't it?"

"He oughtta ground himself he's gonna be like that."

"Wags wouldn't do that."

"Yeah. Well, somebody ought to ground him."

"Maybe if we said something to him."

Knowing they'd already been through that and

there was nothing anybody could say without coming right out and telling Wags he wasn't fit to be a first pilot. When he was the best pilot in the 234th.

"He didn't try to stop you from taking over, did he?"

"No."

"Well, then. As long as it doesn't screw things up . . ."

They had to cover for Wags. He'd do the same for them. Hell, he was only that way for a few minutes over the target. Except for that, you wouldn't want a better pilot. Or a better friend. It could ruin Wags's whole life if it got out. He could just imagine what Major Beck would do to him.

"I can't keep rassling him for the ship every time we get into flak. What if we're in formation? He could get us all killed."

"At least let me talk to him. OK?"

He didn't want to but he'd have to. He'd just have to find the right way of putting it.

Gallegly snorted like a boxer clearing his nose.

"I hope he listens," he said.

Harris woke up around ten. That was early after a night raid. But it had only been five and a half hours long, their shortest mission yet, and he'd been in the sack by three. He woke up without thinking about Hannah for the first time in days, filled with foreboding, knowing there was something unpleasant he had to do. Remembering promising Gallegly he'd talk to Wags.

Wagstaff was alone in his tent, still sleeping, one big foot poking beyond the end of his cot, pushing out the mosquito net. A mosquito was feeding on the toe through the netting. Harris flushed it. The mosquito, heavy with blood, rose sluggishly. Harris clapped it between his palms. Blood on his hands. The first blood he'd seen in five weeks of combat. He'd have laughed about that if he weren't on such serious business.

He wiped his hands on the underside of Silkwood's cot and sat down to wait for Wagstaff to open his eyes. He didn't expect Silkwood back for a while. It was Sunday and they had a chaplain now, with services in the officers' club. Silkwood was the only one of the four who went.

Wagstaff stirred, opened one eye, saw Harris and grinned. He even woke up good-natured. Harris didn't know how he was going to be able to say anything about last night. But he had to. He'd told Gallegly he would.

"Have I missed chow?" Wagstaff said, sitting up and stretching, his huge arms poking out both sides of the mosquito net.

"They'll feed us," Harris said.

When you got back late on a mission you could always get something to eat at the mess hall the next morning.

An obliging cook fed them scrambled eggs and Vienna sausages. Wagstaff ate enough for two, as if he didn't have a care in the world.

"Wags," said Harris, "how about taking a walk?"

Wagstaff looked at him quizzically and nodded.

They walked through the stubble, not talking. Harris felt troubled and uncomfortable, not knowing how to begin.

"Problems with your girl, Tex?" Wagstaff asked.

Not kidding or nosey, just solicitous. It made it even harder to begin.

"No," said Harris.

"Something's on your mind, ole buddy."

Oh, hell.

"About last night . . ."

"What about last night?"

Wags wasn't making it any easier. He must know Gallegly would have said something to him about what happened. Before he could frame an answer, Wagstaff said, very casually, "You dream much, Tex?"

"Some."

What the hell was Wags getting at?

"You ever dream about flying?"

"We get enough of that without dreaming about it."

"You believe in dreams?"

"No. You don't either, do you?"

"Guess not."

Rubbing his chin, not looking at Harris, "I had this dream. I didn't tell you guys about it. You might think it'd jinx us. I dreamed we got shot down."

Wagstaff wouldn't freeze up just because of a dream. Would he?

"Lots of guys probably did after Floogie bought it."

"Oh it was before that. The night we got to Ramat Jonas."

"Before we even flew a mission?"

"I've had the same dream a couple times since then. Nutty, huh?"

Sounding like he was trying to explain, almost like he was asking for help. Big Wags asking anybody for help. That's what was really nutty.

"Sure as hell is," Harris said. Joking, "What gets us Wags, flak or fighters?"

But he already knew. Remembering how Wags

259

had bored into the fighters at Tobruk and what he had said after *Flat Foot Floogie* went down. You could fight back against fighters.

"Flak," Wagstaff said. "One minute we're up there like a big happy bird and the next thing, whammo. Not even knowing what hit us."

"Rugged."

"Last time I even dreamed where it was," Wagstaff said reluctantly.

"Where?"

"Tobruk."

Tobruk was where he'd really screwed up. Maybe that was why he'd dreamed about it.

"Hey. I have the same dream some time too."

Wagstaff stared at him.

"You dream about Tobruk too?" he said incredulously.

"I mean dreaming about the same thing over and over."

Wagstaff appeared relieved.

Half a dozen times since he graduated from Rice, Harris had dreamed final exams were coming up and there was one course where he hadn't cracked a book and didn't know a damn thing. And was sure to flunk, meaning he wouldn't graduate. Worried sick about it. So glad to wake up and find it was only a dream, when while he was going to school he'd never worried about flunking an exam. Just about all the studying he'd have to do or maybe about making a bum grade.

He told Wagstaff about his dream to show how dreams didn't mean anything. Wagstaff thought it was funny.

"Crazy, the thing's a man'll dream, ain't it?" he said.

260

"Yeah. Crazy as a guy letting a dream get him down, ain't it?"

"Roger," said Wagstaff.

Harris couldn't think of anything else to say. Maybe it was enough for Wags to get it off his chest and hear somebody say it didn't mean anything.

"Hey, Tex? Don't say anything to anybody. I'd feel kind of stupid."

"Hell, no."

It made him feel pretty good to know he was the one Wagstaff had picked to confide in.

Gallegly was waiting back at the tent. He looked at Harris without speaking, waiting.

"I had a talk with him," Harris said.

"And?"

"Maybe now that we talked about it he'll be OK."

"What'd you say to him?"

"We just kind of talked."

"Did he get sore or anything?"

"No."

"I'm glad," said Gallegly.

CHAPTER XV

In the afternoon a ground officer came around passing out evasion material — tiny compasses disguised as uniform buttons and other commonplace objects, big white silk handkerchiefs printed with a map of Libya and a document on leathery paper promising a cash reward in both English and Arabic to anyone assisting a downed Allied flyer back to friendly lines. The British called the documents "ghoolie chits." Ghoolie meant testicles. The story was that if the desert Arabs did not turn downed airmen over to the Germans and Italians for the reward the Axis offered for prisoners, they let their women have them for torture.

"You're to have these on your person whenever you fly," the groundgripper said. "And if you have to bail out, take your canteen with you."

"I think he's trying to tell us something," Harris said.

The groundgripper didn't think it was anything to joke about. He took his work seriously.

"Well," he said. "You never know, do you?"

Harris and Gallegly both had sewing kits. They substituted compasses for a button on their flight coveralls and one shirt. It was kind of reassuring in a way. People who ought to know figured if they got shot down they'd probably be able to bail out and were trying to make it easier for them to get back. Maybe Wags would find it reassuring, too, being told so matter-of-factly that even if they did get shot down they could still get back OK. Ghoolies and all.

Harris had supper in the mess hall, feeling no need to visit the Goldblums now that their crisis was over, just as he had felt no need to join Hannah in the fields that day after flying half the night. She knew how he felt without that.

After chow he read the *Palestine Post* at the club. The big story on the front page was about the Axis being driven back in the desert. It shared the news with an account of Nazi hordes held at Stalingrad. Things were looking great for the Allies. A news item tucked away on an inside page shattered Harris's sense of well-being.

The Jerusalem Military Court had sentenced a young Jewish RAF Other Rank to life imprisonment for possession of 10,000 rounds of .303 rifle ammunition. Six other Jews, five special constables and one civilian had been convicted with him and sentenced to terms which ranged from five to twelve years. It might just as easily have been Hannah and Gyorgy, Harris thought, chilled. For the first time he fully understood the gravity of Hannah's position. She wasn't playing games, and neither were the British. He wondered if she knew the Other Rank, Leading Aircraftsman David Sachs, if they were all members of the same gang or if there were little groups all over Palestine. He didn't intend asking her about it. What he didn't know couldn't hurt her and her friends.

He deliberated over taking the blanket into

Aleenah. Last time Hannah had liked him not bringing it because it told her he didn't come to see her just to take her out in the trees. But after what he had let slip out about being in love with her she should know that, blanket or no blanket. They'd gotten all dusty and the pine needles stuck. There wasn't any reason why they couldn't be comfortable. He took the blanket.

Hannah said she couldn't leave the house.

"As you flyers say, I am on alert. I am so sorry, *Liebchen*."

She gave no details and he did not have to ask. That goddam Gyorgy must have an errand for her to run and she could end up like that RAF guy. Why couldn't he do it himself instead of sending a girl out at night? Knowing perfectly well it was because a girl was less likely to arouse suspicion and, being a *ghaffir*, Gyorgy had to be extra careful the British didn't know what he was up to.

Harris could not resist saying, "Hannah, be careful. You know what happened to Sachs."

She stiffened and said, "How did you . . . ?" stopping short.

Because she obviously was not going to talk about it he did not pursue it. He knew there was no way of talking her out of doing whatever it was she believed she had to do.

"You can leave for a little while, can't you?" he said instead.

"With us it is never just a little while, my Michael."

They left the light on and only kissed a little, expecting Gyorgy to come knocking on the door any minute. As time passed and he did not appear, Harris turned out the light and took her in his lap.

"We really should not," Hannah said without conviction.

"He won't even have to know I'm here," Harris said. "Just don't let him in the door. Let him think you were in your room or something."

He had intended to be just loving and tender but before he knew it he had her shirt off. And didn't care about Gyorgy maybe knocking on the door or Tante Frieda asleep in a back room. He fumbled with a stubborn button on her shorts. Hannah seemed not to care about Gyorgy or Tante Frieda either, but suddenly she sat up and said frantically, "No, Michael! No!"

"I love you," he said hoarsely.

"We cannot. Not here."

"Let's go to our place, then."

"I must wait."

"If he was coming he'd have been here by now."

"Do you really think so?"

Wanting to be persuaded.

"I know so."

They hurried to the grove as if racing for sanctuary. Hannah helped him spread the blanket, untroubled that he had brought it. They flung themselves upon it and embraced hungrily, burning with impatience. They made love as if slaking a prolonged and raging thirst. A voice called from the darkness.

"Hannah. Hannah Ruh."

Gyorgy. Calling from the road.

Hannah went rigid as a corpse.

"Gott in Himmel!" she gasped.

She squirmed from his loosened embrace, scrambled into her clothes and plunged away through the pines, leaving him wretched and sick with concern for her.

He dressed slowly. Numb. Gyorgy had known exactly where to find her. To find *them*. Had known all along, maybe. Maybe even spied on them. Humiliation gave way to rage. The son of a bitch! Embarrassing Hannah like that. It was none of Gyorgy's business what she did. He wasn't Hannah's keeper.

Harris crept silently towards the road, stopping when he heard a voice. Gyorgy's. Too low to be intelligible but, astonishingly, not heated. Conversational. Not a word out of Hannah. He could imagine how she felt. It was all his fault, bringing her out here. Could he tell Gyorgy that without making it even more humiliating for her? Knowing he could not.

Gyorgy, louder. For his benefit?

"Shalom, Hannah."

Hannah, scarcely louder than a whisper, *"Shalom."*

Gyorgy turned and walked towards the Goldblums'. Hannah watched him for a moment, then trudged slowly for Tante Frieda's, head down. Harris wanted to rush to her. But he waited. Gyorgy might look back. He wasn't mad at Gyorgy any more, just concerned about Hannah. Gyorgy hadn't sounded as if he were eating her out or anything. And if he'd really been such a bastard he'd have sneaked up on them instead of calling from the road. All that mattered to Hannah, though, was that Gyorgy knew she'd been out in the grove.

He gave Gyorgy time to get inside and ran after Hannah. She walked so slowly he caught up with her at the door. He put his arm around her and said, "Hannah. Sweetheart." She flinched.

She went inside and sat down in the dark, not letting him turn on a light. He groped his way to

266

her chair and put his hand on her shoulder.

"It's all right, sweetheart."

"Is it?"

Dully.

"What did he say to you?"

"About us? Nothing."

"Well, then."

"It was dreadful. So humiliating."

"He did say something!"

Impatiently, "No. Because he knew we had been making love."

"How would he know that? It was dark. He was all the way out on the road. For all he knew we were just smooching."

"Smooching?"

"Petting. Fooling around a little."

"Do you think so?" Wanting to be convinced. "But he knew where to find me."

So she'd thought of it, too.

"It still doesn't mean he knew we were . . . Even if he did. We love each other, dammit."

"It does not seem so much like love now. What we were doing."

He turned on the light and hunkered down next to the chair. He took her hand and kissed it. Looked up at her. She would not return his gaze.

"You trying to tell me you don't love me?"

"Only that perhaps you do not love me."

"That's just swell!"

He stood up, jammed his hands in his pockets and glared down at her.

"You know something, Hannah? Sometimes you make me so goddam mad."

She looked at him at last, taken unaware by his anger.

267

"Just what does a guy have to do to prove it? Ask you to marry him?"

It took them both utterly by surprise. Good God, Harris thought wildly, am I proposing? He couldn't do that. He was in love with her, sure, but there was a war on. He didn't even know how long he'd be at Ramat Jonas or when he'd ever get back. He hadn't even known her a month.

"I mean what the hell," he hedged. "You know I love you."

Hoping she wouldn't take too seriously what he had said.

"Don't you?" he said, his eyes imploring her not to.

"Of course I do," she said without any suggestion of censure for an offer withdrawn.

She was so goddam understanding and beautiful and sweet and pure. He was awash with tenderness and relief.

He sat on the couch and said, "Come here."

"Oh, *Liebchen,* I couldn't."

"Neither could I. Just to talk."

They held hands. Nothing more. Gyorgy was a third presence in the room, unseen but not unfelt.

"What did Gyorgy want?"

"There is work for me to do."

"Tonight?"

"No. Soon."

"I wish you'd stop that stuff. I don't want anything to happen to you. Like it did to that Sachs guy."

"And I do not wish anything to happen to you. But I do not ask you to give up what you must do."

"That's different."

"Why is it so different?"

"I'm in the service, dammit."

"So am I."

"Not really. You don't have to be."

"Tell me, my Michael, if your Major Beck said to you, go home if you wish, it is your own free choice. Would you go?"

"But you're a girl!"

"I am a Jew."

There was just no use arguing with her when she was like this. Maybe Tante Frieda could talk some sense into her head. But Tante Frieda had probably already tried.

Harris wondered where they could go at night now. Not back to the grove, for sure. Hannah might know some place. Now was not the time to bring it up though.

"When do you have to do whatever it is you have to do?" he asked.

"In the morning."

"That makes it tough on Tante Frieda, doesn't it? Having to do all the work herself."

"You may help her if you wish. If you promise not to be too much in the way."

Teasing him about his performance in the fields the week before, no longer so upset about being discovered in the grove with him. He'd show her. He'd never worked on a farm before but he had kept the yard back home between the visits of the coloured man, dug flower beds, grubbed out weeds, tended vegetables. He'd be OK as soon as his hands toughened up.

He did not get a chance to demonstrate. They were alerted for a mission and he could not leave the field.

The 108th was hitting Tobruk again. Harris watched Wagstaff's face when the target was an-

269

nounced. It revealed nothing. Maybe their talk had done some good. Harris was glad they were hitting Tobruk, wishing he could have done it while the big battle was going on and he could have felt he was making a more direct contribution than at Candia.

They would be getting over the target after dark, going in a couple thousand feet lower than the first time. The intelligence officer said they could expect the accuracy of the flak to be considerably less than in the daytime because Jerry relied a lot on visual ranging.

Blonde Job did not test the intelligence officer's veracity. Wagstaff aborted the mission an hour short of the target off the coast between Matruh and Sidi Barrani, saying he didn't like the way Number 3 and 4 engines were running. Bad-mouthing Trombatore over the interphone, which wasn't like Wags at all.

After they landed at Ramat Jonas, Gallegly took Wagstaff aside and they went off together out of earshot in the darkness. The crew bus arrived before they came back. Harris told the driver to wait, wondering what was going on, knowing it had something to do with aborting but with no clue to Gallegly's intentions.

They returned grimly silent, not walking together. Gallegly went all the way to the back of the empty bus. Harris followed him.

"What was that all about?" Harris demanded, whispering.

"You sure straightened him out, didn't you?" Gallegly said bitterly.

He refused to answer any more questions, not in words but by turning away and looking out the window into the night.

It was not until they were in the mess hall for

post-mission that Harris saw one of his eyes was starting to blacken. Wagstaff had a cut lip: They'd been fighting. The enlisted men gathered in a silent cluster, puzzled, ill at ease.

"Dan," said Silkwood. "What happened to your lip?"

"Bit it."

"Does it hurt much?"

"Only when I smile."

It was only then that Silkwood noticed Gallegly's face.

"Your eye, Terry!" he said.

"Shut up," said Harris.

Silkwood stared at him, mystified, his feelings hurt.

Post-mission was short because they had nothing to report except the problem with the engines. The interrogating officer asked Wagstaff and Gallegly how they had received their injuries and if anyone else on the crew was hurt. Wounded was the word he used.

"We bumped heads getting out," Wagstaff said.

Gallegly didn't stay for sandwiches and coffee. He said he would walk back to the tent instead of waiting for the bus. Harris wanted to go with him and find out what happened but thought it would look odd, the two of them slipping off together. Everybody but Silkwood knew damn well Gallegly and Wags had had a fight and he wanted the crew to think it was just something personal between the two of them. It was bad enough they should think there was bad blood between the pilot and co-pilot, without them knowing the reason.

Wagstaff apologized to Trombatore for bawling him out, saying he knew it wasn't his fault about the engines.

"I was just pissed off because we had to abort," he said. "Those engines've got a lotta time on 'em. Maybe we need an engine change. What do you think, Trombone?"

"Whatever you say, sir," Trombatore said, not looking him in the eye.

Before they finished the sandwiches, Wagstaff had him laughing with the others. Harris only pretended to join in, methodically chewing too big a bite of sandwich, impatient to get away and find out more from Gallegly.

Gallegly was waiting for him, still dressed, sitting on his cot with the mosquito net draped over him like a shroud.

"What took you so long?" Gallegly demanded.

"I didn't know you were waiting for me. You wouldn't even talk to me on the goddam bus."

"Sorry."

"I guess there wasn't anything wrong with the engines, huh?"

"Smooth as a baby's butt. Manifold pressure, RPMs, everything. You can ask Trombone if you don't believe me."

"Why wouldn't I believe you?"

"I told him next time he pulled something like that I was taking it to Beck."

"There must be some other way."

"You got a better idea?"

Harris shook his head dejectedly and said, "What did he have to say about that?"

"Acted like he didn't know what the hell I was talking about. You know he can be. I got so mad I swung on him." Reluctantly, "He didn't want to hit me back. Just laughed and backed away. But I kept

272

swinging. So he floored me. And picked me up and brushed me off."

He sounded like he wanted to bawl.

"But I mean it, Tex. Next time he screws up . . ."

Harris was still awake when the planes started coming back from Tobruk. He counted them in, wondering how many people in Aleenah were doing the same. Wondering if Hannah was awake, making sure he got back all right. He wished he was with her, and worried about Wags.

Gallegly's eye was black and purple in the morning. Major Beck thought it was hilarious.

"That'll teach you to bump heads with the thickest skull in the whole goddam group," he told Gallegly.

He wouldn't think it was so goddam funny if he knew what really happened, Harris thought. You sure couldn't tell from the way Wagstaff was acting that they'd had a fight.

He went to Habima to help Tante Frieda, welcoming the escape. Hannah was away again. Tante Frieda put him to work among the tomatoes. He wanted to do heavier work, showing her how his hands were healing, but she wouldn't let him. They had lunch out of doors, sitting side by side with their backs against an outbuilding. Bread, cheese and fruit. Tante Frieda tried to hide it but she was worried about Hannah. It made Harris worry. If Hannah got caught they'd put her in jail just like that Other Rank and his bunch.

He asked Tante Frieda if she knew where Hannah had gone and what she was doing. She shook her head. Hannah never said and she never asked, she said. Harris said Hannah shouldn't take such chances. It took a while to get across. He didn't know all the right words in German and he had to grope for them with her help. It was almost like playing charades.

"Who can tell her anything?" Tante Frieda asked the sky. "That Hannah. Stubborn like a donkey."

Harris told her not to worry. She touched his cheek with horny fingers and said he was a good boy.

"You are good for my little Hannah."

He wondered how much she really knew about them. What Hannah had said to her about him. If Tante Frieda knew where they went and what they did every night after she went to bed. They couldn't go there any more. They'd have to find another place. He was tempted to tell Tante Frieda how much he cared for her niece. But she must already know that or she wouldn't treat him the way she did.

Hannah returned early in the afternoon, changed from her dress into shirt and shorts and joined them in the fields. She looked at Harris slyly and asked Tante Frieda if he'd been more trouble than he was worth. Tante Frieda scolded her, saying Michael had been a great help.

"Better than you when you came first to Aleenah, my fine donkey."

Showing Harris her gold tooth in a conspiratorial grin.

The rest of the afternoon passed quickly. Harris stayed for supper, hardly tired at all, hands OK. Smelling of sweat. They all did, so it didn't matter. They sat around the table after supper, laughing and arguing. Tante Frieda took his side when he disagreed with Hannah about something. Just like at home before Betty Lee got married. They were a family. Except that at home his dad had been the man of the house and here he was, enjoying the

274

attention of two women, wishing he wouldn't have to leave later on and crawl under that goddam mosquito net on that goddam bedroll instead of sharing Hannah's loving bed.

Abruptly thinking about Wagstaff for almost the first time that day, hoping desperately that now Gallegly had warned him about going to Beck, Wags would see he just had to straighten out.

"What is wrong?" Hannah asked. "You are so quiet."

"Just thinking. Wishing I didn't have to . . ."

Not finishing, not feeling as if he had lied because he really did wish he would never have to leave Hannah, realizing he'd never be happy without her. After the war, as soon as he got settled in a job, he'd write and ask her to come to Houston. He knew his folks would like her as much as he did. He hoped Tante Frieda wouldn't take it too hard. Or maybe she would come, too.

"I wish so, too," Hannah said, looking down at her folded hands.

Though they had spoken in English, Tante Frieda, observant, nodded to herself, aware. She left them alone earlier than usual.

"I have a rival," Hannah said. "You are fonder of Tante Frieda than of me."

"She ever talk to you about us?"

"About her Michael, yes. About us, no. She takes it for granted . . ."

Unwilling to continue, uncomfortable.

"Do you, Hannah?"

Remembering his surge of emotion at the supper table, wanting to know if Hannah had had it too.

She looked at him briefly, then away.

"What do you wish to hear?" she said.

275

"The truth."

"Are you so sure you wish the truth? Very well. Yes and no."

"Dammit, Hannah!"

He was serious and she was joking about it.

"Yes, I take it for granted you love me. No, I do not take it for granted something must come of it. What do you take for granted, *liebchen?*"

"The same thing, I guess."

Hannah was right. They couldn't make any plans. He was glad she took it that way and he hadn't said what was on his mind at the table. Life was too uncertain for both of them. Bullshit, Harris. You're just afraid to come right out and commit yourself. Remembering what you thought of guys that fell for girls they'd just barely met and started taking it seriously, afraid to promise Hannah something and realize later you'd made a mistake. Out of sack, out of mind. He didn't really believe that, not about him and Hannah. Not right now, anyway. But who knew how he'd feel, how they'd both feel, a year from now when she was here and he was God knows where?

But why worry about it? Hannah wasn't putting him on the spot. Just the opposite. Whatever happened would happen. Hannah understood that the same as he did. Drift with it. It wasn't like navigation, where you had to keep shooting fixes and correcting for the wind or you could get carried so far off course you couldn't get back where you were supposed to be. He felt vastly relieved, and grateful to Hannah for being so understanding.

He wrapped his arms around her and held her so hard he knew it must hurt. She didn't complain.

"Oh, Hannahle," he murmured.

Hungering.

"Where can we go?"

"Not back there," Hannah said. "I could not."

"There must be someplace."

"Yes."

She left him and returned with a bedspread.

"I, too, can plan," she said.

She led him out past the chickens and tomatoes, among the vines. They made love between the rows. The water pumps made their diligent sound. Jackals wailed distantly in the hills. Each star in the moonless sky was a separate jewel, the patterns as distinct as the star chart in his almanac. Harris lay on his back looking up at them. He showed Hannah Polaris. She already knew it, as well as the Big and Little Bears. But not Orion or any of the other constellations. A breeze stirred the vines. Three or four knots, Harris estimated.

"Not bright, but dependable," Harris said, looking at Polaris's dim gleam.

"You are too modest, *Liebchen.*"

"Not me, *esel.* Polaris."

Esel. Donkey. What Tante Frieda said Hannah was as stubborn as. And Hannah could be, but also yielding and so tender it made his chest hurt.

"Hannahle?"

"Yes, my Michael?"

Dreamy, content.

Watch yourself, Harris. Don't say anything you'll be sorry for. Just drift with it.

Three more perfect days, working side by side with Hannah among the vines where they made love at night, noisy suppers with her and Tante Frieda. Always on the verge of asking Hannah to wait for

277

him until after the war, telling her he would send for her. But resisting the urge, one part of his navigator's mind, the controlling part, clear and analytical. Don't promise anything you may regret some day.

Three days marred only by Gallegly's sombre mood and a nagging concern about what was happening to their crew. Worry that they might have to go to Major Beck. Wishing he was as unaware as Silkwood. Glad he had somewhere to go to get away from it. When he was with Hannah and Tante Frieda nothing else seemed to matter too much. Not even Wags.

At supper Friday night, the third night, Tante Frieda said, "Who is Wendell Willkie?"

Pronouncing it "Vendell Villkie."

She had heard on the radio he was in Jerusalem.

Harris did not know a whole lot about him except that he had run against Franklin D. Roosevelt in the 1940 election and lost. He'd been a few months short of being old enough to vote in 1940 and had been too partial to Roosevelt anyhow to pay much attention to what the papers said about Willkie. He regretted that now. Tante Frieda must think he was pretty dumb to know so little about a man who had run for president of the United States.

"Michael is very naive politically," Hannah explained in German.

Harris knew why she said it. Just because he didn't agree with her that the English were the next worst thing to Hitler.

"And you are so smart?" Tante Frieda demanded, patting Harris's hand.

"It's not fair," Hannah said. "Always two against one."

Two hours later they were in their new haven

among the vines. Harris preferred it to the pine grove even if the grove had held no memories of Gyorgy Weisz calling for Hannah in the night. There were no treetops here to block the sky. A greater sense of isolation and space. A heightened sensation that there was only him, Hannah and the familiar stars. A feeling that time was suspended, that while they were here nothing that happened anywhere else mattered.

They ate grapes plucked from the vines, grapes still touched with daytime warmth. It summoned up memories of his childhood. Wild muscadine grapes from vines choking low trees. Liveoaks dripping with Spanish moss. Wild grapes were round as marbles, purplish black. All seeds and skin but with a burst of sweetness. He had liked the green ones, too, sour enough to bring tears.

He sampled grapes from different clusters hanging near him in the darkness until he found some not yet ripe, looking for that bygone taste. He ate a handful, thinking how long it had been since he was a boy eating muscadine grapes in the woods, mustang grapes they'd been called, he remembered. Only ten or twelve years ago but it was like a lifetime. Running through the woods playing hunter, trapper, Indian, explorer, Tarzan, in all his fantasies never dreaming that one day he would fly over continents and oceans in a bomber, see strange countries. Lie under stars he knew as well as the streets of Houston with a beautiful girl he loved and who loved him. Love hadn't entered his mind in those days. He hadn't even begun to think about girls.

And tomorrow a whole day in Haifa.

"I hope you don't have to work tomorrow," he said.

279

"Don't you know? It's Rosh Hashonah."

Rosh Hashonah. The Jewish New Year. Next to Yom Kippur the most important Jewish holiday. Even back home he'd never known exactly when it fell. It didn't come on the same date every year like the real New Year.

Oh, hell, he thought. It could ruin everything.

"Do you have to go to temple? Services, I mean? You don't have a temple in Aleenah."

"No, *esel*. It means only no one works tomorrow."

That was one thing he found hard to understand about Hannah and the others. All they seemed to think about was being Jews, yet they didn't go to temple or anything, most of them, anyhow. Whereas he'd gone to temple every Saturday until he was thirteen and hardly ever thought about being a Jew. Except that it meant he had to go to temple.

"We can get an early start, then."

Last Saturday, too, he'd suggested an early start, but he'd had to fly and Hannah'd had to do something for Gyorgy. Both of them on missions. Wasn't that a pistol?

"Not even any cloak and dagger stuff?" he said, teasing.

"Not tomorrow. The day is ours. But you may find Haifa unusually dull tomorrow. It is also Ramadan. The most important holiday period for the Arabs."

"It won't be dull," Harris said. "I promise."

At morning chow everybody was put on alert for a Sunday mission, a big one, rumour had it. It meant no one was supposed to leave the field all day without special permission. Harris chafed for half an hour before deciding to go to Haifa anyhow. He could slip across the fields and back without taking

280

the road out of the airfield. Gallegly said he would cover for him. Gallegly had been going to Haifa every chance he got to shack up with his Arab girl in the room he had rented for her and came dragging back at night even later than Harris. Gallegly knew all about Ramadan. It wasn't just a one day thing. During Ramadan she wouldn't eat or drink or go to bed with him until after sunset.

Haifa was even deader than on other Saturdays. There were still plenty of Jews who took Rosh Hashonah seriously. Pross's was closed and they had to find another restaurant. Harris didn't like it as well. Pross's was sort of their restaurant.

He got a room at the Grand Hotel Nasser on Allenby Street. Hannah waited outside. Harris didn't know how strict they were about a man taking a girl to his room.

Making love on a comfortable bed in a locked room was not as great as he had anticipated. It was hot and they were quickly slippery with sweat. Despite the drawn shades the room was full of light. He missed the velvet darkness and so did Hannah. Sweat and harsh light did not make for tenderness and romance.

He missed, too, the sense of space and solitude and time standing still, the cool breezes, the smell of growing things, the sounds of jackals and water pumps, stars overhead he knew like the back of his hand, knew as well as he knew Hannah's body.

But what was wrong most of all was that their two frantic, sweating bodies reminded him of other girls and other rooms. There was a kind of innocence about their lovemaking in the grove and among the vines. There was a rawness to this. With the other girls it had, if anything, increased his ardour. But not with Hannah. With her he cherished that innocence.

He knew she felt the same. They made love only once, then took turns in the tub. Hannah soaked for half an hour. He knocked on the door and offered to soak her back but she said she preferred privacy at her bath. After all the times he had explored her body she was still modest about being seen naked when they weren't making love.

Somehow neither of them felt like going to Mount Carmel. It would probably be dead up there anyhow, Harris thought. There was a NAAFI Entertainments show on the stage at the Armon, *Hello Happiness Revue,* but Harris knew it wouldn't do to take Hannah among all those British uniforms.

They went back to the Arab quarter, which was bustling although the usually crowded cafés were closed for Ramadan, and bought cooked lamb, a roasted chicken, flat bread and, in a Christian shop, a bottle of wine. They took their purchases back to Aleenah in an Arab taxi for supper with Tante Frieda. Haifa had been a disappointment. Coming back to Aleenah was coming home.

CHAPTER XVI

It was another night raid on Tobruk.

When the target was announced, Harris and Gallegly looked at each other and then at Wagstaff. Wagstaff's face was composed. Harris felt his own face grow stiff. This would be Wags's last chance. Either he'd fly the bomb run like he was supposed to or they'd have to tell Beck.

The mission would be different from any other they had flown. The 108th was flying a diversion for an operation the briefing officer did not choose to describe. There were areas marked on the target map which under no circumstances were they to bomb. They included the harbour and a section just outside the town. Strangest of all, they were to orbit the ruined town and make a dozen separate bomb runs, dropping a single five hundred pounder each time. It was a joint mission with B-25s of the 12th Bomb Group, which would be operating several thousand feet below the heavies.

"Do they know we're dropping through 'em?" somebody asked.

Laughter.

The briefing officer let them chatter among themselves for half a minute about the unusual instructions before ordering them to simmer down and continuing with the briefing. If they saw evidence of naval activity off Tobruk they were to disregard it and were definitely not to bomb any surface vessel observed firing.

"They'll be friendly. And they won't be shooting at you. They'll know who you are. But don't fly over them. They're not that friendly."

It must be an amphibious landing they were flying the diversion for, Harris thought. Like the one in the Solomons. If the British took Tobruk they'd trap the whole goddam Afrika Korps. They'd finally got a mission where they were part of the ground action. Hot damn.

The crew bus was noisier than usual on the way out to the planes. Everyone was defending his own theory about the operation. It was a commando raid. An amphibious assault. A diversion to get Rommel's attention while Montgomery launched the real attack at El Alamein. Even that the attack from the sea was itself a diversion for the prolonged, deliberate bombing raid, the whole thing meant to shake Jerry and the Italians and make them think it was a whole mess of planes up there knocking the tar out of them.

"What do you think, Dan?" Silkwood asked.

"They don't pay us to think," Wagstaff said curtly.

Not like Wagstaff at all, not like the Wags Harris knew, or thought he had known. The real Wags would have said something that had everybody laughing. Harris could tell Gallegly was thinking the same thing.

Blonde Job was at altitude in the middle of a long stream of bombers invisible to each other in the night, heading for Tobruk from the desert side.

Everything had been fine so far. Maybe it would stay that way. Wags had to come through tonight and he knew it. Harris started thinking about Hannah instead of Wags between fixes. He was glad he hadn't taken her to the NAAFI stage show. After supper yesterday she had really started in on the English. Earlier in the week, Lord Moyne, deputy Minister of State for the Middle East, had said Palestine was already overcrowded and that the Jews were out for racial domination of the country. He'd proposed settling Jews in Madagascar as a solution.

"You see, Michael," she had demanded, "you see why we must arm ourselves?"

He hadn't argued. He knew better than to argue with Hannah. Anything he said in rebuttal just made him look more stupid about Palestine when she started showing him where he was wrong.

Next time they went to Haifa they wouldn't go to a hotel, he decided. They'd just eat and roam around and have fun. They'd take Tante Frieda with them. It wasn't fair to always be running off and leaving her sitting at home.

Gallegly called him on the interphone, interrupting his cozy reverie.

"Come back to the flight deck for a minute. Over."

Abrupt, non-committal.

Silkwood wheeled around on his stool. Harris couldn't see his eyes in the darkness but he knew they would be questioning. He unplugged earphones and throat mike, removed his oxygen mask and got the walkaround oxygen bottle. He scrambled to the flight deck wondering what it was all about, hoping it didn't have anything to do with Wags.

Trombatore stood behind the pilot positions between Wags and Gallegly, gripping the armour-plate,

285

outlined in the spectral blue fluorescent glow from the instrument panel. Harris reached past him and touched Gallegly's shoulder. Gallegly turned his black-snouted head and gestured for him to lean closer. Trombatore stepped back so he could lean between the seats. Gallegly pulled aside his oxygen mask, his face grim and eerie in the glow.

"Harris," he said above the roar of the engines, "I want you to listen to this."

Wagstaff looked straight ahead, as if fascinated by something going on outside the windshield, not acknowledging Harris's presence.

Gallegly motioned for Trombatore to come closer. He pulled his mask aside again and said, "Sergeant Trombatore, what's our fuel consumption?"

Sergeant Trombatore, not Trombone.

Trombatore looked at Wagstaff, his eyes troubled above his mask. Wagstaff kept looking straight ahead. The aerial engineer held his mask to the side.

"Two hundred gallons an hour, sir."

That was normal. Fifty gallons an hour per engine cruising at 155 knots indicated. What was Gallegly getting at?

"At the present rate of consumption, with what we have in the tanks, do we have fuel to complete this mission?"

Relentless.

Harris's belly knotted. He knew what Gallegly was getting at.

Trombatore looked beseechingly at Wagstaff. Wagstaff kept on looking at the windshield.

"I asked you a question, Sergeant."

Why did Gallegly have to be so iron-ass with Trombone? He'd never pulled any of that officer crap before.

"Lieutenant," Trombatore said angrily, "I'm just a sergeant. If Lieutenant Wagstaff . . ."

Gallegly didn't let him finish.

"I'm not asking what Lieutenant Wagstaff thinks," he snapped. "What do you think?"

"Yes, sir, Lieutenant," Trombatore snapped back. "We got enough."

"Thank you, Sergeant Trombatore." Less severe, "That's all, Trombone. No sweat, OK?"

"Yes sir," said Trombatore, unmollified.

After one quick last glance at Wagstaff he stalked back to the rear of the flight deck.

"What the hell was all that about?" Harris demanded, looking from Gallegly to Wagstaff and back again, hoping what he was thinking was wrong.

"Lieutenant Wagstaff says we're burning fuel too fast. He says we gotta abort."

"He should know," Harris said uncomfortably. "He's first pilot."

Knowing he was letting Gallegly down. But he couldn't turn against Wags. And Wags was first pilot, the one who had to make decisions. The one responsible for everybody on *Blonde Job*.

Wagstaff looked at him for the first time. He slipped aside his mask and said, "Thanks, Tex," his face ghastly in the blue glow.

"Jesus Christ!" Gallegly cried. "OK, abort, you son of a bitch. But I'm going straight to Major Beck."

"It's the first pilot's judgment," Wagstaff said stiffly.

It was the first time he'd ever pulled rank.

"Roger, boss. It's your judgment we're using too much gas. It's mine we ain't. And Trombone's. He knows this goddam ship better than both of us."

287

"That's a matter of opinion," Wagstaff said.

It was awful watching them argue. They were like two strangers, between angry words inscrutable behind their black masks.

"If Major Beck won't believe me I'll tell him to talk to Trombatore. And if Tromabore's afraid to tell him the truth, you're my witness to what he just said, Harris."

"Aw, come on, Gallegly," Harris said, feeling besieged, knowing he'd have to back Gallegly.

"Are you gonna lie for him and leave me out on a limb with Beck?" Gallegly demanded.

"No," said Harris.

They weren't going to turn back just because Wags had bad dreams. No matter how much he liked Wagstaff he wasn't going to let him screw up the rest of them. There were nine other men on the crew, every one of them ready and able to do the job they were sent to do. If Wags made them abort he wouldn't wait for Major Beck to ask him if Gallegly was telling the truth. He'd go to Beck with Gallegly.

"Wags?" he said, wanting to explain.

"Whose side are you on, anyway?" Wagstaff demanded.

"I'm not on anybody's side, God dammit! You know that. But if we abort . . . It's got to be your ass, not Terry's."

"When we run outta gas and wind up with Arabs coming out of our ass don't blame me."

"Do we abort or keep going?" Gallegly said implacably.

"All right!" Wagstaff yelled. "Screw both of you!"

A Wagstaff Harris didn't know. He would rather Wags had hit him than be like that.

Gallegly looked at Harris. "You with me, Tex?" Harris nodded.

"We won't have to tell Beck now, will we?" he said.

They could just tell Wags he had to ground himself. He could say high altitude bothered his ears or something. Then nobody would have to know but himself and Gallegly.

"I guess not. What a way to have to fight a goddam war!"

"I'd better get back to the office."

Nobody had been paying too much attention to the instruments during the argument. He'd shoot a quick fix and give Gallegly a new heading and ETA if they'd gotten off course. He took one last look at Wagstaff, hoping Wags had cooled off and understood it was something they'd had to do. Wags was sitting like a statue, arms folded across his chest, staring at the windshield.

Silkwood was waiting for him. He had to push Silkwood's legs out of the way to come out of the tunnel.

"What took you so long?" Silkwood shouted in his ear. "What did Terry want? Is something wrong?"

"Naw," said Harris. "Gallegly just wanted to shoot the breeze without tying up the interphone."

He hoped Silkwood never found out the truth. Silkwood worshipped Wags.

They picked out Tobruk some minutes before they were close enough to start the bomb run. A faint blush on the horizon, scattered clouds lit with searchlight beams. Then they could see the beams themselves, a tangle of probing, crisscrossing rays. Below them, fires burning, a tiny budding of red as someone's bomb hit. *Blonde Job* headed for the tangled lights.

Silkwood hunched over his bombsight.

"Bombardier to pilot. Follow the PDI."

Blonde Job plunged towards the searchlights and the pinpricks of muzzle flashes at their roots. Straight and level, steady as a train on a smooth road-bed. Gallegly was flying one hell of a run.

Into the searchlights. Beams caught them, let them go. Caught them again. And held. It was bright as midday in the nose. Harris could have counted the rivets.

"Oh, shit," someone groaned on the interphone.

It sounded like a prayer.

Harris realized he was holding his breath. When they had you in the searchlights they had you ranged. Down below, the eighty eights were taking aim. He was beginning to understand how Wags felt about flak. If they got out of this OK maybe Wags'd be cured.

"Bombardier to pilot. Bomb away."

Cool as a goddam iceberg. Bomb away, not bombs away. Like they were on a practice mission over the bombing range back at Albuquerque. How could somebody like Wagstaff be so scared and somebody like Silkwood not be? Maybe the dumb were just braver than the bright.

The words were scarcely out of Silkwood's mouth when *Blonde Job* racked to the right, diving. Right again. Then left, climbing. So steeply Harris fell back against his table. The metal rim bit into his buttocks. He grabbed his lamp to steady himself, let go before he ripped it loose. Still the searchlights clung. Flak blossomed off the left wing, a fleeting orange burst. Right, right, right, diving. A B-24 wasn't meant to dive like that. Climb. Steep. Too steep. *Blonde Job* faltered, mushed, stalled. Harris

290

floated up, weightless. His head touched the ceiling. For a moment he and Silkwood floated side by side, tethered to their stations by mike and earphone cords and oxygen tubes. Chute packs and a map hung in the nose. Harris's octant was suspended a foot above his table. He grabbed for it as the engines surged and the props dug into the thin air. *Blonde Job* steadied, levelled off. Everything fell to the floor in a heap. Harris, cradling his octant, landed on top of Silkwood.

In darkness.

Darkness! They were out of the searchlights. Gallegly had got them out of the lights. What a flying fool.

Orange bursts off to the left again. Closer than before. *Blonde Job* was flung to the side. Flung or was it Gallegly still taking evasive action?

She fell off to the right. Down, down. Oh, God, they were hit! Harris scrambled on the floor for his chute pack. Grabbed them both, thrust one at Silkwood, not knowing if they were over desert or sea. *Blonde Job* levelled off. All four props spinning. Far below, intermittent flashes lit the darkness, long smears, not the pinpricks of eighty eights firing up. They were over the sea and ships firing shoreward. And under control.

Harris plugged in his earphones. They had pulled free in the commotion.

". . . hurt. Call in."

Gallegly's urgent voice.

"Co-pilot to crew. Repeat. Anybody else hit? Dammit, report in!"

Anybody else? Somebody'd been hit!

Everybody was calling in at once. Tail gunner, OK. Right waist, OK.

"Navigator to pilot. OK in the nose. Who got hit?"

"Harris, gimme a heading for Fayid!"

"Who got hit, dammit?"

"Wags."

Wags! Oh, Jesus! They'd made him go.

"How bad?"

"Don't know. Goddammit, Harris, gimme that goddam heading!"

Silkwood shouldered Harris aside, grabbed the walkaround bottle from its clamps and ducked into the tunnel. Harris, in turmoil, turned on his light and scrabbled on the floor for his Weems plotter, computer and pencil. Everything on his desk had hit the floor after the stall. He made a quick estimate of their position off Tobruk, stabbed his pencil into the Mercator, broke the point and, cursing, bit wood from the tip and drew a blunt line to Fayid. Fayid was their alternate field. He always marked the alternate on his chart before a mission. He measured the angle with his Weems plotter, gave Gallegly the heading and asked about Wags.

"They're working on him. What's our ETA?"

Altitude, free air temperature, airspeed. They were indicating 195 knots now and letting down rapidly, getting down to where they wouldn't need oxygen, racing for Fayid. Harris spun his E6B, using his last known wind and an estimated altitude, and calculated the time to Fayid. He gave the ETA to Gallegly and plunged into the tunnel, bumping his head, scraping a knuckle. He was panting. In agitation, not for lack of oxygen. There was enough air to breathe easily now.

Wagstaff was stretched out with his head cradled in Silkwood's lap. Trombatore knelt beside them.

The assistant radio operator hovered over them. Gallegly was peering back at them around his armourplate. The radio operator was cranking handles on his set. The dim light at his position shed just enough illumination for Harris to take in everything. Wags's eyes were open, reflecting the light, and he couldn't see any blood. Maybe Wags wasn't hit too bad. Thank God!

"Wags?" he said.

Silkwood turned an anguished face. He was crying.

"He's dead," he said.

"Aw, no!"

Harris dropped to his knees beside Silkwood and looked into Wagstaff's face. Wagstaff looked surprised, and as if he were about to say something. A joke, maybe, about Silkwood not knowing what he was talking about. Wags wasn't dead. He didn't look dead. He couldn't be dead. He didn't even look like he'd been hit.

Silkwood pointed dumbly at Wagstaff's left temple. Just a little black smudge. Harris touched it. Wet and warm. Blood. Not enough to kill a big son of a bitch like Wags. He wiped his finger on his pants and put his ear to Wagstaff's chest. Nothing. He shifted the ear to Wagstaff's lips. They were wet. A big wet kiss from Big Wags to Tex Harris, who'd helped make him go to Tobruk. No movement, no breath, no nothing. He was dead, all right.

"God damn son of a bitching bastard!"

Cursing fate or cursing Wagstaff for letting himself get killed? Or cursing himself and Gallegly for what they had done. Gallegly was watching him, his face contorted with remorse.

"It's my fault," Gallegly said heavily.

Silkwood jerked his head around and looked at him, bewilderment fighting grief on his face. Harris shook his head at Gallegly, warning him to say no more. Silkwood was not to know, ever. Not because of his and Gallegly's part in it but so Silkwood would never know about Wagstaff. Nobody knew but Gallegly and Trombone and himself. Trombatore wouldn't talk. He'd liked Wags too.

Harris reached out, dry-eyed, and closed Wagstaff's eyes. Thinking, you dreamed wrong, Wags. Flak didn't shoot us down. It killed you but it didn't shoot us down. Remembered thinking nothing could happen to *Blonde Job* because Wags was a lucky pilot.

He helped Silkwood to his feet and sent him to sit in Wagstaff's place, saying, "You got to help Gallegly, Eddie. You're the only other one on the plane with any pilot time."

Knowing time in a basic trainer wasn't anything like time in a B-24. It was just to give Silkwood something to do. Gallegly only needed someone to call off altitude and airspeed when they landed. Trombatore could do that but it was better to let Silkwood.

He took someone's sheepskin-lined flying jacket and put it over Wagstaff's head and shoulders.

"Sir," the radio operator said, "I can't raise Fayid. Something's wrong with my set, I think."

"Keep trying," Harris said.

It didn't matter a whole lot. If they came in lit up and with the IFF on nobody'd be shooting at them at Fayid. And a red-red flare would clear the pattern.

He hoped Gallegly wouldn't mind him telling Silkwood and the radio operator what to do. Gallegly was plane commander now. Until they landed anyhow.

He went to Silkwood, sitting in Wagstaff's place, and put a comforting hand on his shoulder. Silkwood was gripping the wheel with both hands, his feet planted solidly on the rudder pedals. He'd moved the seat to fit his reach. Silkwood took whatever he did so seriously. Harris hoped he wasn't bothering Gallegly too much. Gallegly had enough on his mind.

There was a small starred hole in the window above Silkwood's head. Where Wagstaff's head had been. It couldn't have been much of a piece of flak that killed him. Such a tiny piece to kill such a big man. If Wags had been a couple of inches shorter he wouldn't be lying back there dead. If. If he and Gallegly hadn't made Wags keep going. You could if yourself to death.

He leaned around the right side of Gallegly's armour-plate, the side away from Silkwood.

"I told Silkwood to sit there," he said. "I hope he's not messing you up."

Gallegly shook his head.

"You OK, Terry?"

Gallegly nodded. Harris wished he would say something instead of just moving his head.

"It's my fault as much as yours," Harris said. "But it's not anybody's fault. Just a lousy break, that's all. You sure did one hell of a job getting us out of the lights."

Wanting to keep talking until he got some kind of response out of Gallegly and knew he was all right.

"That was Wags," Gallegly said. "When I couldn't get us out he took over."

A strange kind of joy pierced Harris's grief. While he'd been paralyzed with fear in the nose, Wags had responded like a champion. Doing what a first pilot was supposed to do. If he hadn't been hit he'd have been OK forever after. Harris took poignant comfort in the thought.

"I'm sure glad," he said.

"Yeah," said Gallegly. "At least he died flying."

The bombs, Harris thought. They still had eleven five hundred pounders aboard.

"What'll we do about the bombs?" he said.

"What bombs? Oh. Thanks. I'll jettison 'em."

The pilots could release the bombs from their position.

"Let Silkwood, why don't you?"

Gallegly nodded.

Harris went back to Silkwood.

"You better jettison the bombs, Eddie," he said. "You OK now?"

"I think so."

He started to cry again.

Harris gripped his shoulder.

"Dammit, Silkwood! He'd really be pissed off if he knew you were sitting there crying like a baby."

"Sorry. I'm OK."

Silkwood wiped his eyes and nose on his leather jacket and gripped the wheel again. Eyes fixed on the instruments, playing pilot.

Harris went back to the nose without waiting to watch the bombs hit. He'd better shoot a fix and get a wind, figure a new heading and ETA.

Holding his penlight between his teeth he picked up everything that had fallen on the floor. He shot a methodical three star fix, trying not to think about old Wags lying dead on the flight deck with a jacket over his face. One lousy little piece of flak had changed everything. Except the stars. They never changed. Only the wind. And the stars told you when it did. But they didn't tell you Wagstaff was going to die.

A knuckle burned. He looked at it. Scraped, with a thin crust of dried blood. When the hell had he done that?

He plotted the fix, got a wind, figured the heading and ETA for Fayid. They'd be there in an hour and forty-eight minutes. He started to call Gallegly. Instead, he measured the distance to Ramat Jonas and figured an ETA for their own field. Why did they have to go to Fayid anyhow? There was nothing anyone could do for Wags now. Even the way they were burning fuel at 190 knots they should have enough to make it back home. For sure if they throttled back to 155 or 160, the speed they usually cruised at.

"Navigator to pilot, go ahead."

"Pilot to navigator, go ahead."

It was Silkwood. Taking being in the left seat seriously. Harris would have laughed if Wags hadn't been lying back there dead.

"What is it, Tex?" Gallegly broke in.

Harris asked him about going to Ramat Jonas. Gallegly had Trombatore check the gauges and said fine. Harris gave him the new heading and ETA based on cruising at 160 knots. The radio operator couldn't raise Ramat Jonas. He could send but not receive.

Harris kept shooting fixes to keep his mind off Wagstaff. It didn't work. He kept thinking about him, back there dead. If Wags had had his way they'd already be back home. Maybe in the sack. Not in the sack. Waiting for Beck to land so they could spill their guts to him and dip Wags in the crap. They wouldn't have to do that now. Harris despised himself for the brief measure of relief it gave him. At least for all Beck or anybody else would ever know Wags was one flying son of a bitch who'd got them out of the searchlights over Tobruk. He might even get a posthumous medal. He'd plant the idea in Beck's head if he could. Maybe it was better for Wags this way. He'd be a hero instead of a disgrace to the uniform. Like hell. Nobody wanted to die.

Either way, dead or alive, Wags wouldn't have been their pilot any more after this mission. Beck would have grounded his butt, maybe even had him court-martialled. It wasn't going to seem right, flying with another pilot. But they'd have to. The war wasn't going to stop just because Big Wags had bought it. Maybe Beck would move Gallegly into the left seat and get him a co-pilot. Gallegly had the time to be a first pilot, and Wags had let him shoot a lot of landings and takeoffs. He wondered if Gallegly was sitting back there thinking the same thing, knowing if the thought had occurred to Gallegly he'd be feeling guilty as hell about it. Climbing into the left seat over Wags's dead body, thinking it was all his fault Wags was dead in the first place. Just as he was feeling guilty for wondering who would be *Blonde Job*'s next pilot with Wags not cold yet.

Would he have the guts to tell Hannah he and Gallegly had made Wags finish the mission that got him killed? Hannah. He hadn't thought about her since Gallegly called him to the flight deck. It had been weeks since he'd gone that long without thinking about her. He'd lost Wags but he still had Hannah. It gave him unexpected comfort. Hannah was more important to him than Wags, disloyal as that might be. More important than anybody. He knew that now. Maybe he'd known it a long time and just wouldn't admit it to himself. If he got through this war alive, and he was going to, he was going to marry Hannah.

Suddenly he was consumed with impatience to tell her so. When they got down he was going to Aleenah, no matter how late it was. He needed desperately to tell her. He did not know why but somehow it would keep him from feeling so bad about Wags.

He went back to the flight deck earlier than usual, wanting to be with Gallegly. Someone had covered Wags completely. He was just a pile of jackets on the deck. Just before letdown, when the radio operator began reeling in the trailing antenna, they found out why the radio had conked out. There was only a few feet of wire. The rest had been shot off by flak.

Trombatore loaded a red-red into the flare pistol and slid back the window by Silkwood, the one with a hole in it. The slipstream rushing in the opening made a sucking, whistling noise. Two crimson balls arched out into the darkness.

Trouble aboard.

Gallegly greased her in as carefully as if he were afraid of breaking Wagstaff. Silkwood called off altitude and airspeed in a firm, even voice. Harris hoped he wouldn't start crying again. It would embarrass everybody, Silkwood most of all.

The crash truck and an ambulance sped towards them as *Blonde Job* was coming out of her roll. They drove along beside the plane as she taxied, horns honking, sirens going, red lights flashing, a spotlight playing over wings, engines and fusilage looking for trouble. Someone in the crash truck yelled out of a window but they couldn't tell what he was saying above the noise of the engines.

Gallegly taxied all the way to the revetment. A few more minutes wouldn't make any difference to Wagstaff and *Blonde Job* had to be out of the way when the other ships came back.

A ground officer was waiting angrily when they climbed out of the bomb bays. He stood in the headlights, his face alternately red and white as the lights atop the ambulance and crash truck flashed

"You better have a damn good reason for that red-red flare with nothing wrong!" he cried. "Who's the pilot of this plane?"

"Shut up, you son of a bitch," Silkwood said.

Harris would not have been more surprised if Wags had come walking out.

The ground officer's mouth flew open, then closed with a snap. He was a captain.

"He's dead," Gallegly said flatly.

The ground officer looked embarrassed.

"Jesus," he said. "I'm sorry. Where's the . . . where is he?"

"Flight deck," Gallegly said.

The ground officer turned to the ambulance crew. "Dead man on the flight deck. Bring him out."

"No!" Silkwood cried. "I will."

"You'll need help," said Harris.

He, Gallegly, Trombatore and Silkwood brought Wagstaff out, he and Silkwood at the shoulders, Gallegly and Trombatore at the feet. Wags felt like he weighed a thousand pounds, and cumbersome as a loosely-filled sack. They had to back and twist like furniture movers to get him through the door into the bomb bay and almost dropped him trying to work him between the struts on the catwalk.

"Lieutenant Wagstaff, is it?" the captain said. "How did it happen?"

"Flak," said Gallegly.

"They had us ranged in the searchlights," Harris said. "He got hit right after he flew us out of 'em."

Wanting to start working on Wagstaff's medal. That was the least he could do for Wags. And the most.

"I counted twenty-three holes," the captain said. "You were damn lucky nobody else got hit."

Lucky for us, Harris thought. Not for Wags.

He looked back at *Blonde Job*. Her pink side was flecked with ragged holes, the largest no bigger than a baseball. The voluptuous blonde had a new black navel, slightly misplaced.

The ambulance men loaded Wagstaff into their vehicle as gently as if he were hurt and bleeding instead of already dead. *Blonde Job*'s crew watched in sombre, intent silence. The doors closed and the ambulance drove away, its dim red tail lights diminishing. So long, Wags, Harris said to himself. He was never going to see Big Wags again. His eyes teared. He winked them back angrily.

The ground officer stood with one foot in the crash truck, turned as if to say something, didn't, got in and slammed the door. The truck sped away.

They climbed into the empty waiting crew bus. No one said anything until they got to the mess hall and sat around a long table over coffee, telling Wagstaff stories in low voices.

"Remember that time . . . ?"

"Remember how he . . . ?"

Wags was already a memory. And would become a legend, Harris knew.

It was a while before the other planes started

landing. Twelve bomb runs took time. The returning crews would come into the mess hall full of loud talk about the mission and then fall silent when told about Wagstaff. Major Beck's plane was one of the last to get in.

"Why's everybody sitting around like a bunch'a sick mules?" Beck demanded. Looking at Harris, "Where's that overgrown pilot of yours? He'll pep things up."

"He's dead, sir," Harris said.

Major Beck went stock still, as if somebody had hit him with a baseball bat.

Then he started bawling. Just like Silkwood.

CHAPTER XVII

The sun was lifting off a distant hilltop by the time they got back to the tents. Harris told Silkwood to move in with them for a while and helped him bring over his cot and mosquito net. The cot just fitted in crossways at the end of the tent.

It was difficult sleeping because of the daytime sounds, the heat and thinking about Wags being dead. Harris had gotten over his impulse to rush over to Aleenah right away and ask Hannah to marry him but he hadn't changed his mind. He was still going to ask her. But he wasn't leaving Silkwood until he was sure Silkwood was OK, and he had to keep telling Gallegly it wasn't his fault as long as Gallegly needed to hear it.

Major Beck woke them up and told them to go with him to Wagstaff's tent and get his personal effects together.

"I'm not gonna let any goddam groundgripper root around in his stuff," Beck said.

Harris had told him how Wags had flown them out of the searchlights and Beck said he was putting him in for the Silver Star. Not the DFC, because he had already put the whole crew in for that. *Blonde Job*'s crew had the most combat hours of any crew in the 108th. Harris hadn't known Beck gave a damn about that. He'd thought Beck was just picking on them, giving them almost every mission the 234th flew.

Silkwood let a few tears slip out furtively when they went through Wagstaff's footlocker but he didn't cry. He was too afraid of Major Beck to do that in front of him. Beck had cried himself the night before but right now you couldn't tell he'd ever shed a tear in his life. He was as gruff and ornery as ever.

They found 12,00 dollars in Palestine pounds and traveller's cheques with different signatures on them. Wagstaff's dice winnings.

"I wonder if the big son of a bitch really cheated?" Major Beck said.

"Dan didn't cheat!" Silkwood said fiercely.

"How would you know?" Beck said with astonishing mildness.

"He was just lucky," Harris said.

Yeah, lucky enough to catch a hunk of flak in the head.

Beck divided the money equally between Harris and Gallegly and told them to send it to Wagstaff's folks a little at a time so the envelopes wouldn't be too thick.

"Damned if we're gonna let some groundgripper get his paws on it," Beck said.

He said he'd see to it personally that Wagstaff's watch and UCLA ring got home.

Two enlisted men came in a jeep to pick up Wagstaff's footlocker and duffle bag. Beck made them list everything that wasn't government issue and give him a copy.

While they were making the list, Harris said, "Sir, what's gonna happen to us now?"

Wags was dead but the war was still on. The crew would be getting a new first pilot and it ought to be Gallegly.

"You'll stand down a few days while *Blonde Job*'s getting patched up." Beck looked at a broad thumb as if there was a message written on it. "Group's starting four day passes for combat crews. You guys can take yours whenever you want."

Sounding like he was afraid somebody might take him for nice, Harris thought.

"Yes, sir. That's swell. But I meant about our first pilot. Gallegly's got a lot of time. And Wags was always letting him take off and land. Fly bomb runs too."

Gallegly and Silkwood tried to pretend they weren't listening intently. Beck just glared at Harris a long moment.

"I want any advice outta you, Harris, I'll kick it outta you," he said at last.

Oh, hell, Harris thought. If Gallegly ever had a chance he didn't now. He'd really screwed things up trying to be helpful. He should have known better than say anything to that mean bastard.

The enlisted men finished making their list and gave a copy to Beck. He made them wait until he'd checked everything on it.

"If one goddam thing don't get home they're gonna be some asses in slings," he said.

He started out of the tent, stopped and looked sourly at Gallegly.

"Don't go running off to Haifa tomorrow," he said. "I'm taking you up for a check ride."

He stalked out before anybody could say anything.

"Thanks, Tex," Gallegly said, without joy.

Harris knew he wanted to be first pilot but was

deeply troubled by the way he got his chance.

"You really think we'll get the DFC?" Silkwood said eagerly. "If I got the DFC, my father . . ."

"Sure," said Harris.

Right now getting a medal did not seem very important. He hadn't done anything to earn the Distinguished Flying Cross anyhow. Just gone along for the ride and done his job. Just like everybody else. Doing what he was told the best way he knew how. There wasn't anything all that distinguished about squinting through an A-7 octant and keeping a neat log. He was surprised Beck had put them in. It had to be because they flew with Wags. They were a hell of a good crew though. And Beck knew it. Maybe after he quit feeling so bad about Wags he'd appreciate the medal the way he ought to.

They hung around their own tent for the rest of the day. The enlisted men from the crew came over two or three at a time and sat around with them. One of them had a whole quart of Johnny Walker he'd been nursing ever since they left Morrison Field. They passed the bottle around taking little nips, nobody wanting to take more than his share. Silkwood had only one, ceremoniously, gagging on it. It reminded Harris of the time they sat up all night with Wags after that first raid on Mersa Metruh. He knew now why Wags had made them sit up with him. He'd been scared by the flak even on that easy mission and unnerved by the discovery. Wanting to reassure himself with a celebration.

Trombatore was the first to come over and the last to leave. Harris could tell from the way the crew acted he hadn't said anything about what happened on the way to Tobruk. They told more Wagstaff stories, laughing over them now instead of moping

306

as they had in the mess hall.

"Remember the time at Belem the monkey stole his musette bag and Big Wags chased him halfway across the field to get it back?" said Trombatore. "I thought I'd bust a gut."

"Y'all should've seen him throwing those three limeys around in Haifa," said Harris. "Then helped 'em get away from the MPs."

"He had guts," the tail gunner said. "Nobody had guts like Big Wags."

That made Harris feel good. It was what everybody thought about Wags but him and Gallegly and nobody was ever going to know anything different.

It was the first time the tail gunner had joined the conversation. Harris wondered if all tail gunners were like theirs. Quiet. Sort of apart from the rest of the crew the way tail gunners were on missions. Crouched back there all alone in the turret, not knowing what was going on with the others, the interphone their only link with the rest of the crew. The loneliest position of all was when a tail gunner's plane was tail end Charley, flying wingman on the last ship in the last element, nothing to look at but nothing. Except sometimes flak and fighters.

"Lieutenant Harris," Trombatore said. "Has Major Beck said anything about who's gonna be our first pilot? We were wondering if he's gonna promote Lieutenant Gallegly into the left seat. It wouldn't be right to bring in somebody new."

The other listened attentively and nodded agreement, as if they had talked it over and Trombatore was their spokesman. Maybe Gallegly wouldn't feel so lousy now. They'd all been wondering the same thing. It wasn't like he was the only one.

They were relieved when Harris told them Gal-

legly would be *Blonde Job's* pilot if he got by Major
Beck's check ride the next day. Which he would.
Gallegly was a good pilot. Not as good as Wags,
Wags was the best, but as good as any other pilot in
the 234th.

Officers from other crews dropped by from time
to time to say how sorry they were about Wagstaff,
not knowing what to make of it when they saw
everybody laughing. Silkwood began perking up in a
melancholy sort of way. It was the most people who
had ever been nice to him in his whole life. Harris
knew he didn't have to worry about him any more.
Or Gallegly either. Once it sank in it wasn't his fault
about Wags and he was used to being first pilot he'd
be fine. They'd all be fine. In a few more days it
would be like Wags was just passing through. It was
kind of sad.

Hannah knew right away something bad had happened. He flung his arms around her the moment
she opened the door without even saying *"Shalom"*
and clung to her wordlessly.

"What is wrong?" she said, freeing herself.

"Is it Michael?" Tante Frieda called from the back.

"Wagstaff got killed last night," he said, feeling
callous because it didn't hurt as much to say it as it
would have a few hours ago.

"Liebe Gott!" Hannah said. "My poor *Liebchen.*"

She led him to the couch as Tante Frieda came
out of the kitchen smiling and wiping her hands on
her apron, her expression changing to concern when
she saw their long faces. Thinking, Harris was sure,
there was something wrong between him and Hannah.

308

"Michael's good friend has been killed," Hannah said.

Harris had grown so accustomed to hearing German he was hardly aware she had not spoken in English. Tante Frieda shook her head and made a clucking sound. Harris sensed her sympathy, but also her relief. Her chief concern was that nothing should hurt her little Hannah. He felt a stab of anger at her reaction but got over it quickly. She'd never even seen Wags, just heard him talk about him. How could he expect her to be broken up about it when his own grief was already blunted less than a day after seeing Wags dead on the flight deck? Almost before he was cold conniving to get his job for Gallegly. And if Hannah mattered more to him than Wagstaff did it should come as no surprise to him that she mattered even more to Tante Frieda.

"You were not wounded?" Tante Frieda said anxiously.

Harris shook his head. Not physically, anyhow. Or any other way, at least not as much as he should be.

"Thank God for that," Tante Frieda said.

She went back to the kitchen.

"How did it happen?" Hannah asked.

Harris told her everything, except about them forcing Wags to continue the mission. About Wags getting them out of the lights, about the tiny hole in the window and the tiny piece of flak that killed him, about carrying him out through the bomb bay and Silkwood and Major Beck crying.

"How awful for you," Hannah said.

"It was worse for Wagstaff," he said harshly.

And with some heat. She had touched a nerve. He *had* thought it was awful for him. It was ignoble. To have felt like that when he was partly responsible,

309

when it wasn't him who'd been killed.

"Do not be angry with me, *Liebchen*. But if anything should happen to you . . ."

So contrite, so shaken by the knowledge he'd come so close to death. Aware that no matter how light he made of his work the prospect of death was always there. More like just another girl than a member of an underground group doing dangerous work herself. Hell, she had more guts than he did. He flew missions because it was his job. Everybody approved of what he did. He was even getting a medal for it. If the British caught Hannah, they would put her in prison for life. Most of her own people even believed what she was doing was wrong. If they knew about it at all. The ones believing in cooperating with the British while the war was on. One thing for sure, when the war was over neither one of them was going to have to worry about the other one.

"Hannah," he said, his chest constricting at the thought of the irrevocable step he was about to take. "Hannah, I've been thinking . . ."

Don't beat around the goddam bush, Harris. Come right out and say it.

"After the war . . . Dammit, after the war I think we ought to get married."

She was surprised but less so than he had expected. And, at first, silent. He was disappointed. He had expected a greater display of emotion. An outpouring of affection. Even gratitude.

"I would like that very much," she said quietly, at last. "If you are sure that is what you want."

"Sure I'm sure. Aren't you?"

Wondering if this was her way of telling him she wasn't so sure. But it didn't make sense. She wanted to get married as much as he did.

"Yes. But I was afraid . . ."

She didn't say what she was afraid of. Maybe that he really didn't love her as much as he claimed to. Not enough to get married, anyhow.

He told her how Wags getting killed had made him realize how much she meant to him. More than anything else in his life. How if he weren't in the service they would get married right away. Overseas you couldn't get married without special permission from your CO. And anyway, it didn't seem right to get married before his folks even had a chance to meet her. Not to get their approval, because it was his decision, not theirs, and they were sure to love her as much as he did. Just because he owed them that much. Hannah agreed.

"Maybe even before the war's over," Harris said. "If I get home on leave or something. I'll send for you and we can . . ."

Something in her face stopped him.

"What is it?" he said.

"This is my home. I cannot leave Aleenah."

"I thought you wanted to marry me."

"I do. Oh, so very much. But my place is here, with Tante Frieda."

"I've thought about that. She can live with us."

"She would leave Palestine no more than I."

"Do you want to get married after the war or not?"

He was getting just a little peeved with her. He hadn't expected any objections.

"Yes, but . . ."

"It's settled, then."

"I am afraid not, Michael. When the war is over for you it may only be beginning for me. I will be needed here more than ever."

"Needed? What are you talking about? I need you."

"Eretz Israel will need me more."

"Eretz Israel can get along without you. What difference does one girl make?"

"It makes a great deal of difference to me."

She was getting as annoyed as he.

"You trying to tell me you won't live in the States even if we get married? I thought . . ."

"Must we quarrel, *Liebchen?* So much can happen."

She was backing down. He knew she would.

"OK," he said.

He gave her his Rice ring to wear, hoping no one back at the field would notice it was gone. He wasn't going to tell anyone but Gallegly. They told Tante Frieda they were engaged and she kissed him on both cheeks, delighted but not surprised.

"I thought it would be sooner," she said.

There was a different quality to their lovemaking that night. As if there were no need to be secretive or make as much of every moment as they could. As if they were already married. Harris could tell from the way she responded to him there would be no more of that nonsense about not living in the States.

"You have changed so very much," Hannah said comfortably.

"I know. I'll admit the only thing I had on my mind at first was getting you into the sack. I never thought . . ."

"It is more than that. Much more. You were just another American. Not like a Jew at all. But now . . . now I think you will grow to love Aleenah as much as I."

He sat up.

"What?" he said.

"When the war is over and we are married."

"I told you. We're gonna live in the States. In Houston."

"A moment ago you were so . . . I thought at last you understood."

"Understood what?"

"My place is here. Our place is here."

"Let's get one thing straight, Hannah. When I get back home I'm sending you and Tante Frieda tickets and we're getting married and living in the States. You'll love it. Once you get used to it."

"No, my Michael."

"What do you mean, no, dammit!"

"Try to understand. Eretz Israel will need us."

"*You* try to understand. We're not gonna spend the rest of our lives in this dinky little town a thousand miles from nowhere. Being goddam fieldhands."

"But I thought you were so happy here."

"I was. I am. Because there's a war on and this is where I am and I'd rather be working with you and Tante Frieda than moping around the officers' club or chasing tail in Haifa. But when the war's over I want to get back to real life."

"And this is not real life?"

"Not for me."

"Perhaps you have made a mistake, then."

"What do you mean, a mistake?"

"Saying we will be married."

"Are you saying we won't?"

No answer.

"Hannah? You telling me we won't if I don't do like you say?"

"*Liebchen* . . ."

"Is that what you mean?"

"Must you make it seem an ultimatum?"

313

"That's what it is, isn't it?"

"If you make it so."

Reluctant but committed.

"You're damn right I'm making it so."

If anybody was laying down an ultimatum it was going to be Tex Harris. He'd offered to marry her and it was going to be on his terms, not hers. Who the hell did she think she was?

"There is nothing more to be said then?"

A sad, simple question.

"That's right."

Take it or leave it, Hannah. She wasn't about to leave it.

She gathered up her clothes and began putting them on.

"It is very late," she said heavily. "Tomorrow there is so much to be done."

He followed her to the house, seething, hurt, neither of them speaking.

"You'll change your mind," he said when he kissed her good night. "You'll see."

Only her lips responded, the rest of her held back as if she did not trust herself to stick to her decision. Stubborn. Stubborn as a donkey. *Esel.* Only it wasn't anything to joke about now.

"You'll see," he said again.

She pressed something into his hand and closed his fingers on it, something cool and hard. His ring. She meant it. She really meant it.

He stumbled on a rut in the dirt road. Kicked the ground savagely. Wagstaff killed and now this. Not anything like he expected. Everything had gone wrong since yesterday. Wags dead. Instead of being crazy about the idea of moving to the States, Hannah expecting him to live in Palestine. If that's what

314

she expected she was going to have one hell of a long wait.

Hurt and disappointment fed his anger. Who the hell did she think she was? To hell with you, Hannah Ruh. It made a bitter little rhyme. To hell with you, Han-nah Ruh.

His anger abated, leaving him desolate. Then less so. They'd had a fight. So what. Just a lovers' quarrel. She was probably in her room crying right now, wishing she hadn't been so stubborn, knowing she was wrong and hoping he'd give her another chance. Anybody with a grain of sense would rather live in the United States than a country like this. And Hannah wasn't dumb. She'd realize that when she had time to think it over. Tomorrow they'd make up and be closer than ever.

Han-nah Ruh, I love you. It sounded much better than to hell with you.

He dreamed that Wagstaff was alive. He came into the tent asking where the hell everybody had been all day. Harris woke up joyous, bursting to tell Gallegly and Silkwood the good news, stared into the darkness and knew it had only been a dream. Wags was dead all right. And Hannah wasn't coming to the States to marry him. He couldn't change Wags being dead but he could change Hannah's mind. He'd go over there the first thing in the morning and get it settled. No, better to wait until night. Give her a few more hours to stew and worry about his maybe not coming. And it would be a lot more fun making up at night. Out among the vines.

After breakfast Major Beck took Gallegly up in *Wrecking Crew* to check him out. The whole crew turned out to watch them take off. Gallegly was in the left seat. He didn't even look out to see them

315

waving at him. Beck made him wring *Wrecking Crew* out as much as a B-24 could be wrung out. Stalls, steep banking turns, airborne engine stops and starts, one touch-and-go landing after another. Once Major Beck feathered Number 3 on the final approach and had Gallegly land on three engines. A good way to get them both killed if Gallegly hadn't been such a good pilot, Harris thought.

Wrecking Crew stayed in sight of the field most of the time. By the time the check ride was over, it looked as if half the two squadrons stationed there was outside watching the show, groundgrippers as well as aircrew.

Gallegly came crawling out of the bomb bay exhausted and running with sweat. Major Beck was sweating, too, and looked mad. That didn't mean anything, though. He always looked mad. And sweated a lot.

"I guess you didn't kill me," he said. "That's something. You probably can't fly formation worth a popcorn fart."

"Wags always split the time with him," Harris said.

Beck ignored him. Harris found that encouraging. If Beck was really sore he'd have chewed him out.

"We'll find out the next mission *Blonde Job* flies," Beck said. "If I can find me somebody dumb enough to want to fly co-pilot with you."

Everybody gathered around Gallegly and started shaking his hand. Gallegly was self-conscious, trying not to show too much enthusiasm. Harris knew he was thinking about why it all happened.

It would be a few days before they flew their next mission. Beck said he wanted them to get their four day pass out of the way first.

Silkwood wanted to go to Jerusalem. The Holy

City. That was where everybody wanted to go when they had a few days off. There or Tel Aviv. Gallegly was undecided. He could shack up with his girl in Haifa but wasn't sure he could endure her steady company that long.

"You can log just so much dual sack time," he said.

Harris knew there was more to it than that. Haifa held memories of Wags. They would all rather go somewhere they hadn't been with him.

"Tel Aviv, I guess," Gallegly said.

They both looked at Harris.

"It wouldn't be right to be in the Holy Land and not see the Holy City, would it, Tex?" Silkwood said.

"I don't care," said Harris. "It's up to Gallegly. He's the pilot."

He really didn't want to go anywhere until he'd straightened things out with Hannah. What would be perfect would be if she could get away for a few days and go on leave with him. Haifa, Jerusalem, Tel Aviv. Anywhere. It didn't matter as long as she was with him. And if she was still set on staying in Palestine it would give him four whole days to change her mind.

"Please, Terry," Silkwood implored.

"OK," said Gallegly. "Jerusalem."

Hannah was formal and tentative at first, and hopeful. Her eyes were shadowed, as if she had not slept. Harris could tell from Tante Frieda's troubled face Hannah had told her about their problem.

"Wouldn't you like to live in the States, Tante Frieda?" he said in almost faultless German.

Dr. Freund would have been proud of him, and

astonished, Harris thought.

"My Karl is buried here," she said. "Hannah must decide for herself."

No help there.

"Ask her if she could spare you for a few days," he said to Hannah, the German for that being beyond him.

"I do not understand."

"I've got a four day pass. Starting tomorrow. We could go to Jerusalem. Or maybe Tel Aviv."

Even if they were engaged he didn't know if she would want Gallegly and Silkwood tagging along. If the others went to Jerusalem they could go to Tel Aviv.

He could see the idea pleased her.

But she said, "I cannot."

Regretfully.

"Go ahead. Ask her."

"It is not that. I must . . . Tomorrow night."

That goddam Gyorgy again.

"I'll wait. We'll still have three days."

"I will not return before Friday."

"Oh, damn."

This was only Tuesday. His leave would end Sunday. But even two nights together would be something. They could at least go to Haifa.

"Then I'll just have to wait until Friday," he said. Silkwood and Gallegly could just go without him.

"I do not think so, Michael."

"Why, for God's sake!"

Tante Frieda was looking from one to the other, troubled, unable to follow the conversation in English but knowing they were arguing.

"When we are alone," Hannah said, mysterious, ominous.

318

She would not go to their trysting place after Tante Frieda went to bed. At first she did not even want him to kiss her, stiffening, averting her face. As on the first night he tried.

"What is it?" he demanded.

"It is too painful?"

"What's too painful?"

"Knowing . . . *Liebchen*, I must not see you again."

"What the hell are you talking about?"

"We want different things."

"We want each other."

"Not enough to change."

"We can work it out. Dammit, Hannah, don't be so goddam stubborn!"

Esel. Esel. Esel.

"Is it only I who is stubborn, my Michael?"

Sad but unyielding.

He could see talk wasn't going to do any good. Ignoring her early resistance, he made fervid, unrelenting love to her on the couch, not caring about Tante Frieda sleeping in a back room. When her fervour matched his he whispered fiercely, "Now say you won't see me again!"

But later, spent and grave, she said, "That was the last time for us."

"It can't be!"

"It must be. Better now than later. Last night, when you left me . . . Last night for one moment I thought, I will give up everything and go with you. It frightened me to learn my resolve was so fragile." Determined, "I will not be so weak again!"

The protest died on his lips. Somehow he knew she would not be swayed. Not by words, not by passion. He could not compete with whatever dream she had for the future. A future that did not include

319

him. He felt no anger, only bereavement.

She hadn't said she didn't love him any more. He could take some comfort in that.

CHAPTER XVIII

He woke up Gallegly and said, "Let's go to Beirut instead."

He had to get out of Palestine, put more than miles between himself and Aleenah and Hannah. There would be nothing in Beirut to remind him of her. The Arab who had picked him up on the way to Nahariyah . . . Nahariyah, where it had begun, kissing her salty lips, having fun together . . . the Arab had said it was very French. No rationing like in Palestine, fine restaurants, beautiful women. He didn't know if he could get interested in any other woman, not right now. But he could try. It might help. Nothing helped you forget a woman like another woman.

"What the hell time is it?" Gallegly said, surly at being woken.

Silkwood sat bolt upright and said tremulously, "Yes, father?"

"Go back to sleep," said Harris.

"Oh," Silkwood said. "I thought I was . . . What time is it?"

"Why does everybody want to know the goddam time?" Harris snapped. He looked at the watch with local time, the one with a luminous dial. "Eleven fourteen. You want a time hack, gimme a goddam flashlight and I'll tell you."

"What are you so sore about?" Gallegly demanded, lifting the mosquito net out of his way. "Why Beirut all of a sudden? I thought you wanted to go to Jerusalem."

Harris told him the good things he'd heard about Beirut.

"And it's as close as Jerusalem," he said. "Just up the coast. An easy hitch."

Probably as easy as Jerusalem anyhow. Hitch-hiking was going to be harder now. It was just their luck that at midnight the night before private cars had been taken off the roads in Palestine, except for those with special licences for certain police officers, doctors, industrialists in the war effort and agricultural technicians. It was supposed to be because of the petrol shortage. Harris had wondered if that were the real reason or if it were aimed at the Jewish underground. He'd meant to ask Hannah about it but never got the chance. They'd talked about more important things.

Gallegly thought Beirut was a swell idea.

"Aw, come on, fellows," Silkwood complained. "You said we were going to Jerusalem."

"It's in Palestine," Harris said. "Don't you want to see a new country?"

"We may not get another chance to see the Holy City."

"Two against one," Gallegly said. "You're outvoted."

"If my father found out I had a chance to go to the Holy City and didn't . . ."

"Lie about it," said Harris.

"To my father!"

322

He was shocked.

Silkwood came close to tears when he realized they were determined to go to Beirut but he was adamant about going to Jerusalem even if he had to do it alone. Harris felt bad about that. He didn't think Silkwood could manage on his own. But, when Silkwood could not be persuaded to change his mind, he was not terribly sorry. It was enough to have Hannah and Wags weighing on his mind without Silkwood to look after.

They packed carefully, taking no more than would fit into their musette bags. They took uniforms that had come in their footlockers, Harris field green shirt and trousers, Gallegly pink sports shirt and trousers, and a minimum of other gear. They left their sidearms under their bedrolls and wore their money belts under British bush jackets. Harris packed Silkwood's musette bag for him and tried one last time to persuade him to go with them, giving up when he realized Silkwood was battening on martyrdom. Silkwood watched them go, looking orphaned.

There were hardly any civilian cars on the road but they got a ride into Haifa on a GI truck from their own airfield. They went to Barclays to buy Syrian pounds. The manager sent them to the British military finance office farther down Kingsway. The shops were open and Haifa was lively. Harris wished he could bring Hannah here on a week day instead of always on Saturday, remembering he wouldn't be bringing her any day.

One Palestine pound bought eight Syrian pounds at the finance office, an American dollar, two. They were flimsy, gaudy notes, the higher the denomination the bigger and gaudier the bill. Their wallets bulged. They felt newly rich.

The finance officer suggested they go to the Royal Army transport office near the railway station down by the harbour. There might be something going to Beirut. A two-pip lieutenant at the transport office said there was nothing scheduled, eyed their wings, pursed his lips, and picked up the phone and ordered a sedan for them. He could not have been more obliging. The British were like that, Harris thought, Hannah's opinion not withstanding.

Their driver was an Arab, a wrinkled old man who looked as if he would be more at home on a camel. He spoke some English but was not sociable. Not like the refugee taxi drivers Harris was accustomed to. It didn't matter. Harris didn't think he could tell them much about the pleasures of Beirut.

When they passed Nahariyah, Harris thought about Hannah with cruelly intense yearning but as they pressed northward his mood lightened. He always perked up when he was going somewhere he'd never been before.

Beyond Nahariyah the road skirted the sea along white cliffs patchy with scrub. If it weren't for the blue Mediterranean off to their left it could have been somewhere in West Texas. The road climbed sharply to the border station at Naqura, looking down on a sweeping vista of beach and sea. Harris wished Hannah were there to see it with him.

"You know, I keep feeling like Wags ought to be here," Gallegly said. "Like we went off and left him."

Harris felt guilty for wishing it were Hannah with them instead of Wags.

The border station straddled a narrow cut in a cliff falling away to the sea. Double arched, with IN on one side in English, Arabic and Hebrew and OUT

324

on the other, and PALESTINE in English and Arabic. A Syrian officer came out of the tall, roundish office between the lanes, gave their passes and IDs a cursory glance and waved them on. On the IN side, customs officers were giving a civilian car a scrupulous examination. The front and rear seats had been removed and an officer was on hands and knees inside it.

They drove past the open iron gates on the far side and were in a brand new country. It looked like Palestine without the irrigation. Just like going from Texas into Mexico at Brownsville.

They drove past Tyre and Sidon, just names, not looking biblical, past mulberry groves and silk factories. Into Beirut along the broad, balustraded Corniche, edging the beach.

Harris asked the driver for the best hotel in Beirut.

"Saint Georges," he replied without hesitation.

He took them to a stately, venerable hotel sitting all by itself on a sandy spit thrusting out into the sea. Five stories, angular, flat-roofed with graceful balconies ringing every floor. Trees in tubs, flowers. Hannah would love it, Harris thought.

Inside, it was as different from the Savoy back in Haifa as the Ben Milam was from the Rice Hotel back home. More so. The St. Georges was like a hotel in a movie. The formally attired room clerk looked French and had a French accent. Everybody looked French except some obvious Syrians or Lebanese—because of the money Harris wasn't sure whether Lebanon was part of Syria or not—and an English officer with a major's crown on his shoulder tabs.

"This sure beats the tar outta Haifa," Gallegly said

approvingly.

The clerk gave them a room at the back overlooking the sea. It had its own balcony from which they could look straight down into the water, and twin beds and a bathroom with an extra fixture set in the floor next to the commode.

"Looks like a urinal for a midget," Harris said.

They decided it was a footbath, a good idea for a hotel sitting right on a sandy beach like this one did.

It was twelve Syrian pounds a day with meals. Six dollars but worth it, Harris thought.

They went down for an elegant late lunch in the glass-walled dining-room overlooking the sea. Soup they didn't finish because it tasted of mutton, a salad of unfamiliar greens, some kind of fish that tasted fine despite the strange sauce—Hannah would know what kind of sauce it was, Harris thought—a meat course, vegetables, crusty bread and real butter on the table. All they wanted of the butter, and sugar, too. For dessert, a basket of bananas, dates, figs and tangerines, all tasting fresh from the tree. Harris had never had a fresh date before, only dried. You bit off the end and squeezed. It popped out of the skin sweet and meltingly soft. This sure wasn't like Palestine, he thought. This was the real promised land.

Poor Silkwood.

They changed into swim trunks and hurried down to the hotel's private beach. Sand came right up to a curving outdoor pavilion set with tables. Women sunned themselves in skimpy bathing suits or waded, wearing snug caps. Some of them were dumpy but enough were lithe. Lebanese-Syrian or even French. Maybe he could pick up a French girl, Harris thought. They were supposed to be hot. He felt

326

guilty about it because of Hannah.

The men looked mostly local or French. A few were British. You could tell them from the others not just from their faces because they were so white-skinned except for their sunburned arms and necks.

A raft for diving and sunbathing bobbed in the blue water fifty yards out. Sailboats skimmed along out at sea. You couldn't tell there was a war going on. He wished Wags was here with them. Hannah, too, but not missing her enough to really hurt.

They swam out to the raft. The English major they'd seen in the lobby was sitting on it with his skinny white legs dangling in the clear water. Harris recognized him by his yellow moustache.

"I say," he said to Harris, concerned. "You bloody well forgot to take off your watch."

"It's waterproof," Harris explained.

"Jolly good."

When he learned they were American flyers and it was their first time in Beirut, he offered to show them the night life. He was a signals officer stationed there. Harris and Gallegly looked at one another in silent agreement. It was good to have someone who knew the ropes and if they met some women they could always ditch him.

"I'll collect you in the lobby," he said. "Eightish. Dinner followed by whatever."

"Roger," said Harris, thinking eight was pretty late to be eating dinner. Back at Ramat Jonas and Aleenah evening chow was never much later than five. But when in Beirut . . .

They washed their feet in the footbath and showered. The shower was down the hall. There was a bathtub in their room but they both preferred a shower. Harris had his own reason for not wanting to use the tub. He thought it might remind him too much of Hannah. The only time in months he'd had a tub bath was in Haifa after they made love.

There was time to kill before eight. Harris got into his greens, Gallegly into his pinks.

"We look pretty damn keen if I say so myself," Gallegly said.

Harris agreed. Hannah had never seen him all dressed up like this, only in khakis. He wished she had, not that it made any difference now.

They went downstairs to find a taxi. The driver knew French but not English. Gallegly had enough college French to tell him they wanted to see a little of the city and then be dropped off in the centre of town.

Beirut was as full of contrasts as Haifa, but of a different sort and more cosmopolitan. Broad avenues lined with trees, narrow streets scarcely more than alleys, paved with cobbles or rectangular blocks. Teeming bazaars, swanky stores with French names and French goods, open front local shops. Signs in English, French and Arabic. Arab porters with burlap bags hanging down their backs to pad burdens of ice blocks, crates of chickens, bags of cement, lamb carcasses all white and bloody, threaded their way among automobiles, bicycles, donkey carts, barrows, horsedrawn carriages. On narrow Rue Georges Picot a country Arab driving a flock of sheep blocked their way, ignoring their driver's honking horn and shouted French and Arabic.

The men wore European cut suits, uniforms, pantaloons, flowing robes, tarbooshes, Homburgs and straw hats, the women fashionable dresses and silk stockings or Arab garb, faces painted or modestly veiled. Like the Hotel St. Georges, it all reminded

Harris of a movie. And he was right in the big middle of it.

They dismissed the taxi at the Place de Martyrs, crowded with more people than lived in half a dozen Aleenahs. After a few minutes of window shopping and checking out the women, they happened upon a confectionery shop with cases of French pastries, elaborate ice-cream concoctions and real American beer in cans and bottles.

"We're not eating until eight," Harris said.

"Roger," said Gallegly.

They had eclairs and parfaits and then a leisurely, luxurious bottle of American beer. They bought two cans each to take back to Ramat Jonas to prove to their friends Beirut was the real Promised Land.

"Tex," Gallegly said, "finding Beirut was the best goddam piece of navigation you ever did."

If Wags was just with them, Harris thought. And Hannah. But they weren't. The next best thing was being here himself. With good old Gallegly.

Wags and Hannah, Ramat Jonas and pink Liberators, Aleenah were all too far away to measure in miles, far away in time as well as distance. Was it only three days ago he'd seen Wags dead. Just last night he'd lain with Hannah on Tante Frieda's couch?

The sadness that welled up in him was less from a sense of loss than from his awareness the sense of loss was fading so quickly.

The British major, his name was Harry, took them to a restaurant up a flight of stairs. Lucullus, the best French restaurant in Beirut, he said. The food did not seem all that much different to Harris from that at the hotel, except for a big tray of hors d'oeuvres with just about everything on it except the sardines and anchovies tasting like eggplant.

The major was disappointed when they both ordered the beefsteak, and quietly amused when they ordered American beer while he was still studying the wine list. After dinner he took them to the bar of the Hotel Normandy, across the Corniche from the sea. It was bright and garish but nearly empty, and there were no unescorted women.

"We'd heard you had to beat off the women with a stick in Beirut," Gallegly said.

"Oh ho ho," said the major, who had put away the better part of a bottle of French wine at Lucullus and a brandy from the Hotel Normandy bar. "So it's that you chaps are keen for."

He led them outside and hailed a taxi. He gave the driver an address in Arabic. They threaded through dark streets and narrow alleys.

"You'll find the Mimosa Club amusing," he said. "Lovely little tarts. Inspected weekly by the medical chappies. Officers only."

The taxi stopped before a dark, unprepossessing building with a weatherstained door.

"Here we are then," Harry said. "Out, men, and into the breach."

Harris didn't think it looked like much. Gallegly gave him a what-have-we-got-ourselves-into look.

Harry rapped smartly on the door with the swagger stick he carried. It opened a crack. Light poured out, and laughter. Women's laughter. American music. Harris recognized the record. "Joseph, Joseph." Harry said something in French and they were let in.

It didn't look like a whorehouse. It was classier

than Madame ZeZe's in Belem, more like a lively party in a swanky private home. The girls were young and fine-looking in evening gowns. Some of them hardly more than children. Fair ones and dark ones, mostly dark ones, a few looking almost oriental. The men were all in uniform, British, Free French, some Harris could not identify. Everybody sipping drinks or dancing or whispering in corners in a babel of French and English. A red-faced British officer, obviously drunk, manned the record player.

Harris and Gallegly were the only Americans, drawing immediate attention from everyone not too preoccupied with drinking and dancing.

They drank beer and looked the girls over. None of them seemed to be trying hard to attract customers. If anything, it was the men vying for attention, courting the girls.

There were doors on three sides of the big room. From time to time couples would enter or come out of one of them. A little girl with large breasts but who could not have been more than fifteen left the dance floor with a burly Scot in kilts. She was flourishing a white balloon. As she passed a manic young officer in Royal Navy whites she flicked the balloon in his face. He bit at it playfully and recoiled. It was an inflated condom.

They were in a whorehouse, all right.

Harris listened to the music and watched the dancing, feeling no great urge for a woman. He knew it was because of Hannah. A girl talking with a Free French subaltern kept looking at him. She was a pretty thing, with dark eyes and hair. He thought she might be French. Her interest attracted him. Why not? he thought. When in Beirut, do as

331

the French do.

He asked her to dance. She accepted casually, as if conferring a favour, as if it bored her to be so popular. The French officer looked hurt as they moved away.

Glenn Miller's "A String of Pearls" was on the record player. Harris liked to dance to that one. His partner was a terrible dancer but made up for it by moving his hand down to her warm buttock and breathing in his ear. He started wanting her. She knew it, of course.

"Are you French?" he said.

"How you guess?" she replied.

Something about the way she said it told him she was lying.

It didn't matter. She was stacked and sexy. And different from Hannah Ruh. He didn't think he could stand innocence and honesty. Not just yet.

The room did not reflect its function. A woman's room, obviously, but like that of someone with taste and money. A good carpet and dressing table, an armoire, a deep chair, lamps and a chastely made bed that gave no hint of the countless bodies that had used it.

Harris's companion quickly dispelled the illusion. She stripped away the bedspread with one expert twist, turned back the covers and before he had his shirt off lay naked on the bed on her back gazing at him with feigned desire. She held her fine breasts in both hands and pointed them at him like twin fifties.

"You like?" she said, low and husky. *"Allez, allez,* you make me so hot."

Harris wished she wouldn't treat him like such a rube. He folded his greens carefully. They had to look nice for three more days. Feeling something less than burning desire, he climbed dutifully aboard. She went immediately into a bravura performance, twitches, shudders, frantic pelvic motions. Sighs, gasps, moans, endearments in several languages, exhorting, complimenting. Despite the obvious theatricality, his interest quickened and he adjusted to her gait, enjoying himself. Until he thought of Hannah.

He looked at himself through her eyes. Half-drunk on beer, grappling lovelessly with a stranger. He lost all interest in the woman and what he was doing. The capability remained but not the desire. It was like PT. Just exercise. He ought to bring Silkwood here for a workout.

She became impatient, redoubling her efforts and cries of ecstasy, then angry.

"Why you not finish?" she demanded.

"Maybe you'd better give me a raincheck," he said.

When he explained what a raincheck was she vented a spate of Arabic too intense to be complimentary. He knew he had aspersed her artistic and professional talents. He apologized. Baffled by his continued ability to perform and determined he should not leave the room unslaked, she did a number of things calculated to bring about what he had paid for. He found some of them mildly repugnant.

"Ma'am," he said. "How much for you to stop?"

She did not find it amusing and had at him with renewed determination. Concentrating, shutting out Hannah, he was at last able to oblige.

"Next time you here," she said, "you go with other girl. OK?"

"Roger," said Harris.

But he didn't think he'd be coming back.

Gallegly and the major were waiting for him.

"I thought you fell in," said Gallegly.

333

Harry got the madame, he called her the mana-
geress, to phone for a taxi. On the way to the hotel
he told them if they had another day or so they
might enjoy Aley. It was a little resort town, he said,
five miles or so up in the mountains above Beirut off
the Damascus road.

"Quite nice, actually," he said. "Lovely hotel, lovely
view, smashing food. But nothing there to compare
with the Mimosa, I'm afraid."

Harris took a half-hour shower, not feeling soiled,
exactly, just a little tarnished from the powder, per-
fume and sweat reek at the Mimosa. It was the first
time he'd ever felt the least bit disturbed after being
with a woman. Not counting that last time in Haifa
with Hannah, when he'd been really bothered but
for an entirely different reason.

Gallegly was already sleeping when he got back to
the room, an arm flung across his eyes to shield
them from the light. He was smiling.

Harris dreamed he knocked on Hannah's door
and no one came. He pushed the door open and
there was Wags with Hannah and Tante Frieda,
drinking Russian tea and entertaining them with
stories in faultless German. All of them laughing.
He was less surprised to find Wagstaff alive than to
discover Wags spoke German. And so well.

No one paid him the least attention.

"Hannah," he said desperately. "Will you marry
me?"

She looked annoyed and put her finger to her
lips. He was interrupting Wagstaff. Humiliated,
wretched, he left them. No one watched him go.
Outside, the stars were preternaturally bright. Even
Polaris was like a beacon. It was blinking, sending
Morse code. He tried to read it. Polaris was trying

334

to tell him something. If he could just make it out everything would be all right, but the dots and dashes were too elusive. The stars faded. Only blackness. "Where are we, Tex?" said Silkwood above the racket of engines. How the hell did they expect him to know without any stars to shoot?

Chapter XIX

Breakfast at the glass wall overlooking the Mediterranean was eggs done just right and bacon. Real bacon, not the thick, fatty kind at Ramat Jonas. And sliced bananas with real cream, real orange juice, rolls the waiter said were called croissants and brioches. French. Beyond the wall the sailboats were already out.

Harris looked morosely at his plate. Maybe if they kept going . . .

"Let's go to Aley," he said.

"You're the navigator," said Gallegly.

They checked out of the St. Georges and took a taxi to the Damascus road, their musette bags heavy with the canned American beer they had bought. The driver let them off at the racetrack on the outskirts of town. The track was hidden from view by a wall but they could hear cheering and the thud of hooves.

"You feel lucky?" Gallegly asked.

Harris felt anything but lucky, and he didn't want to waste time at the track. The thing to do was keep moving. He already felt better, knowing he was going somewhere he had never been before.

An open British army lorry picked them up before

Gallegly had finished his first pipe. They lay on top of the load smoking and looking at the scenery. The road climbed all the way. Olive groves, rocky hills, little valleys in bursts of greenery, cedars in dark green clumps, tall and graceful and, beside the road, sharp-smelling eucalyptus. Sheep and goats foraged in stony fields. A solitary white-haired Arab drove an overloaded donkey along the side of the road. Up here in the mountains, Palestine seemed far away.

A Free French officer in an American jeep painted with the Cross of Lorraine drove them up the mountain and through Aley's bumpy main street to the Aley Palace Hotel at the top. Aley looked like a lively one-street town with open air cafés and un-Arab looking shops.

The Aley Palace was smaller and older looking than the St. Georges but no less French. Their room with meals cost the same. The child dressed like a bellboy who showed them to their room tried to take their musette bags but they were afraid he would strain himself. They tipped him a pound. They knew from his response fifty cents was a good deal more than he was accustomed to receiving. Wherever Americans went they always tipped more than the locals. Except Silkwood. He carried his change in a little coinpurse and acted like if he opened it it might blow up in his face.

Their room was larger than the one in Beirut. The furniture had seen better days and they didn't have their own bathroom, just a washbasin with the C and F on the handles that had almost scalded Harris back at the St. Georges before he figured out the C stood for *chaud,* not cold. The day outside their window was as clear as a polished magnifying glass. They could see the Mediterranean sparkling in the distance below the mountain tops, deep green valleys and leaf groves.

"Uber allen Gipfeln ist Ruh."

"Huh?" said Gallegly.

"That's poetry, dope," Harris said.

Wondering where Hannah was right now and what she had been doing while he was fighting the battle of the Mimosa Club.

The toilet and shower bath were down the hall. There was another little footbath in the bathroom. But there were no beaches and sand up here.

"Maybe it really is for midgets," Harris said. "Or little kids."

Remembering how when he was a little kid and his father took him to the toilet at the movies, he didn't want to use the bowl like a girl did and made his father hold him up to the urinal.

"I think it's to throw up in," said Gallegly. "Frenchmen drink a lot."

They asked their waiter at lunch and he said it was a bidet.

"Pour les femmes."

"What do they use it for?" Gallegly asked.

The waiter, whose English was imperfect, pretended not to understand. He was embarrassed. Harris thought it was their ignorance that embarrassed him, not what the ladies did with a bidet.

"I don't think it's their feet they wash in it," Harris said.

"Oh, Jesus," said Gallegly. "Can you catch anything through your feet?"

After a lunch almost identical to that served at the St. Georges they went exploring, trudging down the hill to the town. As in the Arab section of Haifa, there were only men in the open air cafés. They

338

seemed less Arab than the Haifa Arabs. Most of them dressed just like anybody else. They were playing backgammon noisily, shouting and slapping down their counters on the marble-topped counters with sharp reports like rifle shots.

A sign beckoned in English. "American Soda Fountain." There was little even remotely American about the shop. Even the bananas in the banana splits they ordered were sliced up instead of split lengthwise. But the ice-cream reminded Harris of home. Real ice-cream, not the thin stuff they served at the Mount Carmel Hotel. He wished Hannah were sitting with him as she had on Mount Carmel.

Deeper in the town, off the main street, girls were sitting around a public pool or splashing in the water. None of them could swim as well as Hannah. Or looked as good in a bathing suit. Dammit, how far away was he going to have to go to get her off his mind?

Gallegly wondered if they ought to go back and get their trunks and pick up a couple of the girls but the sun was getting low above the mountains and the air was cooling. It was degrees cooler up here than in Beirut. They watched the girls and the girls watched them. The girls began leaving and they went back up the mountain for a nap.

They changed into their good uniforms for dinner. Less than half the tables were occupied. After dinner they went to the little casino off the dining-room. A few bored elderly men and women were playing baccarat, a game unfamiliar to Harris and Gallegly.

"Some navigator," said Gallegly. "I thought Aley would be zippier than this."

They heard music and traced it to its source, a small orchestra playing old American tunes on a terrace jammed with dancing couples. Free French officers, prosperous looking civilians and their handsomely-gowned women. It was busy as the Rice Hotel Empire Room on Saturday night. Harris wondered where they had all come from. The hotel and Aley itself had been half-deserted by day. They'd been the only customers in the American Soda Fountain and had seen hardly anyone except the backgammon players and the girls at the swimming pool.

There was scotch but no bourbon. The waiter suggested cognac. Authentic Remy Martin, he said, as if that should mean something to them. They settled for American ale, sipped it, watching the dancers wistfully, looking for strays. There were none. Everyone was paired off.

The little orchestra played "Pennies from Heaven." Harris remembered the movie. Windows reflected the soft lights. Dancers glided in the ambience. This would sure be a dandy place to bring Hannah.

But he wouldn't be bringing her anywhere. Hannah, why did you have to be like that and ruin everything? You'd be happy in Houston, I know you would.

He felt restless, and jealous of the men dancing so familiarly with attentive women as he would be doing if Hannah were here. They all looked as if they belonged together. He did not envy the men their women. It was just that he wanted his own.

Gallegly was restless, too. They went outside and climbed into a beat-up old car the driver said was a taxi.

"Jeunes filles," Gallegly said.

Harris wasn't interested in finding girls but he did not protest. He wasn't going to ruin Gallegly's leave

340

just because he was all screwed up himself.

The driver took them down the main drag and let them out in front of an open door with narrow steps leading up to the second floor. Strains of Arab music, like a jammed frequency or someone wailing, drifted down. Gallegly gave Harris an inquiring look.

"Why not?" said Harris.

He didn't much care where he went if it wasn't with her.

Upstairs, a woman hurried to greet them, drawn by the natty American uniforms and officer's bars. She looked like a Syrian housewife. She was the hostess.

A busy bar ran the length of the narrow front room. Tables crowded with local men except for two British Other Ranks drinking methodically were ranged along the side overlooking the street. A second room filled with locals, men only, lay behind the first. Weird music, noise and smoke hung in the air.

"Jeunes filles," Gallegly said.

The woman looked doubtful, then thoughtful, nodded and left them. The Other Ranks looked up from their drinks, noticed them and cocked them careless, amiable salutes which Gallegly and Harris returned just as amiably. Harris thought about Wags cleaning up on the three limeys in front of the Haifa Post Office. Hannah'd be sore if she saw him being friendly with British soldiers.

The woman returned with a sullen-faced little girl about thirteen years old. A waitress, judging from the soiled apron ending just above her scratched schoolgirl knees. The little girl stood with her face averted, her arms folded below where her breasts would be if she had any.

341

"Jeune fille," the woman said.

"Christ," said Gallegly.

He gave the woman a couple of pounds and went to the little girl with a five pound note in his hand. She shrank from him. He pulled her folded arms free and thrust the money in her hand.

"Come on, let's blow this joint," he said to Harris, hurrying towards the door.

Harris paused long enough to slip the woman another couple of pounds and, nodding toward the Other Ranks, said, "Drinks for my friends."

The Other Ranks saluted him with raised glasses.

Gallegly was waiting for him out on the street.

"We should have stayed in Beirut," Gallegly said.

"We can go back tomorrow if you want."

They walked back up the mountain to the hotel. It was cold. They could see their breath. From up here in the mountains the stars were even brighter than at Ramat Jonas. As bright as they were from *Blonde Job's* astrodome. There was old not-bright-but-dependable Polaris. Why should Polaris remind him of Hannah? She was bright. But not dependable. If she was dependable she'd have jumped at the chance to marry him and live wherever he goddam wanted her to.

They watched the dancing some more. If it weren't for the uniforms you wouldn't know there was a war on. When you weren't on a mission you didn't notice the war that much yourself. But it was there. Like the wind. Moving you around the way the wind moved your plane. You ended up in all kinds of unexpected places. You couldn't figure the war the way you did the wind and correct for it and end up where you wanted to. But it hadn't been so bad, going where the war took you. Trinidad, Belem, Natal, Africa, Khartoum, Haifa. Aleenah. Beirut, and now Aley. Places that had just been marks on maps before. Some, like Ramat Jonas, Aleenah and Aley, he'd never even heard of.

He was filled with an urge to keep going. When you were on the move nothing you'd left behind seemed as important as where you were going. He knew the closer he got to Aleenah the worse he'd feel.

"Damascus is only forty-five miles from here," he said.

Damascus was farther from home than he'd ever dreamed of going. Ancient astronomers there may have named some of the stars he shot.

"Dancing girls," said Gallegly. "The Street Called Straight. You're on."

They were the first ones down for breakfast. Hot chocolate, croissants and brioches. They gulped it down, anxious to hit the road for Damascus.

They waited at the junction with the Beirut-Damascus highway, waving their thumbs at every vehicle that passed. A 1934 Ford came by stuffed with a man and a woman and bright-eyed Arab children. The driver showed them V for victory as he passed. An army lorry loaded with standing Gurkhas in heavy woollen battle-dress lumbered by. Tough little brown men with squinty eyes, they grinned at Harris and Gallegly showing perfect white teeth. An odd-shaped little French car approached. It was filled to capacity with four civilians in shirtsleeves. Just when Harris was beginning to think they would never get a ride a taxi with two men in business suits in the back seat slid to a halt a few yards beyond them. It started backing up as Harris and Gallegly ran to meet it, musette bags bumping at their hips.

The driver came around the front of the taxi and opened both doors. A heavyset man with olive skin and a glistening black moustache stuck his head out, smiling cordially, and said, "You are going where?"

"Damascus," said Harris.

"Precisely our destination. You are welcome to come along."

Gallegly got in the front seat. The driver shut the door behind him and waited for Harris to climb in the back. The businessmen moved to the sides to make room for him in the middle. Harris put a foot inside, stooped to get in. And stopped.

What was he doing, going to Damascus? You couldn't solve a problem by running away from it. Understanding at last with startling clarity there wasn't any problem.

What a goddam fool he was not seeing something staring him in the face. Hannah wasn't the stubborn one. He was. Worse than stubborn. Stupid. Her reasons for not wanting to leave Aleenah were better than his for wanting to take her away. She was doing something important to her. Important to him, too. She didn't belong anywhere else. In the States she would be just another housewife watching the world go by.

And what would he be? Just some dope with a job that didn't mean anything. Remembering how once he had flown high above strange places. Missing Hannah. And Tante Frieda. Even Gyorgy Weisz and the Goldblums. Yearning for the heat and smells of Aleenah, the sound of water pumps and jackals at night, sitting around the supper table after work. Sleeping with Hannah in his arms. Forever after remembering, always remembering, what he'd had and let get away. He wouldn't even be home. Not really. Home was wherever Hannah was. He was already more comfortable in Aleenah than she would ever be in Houston.

"Come on," said Gallegly.

The men in the back seat were looking at him quizzically.

"I'm not going," he said.

He felt light-headed, elated.

"You were the one who said Damascus," Gallegly protested.

"I've changed my mind. I'm going back."

Knowing he should apologize for leaving Gallegly this way but too relieved to care.

Gallegly got out of the taxi and said, "Thanks, anyway," to the businessmen. The driver slammed the door and got back behind the wheel, scowling. The taxi sped away in a spurt of stones and dust. The businessmen's olive faces were in the rear window looking back.

"Beirut's probably more fun than Damascus, anyhow," Gallegly said, not sounding particularly sore at him.

"I'm going all the way back."

"To the field? We've still got two more days!"

Gallegly looked at him sharply, comprehension dawning.

"Hannah, ain't it?"

Harris nodded, sheepish.

"I knew you had it bad, but not that bad."

They said goodbye in the St. Georges's lobby. Harris was far too impatient to wait for lunch. Who cared about food? He'd kept Hannah waiting two days and he wasn't going to waste another minute.

He took a taxi to the border. He wanted to take it

345

all the way to Aleenah but the driver didn't have papers to cross the frontier. Harris stood chafing with his thumb out. There was very little traffic. It took him two rides and four hours to get to Haifa, where he hailed the first taxi he saw. He went straight to Aleenah without even stopping by his tent to drop off his musette bag. Throughout the entire journey from Beirut he had shuttled between euphoria and raging impatience while planning the rest of his life.

In Aleenah people were standing in front of their houses, talking quietly. Most of them knew him now and said, *"Shalom,"* strangely grave. It was like the day Rommel launched his attack against the El Alamein line. Maybe the Afrika Korps had been reinforced and was trying again. He hadn't heard any news in two days, hadn't really been interested. In Lebanon the war had been too remote.

He scrambled out of the taxi in front of Tante Frieda's, with the neighbours on both sides watching soberly, offered the driver Syrian pounds, which were refused, and had to reach under his bush jacket to get Palestine pounds out of his money belt. He ran up the path and beat on the door without waiting for his change.

"Hannah! Hannah, it's me!"

The door opened. Tante Frieda stared out looking years older, the creases in her face deeper, her eyes red-rimmed and full of pain. She grabbed him and held on, crying and talking.

What was she trying to tell him? Goddammit, why couldn't she speak English? He felt numb all over except for a growing iciness in his belly.

"Dead!" someone cried with his voice.

He pushed her away, wanting to shake some sense

into her, stumbled with her to the couch, the couch where he and Hannah had made love an age ago.

How could Hannah be dead? What right had she to be dead when they were going to be married and live happily ever after? He'd made up his mind back at Aley. She couldn't do that.

But she was dead, all right. Killed in Haifa by an English sentry's bullet. He wanted to die himself. Why couldn't it have been him instead of Hannah? By rights it should have been. He was the one fighting a war, not Hannah.

Stunned grief exploded into rage. That goddam Gyorgy! Sending a girl to do a man's job. He leaped from the couch and flung out the door. He'd kill the son of a bitch!

He ran down the dirt road. People turned and watched him. He'd give them something to watch. He was going to kill Gyorgy Weisz. Kill Gyorgy? What good would that do? It wasn't Gyorgy's fault, anyway. It was Hannah's own choice. She wanted to fight her own goddam war. He had to hit somebody, blame somebody. But he couldn't even blame the British. They'd shot a prowler. He'd have done the same if he was a sentry.

He slowed to a walk, sanity returning. Grief flooded him mercilessly.

They were all watching as he stumbled to the Goldblums' door. It seemed like everybody in Aleenah was watching. Goldblum let him in wordlessly, knowing from his face he'd heard the news. Frau Goldblum stared from the dining-room, wagging her head in mute, helpless condolence.

Gyorgy came out of his room, concern softening his granite face.

"How did it happen?" Harris demanded without

preamble.

Gyorgy led him to his room and sat him down on the narrow bed. He got a bottle of Stock brandy out of his locker and made him take a drink. It went down like water to vanish in the chill within him.

She had gone with Judah and a Palmach dissident to steal Bren guns at the British Number 2 Base Ordnance Depot in the industrial district of Haifa. They had been surprised by the guards, who opened fire when they ran for their truck instead of halting as ordered. Hannah was the only one hit.

Judah had pulled her into the truck. Eluding pursuit, they had raced to the home of a doctor sympathetic to their cause. She had died before they got there.

"When?" Harris asked bleakly.

"Wednesday night."

Wednesday night. She'd died while he was in bed with a whore at the Mimosa Club.

"I want to see her," he said. "Where is she?"

She was already buried. Dead Wednesday night and in the ground Thursday. He would never see Hannah again. Not ever. He began to cry. Gyorgy put a hard-muscled arm around his shoulder and tried to make him take another drink. Harris shook the arm away.

"I'm all right," he said.

Soldiers got killed. Why should Hannah be any different from any other soldier? Just because he loved her and wanted to marry her? He got up and stared dry-eyed out of the window into the dusk. He could see the dirt road that circled Aleenah and the tough Jews who would have been his friends and neighbours some day if Hannah had lived. Across the road was the pine grove where they had lain at

348

night until they learned Gyorgy knew about them.

A sound of engines rolled across the valley from the airfield. In a few more days he would be flying missions again. With no Hannah to come back to. With nothing to come back to. And one day he would climb into his plane and fly away, never to come back. As if none of this had ever happened. But it had happened and he would never be the same. He did not want to be the same. Not the same as he was before Hannah. A rider on the wind, without aim or purpose.

Hannah had a purpose. She'd died for it. If it had been that important to her it was that important to him. What they were doing here, Gyorgy, Tante Frieda and the others, was more important than anything he could ever do back home. He felt closer to Gyorgy at this moment than to anyone. Even Gallegly. The ice in his belly began to thaw.

He turned to Gyorgy and said, "I'll be back."

"Always you are welcome in this house, my friend," Gyorgy said.

"I mean after the war."

"Good. There will be need for much strong men."

Many, Gyorgy, not much. He was going to have to help Gyorgy work on his English. And Gyorgy would teach him Hebrew.

He went outside and stood in the road. It was dark now. He could see the stars. They would still be there when he came back for good. Hannah wouldn't, but they would. The stars would always be up there to tell you where you were.

He walked back to Tante Frieda's, crying again, to get his musette bag.

ESPIONAGE FICTION BY WARREN MURPHY
AND MOLLY COCHRAN

GRANDMASTER   (17-101, $4.50)
There are only two true powers in the world. One is good-
ness. One is evil. And one man knows them both. He
knows the uses of pleasure, the secrets of pain. He under-
stands the deadly forces that grip the world in treachery.
He moves like a shadow, a promise of danger, from Mos-
cow to Washington — from Havana to Tibet. In a game that
may never be over, he is the grandmaster.

THE HAND OF LAZARUS   (17-100, $4.50)
A grim spectre of death looms over the tiny County Kerry
village of Ardath. The savage plague of urban violence has
begun to weave its insidious way into the peaceful fabric of
Irish country life. The IRA's most mysterious, elusive, and
bloodthirsty murderer has chosen Ardath as his hunting
ground, the site that will rock the world and plunge the beleaguered island nation into irreversible chaos: the brutal
assassination of the Pope.